"Remarkable and ambitious . . . A spectacular combination of history, historical characters, and romance . . . Fascinating!"

—*Romantic Times*

"Mary Pershall's four *Roses* have an intoxicating effect on readers!"

—*Gannett News Service*

"Wonderful . . . Her characters are people with warmth, strength and humor, who stayed with me long after the last page was turned . . . Pershall brings them to life."

—*Shannon Drake, bestselling author of Blue Heaven, Black Night and Ondine*

"Five stars . . . The panorama of historical events is finely detailed, and the reader gets a total sense of the times and people of that age . . . A must for your summer reading pleasure!"

—*Affaire de Coeur*

"Every modern woman's fantasy . . . Fascinating!"

—*Wenatchee (Wa) World*

AND NOW, HER NEWEST,
GRANDEST EPIC ROMANCE . . .

Behold the Dream

Mary Pershall
Winner of the 1985 *Romantic Times* Award
for Best New Historical Writer

MARY PERSHALL

BEHOLD THE DREAM

BERKLEY BOOKS, NEW YORK

Mail to the author
may be addressed to:
Mary Pershall
P.O. Box 1453
Soledad, CA 93960

BEHOLD THE DREAM

A Berkley Book / published by arrangement with
the author

PRINTING HISTORY
Berkley edition / July 1988

ISBN: 0-425-10925-9

A BERKLEY BOOK ® TM 757,375
Berkley Books are published by The Berkley Publishing Group,
200 Madison Avenue, New York, New York 10016.
The name "BERKLEY" and the "B" logo
are trademarks belonging to Berkley Publishing Corporation.

PRINTED IN THE UNITED STATES OF AMERICA

10 9 8 7 6 5 4 3 2 1

ACKNOWLEDGMENTS

I wish to acknowledge my deep appreciation to certain individuals who helped enormously in the writing of this book:

Amelie Elkinton, president emeritus of the Monterey Historical Society and historian extraordinary. Bill Getchey of the Sonoma Mission, a descendant of Mariano Vallejo, for the information, legends, and gossip he shared. The wonderfully informative and knowledgeable park rangers of the California Department of Parks and Recreation at San Juan Bautista, Sonoma, and Rancho Petaluma. Marc Godoy, a friend, for his translations.

And to my editor, Mercer Warriner, for her constant support and the lovely things she does to my manuscripts.

Dedication

To Greg, Kip, and Paige

Monterenos and *Angeleno*,
the history is now yours.

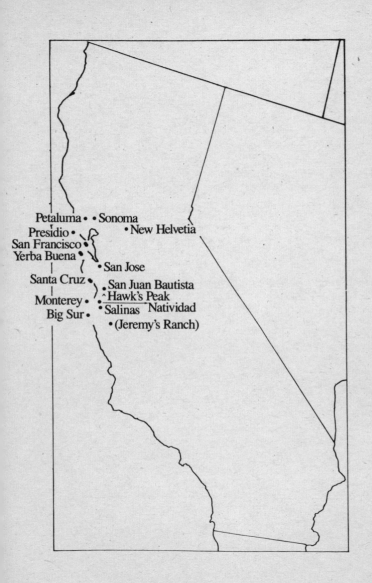

PROLOGUE

It was a land of majestic, snowcapped mountains and distant, hot deserts. Man was drawn through these punishing reaches to fertile valleys, teeming with wildlife: rolling, stretching planes of lush green grasses spotted with blue lupine, indian paintbrush, and wild mustard, cooled by sea breezes and heavy inland mists of fog.

The soldiers came, accompanying the priests, and they established coastal forts to protect the burgeoning missions erected as tribute to God's mercy and justice. The natives who had lived there peacefully for centuries, their existence one of berry and seed gathering, nature's gifts given from tide pool life and swollen rivers laden with fish, submitted their gentle ways before the instant pressure of those who had suddenly appeared to save their lost, unaware souls.

The simple pagan discovered the anguish of his sin and bent before the lash of his savior. For the soldier who followed the priest, life became one of ease, as the land gave effortlessly. He discovered discontentment for what he had known. Generations passed, and the old world was forgotten. The new land was cherished and became part of his soul. Then the old world reached out, demanding of the found riches. The soldier's discontentment with the old ways became one of resentment and struggle. He took the land for himself and his descendants, casting off the last hold of the priests along with the remaining grasp of his almost forgotten once-world. The land became his.

It became the land of the vaqueros, with the metal clink of their glorious rowel spurs, their soft laughter, the bone-chilling excitement of their daring horsemanship, their wide sun-shielding sombreros, and their bright, embroidered costumes. It became a land of rangy, black cattle, grazing in endless dusky herds under the vaqueros' watchful eyes. The land provided unsurpassed wealth, granting an ease of life never before known, giving without harsh season a bounty that required little effort. Where struggle for survival was unknown, pleasure became paramount; graciousness was spawned as the purpose for existence.

These were the halcyon days; it was the time of the dons.

1

"Had you succeeded in this conspiracy, many people would have died. You will not be allowed to plot such foolishness again." An enraged Don Mariano Guadalupe Vallejo glared at the three supplicants kneeling before him.

Ariana tried to ignore the pain. Though her knees had long since become numb, sharp spears of pain radiated up her legs from the three-quarters of an hour she had been kneeling. She could no longer feel her feet. Occasionally she had felt herself waver, and only the fear of fainting had given her the strength to hold herself erect. She would not be the first to give in and further disgrace herself; she had done quite enough of that already.

In the heavy silence, distant ship bells could be heard in the harbor. From somewhere outside a dog barked, accompanied by children's laughter, mocking the tension within Don Mariano's study. Dismissing the sounds, Ariana kept her vision fixed on a small flower in the thin carpet, as she fought a compulsion to glance at her fellow conspirators. She wondered what they were thinking at this moment. For her, there was the additional pain she felt from the don's disappointment in her, making her physical discomfort even more acute.

Don Mariano leaned his hip on the edge of his desk and

his gaze passed over the silent trio. Let them squirm, he thought. Let them wonder about their punishment a little longer, it will serve them well. He studied each in turn, aware of how each struggled to keep his eyes downcast. He wasn't fooled for an instant; not one of them was truly contrite, even now.

He had no doubt that Manuel was responsible for all that had happened. His gaze fixed on the dark, bent head of the young man. As the nephew of Jose Castro, Manuel thought of himself as the leader of the *liberalismos,* the new, young revolutionaries who had dedicated themselves to making California truly independent from Mexico and any foreign influence. The pompous, young pup. His gaze shifted to the slighter form next to Manuel. Rafael could be excused, he thought, if he were inclined to be generous. The boy had been sickly most of his life. His recent acceptance by Manuel and his radical friends had undoubtedly proven irresistible. Then Don Mariano's gaze shifted to the remaining third of the trio, and his heart constricted. The light from the window behind him touched on her blue-black hair, the soft curve of her cheekbones, the heavy-lashed eyes that were respectfully downcast. Ariana, he wondered, why you; why did you do it?

"This is how it shall be," he said, shifting his weight on the corner of the desk. "Manuel and Rafael, you will spend the next six months at my rancho in Petaluma. There you will learn to be vaqueros. Perhaps spending ten to twelve hours a day in a saddle running cattle will help you to reflect upon the errors of your ways. At least it will give you both a useful trade," he added with a grim smirk. He noted the slump to Rafael's shoulders—and the slight jerk to Manuel's. No, Manuel was definitely not contrite; he would bear watching.

"Si, Don Mariano," they both responded.

"You will leave within the hour. Go—now."

As the door closed behind the two young Californios, the don turned to Ariana's bent form. "Get up," he said.

He watched as she attempted to rise. She gasped softly against the pain and wavered as she came to her feet, but he would not help her. And he would not allow her to sit.

"Now you will explain yourself," he said.

Ariana's eyes came up to meet with her uncle's. I will not cower before him, she resolved, I will not. "The *Rifleros*

Americanos are planning a revolt—"

"I do not need an explanation on the activities of Isaac Graham's rabble-rousers," he interrupted sharply. "The Yanqui and his grogshop companions will be dealt with by the proper authorities. I want to know why you felt compelled to become involved with Manuel and his idiocy."

She could not argue that Manuel was an idiot—or at the least an insufferable bully. She had made that decision over ten years ago, when she'd hit him with a rock. The event had not occurred for a noble reason, but because of an eight-year-old's rage against an eleven-year-old tyrant.

"I was the only one who could read the letter." She shrugged. Then, after a slight pause, "Of course, they could have asked you."

The brazen comment caused his mouth to twitch with the threat of a smile. He covered it as he turned and picked up the letter in question. It was from Padre Suarez to Juan Alvarado, warning the governor that from the confession of a dying Yanqui, the priest had learned of an impending revolt by American settlers to take control of California. "How you young fools managed to intercept this letter, I don't know, and frankly it doesn't matter," he said. "Just what did you plan to do about this? Start a war? Take on the *Rifleros* yourselves?" Glancing up, he saw how pale she had grown. "You need not stand there. Walk about, it will take the stiffness from your legs."

She would have liked to refuse his suggestion, to deny the pain that was running up and down her legs, but she knew that in another moment she wouldn't be able to stand it. The last thing she wanted was to cry in front of him. Slowly, she began to move about, unaware that he was watching her with concern. As normal circulation began to return, she stopped before the window behind his desk, hesitating in the warmth of the afternoon sun.

"How much you are like your mother," she heard him say behind her. "You know that she was more than just my half-sister. In our youth we were comrades, confidants. You are much like her; perhaps that is why you have always been so special to me." She heard him sigh. "I fear that I have made great mistakes with you."

Mistakes? she wondered silently. Was it a mistake to love her? Was she to live in the shadow of her mother forever—even now, with him?

"Ariana, you have betrayed my trust," he said.

Oh, Dios, she thought, trying not to cry as she stared at the shimmering water of the bay, its surface moving with the reflection of a thousand, tiny suns. Betrayed him? He, beyond anyone else, should have understood why she had done it. Suddenly, it proved to be too much. Forgetting her resolve, she spun on him.

"How can you deny me what I have done?" she exclaimed. "You once rebelled against your own youth! You were the first to fight against Mexico's injustice. You, with Jose Castro and Juan Alvarado, were the first *liberalismos,* the first revolutionaries who changed the history of California forever! Now, when I have done so little, you accuse me of betrayal?"

He regarded her outburst with amazing calm. "You give me no choice, Ariana, but to make a decision I am loath to make. These are tenuous times; there may even be war. At this moment an order has been given for the arrest of forty of the Yanqui conspirators. It will be done, and the ramifications may cause an uprising of all the foreign settlements throughout California. I will not have you, or those other young fools, involved in it." He paused, studying her lovely, determined face. In that moment, any doubt he'd had about his decision faded. He knew that he could control Manuel and his radicals, but he was not so certain of this one.

She was so much like Rosalinda, he thought, with those large, expressive eyes. Like her mother, she looked deceptively fragile, as well as being self-determined and stubborn. And, *Dios,* she was bright. He wondered if she knew just how exceptionally intelligent she was. He was frightened for her.

With renewed determination, he nodded toward the window. "Look into the harbor. What do you see?"

She frowned even as she followed his gaze. "I see nothing but a ship."

"It leaves for Mexico in the morning. You will be on it. I am sending you to the Convent of Saint Catherine in Veracruz."

Ariana stared from her second-floor bedroom window, her gaze fixed on the ship that lifted on heavy swells in the deep blue water of the harbor. In a few hours' time she would be on it, her world soon gone, lost to the austere, silent confines of a convent. Her damnation made by his words.

Sent away, she thought with anguished disbelief, to *la otra banda,* that other, distant shore that was Mexico. She would remain, he had said, until the reports from the sisters confirmed that she would behave as a proper young woman of her station.

"Do you wish for me to take the veil?" she had cried. "Then I will no longer be in a position to cause you embarrassment!"

"You have never embarrassed me, Ariana," he had replied. "Would I make a decision on such a worthless emotion?"

"Then why is this so easy for you?" she had exclaimed.

"Querida, this is not easy," he had answered. His voice had softened, but his expression had been one of determination. "But it will be done."

She was eighteen years old, and she realized that by the standards of her day, she was well past the age for marriage. Soon she would be a spinster, condemned to the role of a duenna, the ever-constant chaperon that was part of a young, unwed Californio woman's life. A guardian for the chastity of her younger, more conventional cousins. All of that she had long ago accepted, but she could not accept this banishment.

Perhaps she should have said more to him, tried to explain why she had done it. But pride had stopped her, a pride he had given to her. She did not regret what she had done; she would do it all again: to fight for the cause—as he had once done.

The bedroom door opened, distracting her. Grief sloughed away as she felt her emotions harden, slipping into the pit of her stomach.

"Are you ready—*madre Dios!* You haven't even dressed! What have you been doing? The ship leaves in two hours!"

Angular, rawboned, perpetually draped in unrelieved black, Ana Montoya swept into the room. Her angry, suffering eyes darted about with displeasure at the disorder. "You haven't even finished packing!" she clucked.

That voice no longer mattered; Ariana simply didn't care. Her thoughts had taken her too far, and for the first time in her life she regarded the woman with distinctly pleasurable distance. What could she do to her now, after all?

"It is about time that the don took proper steps with you," Ana snapped as she began folding garments on the bed, placing them into an open trunk. "I have told him for years that you were totally uncontrollable. The very idea, going out in the middle of the night, to a remote cabin in Carmel Valley—alone with men!"

"Rafael was there." Ariana shrugged, turning her back on the woman.

"And that made everything all right, I suppose. Of course, as selfish as you are, you wouldn't even consider the fact that poor Rafael is now in the don's disfavor. And don't try to tell me that it was his idea, because I will never believe it! His poor mother had taken to bed, all because of your willfulness! The entire *familia* is in a state of shock over the scandal you've caused—"

Ariana shut out the woman's shrill voice as she thought of Rafael. She did regret his punishment. Her gentle, older cousin had been her only childhood friend. Having been left horribly scarred by smallpox, Rafael emerged from boyhood painfully shy and uncertain, the butt of cruel, childhood jokes. In mutual loneliness, they had found mutual trust and comfort. Then, over the years, their peers began to accept Rafael without ridicule, his disfigurement was less pronounced in a man's body. His acceptance by the *liberalismos* had given him new purpose and life. No, Rafael would be all right.

Sighing, she turned away from the window and her skirt brushed against a table, sweeping a book onto the floor. She picked it up and her hand suddenly trembled as she regarded it with a deep sadness. Her books, too, would be lost to her now. Oh, why had the don given her a glimpse of what life could be, only to take it away? Why had he given her such advantages when they would only increase her sense of loss? What the don has given, the don has taken away. Suddenly the book was snatched from her hand.

"It is the end of these, too, and good riddance!" The duenna smirked at Ariana's flash of surprise and anger. "Don't just stand there—finish packing the items on your dressing table! And don't bother with those perfumed soaps the don gave you for your birthday. The sisters will never allow them. You'll be using good lye soap from now on, be certain of it." As Ariana did as she was bid, Ana carried the book to the shelves which lined the far wall and shoved it into its vacant slot, her expression one of extreme distaste. "I shall advise the don to burn them all."

Ariana's brow arched at the improbability of that occurrence.

"It is unsettling enough that a man of the don's position and breeding would degrade himself by learning to read and write, but that he should have done so with you is absolutely dreadful!" she continued as she resumed the packing. "And I have told him so on every occasion—not that he listens to me. But then, he never listens to me. How I rue the day he came to me and asked me to be your duenna."

He didn't ask you, Ariana thought. You asked him, and I know why.

"Well, it is all over now, isn't it? For once he's made the right decision for you. And none too soon." Ana closed the filled trunk and snapped the locks shut. "The good sisters of Saint Catherine will not put up with your fits and moods, Ariana Saldivar. I warn you." Suddenly she was at Ariana's side, practically shoving her aside. "You will never finish at that pace! I suppose I will have to do it all."

Ariana stepped aside, all too willingly, but not before she saw the woman falter and grow pale. "Your jewels—" she gasped, staring into the empty case. "Your mother's jewels —where are they!" Her voice had risen to an unladylike pitch.

Ariana fought a smile. "I gave them to *Tio Mariano,*" she lied. "For safekeeping. After all, I cannot take jewels to a convent which will not even allow me perfumed soap, now, can I?"

Ana looked stricken. She actually stuttered. "No—of course not." Then panic gave way to frustration and rage. "Look at you! Standing about in your chemise like some common harlot! Get dressed! *Madre Dios,* you're just like your mother!"

Ariana had been moving toward the bed where her dress was laid out, but she froze on the last words. Slowly, she turned about. "Never," she said with control, "never, ever again mention my mother!"

Ana was startled at the vehemence in Ariana's voice. The austere, sullen face slackened with shock. "How dare you talk to me that way!"

"I dare, Ana. Oh, I dare." Inwardly, Ariana was surprised at the icy calm she felt. "How it must have pleasured you, all these years, to have control of me. To take revenge upon the child for what the mother did to you."

"What are you babbling about?"

"I am not babbling, Ana. I will speak very clearly, so that even you will understand. You hated my mother. And with my father, your lover, you tried to find her jewels, the fortune left to her by my grandmother. She managed to foil you and my father's spendthrift ways by giving them to the don for safekeeping—a fact which you did not discover until after her death."

"How dare you—"

"Allow me to continue. After all, as you pointed out, time is growing short. This is the last opportunity we will have to speak of these things. Since I cannot take them with me, you were going to offer to take the jewels to the don for me, were you not? Though I doubt that they would have reached him. Tell me, what are your dreams, Ana; where were the jewels to take you? You did have it well-planned, I admit. I am not expected to return for a long time, perhaps years. And not until then would the theft be discovered. You don't look well, Ana. Do you want to sit down?"

Shock passed and the older woman's face suddenly scrunched with ugly hatred. "You are right about your father—he loved me, not her. But she was a Vallejo, and he was ambitious. And you're just like her—a little whore—"

"Get out."

The sudden authority in Ariana's voice caused Ana's head to jerk, and she stared at her. She looked as if she had seen a ghost. "Someday," the older woman rasped, moving toward the door, "you will suffer as I have. Someday."

As the door closed behind Ana, Ariana drew a calming breath. She could still see the look of hatred on her duenna's face—no, not her duenna. Never again would her mother's nemesis rule her every waking hour. She was simply an old woman, now left to the bitterness of her memories, as Ariana was left to hers.

Exhausted, Ariana slumped into a chair and drew her legs up under her. *Dios,* what was happening to her life? Perhaps she should have tried harder to be content with the structured role of the typical woman of her time. There was security in knowing what was expected and following that path, with no questions, no defiance, no challenges. *Madre* —she would have gone mad!

Had it been the same for her mother? she wondered. Had Rosalinda walked into her lover's arms to rebut codes and mores she couldn't accept? Her mother had stepped off the deeply rutted path life provided, and had paid dearly for it.

Rosalinda Vallejo had run away at the age of sixteen to live with Benito Saldivar. Eventually they had been married, ordered by Don Vallejo as he sought to protect his sister's honor. Then she had died when Ariana was six, disgraced by the final abandonment of her husband. Then not even the don could protect young Ariana from the judgment and condemnation of the family, or familia. Benito Saldivar had never been heard from again, though he was rumored to have died somewhere in the Oregon territory.

The child had been loved, nonetheless—by Don Mariano. Until this moment Ariana had not realized how vital and tenuous those cords of love had been. Fighting back tears, her eyes wandered about the room, coming to rest on the shelves of books lining the far wall. Rainbows of color blurred through her unshed tears, volumes that had been his special gift to her.

She could still remember the first time the don had read to her, after her mother had died. She could recall the emotion in his voice as he had held her in his lap. The words had little meaning while he told her of the future, the promise of worlds beyond her knowledge. She'd lived for those times with him—colorful stories, the secrets he had shared with her. The lonely, abandoned child's life had overflowed with imaginative delights.

She grew in concert with his confidence, his faith exposing her to a rapidly expanding world. Her body changed of its own accord, losing its childishness. Limbs lengthened, curves formed, much to her surprise; these changes were frightening, as no one had prepared her. She couldn't understand the new way in which others began to look at her, with speculation and disapproval, as if they were waiting for something she could not understand. She did not know then how much she looked like her beautiful mother: the same blue-black hair; the same oval face; the same high, delicate cheekbones dominated by large, almond-shaped eyes. Eyes that flashed defiance, countering convention. But she did not know that then.

Thus, she withdrew, focusing upon the only pleasure she

knew, and her mind expanded with what he taught her, reaching for purpose and approval. Her belief structure took form as she observed his wisdom and listened to the recountings of his own past. Was it any wonder she harbored the secret dreams of the *liberalismo?* Wanting to do what he had done, to be part of it? Besides, what other dreams were there for her?

As she had shared his understanding, his wisdom, she had been set apart. Men were drawn to her exceptional beauty and appalled when confronted by her mind. Never once had a man approached the don, asking for the honor to marry her. In a society where men considered education something to be avoided, such in a woman was anathema. No amount of land the don granted for her dowry, not even the fortune in jewels left by her mother, could compensate for her unsuitability. By the age of fifteen she had learned that she needed only to express an opinion to send a man into the arms of another. The child-outcast became a young woman who was appallingly and unforgivably poxed by knowledge and education.

She rose from the chair and crossed to the window, leaning her shoulder against the frame. Her eyes fixed on the ship waiting for her in the bay. I had dreams, she thought, and this would seem to be the end of them. She swallowed hard, forcing back a painful lump of unshed tears. There is so little that I've accomplished! So many things I want to do, to be! Then her entire being protested, denying the finality of what was happening to her. This is *not* the end! How many times had *Tio Mariano* told her that there were new worlds to conquer? That life was expanding, challenging, and each tomorrow was a beginning? "I promise you, *Tio,*" she whispered out loud. "In spite of this imprisonment, you have not heard the last of me!"

2

With the first few rays of dawn a sleek clipper ship cut through the current, rounding Point Pinos with shortened sail. Coming about, she sailed into the natural deep water harbor and dropped anchor. Those on deck burst into activity as the ship's company prepared for port. As the sailors rushed about the polished decks, Jeremy Randolf Morgan stood at the starboard railing, his eyes fixed on the shoreline.

The dark cloak that hung about his tall form lifted in the sharp breeze that swept across the water, but he was oblivious to everything except the object of his attention. His square jaw tightened as his deep blue eyes fixed with intense interest on the shoreline. The prominent mountains gave a solid background to densely wooded heights, reaching down to the breaking water which lapped over the rocky beach. His eyes were drawn to the scattered huts and sun-bleached adobes comprising the settlement of Monterey, nestled between the foot of the mountains and the rugged coastline.

Soft footsteps behind him broke his concentration and he turned. His eyes searched her face for some evidence of her mood as she came to stand at his side. The breeze released silky blond curls from her coiffure, which she had created with such studied care only an hour past. Her beautiful, pale blue eyes fixed on the shoreline.

"My God," she whispered. "It is worse than I imagined."

"Beth—" He modified his voice, regretting his quick anger. "You knew it wouldn't be New York."

She looked up at him. Her eyes were bright with accusation. "No. I knew it wouldn't be New York." She turned away from him. "I will see that the packing is finished."

He turned back and leaned against the railing as he heard the retreat of her footsteps across the heavy planking. What had he expected? She had known the glitter and excitement of the theater and the arts, balls and salons, streets teeming with commerce. And he had brought her to this: a few, ramshackle, sun-bleached adobes amid dusty, rutted streets. The capital of California.

It wasn't her fault; it was his. If she hated him he had no one to blame but himself.

Belowdeck, in the small, cramped cabin she had occupied for the past thirty-four days, Elizabeth Hilton Morgan choked back tears of grief and rage as she threw garments into a trunk. Picking up a delicate lace fichu, she stared at it for a moment, remembering that last time she had worn it. Unwanted memories flooded into her mind. A great sob broke forth, and she sunk onto the edge of the narrow ship's bed, clutching the delicate lace in her hands.

It seemed so long ago, yet it had been less than a year. Her debut season—parties, balls and salons. The glitter and excitement of New York had become her own, veritable feast, and her future lay gloriously ahead. As the exquisitely beautiful daughter of Jonathan Hilton, whose fortune alone would have drawn the creme de la creme of the eastern seaboard's eligible bachelors, Elizabeth was the undisputed belle of the season, a position she accepted with charm, wit, and grace. She had been nurtured to assume the role, and it came as naturally as breathing. She would have a stunning debut, an engagement to the most promising among the bevy of her eager and panting suitors, a wedding that would be *the* social occasion of New York society, followed by the same role her mother had played for the past eighteen years as a leader of New York society. It had all been gloriously planned and assured.

She first laid eyes on him at the Vanderhoorts' Grand Picnic, a sumptuous annual event given among the society couple's luxurious, manicured gardens to honor the season's debs. She spied him over the shoulder of Bradford Stewart, who was attempting to entertain her with a rather tiresome account of his sailing expertise. She barely heard what he said as she tried not to stare, and glancing away with vacant eyes, she smiled at the others in their select group, pretending interest in the conversation. But her mind was focused on the tall, incredibly handsome army officer, resplendent in an immaculately fitted tunic with gilt buttons.

She bided her time, knowing that the information she wanted would come to her soon enough. Never let it be said that Elizabeth Hilton was unbecomingly aggressive. The world came to her, as it always did, by way of others. Not fifteen minutes had passed when one of her very best friends, Amelia Harrison, joined the group. Beth knew immediately, by the gleam of excitement in Amelia's large brown eyes and the flush to her normally pale cheeks, that her messenger had arrived. It only took moments for Beth to detach herself gracefully from the small bevy of debs, including Margaret Winfield, Rosellen Astor, and their ardent suitors.

"Have you seen him?" Amelia asked breathlessly.

"Who?" Beth asked with a look of patient boredom, glancing about the stretching lawns that were sprinkled with the bright, colorful gowns of the ladies.

"Jeremy Randolf Morgan!"

The name caused a slight arch to a fair, manicured brow. "Morgan?"

"Yes, Hamilton Morgan's son! All that money and he is so extremely handsome! Over there, talking with Father and Mrs. Vanderhoort. Major Jeremy Morgan." She sighed wistfully. "He's been in Washington; something to do with the State Department and that awful man, James Buchanan, Father loathes so . . ."

Beth's interest sharpened, and she half listened as Amelia rattled on about Major Morgan's blue, blue eyes and his absolutely devastating smile, as her own thoughts took another course. She knew she needn't bother questioning her friend about Morgan's association with Buchanan; Amelia's understanding of government and power ceased beyond who had attended the inaugural ball and who wore what. Not that Beth's own interest didn't lean in that direction. After all, politics was not a fit subject for a woman. But she did understand associations, and the benefits that could be gained from them.

Hamilton Morgan was part of the Albany Regency, the small, powerful, elite group of men who controlled New York politics. They had been largely responsible for the upsetting victory of James Polk for the presidency and the power-switch to the Jacksonian Democrats in Washington. That was the limit of her understanding, but it was quite enough. She allowed her eyes to shift to the subject of Amelia's exultations, and her interest deepened.

A quarter of an hour later, Beth had just about expended her patience when she found her father with his cohorts in the Vanderhoorts' library. Pausing at the wide double doors leading to the gardens, she smoothed out the pale blue silk of her gown and adjusted the lace of her fichu. Assuming a smile that would show her dimples to their best advantage, she swept into the room.

"Oh!" she breathed, stopping short. Flushing, she backed away a few steps. "Gentlemen, I am so terribly sorry! I did not mean to disturb you."

Jonathan Hilton smiled with indulgent affection at his eldest daughter. "That is quite all right, Elizabeth."

"Indeed," Theodore Harrison agreed. "A young lady need never apologize for gracing a room with her beauty."

"Is there something you need, my dear?" her father asked patiently.

"Well, if you are not too busy—I would like to speak with you for a moment, Father."

He joined her outside, walking with her along the ivy-covered walk that surrounded the gardens. "What is so pressing, Elizabeth?" he asked, nodding to the other couples who passed. "A new gown, perhaps, for the Astors' ball?"

"No, Father. Mother has taken care of that. No . . ." Her brow wrinkled for a moment as she considered how to phrase her question. And then suddenly realizing what she was doing, she drew her fingers across her brow with mild alarm. A lady never frowned; it caused horrible wrinkles. "Father, tell me something important about James Buchanan."

Jonathan Hilton stopped short and frowned. "Why ever would you want to know about our secretary of state?"

"Has he done anything important?"

Jonathan Hilton laughed. "That would depend upon who you are listening to."

This wasn't getting her anywhere and she wanted to stamp her foot with frustration. She hadn't time for her father's illusive humor. "Father, I must know something immediately about what is happening in Washington."

Her father's eyes widened. "My dear, such things will only give you a headache. Now, why don't you go back to your friends? In the time you are spending with your old father, worrying about things that shouldn't concern you, you are depriving the young men of your company."

She glanced impatiently at those who were passing by. Oh bother, there was nothing for it but to come directly to the point. "I need something— Oh, bother, what do you know about Jeremy Morgan?"

Understanding dawned in Jonathan Hilton's brain. "Is that what this is about?" He chuckled. "Why did you not say so in the first place?" He drew her to a bench in the shadows of the arbor. "Now then, what could I tell you? Morgan, heh?" He glanced at his daughter and smiled appreciatively. "A good choice, my dear. Very good. Hamilton is proud of that boy, and he should be. Let's see, what do I know about Jeremy Morgan . . . I will have to make some discreet inquiries about the young man, of course. But for your purpose, I know that he was involved in the Aroostook War under General Scott—" Seeing his daughter's brow wrinkle, he shrugged. "Never mind that. Suffice it to say that he served his country well. So well, in fact, that when Daniel Webster—secretary of state under President Tyler—wrote the Webster-Ashburton Treaty, young Morgan was in a position to contribute to the signing."

"Father, I haven't the vaguest idea what you are talking about," she said impatiently.

"Of course you don't, my dear," he said, patting her hand. "Let's see; how to impress the young man. Ah, I think I have it—"

With little appetite, Beth nibbled lightly at the lobster salad. Not that it would have mattered if she were hungry; ladies never ate more than a few bites in public. Everything had gone beautifully, according to plan, as it always did. Dinner partners were drawn from lots at the Grand Picnic. However, lotteries, as everything else in a well-planned

social society, were easily fixed. Thus, with little finagling,
Elizabeth Hilton's dinner partner was Bradford Stewart.
Amelia had been practically overwrought with excitement
when Beth had told her that Amelia's partner was to be one
Major Jeremy Randolf Morgan. In fact, Beth thought she
was going to have to slap her friend to keep her from
swooning and ruining her plans. Poor, unsuspecting
Amelia, Beth thought. Little did she know that Beth had the
handsome Major Morgan exactly where she wanted him. To
have him as her partner would have been entirely too
obvious. No, indeed, he must come to her. That is exactly
why he was placed at best advantage, directly across the
table from her.

Flower laden, linen-covered tables had been set up under
the spreading maples that scattered over the Vanderhoorts'
vast lawns. Each table held a small group of three to four
couples, as it was thought that the smaller grouping led to
conversational ease and perhaps the beginning of betrothals
and weddings. These were, after all, the purpose of the
"season."

Beth wanted to kick Amelia under the table, and would
have, if her foot had reached. She loved her friend dearly,
but Amelia tended to become hysterical at the least provo-
cation. As the men had left the tables to fetch plates for the
ladies, Amelia had begun to giggle. Margaret and Rosellen
did not help matters as they fell into laughter at Amelia's
nervous titters. Beth wanted to scream. She snapped harsh-
ly at Amelia. Fortunately, it worked for a few moments.
However, if Amelia's constant, nervous chatter was any
indication, she would hyperventilate before the dessert.
Beth envisioned Major Morgan lifting Amelia into his arms
and carrying her off to Mary Vanderhoort's smelling salts.
So much for well-laid plans.

On the other hand, Amelia's silly chatter had managed to
hold the major's interest, in spite of the fact that he looked
rather pained. It was a point in his favor; the man was a
gentleman. And, she thought, it *had* given her time to study
him at leisure. He was incredibly handsome, more so up
close, with dark, softly curling hair revealed by the absence
of his hat. He had dark, full brows and a strong forehead,
which everyone knew indicated intelligence; strong chin,
determining strength; and patrician nose, which bespoke
nobility. Perhaps his family was even descended from

European aristocracy. She would have Father look into that. His skin was a bit too tanned, but that could be forgiven, considering his chosen profession. And, as she had already noticed, his eyes were blue, and he had a rather startling gaze, his irises ringed with a darker shade to emphasize their depth.

There was another reason to thank Amelia for her giddiness: it had distracted Major Morgan from the conversation at the table. Beth was armed with her father's advice, but she hadn't the vaguest idea of how to introduce it. But because of Amelia, he would be unaware of what everyone else had been saying, a fact which served Beth quite well. Taking a sip of her wine, she set the crystal goblet down on the table, carefully forming her next words.

"Bradford, actually I believe that the Webster-Ashburton Treaty had more to do with slavery than with territorial possessions."

Bradford Stewart inhaled his wine. He turned to Beth with watery eyes. "What?" he gasped raggedly.

"I believe I said it," she said lightly, picking at a pickled cucumber on her plate. "The British were far more concerned with the problem of slavery than territorial possessions. Hence, their reluctance to sign the treaty."

Bradford stared at her with confusion, as did the others at the table. "Beth, we had been talking about—"

"Perhaps you don't agree with me," she said quickly as she shrugged a delicate shoulder. "That is your right, Bradford, and I do respect your opinion. You needn't talk about it if you wish."

"I—we'll talk about it if you wish, Beth," Bradford mumbled.

"It is quite all right," she persisted. "Perhaps it is not suitable discussion . . ." she allowed her voice to trail off, touched with regret.

"It is a totally suitable subject of conversation, Miss Hilton."

Beth raised her heavily-lashed blue eyes and affected a look of wonder. His eyes were so very blue, she thought, and a moment of triumph filled her as they regarded her intently.

"Slavery was an issue," he said quietly, in a resonant voice that thrilled her, "although it is overstated to say that the British were not concerned with territorial possessions.

However, they were and are most concerned about our slave trade. They agreed to the treaty defining the boundaries between Canada and the United States. Restrictions upon slavery were seriously discussed."

She smiled at him, allowing a mischievous spark to enter her eyes. "I fear that we are boring our dinner partners, Major. I must apologize for bringing up such a serious matter at a social occasion. Will you forgive me?" She patted Bradford's hand by way of apology, ignoring the puzzled look he was giving her. With a smile of mutual tolerance and understanding cast across the table at the object of her interest, she attacked the lobster. Delicately.

For the next three months, New York society waited breathlessly, watching the courtship of the handsome and wealthy Major Jeremy Randolf Morgan and Elizabeth Forrest Hilton, the belle of the season. Everyone rejoiced when the betrothal was announced at a glittering dinner given by the bride's parents. The wedding, of course, was declared the social event of the season. Amelia was maid of honor, though Beth thought she cried a little too much, and a little too loudly. Nonetheless, it had been a magnificent courtship and a picture-perfect wedding. Beth's life, everything she had ever dreamed about, lay gloriously before her. Before the White House dinner. Before angry words, disgrace, and the end of a brilliant military career. Before exile.

Beth stared at the fichu clutched in her hands. The ship rocked, lifting on a wave, and dropped heavily, bringing her back to the present. Her fingers tightened on the delicate lace and she pulled, ripping it apart, shredding it again and again until it lay at her feet in tatters. Her tears pooled on the claret-colored silk of her skirt, and she heaved a sob, hating what had happened to her life. Everything was gone, lost in the promise of such a grand beginning. "You will pay, Jeremy!" she whispered out loud, trembling. "I swear it, you will pay!"

A deck above, Jeremy's thoughts had followed a similar path. He continued to stare out at the shoreline, though it had become blurred as his thoughts turned to the woman in the cabin below. It had begun so well, and had turned to such bitterness.

He had not wanted to go to that damn picnic, but his

father had insisted, claiming that he had buried himself in Washington for too long. A young man's interest should broaden beyond work, the elder Morgan had pressed. Now that he had been given leave from his duties, he should enjoy himself.

Jeremy had noticed her moments after arriving at the Vanderhoorts' home. There was no one to compare with her. Her hair had first drawn his eye: a light, golden blond, shimmering with highlights in the early afternoon sun. But beyond her physical beauty—the high, delicate cheekbones, the flushed, rosy silk of her complexion, the heavily lashed cornflower blue eyes, a body that moved with grace—it was her impudence and self-confidence that attracted him. One glance at the defiant and mischievous glint in those lovely eyes, and he was lost.

Her outrageous comment at supper had caught his attention, as it was meant to do. In spite of the nervous chatter of his supper companion, he had been quite aware of the conversation at the table. He had been as surprised as Beth's unfortunate escort when she had suddenly blurted out her outrageous statement. As the poor fellow coughed, Jeremy had struggled not to laugh, knowing that there was only one person at the table who could have been the target of such a comment. Delighted, he allowed himself to be drawn into her web.

Indeed, he was flattered that she had gone to such effort. He could have saved her the trouble. He had been about to address her, but such efforts could not go unrewarded. Occasionally he had wondered what she would have done if he had revealed his knowledge of her intrigue at dinner, asking her questions that could only have left her flushed and stymied. But he wouldn't have done so. He was already far too interested in the subject of Elizabeth Hilton.

He pursued her with determination and flourish, and in good faith, and love, he had led her into disaster.

Unwilling to dwell on the negative, Jeremy turned away from the shoreline and his morose, senseless thoughts. Stepping across the now cluttered deck, he made his way amidships, thinking of helping Beth with her packing. He proceeded down the deck, then paused, drawing back to let others pass by him in the narrow confine. He regarded them with some curiosity as they passed, for he had not noticed their presence on the ship before. As he knew all the passengers who had sailed from New York, he assumed that they had joined the ship from a Mexican port and had kept to their cabin.

Two Roman sisters passed by, clad in black, their faces framed in stiff white wimples of linen, their eyes downcast. Between them walked a small figure in a heavy dark cloak and hood. Losing interest, Jeremy would have passed them without more than a slight nod of polite greeting. However, as he stepped around them, sailors chose the moment to recoil the ropes which were strewn along the deck. Ropes became taut, leaping up just as Jeremy passed. As the rope entangled about her skirts, he instinctively moved to catch her as she fell. The sisters cried out, reaching for their companion, but he held her firmly.

Gaining his footing, Jeremy pulled her up against him and was startled to feel a soft, slender form. She struggled to right herself. Reaching down, he drew the thick rope from about her skirt. Setting her back on her feet, he looked down and his breath caught. He found himself staring into an exquisitely beautiful face with golden skin and exotic features. Black eyes, framed by soft, heavy lashes, looked up into his, eyes filled with wonder—and something else he could not define.

She struggled to her feet and drew away, re-adjusting her cloak about her body. The sisters clustered around her protectively, causing him to step aside, but not before he heard her husky voice, soft and compelling. *"Muchos gracias, Senor."*

He watched as they passed down the length of the deck to the sailors who were waiting to assist them into the longboat for shore. As they disappeared over the side of the ship, Jeremy turned and continued on to his cabin, hoping to find a moment's peace with his wife.

3

Jeremy glanced down at Beth, marveling at her capacity to look so composed after the long, dusty walk up from the Custom House where he had gained directions. Every glorious blond hair was in place beneath the ridiculously ornate bonnet she wore. But it suited her; Beth had the capacity to make her surroundings fit her presence, as if by divine right. He fought a smile as she shook dust from the hem of her skirt. He wondered, idly, how the dust had the affront to place itself there in the first place.

"Is this it?" she asked. Her measuring gaze passed over the building with surprise.

"It must be. Larkin is a leading merchant in Monterey. I seriously doubt that the customs agent was mistaken."

The building, quite surprisingly, reflected the colonial style of the eastern seaboard. It was two stories high, with an upper balcony supported by chambered posts, eight-over-eight pane windows, and redwood shingles instead of sun-baked tiles for the roof. The home reflected its neighbors only in the whitewashed adobe brick used for its walls.

They passed into the cool, dark room of the thick-walled adobe. The low ceiling was strewn with merchandise hanging from the heavy beamed rafters: pots, farm implements, herbs, harnesses, even furniture. Burdened tables allowed narrow passage and Beth's eyes widened at the display. "He has an entire mercantile city in here."

"Possibly." Jeremy grinned, picking up a surprisingly

delicate glass vase. "Apparently he's tried to cover every bet."

"I try, lad. I do try."

They turned in unison to find a small man, a few inches over five feet tall, standing in the doorway to a back room. He was dressed in a well-tailored frock coat and matching black trousers of wool, a starched white shirt and a well-folded stock, much like Jeremy's own attire. Mutton chop sideburns surrounded a narrow face, a determined chin, and bushy eyebrows over shrewd, encompassing eyes that were warm and welcoming, while measuring the newcomers. "I am Thomas Larkin. May I be of help to you?"

Jeremy introduced Beth and himself, adding, "We have arrived aboard the Chesapeake, out of New York. I have brought letters to you, from a mutual friend in Pennsylvania."

Beth glanced at her husband with surprise, but it went unnoticed as his attention fixed upon Larkin. The smaller man nodded, his eyes narrowing for an instant before the warmth of his smile returned. "Perhaps, Mr. and Mrs. Morgan, you would care to refresh yourselves after your long journey. Come." He gestured for them to follow and led them past a hallway, into a long storeroom. With a few, brief words to an associate who was unpacking crates in a corner, Larkin disappeared through another door, reappearing moments later with a small, dark-haired, handsome woman in her mid-thirties.

"May I present my wife, Rachel. The Morgans have just arrived from New York, my dear. Considering her long voyage, I am certain that you would wish to offer Mrs. Morgan the hospitality of our home."

Rachel Larkin emitted the same warmth as her husband and, to Jeremy's eye, the same, understated authority. In moments she was leading Beth up the narrow, banistered staircase to the upper floor and the Larkins' private quarters. As the women disappeared, Larkin turned to Jeremy and his easy smile dissolved. "All right, Morgan. I would like to see your letters."

He crossed into the hall and went up the stairs, leaving Jeremy to follow him. At the top, he turned, leading him into a small room at the right of the landing. Apparently it was Larkin's private study, as the walls were lined with books and ledgers. Small tables were similarly covered with papers, ledgers, and odd notes clipped in neat piles. Closing the door behind them, Larkin gestured Jeremy to one of the two uncluttered chairs in the room.

Jeremy drew a small, leather-encased packet from his coat. He handed it to Larkin, who withdrew to the other chair and immediately began to scan its contents. As Larkin relaxed in his chair, Jeremy had a moment to study his host. Jeremy had learned never to prejudge a man, but this one gave him pause. Larkin was a wealthy, successful merchant, first consul to California and, of late, confidential agent to President Polk. He was a friendly elf who was well on his way to becoming a self-made millionaire; a man who had single-handedly averted war in California.

It seemed only moments before Larkin placed the letters on the table beside him and looked up to regard Jeremy with studied interest. "Are you privy to what is said in the packet?"

"I am. The contents were memorized before I left New York. Had we been boarded by officials of the Mexican government, I would have destroyed them."

"What are your instructions?"

The question brought a wry smile. "I am to be 'discreet, cautious, and sleepless.'"

Larkin laughed. "That sounds like our mutual friend." Then his eyes crinkled with mischief. "My own orders from Buchanan said that I was to encourage the Californian's love of liberty so natural to the American Continent. Furthermore, that if California should assert herself and maintain her independence, the States shall render her all the kind offices in their power as a sister republic. Of course, if the people should desire to unite their destiny with that of the United States, they would be received as brethren, whenever this could be done, without affording Mexico just cause for complaint." Larkin chuckled. He wove his fingers together, folding his hands over his stomach. "So tell me, did you actually tell Secretary of War Marcy that he was an arrogant, self-serving power-seeker?"

Jeremy was nonplussed. "I did. How did you—"

"I keep myself apprised, Major Morgan. I must admit, it took a certain bravado, particularly at a White House dinner, in the presence of the president." Suddenly he gave a burst of laughter.

"It suited our purpose," Jeremy said.

"Indeed. Tell me, who chose that particular method for your—ah, release from duty?"

"I did." Jeremy smiled in spite of himself. "I've never particularly cared for Marcy, the champion of the 'spoils system.' The situation merely gave me the opportunity to say what I felt."

"A rare opportunity. I hope you enjoyed it."

"I did. As Marcy himself said, 'to the victor goes the spoils.' Mine was satisfaction."

Larkin grinned appreciatively. Then he sobered, regarding Jeremy steadily. "I do hope that you have come fully committed to your mission. I truly believe that California is the hub of a wheel that will roll our country into the next century. What we will attempt to do here is as important as anything you could have done. Unless you can believe that, I suggest you return to the Chesapeake and sail with her."

"I appreciate your concern, Consul," Jeremy answered. "I am aware of the work you have done here, and respect your right to question my dedication. My presence is strictly confidential. While my orders are clear, I am aware that should we do anything to cause political embarrassment for the government, my career will, indeed, be in the shambles it is now purported to be. Knowing this, I chose this assignment freely. As a matter of fact, my term of duty ended before I left the east. That I am still part of the army is by my choice."

Larkin regarded him silently for a long moment. "Good," he grunted. "That is what I wanted to know. Now let me tell you a little something about myself. What you may not already know," he added with a grin. "Should we be successful, the potential for profit is mind-boggling. If California becomes part of the Union, I shall be a very wealthy man. However, Union or no, I am firmly entrenched here, and nothing will affect the success of my business. I have made peace with the Mexican government, but more importantly with the Californios, those who truly own this land. I count them among my friends. The Californios are those you must come to know, Morgan, if you are to correctly judge the situation. It is they who control California, not the Mexican government. The dons rule her, have possessed her for decades. They rule with a power you will find difficult to comprehend, but you must if you are to achieve your mission."

"What is their attitude toward cession?"

"Some resist, but not all. The most important dons look toward the United States as a firm possibility for their future. We must encourage them. The most important of these is Mariano Guadalupe Vallejo. He is the wealthiest man in California. He owns lands in this area, including a house in Monterey, but controls the north, over one hundred seventy-five thousand acres from the Sacramento Valley to Yerba Buena at San Francisco Bay. The heart of his holdings is in the Valley of the Moon, known as Sonoma, but he is often here, as Monterey is still the center of California politics—in spite of the recent attempt to establish Los Angeles as the capital.

"We have difficult problems to counter, Morgan," he continued. "Mexico is hard pressed to release California from her domination, though it is traditionally indifferent to her needs. The Californios distrust all foreigners, except for those of us who have been here for many years and have embraced this way of life. All others are seen as a threat. Lastly, there are the disputes between the Californios themselves. As young men, Vallejo, Juan Alvarado, and Jose Castro were mainly responsible for establishing California's autonomy. Yet, when it was achieved, and Juan Alvarado became the first Californio to become governor, there was such a falling out between these three that eventually Mexico sent another governor to rule her."

"What happened?"

"What often happens when life-long dreams are achieved." Larkin shrugged. "Without another dream to replace it, purpose is reduced to pettiness and bickering. Alvarado was not an adept governor; he soon became little more than a drunkard. He has since retired to his lands, though with the release of his public responsibilities he has recovered from his destructive vices. But while he was governor, the situation between the three became tenuous. Alvarado became jealous of Vallejo's power; Mariano continuously disagreed with Alvarado's policies. Jose Castro became commandant of Northern California when Vallejo retired from that position, and has been arguing with Vallejo ever since—I suspect from fear of Vallejo's continuing influence and power. This opinion could be supported by the fact that Castro has turned his loyalties to Pio Pico, a Los Angeles don who was appointed governor by Mexico in

'42. An intolerable situation for the northern dons.

"But you will learn more of this in time," he concluded. "The important thing to remember is that Vallejo strongly supports cession to the United States; he is our best ally for a peaceful solution. And your arrival is impeccably timed; Mariano is in Monterey now. In fact, he has invited us to dinner. I think you should come along." He paused, rubbing his chin thoughtfully. "Now then, you will need a cover. I believe that your best guise would be that of an exporter. Lumber perhaps, to Mexico and the Sandwich Islands. Are you well financed?"

"I can manage."

"Good," Larkin grunted. "Do not fool yourself that it will be easy. You are here to assist me, as well as to determine the situation for yourself, with reports to Buchanan. You have much to learn before you will be competent to do either. I suspect that California will prove to be unlike anything you have known before, Major. Do not judge her, or her people, by the standards that are familiar to you. If you do, you will fail."

Larkin's caution brought other concerns to Jeremy's mind. He approached the subject awkwardly. "I understand, and will consider carefully what you have said. However, my wife—does not know anything of my mission. She believes me to be separated from the army. Moreover, she is with child. I would not want anything to upset her."

If he was surprised by the information, Larkin's talent as a diplomat served him well. "You know what is best for your wife, Major." He locked the packet in a desk drawer. "Now, shall we join the ladies?"

Beth looked with dismay about the small room. Lord save her, this was to be her home. The single structure, constructed of the same adobe brick as the Larkins' store and home, was set in back of the main house, in the gardens. Two windows overlooked the street, and there was another window on the opposite wall, near the door to the garden. The furnishings consisted of a bed, two chests of drawers, and a table with straight-backed chairs.

"It has a floor."

She glanced at Jeremy, who was studying the wide planks with interest. "Is that observation meant to be comforting?" she snapped irritably.

"Apparently, not many homes in Monterey do." He shrugged. "The Larkins said that most have trammeled earth floors. They—"

"Jeremy, if you say another word, I shall scream."

"Beth, this is only temporary. I have already informed Larkin that I plan to build a home for us. Fortunately, he has begun construction on three dwellings from which we may choose. In the meantime, can't you make the best of it?"

"Do I have a choice?"

His eyes hardened. "No, you don't. And while we are at it, as apparently we are going to argue, I expect you to be more gracious to Rachel Larkin. Your behavior was deplorable."

"I don't know what you are talking about," she said loftily.

"Don't you? Your remark about the primitive conditions in which she was forced to live was inexcusable."

"It was true."

"Only by your standards."

"Yes, Jeremy, my standards! And now I must live in this—this mud hole!"

"By your own choice, madam. I gave you every opportunity to remain in New York with your family. You insisted on accompanying me. I warned you; I tried to save you from this. You made your choice, Beth; I expect you to live with it."

He slammed the door behind him, leaving her to stare with impotent anger at the empty room. How could he? Why couldn't he understand that she had no choice? How could she have returned to her mother's home, a wife, yet not a wife—and pregnant? Her condition would have excluded her from social functions and the company of her unmarried friends. Moreover, she would have appeared a fool, married to a man who had soundly disgraced himself and abandoned her. All those months before the wedding, she had lived at the pinnacle of society. It would be unthinkable for her to suffer the loneliness of pregnancy while surrounded by scandal and gossip. Stay? She would have died first.

If only she hadn't proved quite so fruitful. Without the pregnancy she was certain that eventually she could have overcome the scandal, but Jeremy had impregnated her almost immediately. At first she had been delighted by the fact, as it released her from her husband's affections.

Though the small room was overly warm from the fire Jeremy had set, Beth shivered. She had suffered through those first months of marriage, and then suspected that she might be with child. Actually, it was not she who had first suspected, but Jeremy.

Like any decent woman of her time, Beth was an innocent on her wedding night. Oh, her mother had talked to her the night before the wedding, though at the time Margaret Hilton's words had seemed insensible. Mostly, Beth recalled her mother's distaste for the subject she had come to discuss, though the fact did not impress Beth. Disapproval was a normal condition for Margaret Hilton. Besides, Beth's thoughts were filled with last-minute details of the wedding. But her mother's few words became horrifyingly vivid less than twenty-four hours later.

"There are certain matters which a married woman must suffer, Elizabeth. However, if your husband is considerate, he will have his way quickly and with little fuss. You must allow him, except when he has had excessive drink. In that event you may bar your door to him. Think of more pleasant matters and it will not be quite so distasteful."

Her mother was wrong. But then, Jeremy was not a considerate husband. He . . . had removed her gown and touched her with shocking intimacy—in places on her body that she had never dared touch.

She shifted uncomfortably in the chair before the fire, wondering why she was allowing herself to recall those moments. Perhaps because she knew that someday, after the birth . . . he would do "it" again. But not for months.

When Jeremy had told her that she was pregnant, she had been horrified. She would never become accustomed to the fact that he could so casually discuss such an intimacy. But he seemed genuinely pleased, even delighted. His gentle teasing eased her embarrassment somewhat, until she asked him how he could possibly be certain. Unfortunately, he told her. She had listened with shock, flushing at the mention of her breasts. When he mentioned the absence of her monthly flux, she was left speechless.

Beyond the disquieting aspects of the physical side of marriage, those first months of her marriage to Jeremy had been everything she had hoped for. She found herself in a new position with her friends, the grand dame of the young set. Sparkling with authority and a husband who unfailingly drew admiring and wistful glances from the ladies, she saw the future beckoning gloriously.

Then, in one horrible night it all changed. Dinner at the White House, angry words exchanged, and disgrace. He had even tried to justify his actions to her, but she had no interest in listening to him. What could he have possibly said to have made up for such humiliation? And then, just when she thought they had been forgiven by their friends, when calling cards and invitations once again were left on the silver tray in the entry hall, he had calmly announced that soon they would be leaving for California! Three weeks later they were on a ship bound for Monterey.

Beth glanced about the small room, the spare, primitive furniture, remembering all that she had left behind. Despair overcame her and she dropped her head to her arms, giving in to an overwhelming rush of self-pity.

"You have a beautiful home, Don Mariano," Jeremy said graciously, while silently thinking of ways to strangle Beth. She was stunning in a rose silk gown, with diamonds sparkling against her ivory skin above the low neckline, and yet, he wanted to throttle her.

The evening had begun surprisingly well. When he had returned to their quarters that afternoon, to inform her that they would be dining with friends of the Larkins, she had seemed resigned. When they had joined the Larkins in their parlor for a glass of sherry before departing for dinner, she had displayed none of her earlier shrewishness toward Rachel Larkin. In fact, she had been warm and gracious, giving Jeremy some hope that the worst had past. He watched his beautiful, young wife as she laughed delightedly at a comment Thomas made, and he felt the same rush of warmth and love he had felt for her before their marriage.

Then Beth learned that they would be walking to dinner. Apparently, it was a normal occurrence, as there were no carriages in Monterey. Larkin had a perfectly splendid carriage ordered for Rachel, he informed them, but it would not arrive from the east for two to three more months. Then, with a glance at the tip of Beth's rose-slippered foot, Larkin good-naturedly suggested that Rachel might lend her some "appropriate" footwear for the trek. And, he added, it would do her well to hike up her skirt to keep the mud from her hem.

Beth did not say a word. She didn't have to; Jeremy had learned to read her silences. They came in degrees, from miff to extreme displeasure to sheer rage. Her mood, as they walked up the hill from the Larkin house, was lurking somewhere between the latter two.

Knowing he was on thin ice, Jeremy nevertheless tried to explain to her in a lowered voice the importance of their dinner host. Mariano Vallejo was one of the most influential men in California. If Jeremy was to be successful in his business enterprises, it was imperative to enlist Vallejo's support. He cautioned her not to speak of their past, particularly of his military career. The Californios were wary of foreigners, particularly those who had been in the military, he explained, and the wrong word could lose their trust completely. As he had hoped, the information seemed to appease her, and he felt her relax against his arm. Any ease he felt, however, was dispelled moments after they entered the Vallejo home.

Jeremy was impressed, as he had been with the Larkin home, by the well-appointed New England influence depicted in the furnishings of the Vallejo parlor. As he turned to Beth to note her reaction, he realized that her attention was fixed on something other than Vallejo's choice of decor. Her eyes were wide as she stared at Vallejo's other guests.

"My word," she breathed. "They . . . are so dark!" Then, to his dismay, her eyes turned to blue ice.

Everyone in the room had turned at their entrance, and Jeremy covered his horror at Beth's comment with a smile. While two of the men present were apparently American or European, the women in their company were dark-complexioned Californios. The third man broke from the group and came forward to greet them. He was tall for a Californio, with a round face, rosy cheeks, and bushy brows over bright, lively, appraising eyes. He introduced himself as Mariano Vallejo and graciously welcomed them to his home. He turned then, and introduced them to the others.

John Cooper, Larkin's half-brother, and William Garner, a tall, blond Englishman, were, like Larkin, longtime residents of the area and heavily involved with trade. In fact, Larkin explained, it was Cooper's influence that had first drawn him to Monterey. While pleasantries were being exchanged, Jeremy grew more tense. Beth was staring coldly at the women. Then, as Vallejo introduced them as Maria Francisca de Garner and Dona Encarnacion de Cooper, he felt her stiffen.

"Your wives?" she asked.

"Si, Senora Morgan," Vallejo answered smoothly. If he was affronted by the question, he graciously gave no evidence of it. Cooper and Garner stared at her.

"Dona Encarnacion is also Mariano's younger sister," Larkin added, smiling at Beth with equal diplomacy.

Jeremy wanted to shake her. "Don Mariano, your home is quite beautiful."

"I am gratified that you are pleased, Senor Morgan," Vallejo responded warmly. "Most of what you see is due to the efforts and talents of our friend, Thomas. One merely has to express the slightest wish for anything, and it miraculously appears upon the next ship in our harbor."

"I do my best, Mariano." Larkin smiled.

"Such modesty, Thomas." Vallejo laughed. "You give new meaning to the title merchant. Your efforts have brought a new standard of living to Monterey. Not to mention your pockets."

"Give a little, take a little." Larkin shrugged; the men laughed.

Rachel smiled at her husband affectionately. "I wish you had given the same attention to my carriage, my dear. I fear that I have ruined another gown walking through those streets."

"Amen," Beth added, arching a brow.

Vallejo sighed. "Ah, Rachel. I have told you that if you would learn to ride as our women you would not be subject to ruining your lovely gowns."

"Ride? Dressed like this?" Beth asked, amazed.

"Quite so, Mrs. Morgan," Cooper answered. "Californio women do not hold to the delicacies of eastern tastes, riding only for pleasure and only when one is 'properly attired.' They are one with their horses. A Californio woman would never walk when she could ride."

Fortunately, Beth was too dumbstruck to respond immediately. Jeremy slipped quickly into the conversation. "Speaking of which, I am in need of a mount. I would be grateful for advice as to where good animals can be purchased. Could you suggest . . ." But the request was never finished.

"Dinner will be served in a few moments," announced a husky, feminine voice.

Jeremy turned, unaware that anyone had entered the room. She came to stand by Vallejo's side and slipped an arm beneath the don's. Jeremy stared into dark, exotic eyes. His own widened perceptibly as a flicker of recognition passed between them.

"Ariana!" Rachel Larkin exclaimed, stepping forward to draw her into a hug. "Oh, my dear, I did not know you had returned! Mariano, why didn't you tell me?"

"A surprise for you, Rachel." Vallejo smiled, glancing down at the young woman with affection. "It was the reason for this particular dinner invitation. Senor and Senora Morgan, may I present my niece, Ariana Saldivar. She has recently returned to us from the Convent of Saint Catherine's in Mexico. It is a very happy day for us."

Jeremy fought a smile. That answered the question about the nuns. Amazing, he thought, this exquisite creature in a convent? She was beautiful, with a creamy complexion of deep gold, and large, expressive eyes that were almost black. Her slender figure was gowned in pale green silk with ivory lace at the neckline. Her raven hair was pulled back severely into a chignon at her neck. The effect emphasized her heavily lashed dark eyes and high, sculptured cheekbones. On the other hand, he mused, a convent would be an effective way to protect such a beauty. Not a bad system, when one considered it. He glanced at his wife. Beth was staring at the other woman and Jeremy tensed.

"By my word," she said. "Were you actually in a convent? How perfectly dreadful."

4

The white, linen-covered table sparkled with fine china, glistening crystal goblets, and heavy Spanish silver. Jeremy was seated on Ariana Saldivar's right, with Rachel Larkin at his left. Beth, to his horror, had been placed at the other end of the table next to Vallejo. In all probability, he mused grimly, their stay in California would prove to be extremely short.

He turned to find Ariana watching him speculatively. "Senor Morgan, I am glad to have this opportunity to thank you properly for saving me from injury aboard the Chesapeake."

"It was my pleasure, Senorita Saldivar." He smiled. "But I must apologize for my wife's rudeness."

"It is not necessary," she responded, nodding to the servants to serve the first course. When she turned back, he was surprised by the glint of humor in her lovely eyes. "She was correct. It was dreadful."

"New England pot roast!" Larkin exclaimed as the dishes were carried in.

"And boiled potatoes." Ariana smiled. "Just for you, Thomas."

"But however did you learn to cook this?" Larkin grinned, his eyes rolling with pleasure as his dish was served.

"I have my secrets," she answered.

"Indeed," Vallejo agreed, watching his niece speculatively. "It appears that you do."

Ariana merely smiled, ignoring her uncle's gaze. "Thomas, I remembered you once saying that if you had to eat one more tortilla you would go mad."

"Tortilla?" Beth asked.

"A type of unleavened bread that is the staple of our diet, Senora," Vallejo answered. "But you could not know, Ariana; Thomas has long since solved that particular problem. Four years ago he opened a bakery. It prepares the leavened bread he prefers, along with other delicacies to suit his Yanqui palate. It has proven quite popular with foreigners."

"Four years ago?" Ariana repeated softly. She picked up her wine goblet, and Jeremy wondered at the sadness of her expression.

Dinner progressed smoothly. As Ariana had fallen strangely silent, in spite of his efforts to engage her in conversation, Jeremy turned his attention to others at the table. Warily, he glanced down the table at Beth. Larkin was dominating his end of the table, barely giving Beth an opportunity to draw breath. Stifling a grin, Jeremy relaxed and enjoyed the well-prepared dinner.

As the roast was served, Vallejo addressed Jeremy. "Senor Morgan, Thomas's note to me this afternoon mentioned that you have come to California with hopes of developing a business in lumber."

"Yes, Don Mariano, that is correct."

"I have suggested redwood, Mariano," Larkin said. "The mountains of Santa Cruz."

"Si." Vallejo nodded. "A good choice. But may I ask, if I am not being too forward, why you have chosen California, and not, say, the Oregon territory?"

"Of course you may ask. California's natural ports, her resources, not to mention her moderate climate, hold great promise for anyone seeking a new life. Articles in the New York *Sun*—which I understand were written by Larkin—caught my interest." He glanced at Larkin, who met his eyes over his wineglass.

"Ah, si. Thomas is California's most vocal champion, though he chooses not to sign his work. However, I understand that his articles have been picked up by many of the newspapers in the eastern part of your country. You are from New York then?"

"No, sir. I read his articles in the *Sun* as I spend a good deal of time in New York. However, my family home is in Pennsylvania."

Beth frowned, staring at her husband for a moment. Pennsylvania? She thought he had always been in New York. Glancing up, she met Larkin's eyes. My word, she thought, why was he looking at her in that strange way? The man looked as if his collar button would pop.

Vallejo gave a moment to his dinner. Then, wiping his mouth with his napkin, he leaned back and sipped from his goblet. "Pennsylvania. Would your father be Hamilton Morgan?"

Jeremy was nonplussed. "You know of my father?"

The don cut into his beef. "Your father is a prominent man—merchant, banker, exporter. He owns one of the largest shipping lines in the states, does he not?"

"He is comfortable."

"Si. Comfortable." Vallejo gave in to a chuckle. "I like that." He took another bite of his beef, chewing thoughtfully. "Pennsylvania. Your new secretary of state, Buchanan, is from Pennsylvania, I believe. Am I correct?"

Jeremy's stomach tightened and he forced himself not to look at Larkin. Setting his goblet down, he smiled. "Yes, I am proud to say that he is. A native son."

"I am certain that you are proud, as your father must be."

"My father, sir?"

"Of course!" Vallejo smiled. "It cannot hurt one's business when a fellow . . . a native son, is in such a position of prominence!"

"No, it wouldn't hurt," Jeremy agreed. "Don Mariano, this wine is delicious. My compliments."

"Again, a testament to Thomas's talents. I merely have to request a French vintage, and it miraculously appears. I believe that Ariana has champagne chilling to serve with our dessert. Am I correct, my dear?"

"Si, Tio," she answered. "And a cake for Thomas."

"Oh, my dear, you spoil me!" Larkin said contentedly.

As he half-listened to the exchange, Jeremy's thoughts were not on food. He was stunned by the don's observations. Glancing covertly at the man as Vallejo exchanged opinions with Larkin over the merits of the coming dessert, he wondered about the depth of the don's questions—and knowledge. Had his observation about Buchanan been innocent? One thing was certain, he would not take this man lightly. If he had been tempted to underestimate him, he would no longer be so foolish.

"Gentlemen." Ariana rose from her chair as the servants cleared away the dessert plates. "We shall leave you to your brandy. Ladies?" The women rose and followed her into the parlor. A servant entered with a tray bearing a carafe, glasses, and a humidor of cigars.

Jeremy observed as the clear liquid was poured into a glass and set before him. He looked up, noticing that the others were watching him.

"Have you ever had aguardiente, Morgan?" Cooper asked innocently.

"No, I cannot say that I have." Noting their expressions, he eyed the glass with suspicion. The others took up their glasses, tossing off the contents with a swallow. Against a silent sigh, Jeremy repeated the action with his own glass. The liquid seared his throat, taking his breath away. For an instant the room seemed to disappear, and there was an explosion of red behind his eyes. Slowly, he began to focus on the expectant expression of John Cooper.

"Gentlemen," he gasped, clearing his throat with effort. "If there is a heaven, I have just swallowed it."

The room filled with laughter. Vallejo clapped him on his back. "Well done, Morgan. It is normal for a Yanqui to follow his first drink of aguardiente with a bucket of water before he can speak again."

Beth shifted uncomfortably in the high-backed chair. In the awkward silence, her gaze passed over the room, then fixed on the two women sitting across from her. Rachel had abandoned them to powder her nose, and their hostess had excused herself to see to a problem in the kitchen. Why were these women simply staring at her?

Suddenly Maria Francisca broke the silence. "Is that your own hair color, Senora Morgan?"

Beth thought she might choke. What an astounding question! "Of course it is!"

"You must not take offense," Ariana said, entering the

room. "Maria did not mean anything by her question." She took a chair next to Beth and began to pour out cups of thick, black coffee. "Before Rachel came to Monterey my people had never seen a white woman. Surely you can understand that her manners and dress were considered quite unusual. Moreover, Rachel's hair is brown, much like our own. Your fairness is thought to be quite unique."

Beth watched as Ariana added sugar, then stirred the coffee with thick sticks of cinnamon. As Beth reached out to accept the offered cup, she glanced at the other two women. The silk gowns they wore were of good fabric, but decidedly plain, except for the bright colors. They were cut deeply off the shoulders, and apparently the women wore no petticoats beneath them. It was an observation Beth had made upon her arrival, and she was still shocked by it. Of course, they would be fascinated by a white woman, she reasoned, particularly one with manners and breeding.

"That is quite understandable," she said with studied graciousness. "Yes," she added patiently. "This is my natural hair color. Many American women have light-colored hair."

"It is very beautiful," Dona Encarnacion said.

Beth smiled, accepting the compliment.

Rachel Larkin returned at that moment. "Well now," she said pleasantly, "what have we been talking about? Thank you, Ariana," she added, accepting a cup of coffee.

"The color of Senora Morgan's hair," Ariana said dryly, sipping her coffee.

Rachel glanced at Beth. "Oh. Yes, it is quite beautiful."

"This coffee is delicious," Beth said with surprise.

Ariana smiled, accepting the compliment.

"Well, Ariana, tell us all of it," Rachel said as she settled into her chair. "How have the last six years treated you?"

"Well enough." Ariana shrugged.

"Come now, tell me. Six years is a long time."

"Yes. It is." Ariana stared at Rachel, and a silent understanding passed between them.

"I am glad that you are back," Rachel said softly. Her eyes filled with compassion.

Beth glanced between the two, wondering at the silent exchange. "What is a convent like?" she asked bluntly.

"It is solitude," Ariana answered. "Contemplation, a

time of peace. A time to find one's soul."

"Of course." Beth hadn't the vaguest idea what she was talking about. "And did you?"

"Did I what, Senora Morgan?"

"Find your soul?"

"Beth!" Rachel exclaimed.

Beth ignored Rachel's protest as she waited for an answer.

"Yes, Senora Morgan. I found it. But that could not possibly interest you. Tell me, are you from Pennsylvania like your husband?"

"Oh no, certainly not. I have spent my entire life in New York." Obviously, this was all that needed to be said.

"You met in New York then?"

"Yes, during my debut."

"Your debut?" Maria Francisca asked.

Seeing the blank expressions on Maria's and Encarnacion's faces, she smiled patiently. Oh dear, how could she explain this? "It is a season for a young woman's presentation to society."

"Oh si, I understand!" Encarnacion said brightly. "It is her *quincienera!*"

"Her what?" Beth frowned.

"Her debut," Ariana said. "It is much the same."

"Oh," Beth said, looking slightly disappointed. Indeed. Much the same? Really! She glanced at Rachel Larkin.

"So, you met Senor Morgan during your debut," Ariana observed. "Was he one of your *chambelanos?*"

"My what?"

"One of your escorts," Rachel translated.

"Oh, no. I met Jeremy at the Grand Picnic, given by the Vanderhoorts—" She looked into blank faces. Sighing, she shrugged. "I met him at a picnic."

"A *merienda,*" Maria said, nodding. "It is a good place to meet a young man."

"Indeed," Ariana observed. "How fortunate that he chose that moment to visit his father. I suppose that was the reason he was in New York—from Pennsylvania."

"Oh, no," Beth tossed. "He was . . ."

"On a holiday," Rachel said quickly.

Beth stared at Rachel. Did the woman think she was without sense? Fuss and bother. Jeremy had cautioned her not to speak of his military career, and that was the last thing she intended to do.

"Was your husband in the lumber business in Pennsylvania?" Ariana pressed.

"I believe that he—" Rachel began.

"My husband has many talents," Beth interrupted, drawing her eyes from Rachel. She smiled at Ariana. "Lumber is only one of them."

Jeremy stared at his wife's back as she walked ahead with Rachel on their return to the Larkin home. Larkin had been silent since they left Vallejo's house, his thoughts on what Rachel had whispered to him when they had managed a few moments alone.

"Morgan, I fear that your wife was going to give you away," Larkin said suddenly. "How can you expect her not to say something untoward, quite innocently, of course, when she knows nothing of your business here?"

"You have been away from the east too long, Larkin," Jeremy said. "My wife is a social creature, a part of that social milieu that has kept her innocent and spoiled. However, she was taught that a woman's energies are focused on her husband's career, and thus her own position in society. She has no understanding of business or politics, Thomas, but her instincts sharpen at the slightest hint of anything that could affect me."

"Forgive me," Larkin grunted, "but I have observed your wife's lack of tact in certain situations."

There was little Jeremy could say to that, and they fell silent. How could he explain to this man about the world in which Beth had been raised? He knew that she would never betray him as long as she was allowed to exist within the stringent confines of what she felt to be her role in life. But what would happen if he were to confide in her, giving her the opportunity to think for herself, and she disagreed with him? That could spell disaster.

Beth had been trained, influenced to believe that she could never comprehend a man's world. Her only duty was to support her husband. For a woman like Beth, an opinion was a dangerous thing. She would turn on Jeremy in a moment. His gaze shifted to Rachel Larkin and he fought a sigh. No, Larkin couldn't understand. What he had observed between Thomas and Rachel confirmed his misgivings. Such love, one that thrived in an obvious partnership, couldn't possibly comprehend the simple fact that his wife loathed him. Keeping her uninformed would assure her support. Should she begin to understand what he was doing, what she had given up for it, she would try to destroy him.

Beth readied for bed behind the screen Jeremy had constructed for her privacy. Angry, she nearly ruined a fine lawn chemise, causing a narrow rip in the bodice. Tossing it aside, she pulled her nightgown over her head, buttoning it to the neck. As she stepped around the screen she was surprised that Jeremy had not yet retired, but was lounging in a chair with a glass of wine.

"It is late," she said tightly. "Do you really need that?"

"Yes," he drawled, his eyes passing over her slowly. "I do."

She tensed uncomfortably, even as she knew that the full, cotton garment concealed her suitably. His look made her squirm, nonetheless. Her discomfort brought suppressed anger to the surface. "Why did you tell Don Vallejo that you were from Pennsylvania?"

His gaze raised to hers. "Because I am. Our family home is in Pennsylvania, my love." He lifted his goblet to her in silent tribute.

It struck her uncomfortably that there was so much she did not know about her husband. "Why couldn't you tell him that you had been in the army? The subject of your career arose among the ladies while you were having your brandy. Oh, don't look so alarmed, I didn't say anything. You told me not to . . . but why, Jeremy? What does it matter now?"

"I explained that to you, Beth," he said wearily. Oh God, it would be so much easier if he *could* trust her. "I am here to start a new business—a new life for us. I must have the complete trust of these people. You may speak of anything else, but if they discover that I was recently a member of the United States military, it could undermine any possibility of my gaining that trust. Larkin's advice to me confirmed this opinion. Trust me, Beth, I know what is best. Beyond that, except for your rudeness when we first arrived, you did well tonight, and I am proud of you. Now go to bed."

She had been suffused with feelings of frustration and outrage as her mind had tossed with questions that preoccupied her throughout the evening. Then, in his dismissal, she seemed to lose the meaning of her question. What did it matter, anyway? she thought, crossing to the bed. Men concerned themselves with such insidious things. They were better not considered. Crawling into bed, she pulled the covers up to her chin. She *had* done well, she thought in the last moments before sleep claimed her. Whatever he was doing, she was certain that she had not spoiled his plan. She recalled her father's oft-repeated words: a new enterprise demanded quick action; one must always be a step ahead of the other man. Yes, she had done well.

Jeremy sat in the silence, sipping his wine. His explanation had been so effortless. A frown, a stern word, and she had forgotten her question. Her response had come as a surprise, bringing him a sudden, stirring moment of hope. Fortunately, he had come to his senses and had dismissed the temptation to confide in her. He groaned, shifting on the hard chair.

What was it that plagued him so? Beth was—almost everything he had ever expected in a wife. She was beautiful. She could charm anyone she chose to impress. She was intelligent, though she didn't know it. She was spoiled to the tips of her tiny toes. In fact, it was that which had first drawn him to her. He smiled. It was her shrewd, calculated plotting that had caught him. She had tantalized him with the heady prospect of peeling away those well-formed social molds; gradually bringing her to realize her own worth. And then it had all quite suddenly ended and he found himself treating her as he had sworn he would never do. Their marriage was exactly like others he had observed and detested. All hope, all expectation, were gone, merely because he had touched her.

Jeremy had been well-versed in the role he was to play as a husband of his time. His father had introduced him to his first whore when he was fifteen. This was the male debut. Along with the carefully chosen harlots that brought Jeremy Morgan into a new, expanding world, there were lectures on the position he would eventually acquire as a husband. Jeremy soon rejected his father's paid offerings, finding his own willing subjects throughout his college years. They were women who gave freely of their emotions as well as their lovely bodies. They were women he cherished, and his moments with them touched upon something deep. But the lectures continued. He listened to his father's diatribes on the role of a husband, and Jeremy saw examples of the elder Morgan's teachings in his mother and her friends: the stoic wife.

"A gentleman does not suffer his wife unnecessary indignities," his father said one evening in the library as they shared a nightcap. "She endures, as no good woman enjoys sexual pleasures as a man does. Have it done quickly, my boy. It will cause her less pain."

There were three members of the human race, Jeremy learned in his youth: men, wives, and mistresses. The latter two were separated by far more than just marriage vows. Mistresses enjoyed carnal knowledge. He had observed this first in his father's exploits and then through his own experiences. In fact, these women demanded it. Mistresses, he found, could experience a climax. Wives, so he had been told, were incapable of it. "Good" women married and spent their entire lives suffering the attentions of their husbands. By the time Jeremy was nineteen, he decided that something was terribly wrong with these attitudes. He decided simply that his wife would enjoy the pleasures of a mistress. His wife's body would be treated with the same consideration as any woman he had touched, bringing her the same pleasure. Surely the experience would prove to be even more satisfying with love.

As a man, the naivete of his youth caught up with him. He knew that his expertise in matters of physical satisfaction was more than adequate. Yet, on his wedding night he began to discover the difference between wives and lovers. He had loved Beth, and he had tried to bring her the satisfaction he wanted for her. That night, she had begun to hate him.

Rachel Larkin glanced at her husband and sighed. "Thomas, surely that can wait until morning."

Larkin grunted as he finished the last few lines of the letter. He glanced up at his wife. "This letter must go out on the merchantman leaving in the morning. Now, what is it that you were trying to tell me?"

"I wasn't trying to tell you anything," she said with fond patience. "I asked you what you thought of Beth Morgan."

"I think she will be the undoing of her husband's mission." He rose from the writing table in their bedroom and untied his stock, tossing it onto a nearby chair. "What did you talk about, before we joined you in the parlor?"

"Not much," she answered, picking up the stock and the shirt that joined it. "Actually, I agree with what Jeremy told you. I think that young woman understands more than you give her credit for. Oh, I don't think that she understands the reasons for everything she does, but her instincts are good. When it is important to her, she handles herself well."

"She's a spoiled brat."

"Yes, she is. But she comes by it honestly, Thomas. She cannot be blamed for her upbringing."

Larkin grunted. "I defer to your judgment, madam. So then, what has been bothering you since we returned home?"

She smiled as she handed him a bedgown. "Am I so obvious?" she asked, crossing to the wardrobe to hang up his jacket.

"Only to me."

"Perhaps it is nothing." She shrugged. Meeting her husband's eyes she answered somberly. "It is Ariana," she said. "It is only a feeling—but as I live and breathe, she is up to something."

Ariana paused, looking up from the letter she was writing to glance about her uncle's study. Everything was the same, she mused, exactly the same. It was as if six years of her life had not passed by at all. She had stepped off the Chesapeake to reenter an unchanged world. She glanced down at the letter before her and tapped the end of the pen against her lips as she composed her thoughts. This world was not totally unchanged, she thought, for she had changed. Yet, she was part of it, and would never leave it again.

She finished the last lines of the missive and sealed it. Just then the door to the study opened, and she slid the note into the pocket of her skirt. She looked up and smiled.

"*Querida,* you are up late," Vallejo said as he came into the room.

"So are you, apparently." She smiled.

"I came for something to read before I slept."

"So did I," she said, picking up the open book on the desk. She rose, crossing to the fireplace. Clasping the book in her crossed arms, she warmed herself from the fire.

"In fact, I am glad to find you here. It will give us the chance to talk."

"About what, *Tio?*"

"I could think of many things," he said leaning against the desk. "We have not had a chance to talk since your return."

"Did not the good sisters report to you? I understood that they did so weekly."

"Of course. And the reports were quite satisfactory. But I would know your feelings, Ariana."

My feelings? she wondered. How should one feel about six long years cloistered behind thick, gray walls? Seventy months of back-breaking work. Plain rationed food; austere women who would speak only when necessary. She had been eighteen years old when she entered the Convent of Saint Catherine and had been horribly lonely and filled with grief.

"I learned much with the help of the good sisters, *Tio,* like the comfort of obedience—to know when one does not question but merely obeys."

He regarded her for a long moment. "Did you receive the books I sent to you?"

"Si," she answered, true warmth entering her voice. "They were—very dear to me. More important than I can say."

"Bueno," he said. For an instant she thought she read regret in his expression. "I would not have had you without the comfort of books, Ariana. There was a time in my youth when I knew such emptiness." He paused, sighing deeply. "Do you understand why it was necessary for me to send you away?"

How strange, she thought. That question once caused her to cry herself to sleep. Now she felt nothing. Her emotions had long since hardened. *"Si, Tio.* I disobeyed you, placing the familia in grave danger."

"No, Ariana. Your only offense was youthfully foolish judgment. It was a difficult and dangerous time. Forty-three of the foreigners who threatened rebellion were arrested and sent to Mexico to stand charges of insurrection. The situation could have been far worse if your hot-headed band had been allowed to interfere. I could not have you involved."

She kept her voice even as she struggled with the anger his words brought. "Yet, the others who were involved were rewarded! Soon after I was sent away, Manuel—who had led my 'hot-headed band'—was made Prefect of Monterey!

Why, *Tio?* Because he was worthy? Because he is Jose Castro's nephew? Or just because he is a man? He has held that position all these years, while only I was punished."

"I did not send you away because of what you did that night, Ariana, but what I feared you would do in the future. I wanted you removed from the temptations of involving yourself in dangerous pursuits. I had been far too lenient with you, and you would suffer as a result. It grieves me that you had to be sent away because of my mistakes. I knew, however, that I was not strong enough to say no to you, and I had to leave it to others to do it for me.

"But you are home now," he continued. "And none too soon. Had I suspected that a revolution would begin in Mexico, I would not have left you there as long as I did."

"I was safe at the convent, *Tio.*"

"Yes, fortunately you were. But tell me—was it as bad as we heard?"

"It was terrible. There were riots; mobs began by destroying Santa Anna's monuments, and soon the rioting spread to the entire city. Even the soldiers mutinied. Only when Herrera took the reins of government was law and order restored."

"Herrera has a reputation for being an honest man. Perhaps he can bring some sanity to the country."

"Perhaps." She paused. "If the radicals agree to his conciliatory policies. But I doubt it. There was still much unrest when I left."

"I know, *querida.* That is why I brought you home, before anything else happened. But now you are indeed home—and we must give thought to your future." He smiled and winked at her. "You are twenty-four years old, Ariana. Far past the time for marriage."

"Marriage?" Her chest tightened.

"Of course." He smiled. "Surely you would not prefer the few alternatives left to a young woman?"

Alternatives? There was just one, and she had spent six years in that life. *"No, Tio.* I do not wish to return to a cloistered life."

"I thought not. Well, we need not discuss this now. You have just arrived home and there is plenty of time." He rose from the desk. "As for me, I have a meeting with Jose Castro in the morning, and I will need my wits about me. He is growing more difficult as the years pass. I am going to bed." He crossed to the door, and paused, smiling at her warmly. "Welcome home, Ariana."

She returned his smile, and the door closed behind him. Slowly, her smile faded, and she stared at the door for a long moment. Married? After all that she had been through? "In a pig's eye," she whispered.

5

Veracruz, Mexico
October, 1844

Ariana tilted her head and assumed an interested expression. She struggled against a sudden impulse to yawn. Laying her napkin on the table, she rose from her chair and went to stand behind her dinner partner. For a moment her eyes fixed on the flesh at the back of his neck where it rolled over the stiff white collar, then her slender hands lifted to his shoulders. She kneaded the soft flesh beneath the heavy wool of his coat as she bent and placed a kiss on the top of his thinning hair.

"You worry too much, dear Mari," she murmured, then turned to sit on the arm of his chair. Her hand slid to the base of his neck. "Your muscles are tense, you will never be able to sleep tonight. How can you lead men and accomplish your goals when you cannot sleep?"

The small, shrewd eyes narrowed and he smiled. "Ah, Ariana, my dearest love. There is no one who worries about me as you do."

"Someone must." She shrugged, knowing that the movement brought his eyes to her bare shoulder and the deep cut of her gown. Her mouth slipped into the pout he always found delightful. "But you do not appreciate what I do for you. Always you speak of armies, weapons, soldiers."

"Have I bored you again, little one?" He smiled indulgently as his eyes warmed.

The pout turned into a smile, and she wrapped her arms about his neck. "You never bore me, my love. I just do not always understand what you are telling me."

"Of course not; and I have bored you. What a comfort you are to me. Someday, when the monarchy is returned to its rightful place in Mexico, there will be nothing but time for us."

"But for now . . . just a little time, perhaps?" Her hand slipped lower, bringing a slight gasp from him.

"Si, Ariana," he answered huskily. "A little time, of course . . ."

Ariana lay still, listening to the heavy breathing of the man lying next to her. She slipped carefully from the bed so as not to awaken him, and crossed the moonlit room to the washstand in the corner. Quietly, she washed, ridding herself of the results of his lovemaking. Slipping into a clean linen bedgown, she crossed to the table and poured herself a measure of brandy. Taking it to a chair near the balcony doors, she settled herself comfortably and sipped the heady liquid. It was a nightly ritual that helped her to forget what had preceded. She laughed softly, quietly, and she felt the biting edges of bile. How simple men were. How pathetically simple it was to control them.

She had been in Mexico for four years. Admittedly, the first one had been wasted, lost in self-pity and grief. Poor little Ariana Saldivar, exiled from home and family, her knees worn raw from hours of prayer and duties scrubbing the halls of the convent. She worked hard, trying to purge her sinful soul of the desires of wanting, of needing more than the restrained life of the obedient supplicant. Then, almost exactly one year after her arrival, she had been called to the Mother Superior's study. Expecting another lecture on sin, Ariana was shocked to learn why she had been summoned: she was to attend a dinner party that night in Veracruz—at the home of Antonio Lopez de Santa Anna, the president of Mexico.

The Mother Superior, a rigid, arrogant woman, made no attempt to hide her disapproval of the invitation, and of the fact that there was little she could do about it. The request had come directly from the president. Moreover, there was a letter—a sealed letter—from Ariana's uncle. With a cluck of her tongue, she reminded Ariana of the impropriety of receiving mail not first approved by her guardians at the convent. But she reluctantly handed it over.

Once in the privacy of her small chamber, Ariana eagerly ripped open the letter. Her eyes feasted on the bold strokes of her uncle's broad hand. The short letter was brief in its greetings as Mariano mentioned nothing of what was happening at home. She was, he informed her, to attend the dinner party at President Santa Anna's home. When the president had learned that Mariano Vallejo's niece was sequestered near Veracruz, he had graciously requested to meet her. Mariano assured her that he knew she would represent the familia well.

Ariana lowered the letter, tears stinging her eyes as she tried to force back the pain she felt from reading the brief, almost terse note. Very well, she thought, I shall go; I will do anything to be away from this place, even for one night! But not for *Tio Mariano,* or for Santa Anna, but for myself.

She was late and kept the carriage that had been sent for her waiting for a full half hour. The few gowns she had brought with her had been packed in a little-used storeroom of the convent. When they were unpacked, it was discovered that mice had made their way into the trunks. All of the gowns had been damaged to some extent. Three gowns were ripped, recut, and sewn together to make one decently fitting dinner gown. She was pleased with the result, as were the two young novices that helped her, both of whom had been trained as seamstresses before their families had given them to the church. The result was a cleverly constructed gown of pale blue silk with a rose underskirt, trimmed about the bodice with two deep rows of ivory lace. Enough lace had been salvaged from the skirt of one of the discarded gowns for a matching mantilla, which she wore over her hair on a high, tortoiseshell comb.

The last-minute flurry had served one good purpose; Ariana had little time to become nervous. Using the half hour carriage ride to gather her wits, she arrived calm and amazingly collected. As they approached Santa Anna's estate, Ariana was stunned. The president's home was a tropical oasis, unlike the rest of the bleak, desolate area, where wars, revolutions, and bandits had left little more than burned out houses surrounded by red, sandy hills, barren of trees and even birds other than the grotesque, black zopilote.

If the grounds amazed her, Ariana was struck speechless when she entered the grand casa. It was illuminated by hundreds of candles, their flickering lights reflecting off crystal chandeliers and wall sconces, creating colorful dancing shadows. The reception room, where she was escorted by a majordomo, was filled with ladies adorned in a rainbow of bright, rich colors and men in uniforms of many nations: French, British, American, and others she could not identify. And then there were dons, in their richly embroidered costumes.

She was escorted almost immediately to the president. As she was introduced to him, she curtsied deeply. She couldn't believe that she was in the presence of this well-known and powerful man who appeared to be nothing like she had expected. Known to be ruthless and quick to anger, he was the essence of graciousness. Tall and angular, he had an expressive face that reminded one of a scholar and a smooth but demanding voice. Ariana was overwhelmed and more than a little fascinated.

In the hours that followed, Ariana's life was changed. It wasn't the glorious decor, or the delicious and abundant food prepared to European taste—though she ate ravenously, not having had anything like it before. Nor was it the delight of being in the company of gallants and beautiful women who actually seemed not to worry about their souls—at least for the moment. It wasn't even the few hours of pleasure and laughter.

It began when she was introduced to her dinner partner, General Mariano Paredes y Arrillaga, commander of the largest army of troops in northern Mexico. A few inches shorter than she, he strutted with self-importance and power. It took her a few moments, when she was barely into the first course, to begin learning about his aristocratic family ties and, by dessert, the fact that his dear, proud wife did not understand him.

Late that night, as she lay on her narrow cot in her convent cell, staring at the thin beam of moonlight that seeped through the tall, spiked window, she thought over everything she had seen, felt, tasted—and sensed. She could not understand why she felt so tense, as if in expectation.

She thought over the past evening, of the many things she had discovered. Besides the fact that the Texans were claiming the Rio Grande as boundary, as well as the Colorado River with access to ports on the Gulf, she had been fascinated to observe the underlying hostility between the foreign factions during the evening, although they were too conscious of diplomacy—or wary of Santa Anna—to make their feelings obvious. But one thing was clear: relations between Mexico and the United States had become seriously strained. Apparently, since August of the previous year, about the time she had come to Mexico, a commission of representatives from the United States and Mexico, with the Baron Roenne of Prussia as mediator, had convened to resolve the extensive debts Mexico owed to the United States. To counter U.S. demands, the Mexicans had tried to introduce claims protesting American support of the Texas revolution five years before. The U.S. dismissed the claims as an affront to their national honor.

It was not the financial dispute that interested Ariana, but the political tensions that existed between the two countries, and above all, that Mexico was in serious trouble. As she listened, she felt an illusive stirring, which grew throughout the evening. This awareness sharpened as she happened to overhear a conversation between the British and French representatives in Mexico as they prepared to leave.

"My friend." The French officer had smiled, slipping into his dress coat. "Whatever else is said, I fear your then foreign secretary, George Canning, was correct as early as 1823 when he remarked on the true threat to our two countries."

"And what would that be?" The British officer frowned, disturbed that he hadn't the vaguest idea what the Frenchman was talking about.

"Only that the line of demarcation he most dreaded was the Americas *versus* Europe."

The Englishman snorted derisively. "I seriously doubt that we need worry about that. Mexico and the United States are too neighborly to be friends."

"Ah, just so," the Frenchman responded with a silky smile. "That is exactly what Canning said. But then, when he became prime minister, he was occasionally found to be in error."

It had been three years since that first, fateful dinner with Santa Anna. That night her life had changed, forming a single, directed purpose. Even now she could still recall the Frenchman's smile and the words he had spoken. Those many hours later, when she was again alone in her tiny convent cell, she had begun to deal with all that she had learned that night. Mexico and the United States were at odds; "too neighborly to be friends." Indeed, Mexico was in trouble with most of Europe, through weakening relations and rising, unsolvable debts. Moreover, as long as Mexico was embroiled in her troubles, particularly with her "too neighborly" northern neighbor, she would have little time, and few resources, to direct her attention to California.

These matters, and others, had been spoken of openly throughout the long evening. She had stood by, listening but unseen, as no woman was seen. What had amazed her at first was how much nonsense was spoken, how little understanding those prominent diplomats and men of position had of history and politics beyond their own countries. More than once she had caught herself about to offer a comment on a blatant error of observation or judgment. But then, attractive fixtures did not offer opinions.

That night, pulling the covers of her narrow cot up to her chin, she had forced herself to relax, and she began to think the impossible. Ideas, dangerous ideas, began to germinate until she realized that she was trembling. General Paredes kept coming to mind, his image relentlessly nagging her. There was no doubt in her mind that he was more than interested in her; he had made it blatantly obvious. She had found his overtures repellent at the time, now they seemed to become . . . possibilities.

Madre, she had thought; could she do it? Reason and emotion battled within her, goaded by her undeniable desire, her life-long need to be part of the struggle against the oppression of her people, which Vallejo had so deeply nurtured in her and which she had been denied. There were so many possibilities, all ultimately preferable to languishing in the Convent of Saint Catherine for an undetermined number of years.

Dios, the irony! All her life her education had been a detriment, besides the satisfaction it gave her. At last her knowledge, her understanding, could be put to good use. All those years of ridicule, contempt, and loneliness. But none of those mattered if she could finally make them mean something! A purpose for those bitter years of frustration and pain.

Suddenly overwhelmed by the possibilities and the hope they brought, she had risen from her bed, pulling a shawl about her shoulders against the chill of the room. Her hands trembled as she lit the lamp on the table, and it took three attempts before a match would catch. Silently chiding herself for her nervousness, she took a few pages of writing paper from the small drawer under the table, and sat in the narrow chair. Then, with forced calm, she began to pen a letter to Monterey; not to her uncle, but to Manuel Castro. She had no way of knowing if her intractable cousin was still in Monterey, but if he was, she knew enough about him to know that his visions—and his revolutionary leanings— would not have changed. In so many ways Manuel was like his uncle, Jose, who had once achieved so much for California with Vallejo and Juan Alvarado. And in other ways, he was more dangerous to their cause—more volatile, more opinionated, quicker to anger, thus prone to rash and disastrous decisions. But, as much as she disliked him, she would need him if her plan was to work.

Sealing the letter to Manuel, she penned another to General Paredes. This second letter was far more difficult. She began the letter, then tried again, crumbling the results and tossing them into the basket under the desk. Paredes would be the key, the entry to all that she sought; everything depended upon him. She knew that she could not approach him with reason; he was not interested in her mind. The problem brought Ariana to the edge of a world she was totally unfamiliar with. On her fourth attempt she allowed fantasy to guide her, dismissing the image of the plump, pompous general, replacing it with an image of her dreams. She read the result and found herself smiling. If he did not respond to her message with the eager anticipation that she expected, she would resign herself to a life in the convent. In a pig's eye.

An hour after she had begun, the letters were finished and

sealed. Then, with the deep feeling of peace that comes from making an important decision and acting upon it, she went to bed, falling into a dreamless sleep.

Lost deeply in remembering, she started when Padredes turned in the bed, moaning softly. Watching him in the gray light that preceded dawn, she held her breath for a moment until he settled. Then she returned to her goblet, taking a sip as her eyes moved over the countryside beyond the open windows of the veranda and the desolate, barren landscape. Veracruz, founded in the seventeenth century by the Viceroy Conde de Monterey. Appropriate, she thought, that the place where she had found purpose to her life should have been founded by a man who bore the same name as the city that was an integral part of that purpose, though so many miles distant.

Fate had played gently with her. Manuel had not left Monterey, and her letter had reached him. She was soon to learn, though not to her surprise, that he was still deeply committed to California as an independent republic. Over the years, since that first letter, it became increasingly apparent that Manuel had difficulty accepting opinions and help from a woman, but he could not deny the importance of the information she offered.

Three months after that first, fateful letter, she had been working in the fields outside the convent walls, weeding the vegetables to be sold for its support. She had heard a voice, urgently whispering her name. Watching the bent sisters who worked alongside their charges, Ariana had edged to the border of the clearing, and slipped into the shadows of the wall. She could barely suppress her joy as Rafael reached out, pulling her into a fierce hug.

Three days passed before she could slip out to meet him again. She had waited and watched over the months, subtly testing the sisters who would prove the most pliable. She was gratifyingly rewarded—as were they—but her plans were well-funded from jewels she had brought with her; the fortune left to her by her mother. Oh, how she blessed Ana Montoya! If not for her ancient nemesis, Ariana would not have thought to sew the jewels into the linings of her gowns. Moreover, Ariana found that it took surprisingly little to bribe her three conspirators. Ariana suspected that their own hatred and resentment of the Mother Superior was reason enough for them to justify their involvement in the plot.

The past years had been fruitful. Ariana had long since ceased to question her ability or the strength she had discovered within herself. She mingled with men in power, plying her considerable wiles as she deftly extracted information. She discovered that she had an amazing level of control over people with whom she dealt. Her ideas were bright, pertinent, accurate—and subtly offered. She had discovered the invaluable talent of making a man believe that his ideas were his own.

She guided Rafael as he gathered the considerable army of men they used; their purpose, to create discontent and civil disobedience among Mexico's population. This, too, proved amazingly simple, using the abject poverty and anger they found. All of this, each tender piece of information, was passed to Manuel, thus creating discontentment hundreds of miles to the north.

Beyond what was accomplished by Rafael's "army," or Manuel's actions in California, the wealth to finance their venture, the information, and the orders came from her. In an age when women were ignored, she had found herself listened to, even revered. To a large measure, the men she worked with had simply been unprepared for the depth of her education and knowledge. At times, she even suspected that they saw her as some sort of Joan of Arc. But she did not care about the reason; it mattered only that they were successful in their mission.

They trusted her and depended upon her. Where other women were ignored, she had become the pivot for these men's ambitions and dreams. The men were in awe of her, and afraid of her. And that old fool . . . she glanced at the sleeping form in the bed . . . did exactly what she suggested, though he did not know it.

She had long since learned the truth about Santa Anna— whose "scholarly" appearance hid his true character. The man, though brilliant, was a lecher, his interests leaning toward womanizing and cockfights. His innate shrewdness and understanding of the Mexican people had kept him in office, but his problems remained. Border skirmishes were frequent, particularly in the Yucatan, where the Texas example had encouraged cessionism and was keeping Mexico involved in a long and costly war. The treasury was depleted, and foreign creditors were hounding him, the debts mounting each year. Most of all, diplomatic relations with Britain, France, and the United States were moving steadily toward a crisis. Ariana had dedicated the past three years to these politics. If Mexico's wretched neglect of California was to continue, leaving California the opportunity to achieve her independence, then Mexico's attention and energy had to remain focused on its own problems.

Not everything had gone smoothly. There had been tense moments for the Californio *liberalismos* when it appeared that the United States was moving toward a purchase of California. Fortunately, this threat had been quickly resolved because of disagreements on the matter within the United States government. A second threat also proved brief when a misguided commander of the United States Pacific Fleet, thinking his country to be at war with Mexico, had sailed into Monterey Bay and claimed possession of the territory. When he realized his error, the errant commander had sailed off with his fleet in disgrace and humiliation.

Ariana recalled the event, laughing softly as she sipped her brandy. Manuel's letters had made light of the incident, but not of the fuel it had provided, flaming the fires of rebellion among California's citizens. Manuel and others working for their cause would not allow anyone to forget the threat to their liberty.

So much had been achieved, each accomplishment leading them closer and closer to their goals. She occasionally had the disjointed thought that the fates were orchestrating events for her own purpose. Two years before, in 1842, the Mexican government replaced Juan Alvarado with a new governor. Though saddened by the event, Ariana knew the feeling was purely nostalgic. Privately, she granted Alvarado his due as the first Californio governor. And he had tried to be successful, before frustrations, disappointments, and perhaps a lack in his own character had led him to becoming a drunkard.

Mexico replaced Alvarado with a Mexican appointee: General Manuel Micheltorena. Jose and Manuel Castro, and even Alvarado himself, had done their part in resisting Micheltorena. Playing on the unrest of the people, they fostered a small revolution against the new governor and his Mexican army. Micheltorena capitulated and his service was short-lived, as within a few years he returned to Mexico, thoroughly beaten. The political situation in California had been left in shambles by his sudden departure. It was a turning point for what Ariana did next.

While Santa Anna was in a particularly sated mood, Ariana suggested that it might prove advantageous to make Los Angeles the new capital of California. After all, she told him, those troublesome Monterenos of the north had far too much power—which was the reason for unrest that caused Mexico so much grief. Take the control from the troublesome north and give it to a new, southern capital in Los Angeles, with the Angeleno Pio Pico as governor.

"The Monterenos would revolt," Santa Anna had responded, accepting the wine she offered.

"Perhaps." She had shrugged, noting that his eyes had fixed on the swell of her breasts revealed as her bedrobe slipped from her shoulders. Staying his hand as it reached for her, she smiled. "But perhaps not, if you appease them with another gesture: Jose Castro as military commandant over affairs in the north. Such a position would be considered one of power, almost equaling that of governor itself. Yet the real power would be in Los Angeles—closer to your own control."

Later that night, Santa Anna agreed. It was a plan meant to appease both north and south, while Ariana knew full well that it would cause further dissension, with blame given to Mexico. Moreover, while Pio Pico mistrusted and resented the northern Monterenos, he loathed Mexico. But then, Santa Anna did not know that.

Beyond everything Ariana had done, however, it was the work accomplished with Paredes that gave her the most satisfaction. This thought brought her back to the present, and she glanced at the packet of papers on the desk nearby. Slowly, she smiled. If all went well, Mexico would be unable to focus on future events in California—a last, great step toward California becoming a republic. She knew the words in the *pronunciamiento* by heart. As she should have; she had helped him to write it. Once published, it would bring about a revolution in Mexico.

She had done all that she had planned, had worked for

these past years. But not without a price, nothing came without a price: his plump, sweaty hands touching her; the smiles, moans, and sighs she evoked as he took her body. The revulsion and pain she had felt that first night with him. And with others, even Santa Anna. The loss of her innocence had been the price, but she did not question it; she would do it all again. She would sooner stop breathing than reject the dreams that drove her. No life was worth that loss, not even her own.

She welcomed the first light of dawn with relief. He was still sleeping soundly and would not expect her in his bed again. Rising from the chair, she dressed quickly and slipped from the room, down the hallway and stairs, nodding to the guards as she passed and made her way to the side door that would lead her to her waiting horse.

She was relieved to find Rafael waiting for her in the small village near the convent, their normal meeting place. She was extremely tired, and there would be less than two hours of sleep remaining before she was required to rise for her duties at St. Catherine's. At desperate moments she had wondered how she could continue. She tried not to think of others her age: cousins she adored and thought about in such moments, their gowns, gallants, and fiestas. Those were the worst moments, returning to the convent, facing what awaited her there. The longstanding battles with the Mother Superior were wearing. And there were the older sisters who watched her, following her with their crow-eyes. They were set in their ways by the lead of the prioress, and their tight, pinched faces mirrored the vapidness of their empty shells. Repetition of prayers replacing passion.

She slipped from the horse and drew Rafael away from the others into the shadows of a crumbling adobe. "The revolution will begin soon."

"Are you certain?" Rafael exclaimed.

"Within a month," Ariana answered with a satisfied smile. "Paredes has written his revolutionary manifesto, protesting Santa Anna's taxation and waste."

"I wish I was as certain as you are that this will work."

"Rafael, besides the fact that Paredes commands the largest force of troops in Mexico and is popular with the army, there are his family ties. They are the conservative pro-Spanish who once supported Santa Anna and put him in power. There is no doubt—once the *pronunciamiento* is published—that Jose Joaquin Herrera will become president."

"And Mexico will be permanently embroiled in its own problems—and we will be finished here," Rafael observed hopefully.

"Si. Soon we will go home, Rafael." She reached out and touched his face gently. "I want it as much as you do. But now it is late. I must go."

As she turned away, he stopped her. "There is another matter, Ariana."

When he hesitated she became impatient. *Dios,* did he not know how tired she was? "What is it?" she snapped, despising her cousin's indecisiveness.

"A problem with one of the men, Santiago Gomez." He shrugged. "I do not know why I mention it, actually—I took care of it. He has been disciplined."

"What are you talking about?" she asked tightly.

"He left camp without permission." Rafael sighed, suddenly wishing he had not bothered her with this. "There is a young woman. None of us have had a life of our own, after all, for some time. He was discovered when he came back into camp."

She stared at him for a long moment. Why did she love him so; he was such a fool. Then, slowly she smiled. "Then there is nothing more to be said, Rafael. As you said, you took care of it. I trust that it will not happen again. After all, while I know that we can trust Santiago, another could be a spy. Everything we have worked for is about to happen. I need not tell you what it would mean if the wrong word was said about what we are doing. All would be lost. It could mean the lives of every one of us."

"Of course. He understands now that we all must make sacrifices."

"Vaya con Dios, cousin," she whispered, quickly embracing him. Then she turned and moved to the edge of the shadows, approaching the man who held her horse. She glanced back at Rafael and smiled. "Anselmo," she said quietly to the man. "I have a task for you."

"Si," the man answered, lifting her into the saddle.

She bent down to him as he handed her the reins of the shifting horse. "Santiago Gomez," she murmured. "Take care of him. And his woman as well."

With a steady look of understanding, the man nodded. Without looking back, she turned her horse and rode from the village, returning to the Convent of Saint Catherine before the bells rang for morning prayers.

6

Jeremy arose early and dressed quietly so as not to disturb Beth. He found Larkin in the storeroom, sorting through his massive inventory.

"Good morning, Morgan." Larkin looked up from his tallies with a smile that made Jeremy wonder if he had just found an overage. "I trust you slept well."

"Very comfortably."

"Good. Rachel and the children are breakfasting upstairs. I am certain that they would be delighted with your company."

Jeremy suppressed a wince. The Larkin children were cheerful souls, but tended to be somewhat lively. Larkin readily admitted that he was somewhat indulgent to his young daughter and two small sons. Their two older brothers had been sent away to school, each in turn, at the tender age of six. It grieved the Larkins to be parted from their offspring, but as there was no established school in California, they felt they had no choice. However, this separation tended to make Thomas overly tolerant of the remaining brood.

"While I would enjoy that," Jeremy said diplomatically, "I'm not particularly hungry this morning. But I could use some information. I understand that all new arrivals must report to the commandant's office."

"Yes, it is the law in California," Larkin agreed as he pried the top off a crate. "Our esteemed commandant and his prefect strive to keep their fingers on the pulse of the comings and goings in Monterey. Their offices are at El Cuartel. Just look for the Mexican flag flying at its peak."

"Which leads me to another problem. I am going to need a mount. Would you direct me to the nearest stable?"

"Out there," Larkin said in a muffled voice as he bent into a deep crate.

Jeremy frowned. "Out where?"

Larkin glanced up and saw Jeremy's confusion. Straightening, he broke into a grin. Setting his papers on a bale of fabric, he strode to the door of the store. "Come with me, Morgan."

Jeremy followed the smaller man through the store and out onto the porch. Jeremy nearly plowed into him as Larkin stopped suddenly. "There."

"Where?"

"There," Larkin repeated impatiently. "Take the one that suits you."

All Jeremy could see was the empty street. There was no movement in the early morning hours but for a few horses that had apparently escaped from their owners. They were dragging hackamores as they grazed from grasses edging the wide, dusty avenue. Suddenly, numbly, Jeremy realized Larkin's meaning, and he regarded the other man with surprise. "Those?"

"Those," Larkin affirmed. "One thing we have in abundance is horseflesh. There was a time, a decade or so ago, when they were so plentiful that they threatened pasture land. They were slaughtered by the hundreds."

Judging the horses from where he stood, Jeremy was sickened by the prospect. They were exceptionally good animals. "They run wild?"

"More or less. They are hardly wild, but they do run free. When you need a mount, catch one. At the end of your ride, release it." With that, he disappeared back into the store.

Jeremy stared at the peacefully grazing horses. Well, he thought, how difficult could it be? Drawing a deep breath he stepped off the porch, bracing himself against a passing feeling that this system was insane.

It took him ten humiliating minutes to catch one, moments that damaged his sense of dignity. He made a silent resolution that before the day was out he would obtain his own mount, along with a saddle for the comfort of his backside.

El Cuartel was a large, adobe structure surrounded by high walls overlooking the bay. Grimly, he noted the lackadaisical manner of the few guards stationed at the entrance. Fifteen to twenty soldiers moved about, and while they noted his presence with a certain amount of interest, no one challenged him as he searched for the commandant's office. He presented his papers to a subordinate, as Castro had not arrived for the day. Then, having complied with Monterey's laws, he left. But not before he had made a thorough visual judgment of Monterey's defenses.

Outside the walls, he reclaimed the horse, which he had tied securely behind a wall of brush, having no intention of subjecting himself to his earlier humiliation. The next hour he spent combing Monterey as it began to awake to the coming day. As he rode slowly through the quiet streets, he noted the thirty or forty scattered houses that were sprinkled in an irregular pattern about the rolling pine-forested climbs edging the Monterey Bay. Few had chimneys, and many had boards and brush on their south sides. An effort to keep out the rain, Jeremy surmised.

He had learned from Larkin that the strange, primitive structures consisted of bricks of sun-baked adobe mud, covered with an overcoat of plastered mud, inside and out, which was then whitewashed with lime made of seashells. The lime coating was added to resist dampness and invading bugs.

The roofs, unlike Larkin's redwood shingles, were of kilned tiles or thatched tules. Window openings and doors were left uncovered or hung with oiled hides. Floors, he had been told, were no more than trammeled earth. He could well imagine the reaction that must have greeted Larkin's use of redwood timbers as supports for his house, allowing for a second story and balcony. Furthermore, the natives must have been quite mystified by the addition of eight-over-eight paned windows, shutters and doors, paneled interior, planked floors, baseboards, and a fine, graceful interior staircase—not to mention an interior fireplace!

However, it had not taken long for the more prosperous and sophisticated dons to see the advantages of Larkin's architecture. Similar structures seemed to be popping up all over Monterey, allowing a promising future for the "Monterey colonial."

Jeremy drew a deep breath of the fresh, salty air, enjoying the opportunity to be by himself. He and Larkin had spent the past three days, and most of the nights, exchanging opinions on the current political situation, its history, and possible ramifications.

Jeremy had spent six months preparing for this mission —one he had come to realize had begun as early as 1838. He smirked, wondering whom he could credit the most for his present situation: Winfield Scott, Daniel Webster, his father, or his father's friend and old schoolmate, James Buchanan. But one thing was certain, it had begun three thousand miles away in the rich, fertile Valley of the Aroostook.

With his years at Harvard and West Point behind him, the fresh, green, twenty-year-old Lieutenant Jeremy Randolf Morgan was assigned to serve as an aide to General Winfield Scott. As it happened, the event in the young officer's life coincided with a momentous decision by a group of lumbermen from New Brunswick.

The Treaty of Ghent had failed to provide a firm northeastern boundary, dividing Canada from the United States. Conflicts had continued, without resolve, until the Canadian lumbermen decided to take matters into their own hands. They entered the Valley of the Aroostook, and summarily began to chop down trees. In what would later be referred to by the locals as the "Restook War," the loggers were expelled by Maine's militia. The conflict continued, however, until Winfield Scott was sent to the area with a small army, including the young Lieutenant Morgan. Scott deftly arranged a treaty whereupon both sides would retain the territory they actually occupied. Now it remained for the governments of the United States and Great Britain to form a formal treaty on the matter.

By 1842, nothing had been resolved. Any attempt to do so was further complicated by the fact that Massachusetts held title to lands in Maine, and both states had to agree to any resolution. It was then that Alexander Baring, Lord Ashburton, arrived in Washington with the intent of working out a treaty over the boundary dispute. Secretary of State Daniel Webster called for Scott, and began serious briefings with the general on the Aroostook matter. Scott brought along his aide, whose pragmatic and discerning opinion he had come to enjoy. Within the first hour of the conference, a stunned Webster and Scott were to learn, from a somewhat reticent Lieutenant Morgan, that he might have some influence with Lord Ashburton. It seemed that his mother had grown up with the English baron's American wife. He had known both Lord and Lady Ashburton since childhood.

Diplomats, geographers, historians, and surveyors had failed to settle the fifty-nine-year-old dispute. Yet, Ashburton and Webster were to resolve the conflict, which now included added complaints involving African slave trade. Pressures from both countries became bitter, fueled by the British belief that they had every right to "visit" American ships in order to verify that they were, indeed, American. Of course, if slaves were discovered, it was the British right to free them. In their outrage, the American southern states put considerable pressure on their government.

All concerned knew that the situation had become totally out of hand when further complications were added from sources demanding the acquisition of the Oregon and California territories. The original purpose of the negotiations, to determine the Canadian/United States boundaries, was being overshadowed by the pressures of these special interest groups from both countries. In their meetings, Webster and Ashburton began to show the strain from these pressures, and compromise looked less and less certain. It was then that Jeremy made a decision of his own: to remove the two men from the stricture of formal negotiations and the demands of those who invariably attended the meetings. He suggested to his mother that she plan a small, quiet dinner party.

It came as no surprise to her son when Caroline Morgan drew Lady Ashburton into her confidence. The date for the fateful evening was decided, and on that evening a small party gathered at Caroline Morgan's table: her husband and son, the Daniel Websters, and the Ashburtons. She served a sumptuous dinner with fine wines, and deftly encouraged relaxed, unguarded social conversation. Then, when the brandy and cigars were served and the ladies made ready to depart, they offered some advice.

Glancing at her son, Caroline Morgan suppressed a smile. "It would seem to me that your solutions are simple," she said, laying her napkin on the table. "But then, I am only a woman. When I am given a decision to make, I simply make it."

"But our world is so much simpler than theirs, Caroline," Lady Ashburton observed.

"Yes, without doubt. However, though on a much smaller scale than our husbands, we make daily decisions settling disputes, balancing the lives of those we love."

"Yes—" Lady Ashburton agreed thoughtfully. "And our talents, or lack of them, affect those lives. Our world may be small, but no less important to us." She glanced at her husband affectionately. "My dear, you have always said that without my talents of intricate planning, your life would crumble."

"Indeed it would," Lord Ashburton agreed quickly. The man was no fool.

"Well," Caroline Morgan said, arching a fine, dark brow. "Let me assure you that if we allowed ourselves to anguish over every decision, then absolutely nothing at all would get done! When we are faced with conflict, we merely sweep all accumulated pressures aside and make our decision. After all, we alone are responsible, therefore we draw the lines and simply ignore those who would disagree."

Remembering, Jeremy smiled. Then he laughed out loud, the sudden sound causing a passing dog to ruffle its back and bark at him. Soon after the fateful dinner, Webster and Lord Ashburton agreed on a compromise. And, although it caused considerable dissension on both sides, the treaty stood. The outcome had further ramifications, of a more personal nature. Jeremy was promoted to the rank of captain, with Webster's and Scott's personal commendation. A year later, due to the quality of his service to General Scott, he was a decorated major in the U.S. Army. There was no doubt about it, Jeremy mused, glory was not only found on the battlefield. In fact, he had his mother to thank for his present situation.

Sweeping personal reflections aside, Jeremy began to consider what he had learned from Larkin these past few days, added to what he already knew. Concern over possession of the Oregon and California territories had begun long before Aroostook, though that event had been his first exposure to the problem. And, it was that exposure that had led to Buchanan's choice when faced with the situation a little over a year ago. One of Polk's campaign promises included the acquisition of the territories. Soon after his election, though he would not take office officially until March, Polk had instructed Buchanan on the matter. Hamilton Morgan had approached his son while Jeremy was on leave—a leave that he now knew had been carefully orchestrated. Throughout the turmoil of his courtship of Beth, Jeremy had been faced with the most salient decision of his life.

Thus, he had found himself at a White House dinner for the newly inaugurated president. Deliberately insulting the secretary of war, William Marcy, he was summarily disgraced, dismissed from the service and, with a recent bride, found himself sailing for a new life in the far west, a life as a confidential agent with instructions from the president and the secretary of state.

Jeremy had been well informed about most of the principal players. He knew of Garner and Cooper, along with the major immigrants to California he had not yet met. "John Cooper: half-brother to Thomas Larkin. Emigrated to California in 1823; embraced Catholicism, became known as Juan Bautista Cooper; married Dona Encarnacion Vallejo, younger sister of Mariano Vallejo. Holds large rancho in Big Sur. A deformed left hand from a childhood accident. Influential in California affairs.

"William Garner: married Maria Francisca Butron, heir to the large La Natividad rancho. Born in London of an educated father. Assigned by his father aboard a whaler to learn the trade. Deserted ship at Santa Barbara. Established a lumber business in the Santa Lucia Mountains. Involved with the *Rifleros Americanos,* but not sent to prison in 1840 due to influence with the authorities."

He was well versed about most of the important Californios as well: Mariano Vallejo, his nephew Juan Bautista Alvarado, and his cousin, Jose Castro. The three had been largely responsible for the secularization of the Catholic missions. It was this trio who had thrown off Mexico's stranglehold on California.

He had known, even before their meeting, that Vallejo was exceptionally educated, that he favored annexation to the United States. Alvarado had become a drunkard and was prone to serious disagreements with Vallejo. Castro had been appointed by Mexico as commandant in northern California, in a surprising move following the establishment of Los Angeles as the new capital. The three *liberalismos,* once the leading rebels of California, had long since had a parting of the ways.

These details, along with other items, Jeremy mentally filed in expectation of people he expected to meet. He was well versed in the history of the Catholic missions and their demise, the control gained by the descendants of the early soldiers who once accompanied the mission fathers, and their ascent to power, now the dons who controlled California. In addition, he was familiar with the struggles that had developed between the forces of the north and south, recently settling into a government in Los Angeles under the dubious leadership of Pio Pico, who had little influence with the powerful dons of the north such as Mariano Vallejo. California was a hotbed of revolution, within her own borders, as well as against any possible foreign influence.

He was well informed on the subject of Thomas Larkin, and the obstacles the man had encountered these past years. If he had not felt so before his arrival, he had since gained tremendous respect for the consul. The man was a phenomenon. Moreover, he seemed to wield his influence unconsciously. Not as an accident—Larkin was shrewd if nothing else. But his efforts were given with total energy, his decisions made with instinctive accuracy. Arriving in Monterey virtually penniless, he had constructed a home that Jeremy suspected would alter the architecture of California.

Larkin was unsurpassed as a merchant, rivaling any that Jeremy had seen in the east. He had imported an iron strongbox when he discovered that there was simply no place for the citizens to keep their valuables. Thus he had created the first bank in California. He had opened trade to the Sandwich Islands and Matzalan, creating a monopoly of trade that rapidly blossomed into a fortune. He had opened the first soap factory in California, on the Salinas river. He had opened the first bake shop; he was the first press agent for California; the first subdivider of land. He had achieved all of this, while being the only foreigner in California to own land and operate a business, and while retaining his own religion, against California law. And, he had not accomplished his goals by marrying a native daughter. Was it any surprise that in 1842, the man had practically single-handedly averted war?

One day that October, while sailing off the Peruvian coast, Commodore Thomas ap Catesby Jones, Commander of the Pacific Fleet, had received reports that convinced him the United States was at war with Mexico. The commodore's orders were clear. In such an event he was to sail to the Pacific coast and take possession of California. He did so without delay, stunning the small garrison of Monterey with the appearance of his small, but undeniable fleet.

Defenseless, the garrison surrendered. Thomas Larkin, rowing madly against the resisting current, appeared aboard the flagship where he assured the commodore that, without question, the United States had not declared war against Mexico. The flustered and chagrined commodore lowered the flag. At Larkin's insistence, he gave a grand ball as an apology to the outraged citizens. The following day, demoralized and facing the condemnation of his government, he sailed away.

Larkin began again, soothing feelings of new mistrust against his government, plotting new ways to lead the Californios to cession with the United States. Then, in Larkin's new position as consul and secret agent for President Polk, he received aid in the form of Major Jeremy Morgan.

Challenges, Jeremy thought. At least life never seemed to prove boring. The road left the perimeters of the town, disappearing into a densely wooded forest where a few small cabins were scattered about the fringes. Losing interest in his morning's sojourn, Jeremy pulled his mount's head about to return to the Larkins'. Then he saw it. Tied up before one of the cabins set back from the road, it was one of the most magnificent horses he had ever seen. Saddled with a high, pommeled Mexican saddle was a coal black stallion.

With hopes that he might be able to purchase the animal, or at least obtain one from the same bloodline, he decided to wait for the owner. Moments later, the door to the cabin opened. A small figure clad in a long, colorful woven serape and a round-brimmed, flat-crowned hat, stepped into the sunlight. Jeremy's brows lifted with surprise. "Well, well," he murmured. It seemed that Senorita Saldivar had an early morning assignation. Either that or she was just concluding a long night. He watched as she approached the stallion and effortlessly swung into the saddle. He had caught up with her before she had gone more than a hundred yards. "Good morning."

Startled, she frowned for a moment, checking the impulse to glance back at the cabin. Dark eyes flashed with displeasure from beneath the wide brim of the hat. "Senor Morgan. What are you doing out at this hour?"

"I am an early riser, Senorita Saldivar. As are you, apparently."

"Apparently."

The lady did not seem pleased to run into him, a fact which deepened his interest. "Forgive my surprise, Senorita. I was under the impression that a young lady of Monterey does not wander about without an escort— preferably the company of her duenna. Was I misinformed?"

Ariana glanced at the Yanqui with irritation. Damn the luck. Her efforts, since her return, had proved difficult. So much had been achieved during her years in Mexico; now, with such mistakes as this, she could be reduced to the insipid, useless life she had once known. She would just have to be more careful. But it could have been worse, she reasoned, had those she had just met with followed her from the cabin. If it was known that Bernard Garcia was in the area, there would be the devil to pay. Not to mention her uncle's reaction if he discovered that she was consorting with one of Garcia's ilk. Or the fact that Garcia probably would have murdered Morgan on sight.

Bernard Garcia, known as Three-fingered Jack since three of his digits had been shot off two years before during the insurrection against Governor Micheltorena, was one of the most notorious and bloodthirsty bandits in California. Along with his cohorts, including Juan Padillo who was with Garcia in the cabin, and Joaquin Murietta, they terrorized the communities from Sonoma to Los Angeles with their thieving and butchery.

Garcia, thick set, pockmarked, with full lips and small, cruel eyes, was as fierce looking as he was just plain mean. His and Padillo's idea of entertainment was to lasso a victim and drag him behind a horse, then tie him to a tree and use him for knife-throwing practice. But Ariana was safe with the dubious duo. To her astonishment, Garcia had found her in Mexico. He had sought her out to pay his respects. He had heard of the *liberalismo lady,* and he pledged his support, wanting only to serve her. Thus, they were all too willing to keep the foreign settlers unsettled. The pot was sweetened by the fact that they happened to hate all foreigners, and Ariana paid them with Vallejo horses, which were considered to be the finest in California.

"You were not misinformed, Senor Morgan," she said pleasantly. "However, I am no longer under the control of a duenna. Since my return, my uncle has allowed me a certain amount of freedom. Due to my age, I imagine. A Californio woman is customarily married by the age of sixteen."

He thought for a moment to respond with a compliment, but dismissed the impulse. He sensed that Ariana Saldivar was not a woman susceptible to flattery. Instead, he merely smiled. "Your horse gave you away."

"Pardon, Senor?" She managed to retain her composure, but her stomach knotted.

"Your horse," he repeated. "It is one of the finest animals I have seen. Are there others like him? I would be very interested in purchasing one."

"There is no other like El Oro, Senor Morgan. But there are many fine horses at my uncle's rancho in Sonoma. I suggest that you speak with him. Now, if you will forgive me, I am late."

As he watched her ride away, he recalled John Cooper's words: how a Californio woman never walked when she could ride. From her exceptional command of the powerful stallion, it was obvious that Ariana Saldivar had spent her life in a saddle. Then his gaze shifted to the small cabin nestled at the edge of the wood, and he wondered about the identity of her lover. And he wondered why he cared.

He returned to the Larkin house midmorning to find Larkin waiting for him. "You are in luck, Morgan! We have been invited to a *merienda* at Point Lobos!"

"A *merienda?*"

"A picnic, Morgan! A California picnic! What luck; everyone you need to meet will be there!"

The heavy bank of morning fog had burned off by late morning. The sun spread its warmth over Point Lobos, a craggy outcrop overlooking the deep cobalt blue of the Pacific. The point was covered by twisted and bent cypress, and dense pine and fir. The thick, lush underbrush of fern was sprinkled with rhododendron with large red and pink blossoms. High, white-foamed waves crashed against rocks, seeping into tide pools teeming with miniature life, which scurried about in the brief moments before the swirling foam was pulled back to the sea.

Trestle tables had been set up in the cool, crisp air under pine and cypress. Pits had been dug under spits to render whole pigs and halves of beef which turned, crisping and deepening in color with each circle, fat snapping as it dripped to the red-hot shimmering coals below. Above, sea birds dipped, made curious by the smell of the cooking meat. Seagulls, bravest in their voracious appetites, drew near, some landing, waddling close, hesitantly squawking in anger as their courage failed them and they rejoined their companions in flight.

Plump, brown hands turned dough for tortillas, slapping it from palm to palm, flattening, spreading, tossing it into pans over a fire before twisting off another portion. Laughter and gossip were exchanged as others stirred heavy pots of frijoles, refrying the beans with cheese and heavy spices in drippings from the beef and pork. Bladders of pig and goat were stuffed with vegetables and meat, wrapped in corn husks and set into coals to steam beneath the turning meat.

Beth sat on a blanket spread beneath a cypress, watching the goings-on. She felt at once left out and content to be so. The language was incomprehensible; indeed, she felt it intolerably rude that even those who she knew spoke English perfectly well chose to jabber on in Spanish in front of her. Moreover, it shocked her that the women were doing the cooking. She knew that they had Indian servants for such tasks, yet for some unfathomable reason, merely because it was a party, they chose to perform the tasks themselves. Apparently it was a custom, or so she had been told, although the reason eluded her. The prospect of dealing with such menial chores as part of a celebration was beyond her comprehension.

Loneliness gripped her suddenly, and she had to fight back tears. Everything had moved so quickly. Much had happened in just a few months. How could her life have changed so? This wasn't real, she thought. But it was.

Bitterness stirred in her, touching ugly places.

Across the clearing, Jeremy stood with Larkin. As the other man talked, Jeremy was half listening, distracted by the vacant expression on her finely boned face. He knew she was unhappy, just as he knew that there was absolutely nothing he could do to help her.

"You have met Soberanes, de la Torre, Estrades, de la Guerra, among others," Larkin was saying. "Alvarado is Vallejo's nephew, Castro his cousin. Together with Mariano they were among the first in California to resist the laws of the Mexican government."

Jeremy observed the two under discussion. "If he is so resistant to Mexican rule, why does Castro remain as her military commander?"

Larkin pursed his lips in thought. "Morgan, Vallejo once remarked to me that 'in the breast of the Californio, love of family is stronger than selfish and vile interest.' Keep it in mind. They do not despise Mexico's government as much as they revile Mexico's disinterest in California's affairs. The 'familia' is their family by blood. California is the body of the family. Part and parcel. They take their positions because that is what exists. They will retain their positions because they are the authorities in California. It is my hope that a peaceful cession will draw them into positions of authority under our own flag."

"And if there is war with Mexico?"

Larkin sighed. "Then we must hope that they are not backed against a wall. If their freedom to choose is threatened, they will certainly align with old loyalties. And that is why I have struggled for a peaceful solution." He brightened suddenly, his stern face softening into a smile. "And there are others who will help our cause."

Jeremy turned as two men approached.

"Morgan, you know Cooper, may I present David Hartnell, one of our more prominent Yankee Californios." Larkin's eyes glinted with humor.

Hartnell laughed at the description. "You must be Morgan. Welcome to California."

David Hartnell, Jeremy thought. Settled in California in 1822. Agent for the English company, John Bigg. Helped to establish the tallow and hide industry, later the territory's main form of currency; known as "California banknotes." Owner of the Alisal rancho. Married Teresa de la Guerra, daughter of an influential Santa Barbara don. Has served in official positions under various California administrations.

Jeremy smiled. "Word seems to travel swiftly."

"Indeed it does," Hartnell said. "We knew of your arrival within hours. There is little else to talk about, Morgan, as starved as we are for news."

Somehow, Jeremy doubted that.

"So," Hartnell said. "How do you find it?"

"California? I can hardly give an opinion as yet."

"Don Mariano was quite impressed with you the other evening," Cooper interjected. "A sizable stroke of luck for the success of your lumber business, Morgan."

"Short of marrying a Californio woman," Larkin tossed, grinning.

"For some of us," Hartnell countered, agreeing. "Though it is not a requirement for success—wouldn't you say, Thomas?"

"But it's a far easier path—for one who is fortunate enough to find the lady of his choice among the fair ladies about," Cooper observed.

"Indeed, it's a sore point for many of our young Californio friends," Larkin commented dryly. "The fact that so many Americanos have captured the hearts of the dons' daughters, and have thus acquired large grants in the bargains, is a sore issue. Jose Castro once remarked that 'a caballero could not woo a senorita if opposed in his suit by an American sailor. These heretics must be cleared from the land!' Fortunately, the threat has eased. Besides, once a man takes a Californio bride, he becomes *familia*."

"Well, one thing is certain," Jeremy mused, glancing about. "They certainly know how to throw a party."

"Oh, Morgan, you haven't seen anything yet." Cooper laughed. "Celebrating is what the Californio does best. The entire purpose of his life is given to it."

Jeremy frowned. "But what of their businesses?"

Hartnell shook his head. "The Californio has a certain disdain for practical affairs."

"Indeed, Senor Morgan." A voice came from behind Jeremy. *"Poco tiempo,"* Vallejo added, joining them.

Jeremy glanced at the other three men. If they were embarrassed from being overheard, they gave no evidence of it. *"Poco tiempo?"* he repeated.

"Si. Translated it means too little time. It is a saying of my people which means, since there is not enough time to do it today, we may as well wait until tomorrow."

"Or *no se apure,*" Cooper added. "Don't be in a hurry."

"Or the old *manana* habit," Hartnell said. "Have satisfaction for what you are doing today. Don't worry about tomorrow."

Seeing Jeremy's confusion, Vallejo smiled. "It is a gracious and giving land, Morgan. We descend from many generations who have had to expend little effort for survival. Thus, graciousness and pleasure have become a way of life."

"Don't overlook the fact that you inherited your way of life from your ancestors, Mariano," Larkin said wryly.

"The *Gente de Razon,*" Vallejo agreed, nodding. "Under the old Spanish military system, soldiers were discouraged from any personal initiative. It was a punishable offense. When these early Indian fighters settled in California, their lack of efforts extended to their personal lives."

Jeremy thought about that for a moment. "Your people must have been rather shocked by the Yankee work ethic."

Vallejo laughed. "Very astute, Morgan." He exchanged a look with Larkin. "He learns quickly."

Larkin nodded. "Yes, apparently. He should be quite successful in his business ventures here."

"Indeed," Vallejo agreed. "Si, Morgan. The desire of your people to work, for the mere sake of working, quite stymies my people. In fact, because of the energies you put into your business enterprises, the first Americans and British here were thought to be spies."

"Spies?" Jeremy repeated.

"Si. What other reason could be given to it? My people could not believe that their interest in work was honest."

"From what I have heard, you managed to put forth some effort on occasion. As in the revolt against Mexico a few years ago."

"We do have our passions, Morgan. In my youth I was a *liberalismo,* a rebel," Vallejo said, his dark eyes glinting mischievously. "Politics were our fodder. Besides, it was necessary to rebel. While Governor Micheltorena was a good man, in spite of the fact that he was from *la otra banda*—that other shore that is Mexico—he brought *cholos* —scoundrels—with him for an army. The scum of Mexico, convicts, to rule us! They had to be expelled."

"Yes, you accused them of stealing chickens, as I recall," Hartnell said, stifling a smile.

"That, too," Vallejo observed somberly.

Cooper winked at Jeremy. "Our esteemed dons, particularly Vallejo and Alvarado, had made the expulsion of Mexican governors their chief sport."

Vallejo's mouth worked with a smile. "You give me too much credit. Part of me regrets that Micheltorena brought such rabble with him. He was not only a good soldier, but a scholar and a gentleman as well. If not for the fact that he was Mexican, I believe that he would have done well for California. Instead, now we have Pio Pico."

"Isn't he an ally of Castro and Alvarado?" Jeremy asked, remembering the information he had crammed through in preparation for his mission.

"Yes, he was, and still is, more or less," Vallejo answered. "However, there have always been rivalries within California. Once there was the division between the Abajenos, the southerners, and the Arribenos, the northerners. Then, when Los Angeles was chosen by Mexico as the capital, the rivalry sharpened. Now it is the Angeleno in contest with the Montereno. We in the north do not recognize the southern capital. It will remain in Monterey."

"And to the victor will go the spoils," Jeremy murmured.

"What was that?" Hartnell asked.

"Nothing," Jeremy answered. "Just a remark made by Secretary of War Marcy."

"Ah, yes." Larkin smiled. "Your good friend, Marcy."

"He is a friend of yours?" Hartnell asked, his eyes widening.

"Not exactly." Jeremy smirked, ignoring Larkin's chuckle. "But I've known him for some years."

"Well!" Cooper brightened. "If the situation with Mexico worsens, that could be quite advantageous. Close ties to the secretary of war couldn't hurt."

"I wouldn't count on it," Jeremy answered.

Rachel finished roasting the peppers and dipped them into a bowl of water to cool. After dabbing her forehead with the hem of her apron, she untied it and tossed it onto the end of the table that had been set up under the trees for food preparation. Glancing about, she stretched, rubbing the small of her back against the dull ache that had grown over the past quarter hour from bending over the fire. Then she spotted Beth Morgan, who was sitting under a tree at the far edge of the clearing. Rachel watched her for a moment, then sighed, shaking her head.

"May I join you?"

Beth was startled. "Oh—of course."

Rachel sat down on the edge of the blanket and spread out her skirt. "Are you enjoying yourself?"

Beth glanced at the woman. Was she serious? "It is peaceful."

"Yes, it is," Rachel answered, ignoring Beth's underlay of sarcasm as she glanced about the festivities. "The music is lovely, don't you think?" she asked, referring to the soft strains of the guitars.

Beth glanced at the players who were perched on upright boxes across the grove. "I suppose so." She swallowed heavily. Then, her eyes strayed to Rachel. "How were you able to stand it when you first came here? Did Thomas give you a choice—to come here, I mean?"

"Thomas had nothing to do with it." Rachel smiled. "When I left the east I was Rachel Holmes, not Larkin. My husband was stationed in the Sandwich Islands, and I journeyed there to be with him. I met Thomas on the ship."

Beth regarded Rachel with surprise. "But I thought—" No, she had assumed.

"I was married quite young," Rachel continued. "Soon after our marriage, my husband was assigned by his church to a mission in the islands. He went ahead to establish our home and I followed a few months later. Thomas . . . Thomas was an unexpected presence in my life. While it all was quite proper—" She paused, smiling as she remembered. "There was something about him. However, when we docked in Hawaii, I did not look back as the ship sailed on but set myself to rejoin my husband—only to find that he had died a few weeks before my arrival."

"Oooh— Whatever did you do?"

"Do?" Rachel smiled. "I did the only sensible thing. I wrote to Thomas."

"You came here—by choice?"

"Indeed I did. And it was the best decision I have ever made. After all, Elizabeth, what does it matter where we are if we are with a man we love?" She saw the distant look her

words brought to Beth's eyes. Oh dear, she thought, so that's
how it was. She had suspected that there was deep trouble in
the Morgan marriage. "We corresponded for a time, and
then Thomas returned to the Sandwich Islands. Soon we
sailed for California. Because we were not Catholic, and
could not be married in California, the wedding was
performed aboard ship by the United States Consul, Jones,
of Honolulu, who accompanied us on the voyage. But oh,
Beth! When we disembarked in Santa Barbara, I found that
a wonderful wedding celebration had been planned. From
those first moments, I fell in love with California and her
people. How could I not, when such warmth and love was
shown to me, so unreservedly? The governor and all the
important dons and dona's were there, decked out in their
finest. The celebration lasted for three days. I have never
regretted one moment of my life since."

Beth knew that Rachel's words were meant to comfort
her, but she could not manage more than a perfunctory
smile. Rachel's story had only served to depress her more.
After all, Larkin had quickly established himself in a new
country. Rachel was immediately accepted as his bride,
sharing his position. Wasn't that proven by the fact that
even the governor had been present at their celebration?
But what was there for her besides the disgrace that
shadowed them? Jeremy was nothing here, and thus neither
was she. Merely an immigrant, seeking to begin a new
enterprise that was laden, in her mind, with failure. It had
not escaped her that Rachel was regarded with respect by
the Californios; the men nodded to her, the women
curtsied. They called Rachel "Dona Yanqui"; to Beth they
were barely polite.

Rachel watched Beth's sullen face, and she sighed. "Try
to accept your life, Beth," she said softly. "As foreign
women, we have so much freedom here. More than you
could possibly imagine. You might find everything you
want, if you would give it a chance."

Beth watched Rachel as she left to return to her chores,
and she leaned back against the trunk of the tree, thoroughly depressed. She glanced down and irritably brushed an
insect off the pale blue lawn of her skirt. Looking up, she
sighed, noting the attire of the Californio men: the short,
silken jackets, the gaudy waistcoats, white silk shirts open at

the neck, the flaring trousers decorated with gold or silver buttons running down the side seams. Some sported the ever-present serapes of heavy wool worked with colorful embroidery. The women, heaven help her, were gowned in rich silks and satins, with bare arms and shoulders—in broad daylight! Some wore heavy lace mantillas about their heads, lifted with thick combs, others had thrown Chinese silk shawls about their shoulders to ward off the chill air. Never in her life had she felt so appropriately underdressed.

No, never, in spite of Rachel's words, would she accept her life here. In fact, the thought of doing so terrified her, as that would mean forgetting everything important to her. To accept this life would be to give up, to admit that her life had changed forever. She would never, ever do that.

Jeremy brought her a plate of food, sinking down on the blanket next to her. "Try the empanada," he said, biting into a steaming tortilla. "They're delicious."

Stiffly, she took the plate. In silence she nibbled at a sweet pepper. "How thoughtful of you to finally join me."

He frowned at the sharp edge in her voice. Controlling himself, he set his plate on the blanket and leaned an arm across a bent knee as he glanced about. "I did not come here to hide in a corner, Beth." He looked at his wife and noted the sadness in her eyes. In spite of his irritation, he softened. "Beth, I know this is not easy for you. But you could try."

"How could you just leave me here?" she asked, swallowing.

"Nothing was keeping you here. Why didn't you join the other women? Rachel tried to talk to you—I watched your face, Beth. You weren't even polite to her, were you?"

She turned and glared at him. "You don't even know what was said, and you assume that I was being rude!"

"Well, you were, weren't you?"

"What good would it do if I denied it?"

"Oh, Beth, please," he said, feeling deeply tired. "I'm sorry. Eat your supper. It's really quite good. Later there is to be dancing." He reached out and lifted her chin. "We have not danced for a long time, Beth."

The feel of his fingers on her face warmed her unexpectedly. She stared into the deep blue of his eyes, the suggestive promise of pleasure, laced with humor, that she had not recognized for so very, very long. In spite of herself, she smiled timorously. "Dancing? Oh, Jeremy, that would be nice."

"Then eat, Mrs. Morgan, for you will need your strength." He smiled. "And try this—" He reached for an earthen flask he had brought with the plates. "It is a cordial called angelica. It's quite delicious."

The afternoon air grew chilly, and Jeremy draped a shawl over her shoulders. She looked up at him and smiled, a certain glow illuminating her eyes. His hands felt good, wonderfully possessive—and safe. She felt positively giddy. Lord, what was the matter with her? Perhaps it was the angelica, she thought, which was delicious, and she had drunk quite a bit more than she had intended. But it made everything so much easier to bear . . .

It had been a marvel, the afternoon. Spicy foods warming her pleasantly. Language that had once seemed coarse lifting to her ears in soft, soothing, almost musical, phrases. Dark faces and warm, deep brown eyes. Manners laden with regal grace. The deep timbre of her husband's voice melding with his touch, seeming almost welcome. Definitely welcome. She resisted the sudden impulse to giggle. If only Amelia Harrison could see her now. She would have vapors. She leaned against Jeremy's body, reveling in its support as her gaze traveled happily over those gathered about the boards that had been set up for dancing. My word, she mused, how pleasant the day has become.

The lively strains of the guitar and violins began again, as dancers took to the boards. Jeremy's arm slipped about her shoulder, and she glanced up at him. As he watched the dancers, she realized that the gesture had been unconsciously natural, one of simple, easily given affection. The realization brought a tingling sensation to deep, ignored parts of her. She stiffened, a response that went unnoticed by her husband. She boldly slipped an arm about Jeremy's waist. The gesture drew his attention, and he looked down at her. His eyes were questioning, then they darkened with wonder. But the moment passed quickly as the music suddenly stopped. The silence drew his attention, as well as her own.

The boards were cleared of dancers. Shadows had deepened in the approaching dusk. Illumination from the lighted torches set about the clearing cast a wavering light over the dance floor. At the center, alone, stood Ariana. The crimson silk of her gown reflected the burnished light. The deep silence of the gathered crowd seemed to heighten the angles of her body as she stood in preparation for her dance. Her ankles were bound with a dark sash; on her head was a glass tumbler of water, precariously balanced by the tall tortoiseshell comb set into the thick twist of her dark, bound hair.

The melodious refrains of a lone guitar began. Ariana's body turned to its haunting melody. Beth watched her move, fascinated, transfixed. Slender, bare arms lifted upward, and her crimson, silk-clad waist twisted. Full breasts pressed tightly against fabric as heels clicked in sharp rhythm against the boards. The sound increased, tapping in Beth's brain as the slender body moved. Skirts swirled, exposing trim, bound ankles, calves, and thighs. Hips undulated in the blatant seduction of the dance. Ariana's hands rose, and she began to clap in time to the music. The watchers joined in, the sound building in momentum, drawing, encouraging, their murmurs lifting to shouts, cries that heightened the intensity of the scene.

Beth's breathing became ragged. The crowd watched the glass expectantly, but Beth's eyes were fixed on Ariana's body. The turns, the steady, measured clicking of the heels. She swallowed heavily and glanced up at Jeremy, fixing on the angles of his profile. How had she forgotten how devastatingly handsome her husband was? she wondered. And it came to her in a moment that seemed totally to overwhelm her. She wanted him. Her breast rose heavily, and she pressed against him, exalting in the realization. Slowly, she again lifted her gaze to his profile.

He was unaware of her emotions, of her sudden, embarrassing need. He was staring, not at his wife, but at Ariana Saldivar. His arm was about her, holding her tightly against his side, but his eyes were fixed on the boards, the clicking of the dancer's heels, and her lithe, supple body.

Beth shifted her gaze back to Ariana, and her eyes darkened. The rhythm began to pound in her brain, and she burned with the passion she had seen in her husband's eyes. For the first time in her life, so swiftly upon the tail of her first awareness of passion, Beth knew jealousy. Her gaze narrowed on the beautiful Californio. At that moment, she felt her heart shift, and she knew sudden, sheer hatred.

7

A sudden downpour of rain and the appearance of an American man-of-war in the harbor brought about a swift packing of horses and ox carts. The *merienda* shifted from Point Lobos and was reorganized at the Custom House. Children were scuttled off to nearby homes, where they were put to bed. The fact of a strange bed was accepted as a matter of course by even the youngest child. From birth they had learned that no respectable *merienda,* fiesta, rodeo or wedding was over until it was over, often lasting for two or three days.

Situated comfortably on a bale of cotton in the Custom House, Jeremy accepted a tankard of rum from John Cooper as he toweled his dripping hair with his free hand. "Has your wife left us?" Cooper asked, glancing about the long room to the few childless women who had remained.

"She returned home with Rachel. Thomas seems to have a particularly satisfied gleam in his eye," he added, grinning as Larkin wrestled a barrel of rum across the wide planks of the floor.

"That man-of-war brings a heady prospect of profit." Cooper smiled. "I expect that our ranks will soon swell considerably. It should be quite a party."

"Not if that rain doesn't let up," Jeremy observed, tossing the wet towel on a nearby heap with others. "I doubt that they will chance their longboats until morning."

"I've known them to chance a raging storm for a pot of rum." Cooper laughed. "Those sailors have not seen port since the Sandwich Islands."

Jeremy, Cooper, and the tapped barrel of rum were soon joined by the other men, including Larkin, who now had his stores well in hand. The women remained clustered at the other end of the long, narrow room, chatting among themselves in apparent contentment. When Jeremy's gaze traveled to the group for the third time, Vallejo suddenly laughed.

"You wonder about our women, Morgan, and why they do not join us."

"It occurred to me." Jeremy shrugged. "Women in my culture would certainly have included themselves."

"Oh, but they are included," Jose Castro said. The short, plump, round-faced commandant regarded the women solemnly. "As you can see, they are here."

"Jose refers to a great advance in our culture," Vallejo offered, smiling at Jeremy's look of skepticism. "In fact, we have become quite civilized toward our women. There was a time, not too many years ago, when such an occurrence would have been looked upon with great indelicacy. The strict customs between men and women ran deeply, Jeremy. The church considered it sinful for a male relation to sleep in the same house where unwed females slept. No male child after the age of three would be allowed to do so. Often they ended up sleeping in an open field if nothing else was available. Brothers were scarcely permitted to converse with their sisters, unless in the presence of a third person."

"And that person was always an elder," Garner interjected. "When I first arrived in California, on occasion I would observe a girl rushing out a back door when her brother entered through the front."

"Do not look so shocked, Morgan," Vallejo said. "The church had great influence in the heyday of the missions." He glanced in the direction of the women. "It will take a long time to undo much of what they did. Do not misunderstand me, however. We are Catholic, and will always be. It was the—strictures upon our growth that led to dissension."

And the strictures upon owning land, Jeremy thought. Mission land, which you now hold.

"The absence of secular education concerns me the most," Larkin said, topping off his tankard from the barrel. Jeremy knew he was referring to his bitter regret at having to send his young sons so far from home to receive an education. However, he wondered silently, would it have been any different for the Larkins if the church had allowed schools with secular teachings? There would have been Catholic religious training as well, and Larkin was Protestant to the core.

"The church isn't solely to blame," Vallejo said, his voice touched with a deep bitterness. "On occasion the government attempted to establish schools. Their practice was to give the task to some illiterate soldier who knew better how to discipline than teach. One such experience almost destroyed my interest in learning."

"But the church condemned *telemachus*," Larkin argued.

"Indeed." Vallejo sighed. "The forbidden word." He glanced at Castro and broke into a grin. "Jose and I were once unofficially excommunicated for our resistance to that edict."

"That was your fault, Mariano," Jose observed.

"Si, I accept the blame." Vallejo shrugged. "When I was in my youth, Morgan, I had a great drive to learn, yet all learning but that of the church was forbidden. It was considered *telemachus*, or the forbidden word. Then, upon discovering that a small library was owned by the captain of a visiting Spanish vessel, I sneaked aboard and—'borrowed' it."

The men laughed, knowing the outcome of the story. "Well?" Jeremy prodded impatiently. "Were you caught?"

"Of course. Alas," he sighed with mock sorrow, "I was betrayed by my sweetheart who reported the sin to the priest."

"Your sweetheart?" Jeremy smirked, arching a dark brow. "Obviously, not all young women ran out the back door at the sound of a male voice."

The room erupted in laughter. "You have me there, Morgan." Vallejo grinned. "In matters of men and women, there is always a way—and enough exceptions to cause you to doubt the rule."

"Sorry for interjecting a note of discord." Jeremy smiled. "Go on with your story."

"Ah, well. At first I did not know of my love's betrayal. In the meantime, armed with our treasure, Jose, Alvarado and I formed a secret junta, pledging ourselves to the study of politics and history. This was serious, Morgan. It went solidly against our elders who were firmly attached to 'king and pope.' It was a youthful rebellion against our elders, who seemed to feel it necessary to pray at the break of dawn, at noon, at sunset, and at bedtime—to the exclusion of all other thought. However, it was soon after that the priest hauled us by our ears before him. He demanded the *telemachus*—apparently the fact of my theft of the books bothered him less than the prospect of our reading the books, thus subjecting ourselves to the forbidden word. In the way of youthful courage and conviction, and to the horror of our families, we staunchly refused his demands."

"And then you were excommunicated."

"Unofficially."

"How can you be excommunicated unofficially?"

"The priest never carried through on his threat. He used it only to frighten our families. Which it did. They brought pressure upon us to return the books. However, we stood fast. I still have those books somewhere."

"That moment began a new freedom in California, Jeremy," Larkin said, filling a new round of tankards from a pitcher he had drawn from the barrel. "That first, tender resistance grew. The junta's objectives were education, a reduction of the power of the church, freedom for men to express themselves, freedom for bondsmen, and a beginning of self-government for California. While it is not normally in the Californio character," he added, glancing at Vallejo with a smile. "Mariano is being modest. What he, Castro, and Alvarado did was not only courageous, but the beginning of freedom from Mexican domination."

Just then the door opened, allowing a sweeping gust of cold air and wind into the room. Everyone turned to the interruption as Hartnell rushed to close the door and greet the newcomer. A heavily cloaked man had come into the building, rain dripping in a steady stream from his great coat. Hartnell took the cloak, and a few words were exchanged. For those watching, the removal of the coat answered silent questions. Of medium height, with sandy, curling hair that dripped rain onto his collar, the young man wore the uniform of a lieutenant in the United States Navy. Hartnell ushered him over to the group that was clustered about the large, iron stove.

"Gentlemen, may I present Lieutenant Joseph Revere of the U.S.S. *Portsmouth.*"

"Gentlemen." The young lieutenant nodded in greeting, momentarily flustered as a tankard of rum was pushed into his hands. "My—I wish to convey greetings from my captain."

"We assume that, Lieutenant." Larkin smiled affably. "Warm yourself, or you will not be able to convey anything. How many of your men should we expect this evening?"

"Only two men came ashore with me. They are waiting by the longboat—"

"Good Lord, man!" Larkin turned even as two of the Californios were already moving toward the door. He turned back to the drenched, half-frozen officer. "Only two have come with you? This is a hospitable port, Lieutenant Revere, as your captain will find."

Jeremy watched the young officer's expression as it worked uncomfortably. The hazel eyes shifted to the others, as if he were seeking something. Jeremy's eyes narrowed slightly, and before Larkin could introduce him, he slipped off the cotton bale. "Perhaps I could be of service. Jeremy Morgan," he said, offering the officer his hand. "I could take Revere to his lodgings. I'm certain that he will be in no mood for festivities after an undoubtedly tiring voyage, not to mention the difficult one to shore."

"Yes," Larkin said, pausing. "Yes. A good idea, Morgan. I think that Rachel could put him up for the night. His men could stay with you, Garner, could they not?" A surprised look from the other man was followed by a resigned shrug. "Good. See to it, Jeremy. I will see you later then, Lieutenant."

The rain was coming down steadily when the men left the Custom House, curtailing any conversation but a few, brief shouted orders as they met with the others coming up from the beach. Nothing more was said until they reached the Larkin house, where they were met by Rachel, who ushered them into the upstairs parlor. Divesting themselves of their wet things, they remained by the hearth, sipping warm brandy, while Rachel took their coats to dry by the kitchen fire.

"You are very kind," the officer said, glancing at the door as it closed behind Rachel. "I did not wish to inconvenience anyone."

"You haven't."

"Nevertheless, please extend my gratitude to your wife. I would have done so myself had she not left so quickly."

"Rachel?" Jeremy glanced at the door. Then he smiled. "Rachel is used to sudden guests, and knows when the situation is not a social one. But she is not my wife."

"But—" Revere frowned, his hazel eyes mixing with confusion and embarrassment. "I apologize, Morgan. I thought—"

"You thought that I seem to be rather at home here. It is the way of our host and hostess, Revere. This house is the hub of Monterey, as you will find out for yourself. Larkin is more than just the consul here, he is the pivot to everything that happens here."

"Larkin?" Revere's sandy brows arched with surprise.

"It was Larkin you came to see, wasn't it? Privately?"

Jeremy admitted that Revere covered his reaction well. "Thomas Larkin? I would, of course, present my captain's compliments to the consul, as well as to the commander of the military government in Monterey."

"Of course. And you came ashore—alone but for two men—to pay those compliments. In a raging storm? A delay, under the circumstances, would have been quite acceptable."

"The weather did not seem difficult when we started out." The officer averted his eyes as he sipped his brandy.

"Stick to that."

Revere looked up. "Pardon?"

"Nothing," Jeremy answered, settling more comfortably into his chair. "Revere—" he said after a moment, hesitating on the name. "I don't suppose that you are related to our country's illustrious ancestor, Paul Revere?"

"My great-grandfather," Revere answered absently.

At that moment the door opened, and Larkin came into the room. "Well, Morgan," he said affably. "I see that you made our guest comfortable."

"No, you can thank Rachel for that. If anything I've caused him discomfort."

Stunned, Revere rose quickly from his chair. "Mr. Larkin, I'm so sorry. I did not know who you were . . ."

"No need to apologize," Larkin said abruptly, waving the officer back to his chair. "Since you have come ashore alone, I presume that you have a message for me." He noted the officer's lack of ease as he glanced at Jeremy. "Do not concern yourself with Morgan, here. You may speak freely."

Revere looked unconvinced. Then, as the other two men waited, he sighed. "I have come ashore to bring you a message, Mr. Larkin, but it is unofficial. The *Portsmouth* is here to take on supplies. Meanwhile, I have been given—special leave to acquaint myself with the area. I am a bit of an amateur chronicler, you see, and I hope to note some observations of the land and the people."

Jeremy vacated his chair for Larkin, who had moved toward the fire to warm himself. "Of course," the consul replied, rubbing his hands to the warmth of the flames. "And what is the message?"

Revere hesitated, glancing at Jeremy who had turned to stare from the window. "I have been instructed to inform you that the British are in close waters. Commodore Sloat, Commander of the Pacific Squadron, is presently off the Sandwich Islands. I have been told to inform you—that the navy is near."

"Please convey my compliments to your captain. Assure him that we can offer him all the comforts our port can give."

"I will convey your regards—and your kind offer, sir. However, the *Portsmouth* will be sailing for Yerba Buena in the morning."

"I see." Larkin grunted, then after a moment said, "Well then, perhaps we can be of assistance in your own efforts, Lieutenant. Besides studying our area, you might enjoy a trip northward. John Sutter's fort at New Helvetia is not to be missed. In fact, I think you might find it most enlightening."

"I would appreciate any effort in my behalf," Revere replied. "It is my intent to come to know the territory quite well before the *Portsmouth's* departure from California."

Jeremy half listened to the conversation behind him. His attention had been caught by something in the street below. Two people walked along the shadows of buildings in the rain. He had idly followed their progress since they first had come into view. Then, as the rain began to let up, something familiar about one of the pair struck him. Now curious, he watched as they slipped through the gate leading to the Larkins' gardens. He turned back to the room and waited for a pause in the conversation. "Gentlemen, if you will forgive me, I shall be off to bed. It has been a long day."

"Of course, Morgan," Larkin said, somewhat nonplussed by his abrupt departure.

Jeremy ignored the consul's puzzlement as he set his unfinished brandy on a table and left the room. Making his way down the stairs, he left the house by the back door opening onto the gardens. He closed the door quietly behind him and slipped silently into the rose arbor, his mind fixed on the shadows below an acacia tree at the center of the garden.

"Do you honestly believe that he is returning to California only to survey for their maps?" Ariana asked.

"He was here before for that purpose. He even wrote a book about it," Rafael insisted.

"Si, so he was. But this is different. According to Paredes's letter, the Mexican consul in Washington reports that this expedition shows evidence that it will be a military one. The men he has gathered for this venture are soldiers. *That* he did not have before. If you doubt my suspicions, cousin, then why the urgency to discuss it?"

Rafael sighed. "Because Manuel's suspicions are the same as yours. What are we going to do?"

"Do? Whatever I must. Go now. I must return to Rachel before I am missed. And no one must find you here."

Jeremy stepped back to the door to the house. He opened it behind him, then let it slam shut. Clearing his throat, he stepped back into the arbor, his feet crunching on the crushed oyster shells of the path. As he emerged from the other end, he saw a shadow slip through the gate. "Senorita Saldivar!" he exclaimed, stepping into the moonlight. "How delightful to find you here. I see that you were in need of some air, as well."

"Senor Morgan!" she said, startled. *Dios!* she thought. Why was this man always appearing at such inopportune moments? "Has everyone retired?"

"I left early to have a nightcap with Thomas. No escort, even at night, Senorita? Whatever would be said?"

"I returned home with Rachel. Besides, these gardens are quite secluded."

"Does your uncle know you are here?"

"Of course. When he is ready he will come to collect me."

Collect? An odd choice of words, Jeremy thought, like pocketing a possession. Names and words kept running through his head: Paredes, survey, Mexican consul . . . "Well then, perhaps I could keep you company until he arrives."

"If you wish, senor, but I assure you that it is not necessary."

"Perhaps not, but it would be my pleasure."

Ariana plucked an azalea from a full, fragrant bush along the path as she deliberately turned away. Something deeply disturbed her about this man. On the surface, he was totally charming, a quality supported by his startling, handsome features and well-formed, trim body beneath the exquisite cut of his clothes. His easy, assured manner made it obvious that his background was one of wealth and breeding. Nevertheless, there was something else, an underlying strength that seemed to mock his almost frivolous manner. The fact that he kept it suppressed sharpened her curiosity. "It would be rather pleasant to have some company—if your wife is not waiting for you."

"Beth retired hours ago," he said casually. He peered at her through narrowed eyes, wishing that there was a full moon instead of the meager sliver that cast her face into shadows. "Who was with you when I came into the garden?"

The blunt question startled her, but she knew that it would be worse than useless to deny it. Obviously he had seen Rafael slipping away. She weighed the possibilities quickly, deciding upon the one lie he would most readily believe. "Senor," she said softly, stammering slightly. "Please do not tell my uncle, I beg of you!" She dropped her gaze, feigning embarrassment, and missed the arching of a dark brow, the slight smile.

"You are telling me that you have a secret lover, Senorita Saldivar?"

She held the flower to her nose in a gesture of embarrassment.

"Well, well," he said. She wondered at the hint of laughter in his voice. "Never fear, Ariana, I wouldn't dream of telling your uncle . . . such a story."

"Thank you, Senor," she said in a hushed, grateful voice. Then he reached out and took her arm, turning her back to him. Surprised, she almost cringed as he bent toward her.

"I would be careful, if I were you, Ariana," he murmured. "Such dalliances could find you in serious trouble."

She pulled away from him, stepping back. "I—I will remember your advice, Senor. Now if you will excuse me, Rachel is certainly waiting." She turned and hurried through the arbor, wondering at the soft laughter that followed her.

A single candle cast deep shadows around the small room, and wavering forms flickered against the walls. Beth stood before the mirror appraising the young woman looking back at her. Pale hair fell to her hips, barely concealing a body that was still quite slender, she thought, in spite of the fact that her pregnancy was showing with a firm swell of her stomach. She could see the outline of her breasts, the darker hue of her nipples pressing in relief against the thin fabric. The candle behind her illuminated the soft outline of her hips, the length of her legs.

Hesitantly, she reached up and unbuttoned the small pearl buttons at the neckline of the bedgown, releasing the bodice to a deep point between her breasts. They were fuller, tenderer than before. She opened the bodice and stared. Lifting a hand, she reached into the opened neckline to touch a breast, feeling the warm flesh beneath her hand. What pleasure did it give him to touch her body like this? It felt strange to her. She had never touched herself this way before.

She let her hand trail over her breast, pausing at the nipple to fondle it as he had so often done. A small, tight feeling of warmth darted through her belly. There were women, she knew, who gave themselves to men for pleasure. Did they like being touched like this?

Her hand slipped lower, over her gently swelling stomach, and paused. Then she drew her hand away, clenching it in a fist at her side. She trembled. What was she doing?

She left the mirror and crossed to the chair by the window, suddenly needing to focus upon something else. Her hand still felt the warmth of her body, the memory lingering as she sought to still her emotions. The garden beyond the window was dark, illuminated in shadows by the moon. Trim rows of box hedges framing azaleas and budding roses ran through the garden. Her gaze moved to the rose arbor. Where was he? she wondered.

Her fingers drummed idly on the arm of the chair as she glanced about the small room. Soon they would have a home of their own; Jeremy had promised. Larkin had begun construction on the house months before their arrival, and it would be ready in a few weeks. A month at the most. Perhaps Monterey wouldn't be quite so bad, she thought, if she had a home of her own. Not that it could compare with what she had left in New York. But anything was better than having so little privacy and control.

Freedom, Rachel had said. Freedom to do what? Beth's fingers increased their impatient drumming. And then her wandering eyes fell on Jeremy's brandy decanter. She stared at it for a moment. She had never tasted brandy; the angelica had helped her through the afternoon.

She poured herself a snifter and returned to the chair. She had watched Jeremy sniff it first, and she imitated his actions. Her nose wrinkled as it burned from the heavy, unpleasant aroma. Then she tasted it, coughing as it seared her throat. By the third sip it didn't taste quite so bad. In fact, a pleasant warmth had spread over her body. She giggled suddenly, visualizing her mother's reaction if she could see her daughter now. But she couldn't. Beth suddenly felt quite euphoric. She took another sip.

In New York, her mother reigned, ruling all those about her, and would continue to do so throughout her life. If her maternal grandmother was any evidence, Beth's mother would live to be ninety. Beth realized at that moment that she was free, for the first time in her life, from the rigid dictates and standards of others, including Margaret Hilton. Jeremy certainly never seemed to impose upon her. Well, hardly ever. In fact, it often had left her confused and angry. Her father had always made it quite clear what he expected of her.

As she took another sip from the snifter, she was surprised to find the glass empty. Rising, she refilled the glass—a more generous measure this time—and settled into the chair. Some time later, she struggled against a yawn. No, she thought, fighting fatigue. She didn't want to lose this feeling. What if it never came back? She shifted in the chair and glanced from the window.

It was then that she saw them, as they stepped from the

deep shadows of the acacia tree into the moonlight. Staring, Beth felt herself harden, her emotions plummeting into numbness as she watched her husband draw Ariana Saldivar into the moonlight. She tried to draw away from the window, shaken by the sight of her husband with another woman. But she remained transfixed, as if some compelling force was making her watch. She watched Ariana turn away from him and pluck a flower, holding it to her nose to breathe in the fragrance. So, she had been right. Senorita Saldivar was nothing more than a—a flirt.

Jeremy's hand reached out and turned the young woman around, drawing her to him. Beth's breath caught as she watched her husband's head bend down. She couldn't draw her eyes away as she anticipated the kiss that the tender scene was certainly leading to. She felt a strange excitement stirring within her, more sharply than before. Unconsciously, her hand moved to her breast, touching it. She held her breath. Then, unexplicitly, Jeremy moved away from Ariana. Moments later, Ariana left the garden.

Beth stood before the fire, welcoming the heat against her skin. She struggled to steady her emotions as she tried to fix upon what she would do; how she should react when he came through the door. Confront him with what she had seen? But then, what had she actually seen? She heard the latch, felt the cool rush of the night air through the thin fabric of her nightgown. She pictured him standing there. She could feel his surprise to find her still awake, just as she knew that the outline of her body was sharply defined in the fire's light. The awareness brought a returning rush of excitement—and something more. A surprising feeling of power.

"Beth?" She heard the door close behind her. "I thought you would be asleep. Is something wrong?"

Slowly, she turned, and she heard the intake of his breath. She felt a heady rush of control falling into her hands and felt strangely light-headed. She drew a calming breath. "You are late, Jeremy."

"I didn't know you were waiting up. What is it—couldn't you sleep?" Suddenly he looked concerned. "Are you all right? Are you feeling well?"

"I was waiting for you," she said, shrugging her shoulders. She moved from the fire, gesturing to the small table nearby. "Would you like a nightcap?"

"Yes," he said after a moment's hesitation. "Is everything all right?"

"Why do you keep asking?" she said. "I told you that everything is fine." She handed him the glass. He took the chair near the fire, watching her warily as he sipped the liquor. As she sat next to him, she was acutely aware as his gaze traveled to her, passing down over her body, pausing at the unbuttoned bodice. She leaned back, resting her arms on the arm of the chair, knowing that the movement caused the bodice to gape open.

"Did you enjoy your evening?" she asked.

"Yes, I did." What in the hell was she doing? And then he saw the snifter on the window ledge beyond her shoulder. "Beth, have you been drinking?"

She followed his gaze, and reached around to pick up the glass. Taking a sip, she shrugged. "Yes, I have. Is there something wrong with that? You often have a nightcap."

He glanced at the decanter. "Apparently, you've had a couple."

"So?"

"You're not going to feel very good in the morning."

"Oh? Why?" she asked, slurring the last word.

He was tempted to tell her. She had probably never seen anyone with a hangover. Jonathan Hilton would only show his best face to his family. He undoubtedly reserved his less controlled moments for his club and his mistress. "Never mind. We'll discuss it in the morning."

"Was there a problem this evening—after I left?" she asked.

"No—why do you ask?"

"I saw you with Ariana Saldivar in the garden."

"I was just being courteous. There was no problem."

"That's good." She sipped from her glass, thinking about his answer. It was probably just as he said. After all, they really hadn't done anything untoward. They were just talking.

Jeremy stared at his wife's breasts. They had never been offered to him quite so openly before. Her gaze was fixed on the fire with a calm expression. Perhaps she wasn't aware—but then that was unlikely, even with the liquor. Beth hid behind her modesty like a shield, one that was never, never lowered. A gleam of speculation entered his eyes as he wondered how far this might go. His conscience tugged at him briefly. Did he really want to take advantage of the fact that his wife was drunk? Hell, he thought, why not? She was his wife, not some virgin he was about to compromise. He was tantalized by the prospect of taking an unguarded, willing Beth. She might even find some pleasure in it—and remember it later. Perhaps he should have thought of it himself. Setting his glass down, he reached out and took her hand, helping her from her chair.

"Come here," he said, drawing her into his lap.

She regarded him with speculation, but she didn't resist. He settled her into his lap, then kissed her lightly, testing the waters. To his pleasant surprise, her lips opened under the gentle pressure. Then, to his amazement, she began her own eager investigation of his mouth. His hand lifted to her breast and began to caress the tip, which quickly hardened at his touch.

A deep ache began between her legs when he touched her; rays of heat darted outward, upward to her breasts. She regarded the sensation with curiosity, focusing on it, as one who was observing a new, interesting phenomena. She smiled inwardly, realizing that she wanted to know what it was like, how it would feel to be one of those women who . . . Slowly, her fantasy began to flame. As his fingers unbuttoned the rest of her gown and his hand slipped beneath, she felt herself in a dance, torchlights playing over her body. As the gown was drawn from her, lights played across bare calves and thighs. As his mouth claimed a breast, she gasped. Molten heat shuddered through her. She turned in the dance, heels clicking, hips undulating. Her arms moved upward to the music, slipping about his neck, pulling his mouth down to hers.

8

Distracted by the heavy rain against the windowpane, Jeremy threw down the pen impatiently and leaned back in his chair. The latest missive to Buchanan lay idle as he stared at the trailing rivulets that ran down the window to collect in a puddle along the sill, seeping under the frame. Damn, he thought, that window was still leaking.

He glared at the puddle, then suddenly realized the absurdity of being angry with a window. With a resigned sigh, he glanced about the room. He had never wanted this house. He had bought it only to please Beth. Please Beth— he smirked at the thought. That night of the *merienda,* months before, he had begun to believe that there was hope for them. Since that night, while she occasionally had shown other moments of passion, he had begun to believe that they had nothing to do with him. She had become even more restless and withdrawn. He suspected that nothing would ever make her truly happy. Not even their son.

The thought made him stir restlessly as his anger returned. He had thought that all women loved their children. No, that wasn't honest. He doubted that his mother had ever really loved him. Or his younger brother David, or their sister Amanda.

Outwardly the epitome of the successful wife and mother, Caroline Morgan had lived in silent pain. Jeremy had been aware of it from his earliest recollection. When he thought of Caroline Morgan, he thought of loneliness. It had always been there, behind the bright enthusiasm with which she met her daily affairs, gleaming in her eyes like a badge that a silent, brave soldier carried home from a war. The mark of Caroline Morgan's life. Once he had thought that he had been responsible for putting it there. As a child, he had tried to atone, to change the desolate look at all cost: a flower offered from the garden; a story to amuse her, even making it up at the cost of his own dignity. Anything, everything, to change that look to one of approval. He was ten before he realized that the pain was for his father.

He soon discovered that David and Amanda needed him. Not that they sensed the emptiness that he felt. They seemed unaware of their mother's pain. In the physical absence of their father and the indifference of their mother, he became the pivot of their world. He protected David's rambunctious errors from the stern discipline of their parents. A natural student, he helped David through the pain of his studies—they seemed to be so difficult for him, as if they were some unnatural act. With effort, David eventually matriculated at Yale Law School, though Jeremy knew that his mind was on dragons, castles, and unarticulated dreams. Amazingly, David finished his years at Yale, met a lovely girl, married her and settled down. Well, not quite. Law was soon abandoned, against Jeremy's raging protests, for the smoky form of dreams. Then, one day, David dropped a sheaf of papers on Jeremy's desk, his hazel eyes bright with expectation. Upon reading the manuscript, Jeremy had to admit that it was quite good. Jeremy reminded himself that he also had made a career change, from Harvard to the Point. Proud of David's obvious talent, he made a few contacts and celebrated with his brother when the novel was accepted and published.

Through the years, Jeremy was there for Amanda, accepting her roses, soothing the tears of a bruised knee, placing himself bodily between his little sister and the terrors of bad dreams in the dark, frightening hours of the night. He was there for her when she thought herself in love with a classmate of David's, comforting her through the pain of disillusionment, blaming himself for not protecting her as she cried through the betrayal. And then he had seen her happily married to one of his classmates at Harvard. Oh, he had orchestrated the relationship with finesse. If only he had been so successful with his own life.

The night his son was born, he had damned this house. It was too small. It seemed pathetically plain in its straight, angular lines. The small rooms mocked him, as did the furnishings. He should have waited and built her a house of their own design. But that would have taken months more, and he could not abide the thought of living with her in that small room behind the Larkins' house.

The house had been ready a month after the *merienda*. Their son had followed two months later amid a night of cries that had torn through his brain, accusatory screams that even brandy could not blot out.

When he saw her soft and golden, so weary from her efforts, with their tiny son tucked away in his cradle near the bed, he had felt a bittersweet squeezing in his heart. Then she had opened her eyes and the feeling was quickly dispelled. She had looked at him with a distant resolve that, once again, seemed to have nothing to do with him. Or their son. She would not hold him, and a wet nurse was brought in. She rose from her bed on the twelfth day and went about her life as if their son were to be merely tolerated as though he were part of some distant universe.

He took his pocket watch from the narrow pouch in his vest, clicking open the cover. Two o'clock; Revere should be here soon. His letter had said that he would be returning to Monterey the morning of December 2. He slipped the watch back into his vest, wondering why the prospect that Revere would not come suddenly depressed him. "The shade of melancholy boughs, lose and neglect the creeping hours of time." Shakespeare's words flitted oddly across his brain.

He missed Revere. Over the months, their friendship had quickened, forming into a strong bond. Revere had long since been taken into his confidence. His astute observations and unwavering loyalty were welcome to both Jeremy and Larkin. And, beyond his shrewd, discerning mind, Revere had an underlying humor and a propensity for bad puns that made Jeremy laugh when there was nothing to laugh at. He missed him.

"Senor Morgan?" Selena, the mestizo maid he had hired when they moved into the house, stood in the doorway to his study. He turned toward the interruption with annoyance. Would the woman never learn to knock before she entered? "What is it, Selena?" he grumped.

"You have a visitor, Senor."

His mood lightened, then sunk when William Garner pushed past the small, dark-skinned woman who seemed to shrink before the stern glance of the Englishman. Jeremy regarded Garner with irritation, forcing a placid smile. His anger toward the maid dissolved beneath a sudden feeling of protectiveness. "That will be all, Selena. Thank you."

For a moment she regarded him with surprise, which quickly disappeared beneath her normal, indifferent expression. Then Jeremy frowned as Garner helped himself to the sherry decanter. It wasn't that he disliked Garner, exactly. The man had many redeeming qualities, and could be counted on for a wealth of information, but he tended to whine. "To what do I owe the honor of this visit, Will?"

"Just passing by," Garner answered, dropping into a chair on the other side of the desk. "Christ, Morgan, do you realize what it costs to purchase a lot in Monterey now? Thirty-one and one half cents per yard of front line!"

Did the man think that he had found this house under a rock? "Yes, I know," he said patiently. "A rather good buy, I think. After all, one is granted one hundred yards of depth which costs nothing. If you purchase a normal one hundred feet of front line, you gain a plot of ten thousand square yards for about thirty-four dollars. Not a bad bargain." Jeremy smiled at Garner's frown. "You should return to the east for a time, my friend."

Sensing a lack of support, Garner changed the subject. "My horse became lame when I was near the Ramerez rancho yesterday. The son of a bitch offered me a mare to ride!"

Jeremy's mouth twitched with a smile. To a Californio, a mare was beneath consideration; only stallions were worthy as mounts. To offer a mare as a saddle horse was nothing short of an insult. "Perhaps there was nothing else available," he offered in a deliberately appeasing voice.

"Humph," Garner snorted, turning the sherry goblet on the arm of his chair as he glared out of the window. "Ramerez never liked me."

Quite possible, Jeremy thought. Garner meant well, but he was a bigot.

"Odd about what has happened in Mexico."

Jeremy glanced at the unfinished letter to Washington. Consciously, he picked it up and slipped it into a folder on the corner of his desk. "Odd? How?"

"Really, Morgan! I know that your mind is full of timber and lumber prices, but surely even you must know what is going on? Then, perhaps you don't—you should get out more. The rumors that have been seeping up here over the past months are true. There's been a revolution in Mexico. Herrera is the new president. Some general, Paredes I think, was responsible . . ."

Paredes. Mexican consul. Words flitted through Jeremy's brain.

". . . Rumor has it that Washington's trying to negotiate with Herrera for a purchase. I tried to discuss the matter with Larkin, but the man, as usual, is not talking. Closed as a porthole in a storm, our consul. Has he said anything to you?"

"Not a thing."

"Typical." Garner grunted. "You would think that it did not involve us." He took a sip of his sherry. "Do you think that Polk is trying to buy California?"

"I wouldn't know."

"Well, I don't think he will. Damn Mexicans are too embroiled in their own problems to worry about California. By the way, I've heard that John Fremont is in the area again—at New Helvetia. It's said that he's brought an armed force with him. How does an officer in the Topographical Engineers warrant bringing an army with him? What's wrong with those fools in Washington? Don't they know what this could mean to our Californios?"

"I couldn't say." Jeremy had recently wondered the same thing. He had received no official word on Fremont's arrival as yet—nor had Larkin. Fremont. Paredes. Mexican consul. What in the hell was Ariana Saldivar up to? He had watched her over the past months, but to all appearances, except for that one night, she seemed to be nothing more than she appeared: a beautiful woman and a gracious hostess for her uncle.

"Well, I have long given up trying to understand Washington's reasons." Garner snorted. "Morgan, have you ever seen a vaquero work with a lasso?"

"Huh?" It was almost impossible to keep up with Garner's train of thought.

"A lasso. Damnedest thing I ever saw. Never will get used

to it. A Californio can lasso a man, drag him, wring his neck and release the rope as quick as we could shoot him. I've seen them do it while fighting Indians. Better than a brace of pistols."

As usual, Jeremy marveled at Garner's observations. He had learned quite a bit from the man, once he had learned to temper the man's prejudices. Before he could respond, Selena appeared to announce another visitor. This time, however, her face was softened with pleasure, and Revere appeared in the doorway. Jeremy could have sworn that the man patted Selena's bottom as he passed by.

"Jeremy! God, what a time I had!" Revere said, his eyes leering comically at the suddenly flustered maid. His mouth still open, he came to a sudden halt that threatened to topple him. "Well!" he exclaimed with a slight pause. "Garner! What a delight to find you here! How are you?"

Garner's voice raised with Revere's infectious enthusiasm. "Revere! Welcome back!" His blue eyes warmed with expectation. Garner had the look of one whose day had developed particularly well, and he visibly settled in his chair.

Revere's eyes flickered with a moment of dismay, then gleamed with a wicked glint. "What luck that you are here, Garner!" His voice rose with a new surge of enthusiasm. "God, the sightings I made were incredible!" He slung the heavy pack he carried onto Jeremy's desk with a thump. "The sketches I made are magnificent, if I do say so myself! Why, I have seventy-four pictures of flowers in here. Can't wait to show them to you! Wait until you see the wild mustard—"

Jeremy almost laughed out loud at Garner's panicked look. Rising quickly from his chair, Garner set his glass on the edge of Jeremy's desk, not noticing the odd watering in Jeremy's eyes. "Much as I would enjoy seeing them, Revere, I fear that I have pressing obligations. Another time, perhaps."

"Are you certain?" Revere asked, feigning disappointment. He glanced at the pack. "The Indian paintbrush was particularly magnificent."

"I am certain—as much as it grieves me," Garner assured him, moving quickly to the door. "Jeremy, thanks for the sherry." The door closed behind him.

"Joseph," Jeremy drawled. "You never sketched a flower in your life." Revere grinned happily. Jeremy laughed at the inane expression. He gestured him to the vacant chair. "I'm glad to have you back. How was your trip—beyond the flora and fauna?"

"Fabulous," Revere said. "Have you ever been on a bear hunt, Jeremy? God, you wouldn't believe it! But don't worry," he punctuated the words with a grin. "I shall only regale you with the 'bear' facts."

Jeremy groaned.

The soft light from the oil lamps flickered tentatively, casting the small room in soft, wavering shadows. The afternoon had passed quickly, and Jeremy and Revere had been joined by Beth for dinner. Jeremy thought briefly on the meal, noting the surprisingly animated behavior of his wife. It pleased him that she liked Revere. Her usual pinched, strained expression eased in Joseph's presence. Her voice became soft, her manner more gracious. He only wished that there were more to remind her of home; then perhaps their life would be easier.

"You are a lucky man, Morgan," Revere said as the two men sat by the fire in Jeremy's study. His expression was almost wistful. "The boy is delightful. I think he recognized me."

"I'm certain he did."

"Well? Have you named him?"

"Hamilton. After my father."

Revere thought upon the name for a moment. "Good. It suits him, somehow. Although, I must admit, I am somewhat averse to family names. My parents considered calling me Paul." He visibly shuddered.

"Understandable. Moreover, an honor I should think."

"You think so? God, man, I would have spent the whole of my life living up to it!"

"I see your point. Now tell me of your trip. Aside from bear hunts."

"Always to the meat of it, aren't you?" Revere quipped, making Jeremy squirm. "Morgan, you should loosen up. Go on a hunt with me, get away from all of this!"

"Perhaps I will, sometime. Now tell me of your trip."

Revere sighed, then leaned forward and shoved the

packet across the desk toward him. "It is all in there: names, facts, dates. John Charles Fremont left Sutter's fort and traveled to Yerba Buena with a small party of men. He left the rest in New Helvetia. When I departed, he was visiting with Vice Consul Leidesdorff. Unless he is delayed, he should arrive here in a few days."

"Did you meet with him?"

"No. He had left Sutter's fort just before I arrived. Sutter is wary of him."

"Why?"

"You read Sutter's letters to Larkin." Revere shrugged. "He thinks the man is ambitious to the exclusion of reason. His opinion hasn't changed."

"It's unfortunate that you couldn't form your own opinion."

"Perhaps. But I trust Sutter, Jeremy—"

John A. Sutter, Jeremy mused. A German Swiss, he arrived in St. Louis in 1834, a fugitive from debtor's prison, having left a wife and five children in Switzerland. Arrived in Monterey in 1839, when the quarrels between Governor Alvarado and Vallejo were at their worst. Alvarado granted Sutter land on the Sacramento River, with the intent of curbing Vallejo's power in the north. Over the years, New Helvetia had become a major trading post and overland gateway to California.

"—be that as it may," Revere was saying. "It seems that shortly we will have the opportunity to judge for ourselves."

"In a desperate situation," Jeremy said quietly.

"Is it that bad?"

"Polk's attempt to purchase California has failed. Yet, his orders remain constant—to appease the Californios, bringing them to our reasoning without giving any assurances. The last thing we need right now are American soldiers coming into the area."

"We don't know that Fremont is here for anything but a mapping expedition."

"No?" Jeremy snorted. "Joseph, Fremont's father-in-law is Thomas Hart Benton. Chairman of the Senate Military Affairs Committee. He is a personal friend of the president. Polk often consults him on military affairs. Benton is an expansionist and has long led the congressional demand to take California. It does leave one to question Fremont's sudden appearance. Dammit! Why now!" he exploded, hitting the desk with his fist. "Even Vallejo will not be able to counter this threat!"

"Perhaps it won't be as serious as you think," Revere said quietly.

"Perhaps," Jeremy grumbled. "However, without appearing unduly pessimistic, remember that Micheltorena was soundly berated by the government in Mexico for allowing Fremont free access during his last visit. Castro is not about to subject himself to such censure, particularly in light of the fact that our zealous Captain Fremont has chosen to bring a small army with him on this particular journey."

"On the other hand, Jeremy, suppose that the Californios do object? What can they do about it?"

Jeremy glanced at Revere with a smirk. "Very little, militarily. There are less than one hundred soldiers stationed in California, and only a few of the officers are professionals. Monterey's man-of-war is so decrepit that it cannot tack against the wind. As for cannon, when your ship arrived, the powder magazine was so low that Castro had to borrow explosives from a frigate to fire a salute."

"The situation sounds less than desperate."

"That depends upon how you view it. A few more months—just a few more months—and the Californios would have accepted cession peacefully."

"Do you believe that?"

"Yes." Jeremy sat up and unlocked the drawer in his desk. He rifled though the papers and pulled out a packet, dropping it on his desk. "These are speeches made at a recent, secret meeting of the dons. Jose Carrillo was there to speak for Governor Pio Pico."

Revere's eyes widened and he whistled. "Where did you get them?"

"It doesn't matter—the contents do. Carrillo spoke first, condemning Mexico. It was the one theme that everyone present agreed upon. He spoke passionately about Mexico's neglect, even to refusing to provide for California's defense. Yet, he effectively noted that Mexico was all too willing to send soldiers and civil officers to oppress California's people."

"That's an old complaint," Revere observed.

"Yes, but that was just the beginning. Carrillo complained about the hordes of Yanqui immigrants who were coming into the country, cultivating farms and vineyards, erecting mills, establishing new settlements. He feared the displacement of his own people. To preserve California's identity, he called on those present to choose an alliance with France or England."

"What?" Revere gasped.

"He pointed out that California could not maintain independence against Mexico without foreign help. He saw either France's or England's armies and fleets as the means of accomplishing this."

"Oh, my God," Revere groaned. "Then perhaps we should be glad that Fremont is here, after all."

"You haven't heard all of it," Jeremy frowned, tapping the packet. "The dons, almost to a man, responded favorably to Pio Pico's message. Then Vallejo spoke. Read what is here, Joseph. Vallejo agreed that it would be idle and absurd to continue to rely upon Mexico. He said that California is a noble country, destined to become great and powerful; therefore he could not agree to a dependency upon a foreign monarchy, one that he felt would be, like Mexico, indifferent to their interests and welfare.

"Oh, he threw everything at them—even invoking the history of the Britons and Saxons, and the conquering armies of Rome," Jeremy continued, smiling as he glanced at the envelope, recalling Vallejo's words. "He reminded the dons that they were republicans—badly governed, perhaps, but republicans nonetheless. In order to throw off Mexico's galling hold, and proclaim independence of her forever, California would need help to establish its position. And for that there was a third alternative: annexation to the United States. He called the United States the freest and happiest nation on earth, destined to be the most wealthy and powerful. And he pointed out that she is California's neighbor. With such an alliance, California's people would not merely be subjects of a foreign power, but fellow-citizens, with all the rights held by a free people, and with freedom to choose their own government and laws. And he prevailed, Joseph. There was an explosion of support—except from Carrillo, of course, who couldn't speak for the governor. But privately Carrillo concurred. Can you understand now why Fremont's appearance is so inopportune? We are so close, and he could destroy everything!"

"I never realized," Revere said, staring at the papers under Jeremy's clenched fist. "Perhaps he won't come," he added hopefully.

"Perhaps his horse will find a gopher hole and he'll break his neck. Short of that, he will be here. I rather imagine that he sees it as his destiny." Jeremy stared off into space for a moment, his forehead heavily creased with thought. Suddenly he sighed. Taking up the papers he slipped them into the drawer and locked it. Leaning back he picked up his goblet. "Well, there's no use worrying about it anymore tonight. So, tell me about your bear hunt."

9

Beth's ivory fan fluttered impatiently. The windows of the Larkins' parlor were open to allow a breeze, and from somewhere below a determined frog sent its rasping message to a prospective ladylove. The sound grated on her nerves. *A brave front,* her mother would have called it. Not that she particularly cared what Jeremy was doing—as long as his actions did not reflect poorly on her. Besides, the time away from him allowed her to avail herself of Lt. Revere's company.

In spite of her resolve, she stiffened at the sound of deep, feminine laughter amid the conversation of the Larkins' other dinner guests. For a moment, she felt that she could positively commit murder. Whenever Ariana Saldivar was near—a fact which seemed to repeat itself with irritating regularity—Jeremy gravitated to her like a love-sick puppy. Oh, he managed to conceal it from others—always the perfect gentleman—and their conversation was always totally appropriate. Mostly, it seemed, they talked of politics. The fact only confirmed Beth's low opinion of the woman.

"Mrs. Morgan?"

She turned to find Revere at her side with the glass of requested sherry punch. "Why, thank you, Lieutenant." She took the glass and smiled up at him. "Please, we have known each other long enough—and as my husband's dear friend, certainly it is appropriate for you to call me Beth. Or Elizabeth, if you prefer."

Revere smiled awkwardly. Why, the man was actually embarrassed! Beth thought. Revere's innocence—if it could be called that—intrigued her, not to mention his impeccable family lines. Certainly the man was not as innocent as he appeared; after all, he had traveled around the world, more than once, and he was hardly a child. However, the challenge was definitely there. The fact that he had become close to Jeremy only increased her interest.

The night of the *merienda,* Beth had been stunned by the feelings Jeremy had invoked in her. Over the next few days she had thought of little else. She had encouraged repeat performances from him. She no longer felt repulsion from his touch; in fact the experiences were quite pleasant. But she could not recapture the intensity of that one night.

As the weeks passed, she began to realize that it wasn't the act itself that was at fault, but Jeremy. It wasn't just that she didn't love him anymore; in fact, she suspected that love had little to do with it. She had begun to understand why men prefer mistresses for physical fulfillment. Daily life with a person, along with the resentments and antagonisms, simply sapped passion.

A brave front, Mother? You simple fool. Beyond the excessive time that Jeremy spent on his lumber business, she hoped that Jeremy would have an affair—as long as he was discreet—leaving her to her own devices.

Sipping from the punch, she glanced covertly at Revere, wondering how she could manage to get him alone. Then Rachel announced dinner.

They were well into their second course when an officer from the Custom House was announced. He rushed to Larkin's side, stammering an apology to the guests before bending to the consul's ear. Larkin visibly stiffened at the message. He murmured something to the messenger, then rose from the table. "I fear that there is a matter requiring my attention. Please, go on with your dinner. Rachel, my dear, my apologies for the interruption." He moved from the table to the door, passing behind Jeremy's chair. "Morgan, may I see you for a moment?"

When the door to the hallway closed behind them, Larkin turned, obviously agitated. "Well, Morgan," he said in hushed tones. "It would seem that our visitor has arrived."

Jeremy's dinner suddenly felt like lead in his stomach. "Fremont?"

"Yes. He has arrived by ship. He sends his regards and awaits a meeting with me."

"Aboard ship?" Jeremy blinked. "With so many men I would have expected him to come overland."

"I agree. Do you think that it is possible that he has come alone?"

"I'm afraid to give him that much credit."

"Well," Larkin said grimly. "We will soon find out."

"Do you want me to accompany you?"

"Yes, but you had better remain here. If we both leave, Garner and Cooper will be unduly curious. I want to handle this matter as discreetly as possible. At least until we know what he is about."

When Larkin left, Jeremy rejoined the others. He ignored the curious looks cast in his direction, particularly the hostile glare from Beth. He had become so accustomed to that response from her that it had ceased to affect him. Ariana's, however, amused him. She wore a look of innocence, but there was a brief, expectant gleam in her eyes that had given her away. He returned to his chair between Rachel and Ariana, quite ignoring Ariana as he gave his attention to his hostess.

Conversation at the table seemed to return to normal, but Jeremy could only imagine what lurked beneath the surface. The tension in Monterey that had increased over the past weeks seemed to be coming to the fore at the table. When not addressed directly, Garner and Cooper seemed lost in thought. Pablo de la Guerra and Rafael Estrada looked strained, angry. The ladies' conversation seemed forced. Revere, who was Beth's dinner partner, kept glancing at Jeremy with speculation, much to Beth's irritation. Poor Beth, Jeremy thought. There was nothing more serious for her than when a social evening was spoiled by the hideous aspects of politics. Ariana, however, was oozing with questions; he could feel it.

Strange thoughts passed through his mind as he finished his dinner. His life seemed suddenly filled with the complex emotions of women. Beth's sudden response to him the night of the *merienda*—passion offered, then withdrawn again. Her new, unexplained coolness after the birth of their son. His awareness of Rachel's loyalty to Larkin. Ariana, her dark, sultry beauty that seemed to conceal inner secrets that continually warned him of a threat to be treated as he would an enemy. Had he not been taught that women were simple creatures? His life seemed to be contradicting such dictates in a maddeningly confusing way.

Beth ate an uncommon amount of dinner. There seemed little else to do. The heavily spiced beef was distracting, the bread occupied her fingers as she buttered it heavily. Even so, a bite of the bread stuck cumbrously in her throat as Jeremy's voice eluded her. "Listen carefully to the words of your husband." Old habits died hard, and her mother's words echoed in her mind. "A good wife will catch upon the most idle conversation, for a man is never given to gossip. A wife must give support, knowing that business is ever on his mind. You will benefit by his success, even as you will fall with his disgrace." Beth gathered her lower lip in her teeth, biting softly. She had not brought disgrace to him; he had done that by himself. And to her as well. Then, to her relief, Rachel rose from the table and suggested that the ladies might wish to retire.

Beth stood before the mirror in the bedroom allotted to the ladies. She checked her hair, tucking a wayward strand into place. Studying her reflection, she objectively appraised what she saw. Due to her efforts, her body was still trim, although it wouldn't be for long if she continued to eat the way she had tonight. It took a moment before she realized that another reflection had joined hers in the mirror. She tucked away another curl, pretending indifference.

"Your gown is beautiful," Ariana said. "But tell me, is a corset uncomfortable?"

"Not when one is accustomed to wearing them," Beth answered. "But they would be . . ." she added, allowing her eyes to drop to the reflection of Ariana's unbound waist, "for one untutored in the refinement."

"It seems unnatural to bind one's body in such a manner," Ariana said, with a look of honest curiosity. "Does it pinch?"

"Certainly not," Beth lied. She thought briefly of the intense discomfort she had felt during her pregnancy. In fact, her insistence on wearing one into her sixth month had led to serious arguments with Jeremy. "No lady of breeding would appear in public without her body so bound."

"It would seem to squeeze the organs uncomfortably."

Beth flushed at such a blunt mention of matters not socially referred to. "The 'hourglass' figure suggests a lady's innocence."

"Innocence?" Ariana digested the words. "Do you mean a virgin?"

Beth reddened. "Well—yes."

"But you are married. Why would you seek to deny the fact that you are a woman?"

"Well—" Beth stammered. What an impudent question! "It is not seemly to—demonstrate it."

Ariana frowned. Then she smiled at Beth's reflection. "It would seem to make your husband a fool. Beyond that, your child would prove you a liar."

Beth stared with horror at Ariana's departing reflection. Speechless, she could only stare as Ariana joined the others. Suddenly, she had to lean against the bureau as she fought against a sudden difficulty in breathing. The room was stuffy, in spite of the opened windows, and she had the strange feeling that the walls were closing in on her. The sensation was heightened as she realized that she had no place to go. It was too early to rejoin the men. To leave suddenly—and return to that ridiculous little house, the empty walls of incessant boredom accompanied by the squalls of a fussy baby, was inconceivable. It was the first evening since Hamilton's birth that they had spent in some semblance of sociability. She had no intention of seeing an early end to the evening.

The others were gathered on the wide bed, talking. Fearing that she might faint, Beth took a deep breath and tried to focus on what was being said. "I now have over three hundred and forty pieces of copper for my apron," one of the young women said with obvious pride, bringing sighs and exclamations from the others. "I well expect to have well over four hundred."

Now breathing almost normally, Beth felt a prick of interest in the strange conversation. She strolled over to the bed. "You save pieces of copper to wear in your apron?"

The others laughed. "On it," Rachel corrected with a smile. "It is an apron for under a saddle."

"You are talking about her horse?" Beth asked with a blank expression.

"Si," Ariana answered. "The saddle apron is embroidered in silks of many colors, along with gold and silver thread. Sectioned in six or eight parts, which is burnished with small pieces of iron or copper, to make the sound of bells as she rides."

"Rides where?"

"To her marriage."

"She rides on a horse to her marriage?"

"Si." Ariana looked at her steadily, though her voice was deceptively soft. "Such is our custom, Senora Morgan."

"How odd."

The room became silent. Rachel rose from the bed, her eyes snapping angrily. Before she could respond, Ariana spoke. "Si, I rather imagine that it is, to one who is unaccustomed to our ways. Moreover, I am certain that I would find many things quite strange, should I travel to your country. Rachel, it would seem to me that you have been amiss." She smiled at Rachel's bemused look. "I know that you have not told us of the customs of your country because you do not wish to embarrass us. How backward our ways must seem by contrast. But change is coming, dear Rachel, as it certainly must. Therefore, I, for one, must learn everything that I can." She ignored Rachel, whose eyes had widened, her mouth slightly ajar. "I must, if I am to—confront what is ahead of us. Perhaps, Senora Morgan, you would consent to be my teacher? This ignorant subject would be most grateful."

For the second time in fifteen minutes Beth was speechless. "Of—course," she stammered. Then, as the depth of the compliment registered, she smiled graciously. "Of course, Senorita Saldivar! I would be most pleased to do so."

"I would be eternally grateful," Ariana said with a smile.

Beth's heart seemed to have caught in her throat. Then it settled back in her chest and began to beat irregularly. Thomas had returned just as the ladies rejoined the men, accompanied by one of the most refined and handsome men Beth had ever seen. Well built, though of medium height, he had dark, curling hair, a well-trimmed beard, a sharp, chiseled nose, and dark, penetrating eyes. But more than that, he seemed to have stepped out of the finest drawing room in New York. His manners were impeccable, his speech refined. As his lips touched the back of her hand, she felt transported, and that mystical, lovely drawing room formed about her.

"Captain Fremont?" she repeated the introduction. "Oh!" she said, her eyes growing wide. "Not John Charles Fremont! I know your father-in-law! Senator Benton is a dear friend of my father's. We often had the pleasure of entertaining him in our home."

"The pleasure is mine, Mrs. Morgan," he said smoothly.

"I adored your book, Captain Fremont! Is it true that your dear wife helped you to write it?"

"It was a joint venture. Jessie will be thrilled to know that you enjoyed it."

"Beth?" Ariana joined them, using the address that Beth had graciously allowed her to use. "I would be most honored to meet one of your countrymen."

"Of course. Ariana, you are fortunate—Captain Fremont is one of our most prominent adventurers." She made the formal introduction while noting Fremont's graciousness as he bowed over Ariana's hand. Such a gentleman. It was kind of him to be so polite to the natives. The captain must be, by virtue of his experiences, quite used to handling himself in such situations.

"Senorita Saldivar has, just recently, become my very special ward, Captain." She laughed delightedly at Fremont's look of puzzlement. "She has asked me to instruct her on the ways of polite society. I shall endeavor to do my best in teaching her the manners and customs of a young lady."

"I am certain that she is in good hands, Mrs. Morgan." Fremont smiled. "Though my visit to Monterey will be brief, you must tell me if I can be of help in such a worthwhile endeavor."

"Oh, Captain Fremont," Ariana responded softly. "I could never expect such an imposition upon your time."

Beth smiled. "Senorita Saldivar is of one of the best families in California."

"Indeed," Fremont said.

"Oh, yes. Her uncle is Mariano Vallejo. He is a don in California and quite prominent."

"Indeed," Fremont repeated. His gaze touched on Ariana indulgently. Then, as Beth continued to gush happily, his eyes lifted to note the others in the room.

* * *

From where he stood across the room, Larkin's eyes never left Fremont or his small bevy of admirers. "Morgan," he muttered in a voice that was heard only by Jeremy and Revere. "Do you think it wise to allow Beth free reign with our visitor?"

"You brought him here," Jeremy answered.

"I had no choice!" he murmured unhappily. "And you can wipe that confounded grin off your face; I see nothing amusing about this situation! He would not remain aboard ship. Moreover, he insists upon paying his respects to Castro tomorrow. I certainly cannot have him doing so without my being there!"

"You worry too much, Larkin," Jeremy drawled. "He couldn't be in safer hands. The last thing in the world Beth wants to discuss with him is politics. I rather imagine that at the moment she is pumping him for details of the latest gala he attended before his departure."

Revere was watching Beth from a different point of view. He recognized the cow-eyed look she was giving to Fremont. Why couldn't Jeremy see it? Dammit, he valued their friendship. How could he point out the fact that Beth's interests had begun to roam beyond her marriage? It had taken the greatest mincing on his part to avoid what Beth Morgan had so blatantly, and insistently, been offering to him. He should be relieved that her interests seemed to have shifted direction. Instead, it filled him with regret. He could have continued to handle Beth, as he simply had no interest in her. But then, Fremont did look rather bored. Or was this wishful thinking?

Jeremy's attention was not on his wife; it was on Ariana. She was clearly after Fremont. Ariana Saldivar was becoming more interesting by the moment. His instincts, which had never failed him yet, suggested that Ariana bore watching—no matter how careful she had been in the past few months.

Forty-eight hours later, to Beth's disappointment, Ariana's intense frustration, and Larkin's and Jeremy's relief, Fremont left the area. But not without a few tense moments. The morning after his arrival, Manuel Castro, as prefect, sent a message demanding to know the reason for Fremont's presence in the area. Later that day, a meeting was held in Jose Castro's office. Present with the commandant and prefect was Larkin, former governor Alvarado, and Fremont.

Manuel demanded to know why United States troops had been brought into Alta California, and why their leader had chosen to visit Monterey. Fremont assured those present that his intentions were to survey and map the area, nothing more. His men were armed, he assured them, because of reports that many notorious bandits roamed the area—an observation that no one present was prepared to deny.

A somewhat appeased commandant agreed to allow Fremont and his men to remain in California, with the stipulation that they quarter for the winter in the San Joaquin Valley. However, under no circumstances were they to visit populated areas. Fremont readily agreed.

However, in his wake the ambitious adventurer left a mixture of diverse opinions as to his character and purpose. Then, two months later, opinions converged to the musical accompaniment of Josepha Estrada's four-hundred-and-twenty-six pieces of copper.

A morning in early March had been named as the wedding day of the shy, diminutive young maid to her handsome and exceedingly eager bridegroom, Juan Hernandez. Both came from important families, and no one of any social standing within a two-day ride would have considered not attending.

Totally dumbfounded, Jeremy stared at the display before him. A stirring itch of amusement threatened to crack his serious composure. Around him, men passed through the house, pausing to grunt and sigh with awe over the wedding gifts the bridegroom was presenting to his bride. Jeremy stood there, transfixed for want of a proper response. He suspected that Larkin had deliberately placed him in this situation. He had merely said, "Come on, Morgan, I want you to see something! You're going to be impressed."

Before him lay a vast display of ruffles, lace and delicate ladies' undergarments. As he stood there with an appreciative look plastered on his face, he interpreted the comments of the men passing through. Apparently, the bridegroom was expected to provide the bride with six articles of every type of clothing that she would need in her marriage.

Recovering, Jeremy stepped out onto the porch of the hacienda with Larkin. The consul's hands were clasped behind his back as he rocked back on his heels. Both men's eyes were fixed steadily on the festivities in the courtyard.

"I thought the ivory lace was particularly nice," Jeremy drawled, lighting a cheroot.

Larkin cleared his throat. "Yes. It was." The consul drew a kerchief from his pocket and coughed into it, then wiped his eyes before the square of linen disappeared once again into his pocket.

"I owe you one, Thomas," Jeremy said.

"It is fortunate that Estrada is not a poor man," Larkin observed, chuckling. "He must provide everything that is necessary for the occasion, including the feast to feed this mob. I suspect that only half of those here were invited."

"Really," Jeremy observed with interest.

"Oh, yes. No one would ever be turned away from such an occasion. And, by now you know that it will probably last for two or three days."

"What if he simply could not afford it?"

"Then the honor of the familia comes into play. His relatives, even including distant cousins, would see to it. Their honor is at stake."

"Elopement would seem a preferable alternative," Jeremy observed dryly.

"Never, Morgan! Such a thing would only bring disgrace."

"As in the case of Ariana's mother?"

Larkin's head jerked about. "How did you learn of that?"

"It doesn't matter."

"Yes, it does. You continually surprise me with the facts you ferret out, Morgan. How do you come by them?"

"Grogshops are ripe with gossip."

"You could easily die in one of them." Larkin grunted.

"I could die in bed." Jeremy shrugged. He was aware of Larkin's frown, as well as the fact that the man's strict morals guided his disapproval. "There are many ways to gather information, Thomas. You have your way, I have mine." He paused. "There was considerable reaction to Fremont's visit. The settlers are primed. They see him as the great deliverer of their freedom."

Larkin shook his head unhappily. "The Californios will hardly see him in the same light."

The statement seemed so obvious as not to require an answer, and Jeremy remained silent. After a moment,

Larkin turned to him with a frown. "What do you know of Ariana's mother?"

"Only that she eloped with someone that her familia did not approve of. That he abandoned her when Ariana was a child."

"Ariana's father was Benito Saldivar," Larkin said with a sigh. "He came from a prominent, well-to-do family in Mexico. A first son with advantages—all of which he rejected for the grand, glorious dreams of a *liberalismo*. He migrated to California, accepted it as his home, and steadily proceeded to gamble away his inheritance."

"Gambled?" Jeremy snorted. "He hardly sounds like an idealist."

"I've warned you not to judge these people by your own standards. Gambling, to the Californio, is an addiction welcomed by the majority—but then I cannot expect you to understand until you have experienced it for yourself. Moreover, I am certain that you will, before too much longer. In any case, Benito soon found himself married, with a child, and soon paupered. I never knew the man, and certainly not well enough to call him a rascal, although miscreant is the term often applied to him, when he is mentioned at all by the Vallejos."

"What of her mother? Tell me about her."

"Ah, well. Rosalinda Vallejo was an exceptional young woman. Beautiful, intelligent, but far too resolute for her own good."

"In what way?" Jeremy asked, his gaze shifting to Larkin with interest.

"In every way," the shorter man answered grimly. "Rosalinda had her own particular way of viewing life; she met it without compromise. I don't know what she saw in Benito—freedom, perhaps. Or a simple rejection of normal values. Independence is not a trait encouraged in a Californio woman, Jeremy. Modesty and obedience are far preferable. But then, perhaps we share that view, however much authority we may have lost over our women, eh, Morgan?" Larkin grinned.

Jeremy's eyes had fixed on the group of women who sat on benches under a large, spreading oak near the corner of the casa. He was struck by the diametric difference between Beth and Ariana. His wife's fair, blond, delicate beauty contrasted sharply with Ariana's light-olive skin, her blue-

black hair, and dark, challenging eyes. While Ariana stood
back from the group, watching what was happening beyond,
Beth seemed to be holding court, commanding the attention of the other women. He could imagine an assortment
of subjects for her lecture, none of which would change the
condition of her tiny world. Watching, he felt a stirring of
pity. Beth honestly thought that her companions were
hanging on her every utterance for reasons beyond mere
politeness. In fact, she would never consider any other
reason for their attention.

They had argued heatedly over Beth's continuing conde-
scension toward the Californio women, a matter which had
come to a head when she had blithely informed him of her
"arrangement" with Ariana. He had been totally appalled,
an emotion which turned quickly to concern. There was
only one reason why Ariana would seek out such a liaison
with his wife, and he was certain that it had nothing to do
with learning how to be a proper "Yanqui woman." Mentally, he had recounted past conversations with Beth, and
finally assured himself that he had not told her anything
that could compromise him or his mission.

"Ahh, it is beginning!" Larkin said with pleasure, distracting Jeremy's thoughts.

A magnificent roan stallion was led into the hacienda
courtyard, its neck proudly arched, prancing skittishly as if
sensing the importance of the occasion. There were silver
mountings on the bridle and the overleathers of the saddle
were heavily embroidered in bright, cheerful colors. Then, a
buckskin, as fine as the roan, was brought in. Dressed with
its own display, this second horse caused Jeremy's eyes to
widen with amazement. The overleathers completely covered the hindquarters of the animal. They were heavily
embroidered in silk, and encrusted with tiny pieces of
copper, which tinkled like bells as the horse shifted nervously.

Jeremy found that he was thoroughly enjoying himself
over the next few hours. Even Beth seemed to enjoy herself,
displaying honest curiosity without her usual tactless comments. She had drawn to his side as the Larkins explained
the customs of a traditional Californio marriage.

When Josepha Estrada's parents had announced the day
of the marriage, a godmother and godfather had been
chosen for the children who would come from the union.

When the horses were brought before the hacienda, the groom mounted with the future godmother in his lap, and the bride was lifted up before the prospective godfather. Thus they rode to the church, with the wedding party and guests following behind. After the ceremony and mass, the newly married couple rode back to the casa on the groom's mount, while the godparents rode behind on Josepha's horse, coppers ringing in celebration of the event.

Having ridden ahead, bachelor-friends lay in wait. When the bridal pair arrived at the rancho, the groom was kidnapped, to the great amusement of all. His spurs were seized and held, until the laughing groom ransomed them for a good-sized bottle of brandy. Then the occasion became solemn, as the bridal pair entered the casa where they were met by the elder members of their familias. There they knelt before their parents, and amid a great deal of tears, they were blessed. At that moment the best friend of the groom signaled for the music to start, the food to be set, and the merriment to begin.

Jeremy had never had so much food or liquor pressed on him from every source. Everyone seemed to be intent upon allowing no one to survive the day without overeating or becoming totally inebriated. The highlight of the first day's festivities occurred when everyone gathered about a deep, steaming pit that had been dug the day before. The crowd fell silent as layer upon layer of leaves and earth were peeled away. At last, a large, steaming, linen-wrapped bundle was lifted from the pit and placed upon a row of planks. Slowly, the wrapping was drawn back—to the approving sighs of those gathered—exposing a large, steaming bull's head.

Jeremy swallowed. A quick glance at Beth found her staring, horrified. Her face had drained of color.

With great ceremony, the fleshy cheeks of the head were sliced off, and the eyes were plucked out. Most solemnly, they were presented to the bride and groom. As the groom popped an eye into his mouth, Jeremy felt Beth waver, and he reached out an arm, catching her as she slumped against him.

And the celebration continued. Days and nights of food, drink, and dancing. There was a novillada, a type of amateur bullfight, and an exciting exhibition of *Corrida de Toros,* or Tailing the Bull. While Jeremy was often appalled at the cruelty to animals that ran through the Californios' games, this last event gave him an exhibition of the Californios' skill on horseback that he couldn't help but admire.

As the spectators watched from a safe distance on horseback, a group of wild bulls were herded together, and then they were stampeded. The vaqueros took off after them, scuffling as they vied for position, each after the largest and wildest bull. The vaquero who first managed to grab the bull's tail secured it under his knee. Then, guiding his horse sharply away, he threw the animal. It was explained to Jeremy that strength was not what gave the vaquero the advantage, but skill: the control of his horse, the position of his body, and the sense of timing.

Following the event, Jeremy was amazed at the damage to the riders who returned with bloodied hands gnashed open and pulpy. It seemed that the bulls gave as good as they got. But then, from what he had observed, the rangy, black California bulls were the meanest specimens he had ever seen.

As they rode back to the rancho, Vallejo studied Jeremy for a moment. "Morgan, you have been paid a very great compliment." He smiled at Jeremy's puzzlement. "The vaqueros have asked me if you would be interested in participating in one of their events."

"Not the one I just saw."

"No, not that one." Vallejo laughed. "Tomorrow they will play *Carrera del Gallo*. It is a singular honor that they have asked a Yanqui to participate. Think about it." With that, he rode on ahead.

"It is an honor, and would go a long way in establishing you with these people," Larkin observed.

"What is *Carrera del Gallo?*"

"Pluck the rooster."

Jeremy stared at him. "I don't think I want to know what that means."

"Probably not."

The two men rode silently for almost a quarter of a mile. "You were right, Thomas," Jeremy said suddenly. "It would have been a great mistake for me to judge these people by my own standards. They live a totally different way of life."

Larkin's expression became solemn as the casa came into view. "They are a unique people, Jeremy. Living in a unique land." He paused, and then there was a heavy sadness in his voice. "These are the halcyon days, Jeremy. I fear that we shall not see their likes again."

On the third morning of the wedding festivities, Jeremy found himself staring at the array of food. He was hungry, but his mouth burned from hot peppers which seemed to be present in every dish, a condition numbed only by aguardiente, which was offered liberally. He had managed to control his consumption of the potent, colorless brandy by carrying a glass of water about with him. He would gesture with it, with a happy roll of his eyes, when someone sought to refill his glass. However, he could not claim sobriety; he had long passed it. Revere, he noted blearily, had lost all traces of shyness, becoming an extremely flirtatious fellow, regaling the ladies with considerable finesse and enlisting a goodly amount of giggles. Garner had fallen asleep under the oak by the corner of the casa. Cooper was telling bawdy stories, to the thorough enjoyment of his Californio companions who were little better off than he. But what brought a grin to Jeremy, growing into a deep chuckle, was Larkin. Prudent, controlled, Protestant Larkin was sauced to the gills. It was the only time Jeremy would ever see him out of control. As he listened to Cooper's colorful recountings, the consul was giggling.

Setting his glass on the corner of a trestle table, Jeremy scanned the display of food. Choosing an innocuous-looking morsel, he glanced about. Californios certainly did know how to throw a party, he mused. No pretenses, no affections. No consideration to "social form." Just one damn good party.

"Is that hot?"

Jeremy looked down to find Beth at his side. She was staring at the food in his fingers.

"I don't know. If there's a pepper in it I have two out of three chances of surviving," he observed, examining it. "I have been told that there are three kinds of peppers: warm, hot, and go see God."

"Try it."

"Me first?"

"Yes."

He popped the pastry-covered morsel into his mouth. Beth scrutinized his face as he chewed. "Good," he grunted. Sighing, she chose a similar piece from the tray on the table. "The food is delicious, Jeremy, but sometimes my life flashes before me when I bite into it." She popped it into her mouth. "Why does all their food require—" Her eyes suddenly grew wide. Her cheeks flushed and she gasped. "Damn you, Jeremy Morgan!"

He laughed and offered her his glass. "I'm sorry, Beth, I couldn't resist." Seeing her desperate need and the look of horror in her watery eyes as she stared at the glass, he pushed it into her hands. "It's only water," he whispered.

She drained the glass, then set it onto the table and glanced up at him, her eyes dancing with humor. "Water, Jeremy? How very clever."

He smiled at her response, enjoying her mood. "A small ruse." He shrugged. "You once had a hangover from my brandy, remember?" He smiled at her wince. "Aguardiente is worse."

"Impossible."

"No, it's not."

"Why would anyone do that to himself?"

"Men have been asking themselves that question since the first grape was fermented. But only the morning after." He marveled at how unguarded she looked. Her eyes were bright, her cheeks becomingly flushed, and she looked—happy. He was captivated, remembering the beautiful, perky young woman he had married. Perhaps if he just tried a little harder . . . "Are you enjoying yourself, Beth?" he asked softly.

She didn't answer and merely stared at him for a moment. She appeared confused and licked her lips in an unconscious gesture of nervousness that touched him deeply.

"Morgan!"

A deep voice drew his attention. Instinctively he reached out and drew Beth to his side, not wanting to relinquish the moment in spite of the interruption. "Hartnell," he said with surprise. "Have you just arrived?"

The man sighed. "I must apologize to our hosts for my absence, but it could not be avoided. The damnedest thing—" He glanced about the gathering. "Where is Larkin?"

"Over by the corral," Jeremy said. "But whatever your problem is, I don't imagine that Thomas is in any condition to handle much of anything at the moment." Seeing the other man's confusion, he grinned. "This is proving to be quite a party. Our consul has succumbed to its temptations."

"Damn," Hartnell grumbled, glancing about with a disturbed frown. "Well, it can wait until tomorrow."

"Anything I can help with?"

"No—it's just something I thought I should advise him about. Damnedest thing. Two days ago a large party of men showed up at my rancho. At first I thought they were criminals—grubby, clad in dirty buckskins, unshaven, carrying weapons. About sixty of them. But it turned out to be nothing. Their condition was merely due to exhaustion. Turned out they are Fremont's men—"

"Fremont?" Jeremy interrupted sharply. Cold settled into the pit of his stomach. "He's supposed to be in the San Joaquin Valley."

"Well, he's not. They've spent the past two months in the Santa Clara. I told them they could make camp on my rancho—couldn't do anything else, under the circumstances. Quite a conversationalist, Fremont. Has some fascinating stories. But I should tell Thomas that he is here."

"Yes," Jeremy answered grimly. "Beth, I'm sorry, but I must find Thomas." He pulled his arm away and leaned down to brush her cheek with a kiss before turning back to the other man. "Come on, Hartnell, I'll help you find him."

The two men disappeared into the crowd, leaving Beth to stare after them. Once again, a promising moment with Jeremy had been missed.

10

Ariana slipped through the door, shutting it quietly behind her. Turning to the darkened porch, she drew a deep breath, welcoming the cool night air. One more moment with that insufferable prattle and she would have gone mad, she thought. Ana Montoya was gone and buried these past few years, but there were always others to take her place: a continuous line of aunts of all ages, shapes, and temperament to guard against a threat to her chastity.

She stepped into the shadows of the wide overhang and strolled along the building, pausing to sidestep the windows that cast bright squares of light on the porch. Her chastity, she mused. She visualized the shocked expressions of the aunts if they knew that their efforts were far, far too late. *Dios,* she thought, so much fuss, over what? Her body had value; oh, she had proven that. But not in the way her insipid aunts and cousins thought. It was valuable for power, a power they could not even begin to suspect. They were all fools to give themselves so cheaply . . .

A nagging thought had pressed on her relentlessly since her return. It had come unbidden, and never before had she realized it so acutely. Women had absolutely nothing to talk about. They chattered, they pondered the mysteries of babies, husbands, and the "forbidden." The latter subject was swiftly stifled by the older woman. Speculation for the innocent was dangerous, Ariana realized. They would wonder, their ripening bodies curious, and that could not be allowed. Their husbands would tell them all that they needed to know, they were told. Ariana snorted softly. Their husbands would take their pleasure and leave them as mystified as before, or leave them wondering why they had wondered about it in the first place. And what would they have then, her wondering sisters? Babies, servitude, and obedience. The simpering fools. Although they didn't even realize it, the only power they would ever have was what they had now: the power of their virginity. It was the one thing they could offer that men would come begging for. The one time in their lives when they were in control.

Taking a deep breath, Ariana turned her thoughts to more important considerations. Damn Beth Morgan. She wondered if she was wasting her time with the woman. Her husband was only a merchant, but he was undeniably close to Larkin. The friendship Jeremy had developed with the consul should have made him invaluable. If only Beth Morgan had a brain in her head, she should know something beyond the fact that Fremont had returned!

Ariana shook her head and smirked. She wondered if Morgan knew how attracted his wife was to the adventuring American officer. If Ariana was right, and she usually was about such things, Beth Morgan would do practically anything to get into John Charles Fremont's bed. If only Ariana could find a way to arrange—and use—that information. Musing on this possibility, she glanced about the shadows and started. A tall figure leaned against a roof support at the end of the porch, the soft glow of his burning cheroot glowing in the dark. *Muy bien,* she thought. What a coincidence.

"Is the card game too much for you, Senor Morgan?"

His head turned. "Senorita Saldivar. What are you doing out here?"

"The same thing you are," she answered, coming to stand beside him. "Escaping." She heard his deep chuckle in the darkness.

"Yes, I am. Thomas warned me that your men gambled in earnest, but I admit that I wasn't prepared." His voice grew solemn. "I watched a man play away his land tonight."

"That bothers you?"

"Yes. Shouldn't it?"

"Many of your countrymen have been pleased to discover our men's passion for gambling," she said, pausing as a coyote yipped from somewhere beyond in the trees. "They have gained a great deal by it."

"The prospect holds no pleasure for me."

"You are wealthy, aren't you?"

"I'm comfortable."

"Perhaps that is why you feel no compulsion to take advantage of what you've discovered tonight."

"That temptation is not based on a lack of wealth but a lack of principles," he countered.

"Oh dear, I've angered you," she observed. "But then, I've encountered few Yanquis with principles, Mr. Morgan. You will have to forgive me if I assume that your intentions are similar to those of the men I have known."

"But considering those you have known most of your life, such as Larkin, Cooper, and Hartnell—and I presume that they are excluded—it would seem to me that you have not had the opportunity to know many Yanquis. Having been sequestered for so many years in a convent. You *were* in a convent, I believe."

"Si—" *Dios,* she thought. Be careful. "And you are correct, Senor, I have known few Yanquis other than those I grew up with. They consider themselves Californios. I fear that I am guilty of judging others by the actions of a few that I have met."

"I see," he said, drawing from the cheroot.

She watched the brief, glowing spot of red. What had he meant by that? He spoke, but he said nothing! "If you had remained in the game, Senor Morgan, you might have seen the object of your pity lose far more than just his land."

"More? He had nothing more to lose."

"Oh, but he has, much more. There is no debt of honor more important to my people than one given by his word. He is still playing; I have little doubt of it."

"He has nothing to bet."

"He will bet what is held by members of his familia. His cousin's horse, or his uncle's land."

Jeremy dropped the cheroot and crushed it with his boot. "Who would accept such a bet?"

"Anyone at that table who does not care about him—but understands that the bet will be honored." She smiled grimly at the silence. "It will be honored, Senor, do not doubt it. In the morning the winner of the bet will present himself to the loser. The uncle will take his family and relinquish his lands, for not to do so would dishonor him."

"That is insane."

"That is the truth. Oh, the nephew will be dishonored among his familia for what he has done, but that is a matter only for the familia. Our people never press the game to such extents, in spite of their passion for it. But not your people, Senor Morgan. No, they are learning quickly, and do not hesitate to take advantage of it. Much land has fallen into the hands of your people over the card table. And much more will follow."

"Then why don't your men simply stop?"

"Because we have lived our ways for a long time; our beliefs are deeply embedded. Money is not considered important." She sighed. How to explain this? "In your room, did you notice a bowl filled with silver coins?"

"Yes, I did." He frowned. "On the bureau."

"What purpose did you give to it?"

"I thought that it had been left there by someone—forgotten."

"No, they were not forgotten. They are for you. Or for any traveler who rests in this house and is in need of coin. Moreover, if you were in need of a mount to continue your travels, one would be given to you. Such is our sense of graciousness."

"Why are you telling me this?"

"You expressed concern. I thought you should know."

He seemed to digest what she had said, but his next question caught her by surprise. "Tell me, are you learning a lot from my wife?"

"Si—she has been most helpful. There are many things that I want to learn from her."

"I can imagine."

The pause that followed became awkward. "Why are you in California, Senor?"

"Why are you?"

"Pardon?"

"What now? Marriage?"

She relaxed. "If my uncle has his way," she lied. She knew that her age, if not her education, had practically removed all possibility of that threat. But she had no intention of discussing such personal matters with him.

"You do not sound particularly pleased by the prospect. Is there something else you want?"

"No. There is nothing else in a woman's future. I merely —want to wait."

"To meet someone you can love?"

She had the uncomfortable feeling that he was toying with her, though his tone of voice seemed sincere. "Perhaps. Though I doubt that I will have any choice in the matter. Did your wife choose freely?"

"Oh yes. Our women choose freely, Ariana. And they live with the results of those decisions."

She wondered about the slight edge to his voice. "Your women are fortunate, to be able to decide about their futures the way a man would. Beth was telling me about Captain Fremont's wife, that she even helped him write his famous book. It is difficult to imagine such a thing. But then, it would seem to have its disadvantages. It must be difficult for Senora Fremont—to have her husband gone so much from her."

"She might be grateful."

"Perhaps." She laughed. "Do you think that Captain Fremont will be here long?"

"I have no idea," he answered.

Ariana bit her lip with frustration. Perhaps the fool didn't know anything after all. It would certainly explain why Beth Morgan was so addlebrained. Any other man would have been eating out of her hands by now, proving his machismo with his great, overwhelming knowledge of matters she could not possibly comprehend. She had never wasted her efforts on the wrong prey before, and she would not begin now. "This has been most pleasant, Senor Morgan. However, I must return before I am missed."

"Whatever you think best, Senorita Saldivar. A good night to you."

"Si—" she said, hesitating at his almost curt dismissal. "Good-night."

As she turned to leave, his voice reached her through the darkness. "I hope that you find what you are looking for, Ariana. And that it does not prove to be too costly."

Jeremy shifted uncomfortably, slumping down into the chair in Larkin's parlor. It was insufferably warm, one of those days that appeared suddenly when one was least prepared for it. The air was heavy, adding to the lethargic feelings that involuntarily drew one's thoughts to prospects of naps stolen beneath dark, cooling shadows of spreading trees. The brain seemed dulled as it attempted to focus. Jeremy listened to the others, interjecting comments occasionally, while suspecting that they were feeling as lazy as he was.

"He could be exactly what he represents," Hartnell drawled. "Perhaps he is just here to map the area."

Jeremy snorted derisively. "You don't bring sixty men armed to the teeth with you for the purpose of mapping topography."

"He's right, you know." Revere yawned.

"Indeed," Larkin agreed, mopping his brow with a kerchief. "But he was the ultimate of courtesy when we met with Castro last January. There was nothing to suggest otherwise in the letter he sent to me after he left. He assured me that he was here for peaceful purposes."

"He was given the condition that he withdraw with his men to the San Joaquin," Jeremy observed dryly. "Instead, he removed himself to the Santa Clara. And now he is back."

"A fact which Castro has chosen to overlook," Cooper said.

"Yes, for now. A reaction by our sometimes commandant that is not surprising. But what will happen, I wonder, when other pressures come to bear? The settlers see our topographical engineer as their savior."

"You are too grim, Morgan," Cooper said. "Dammit man, I think you always look for the worst possible scenario."

"You are probably right, Cooper," Jeremy answered pleasantly. *And I am usually right,* he added silently.

"Well, at the moment everything seems to have worked itself out," Larkin observed. Jeremy sensed the doubt in the consul's voice, but he let it pass. "I must say, it was quite a wedding . . ."

Jeremy listened idly to the conversation that followed, as his own thoughts turned to the morning of their departure for home after the wedding, when he had had the worst argument ever with Beth. *My God,* he thought, for every step forward in their relationship, there seemed to be two or three backward. It began when she informed him that she would not be returning home with him. Ariana, it seemed, had invited her to spend a few days at Angel Castro's rancho. A splendid opportunity, Beth had informed him, as the man was the uncle of the commandant. Jeremy was concerned about his lumber business; such an association could only benefit him. Besides, she added, Ariana needed her. God, he thought, how could she be so totally blind and such an unmitigated fool?

She continued to place herself in situations that emphasized her foolishness, lording herself over everyone with her superior attitudes and her observations of life. And he had to defend her, to each and all. He had to pretend that he did not notice her rudeness, smiling through her social blunders, defending her outrageous behavior. Had they remained in the east, she would have been the epitome of correct social behavior, a true success. And that was what she had been raised to be: spoiled, self-serving, confident of her position, a charming bon vivant.

"Morgan?"

Jeremy started, realizing that his thoughts had drifted. "I'm sorry, Cooper. What did you say?"

"We were merely discussing your expertise." The man grinned.

"In what?"

"At *Carrera del Gallo.*"

"Well. It was accidental. Frankly, I found the sport appalling." And he had. Beth was not the only one who occasionally found herself out of her element. Pressed by the vaqueros, he had found himself on horseback, riding hell-bent for chickens. They had been buried in the ground with their heads and necks exposed. The object of the game was to ride at a dead run down the line, bending from the saddle to extract a protesting fowl and carry it to the finish line. Oh, it proved to be easy enough. The military had taught him the horsemanship required, where a fallen rifle had been the object. But a retrieved weapon was not covered with blood, nor did it protest with pain. Perhaps, he reflected in an objective moment, Beth was more honest than he. She lived her life the only way she knew—without compromise. She would have looked upon the prospect of that bloody game with horror, and expressed her feelings without regard to the sensibilities of local custom. She might have caused a minor scandal, but she would have stood her ground. Instead, he had forced back a nauseating lump in his throat and accepted the challenge with a grin.

To do less would have compromised his position with these people, and thus his mission.

Beth pushed a damp tendril away from her ear as she fanned herself ineffectively against the oppressively warm afternoon. "My word, is it always so hot in the Salinas Valley?"

"No, Senora, this is unusual weather," one of her companions answered. "Your people normally complain of our wind, but I think that is preferable to this. It is when the wind stops that one suffers."

Beth glanced at her companions. The three young women, daughters of Don Angel, were lovely. And they did not appear to be suffering. All three were composed and totally unaffected by the heat. Circumventing a siesta, to the dismay of their duennas who had left them in Beth's care and retired to their rooms, the women were sitting on the shady veranda of the casa.

Ariana, as usual, had disappeared somewhere, to Beth's growing irritation. Ariana was entirely too free with her solitary walks, Beth thought. A young, respectable lady did not take walks alone. Moreover, it was a strange situation, considering the Californio attitude toward women, which was quite strict. These rules were, in fact, more rigid than the customs of her own youth. Yet Ariana was given extraordinary privileges that were supported by Vallejo. Beth could not fathom why.

Beth became aware that the back of her dress was damp. She shifted to allow air to reach it when memories struck, and she laughed. "A lady does not perspire, Elizabeth," her mother had said, with an expression that supported her distaste for mentioning the subject at all. "At the very most, she will glow."

Beth's laughter drew bemused glances from the other women. Seeing their questioning looks, she explained, adding, "My mother was quite wrong. I am most certainly a lady—and I'm sweating like a pig." The Castro sisters laughed, even as Beth felt mild shock that she had said such a thing.

"Tell us about your *nino,*" Alicia Castro asked Beth. "Is he beautiful?"

"Of course he is beautiful!" Teresa said. "All babies are beautiful to their mothers. It is rude to ask such a question!"

"It is all right, Teresa," Beth said. "Yes, I suppose that he is beautiful. I never thought about it." She saw the surprise in the faces of the others and felt a twinge of guilt. "Babies have always looked the same to me." Tiny and helpless, she added silently. Really not people at all.

"But surely your own—" Francisca said softly.

"Oh, yes," Beth said quickly. "He is beautiful."

"You must miss him."

"He is in good hands. Selena is quite capable."

"Selena has many brothers and sisters." Alicia nodded approvingly. "She is the eldest, and responsibility for the younger children has always been part of her life. She is a good choice for your baby's nurse. That is an important responsibility for a mother—to choose her baby's nurse."

Beth smiled, a strained effort that did not reach to her eyes. Why were they insisting on this prattle about babies?

"It must be wonderful to be married," Teresa said in a hushed tone as her dark eyes darted to the closed door of the casa. Beth realized that whatever was behind Teresa's words, it was not something of which her napping duenna would approve.

"Why do you think that it is wonderful?"

"Why?" Teresa looked confused. "To live with a man— especially one as handsome as Senor Morgan. To be loved—" Her sisters appeared equally embarrassed, but their dark eyes were expectant as they waited for Beth's answer.

"You want to know what it is like to have your husband make love to you," Beth said.

"Si," came the soft reply.

Beth felt the awkward silence that followed. Never in her life had she spoken openly about the subject. With her own friends the subject had been discussed amid nervous giggles and innuendos, and, of course, it contained an incredible lack of truth. Mary Ellen had once remarked, with lofty authority, that babies came from ingesting too many spicy foods. Beth's lips twitched with the memory—that theory would certainly account for the large number of children that Californio couples seemed to produce. Perhaps spice had an effect, she mused, but it certainly did not produce the result by itself.

"It is not my place—" she said doubtfully, but their crestfallen expressions gave her pause. "Oh, dear." She sighed, as much for her own confusion as theirs. What did they want from her? This wasn't her responsibility. But then, no one would tell them, particularly not those self-suffering elder women in the house. Well, she mused, what should she tell them? What she once experienced with Jeremy, or the more pleasant version? Her lips twitched with a smile. If one of the duennas woke up, there would be the devil to pay. But it could be exciting to talk about the pleasure . . .

Ariana slipped under the breezeway separating the kitchens from the main part of the casa. She entered Angel Castro's study through the veranda doors. The house was tomb-quiet. The older women were still napping at the other end of the house, and apparently Beth was still on the front veranda with the Castro sisters.

Ariana smiled grimly, blessing her luck. Manuel had been late in meeting her, and she'd had no choice but to wait for him. With Fremont's presence in the area, Garcia's work was more important than ever. Fremont was becoming a catalyst for the American settlers. From what they had learned, the officer had spent his time in the Sacramento and Santa Clara valleys encouraging the Yanquis to take a stand against "Mexican oppression." Only one thing could distract them: threats to their homesteads by an Indian uprising. Garcia was a master at stirring up the Indians.

With a little more luck, she would have just enough time to write to him. She just hoped that Padillo was with him, because Garcia couldn't read. But there was nothing to be done for it—Manuel couldn't leave Monterey without arousing the commandant's suspicions. If she tried to send word with Rafael without the letter to back him up, Garcia would probably murder him before he could open his mouth. She rifled through the don's desk and found some writing paper and a pen.

Beth paused, noting the stricken looks on the young women's faces. My word, she thought, perhaps I shouldn't have tried to explain this. I've shocked them. And then she realized that their expressions of horror were directed at a point beyond her shoulder. She turned in her chair and gasped.

Below them at the foot of the steps, having suddenly appeared from the shadows of the locust trees shading the corner of the casa, stood three men. They were clad in buckskins heavily laden with dirt and grime that tarnished the soft, natural color of the leather. Their garments were matched by scruffy beards and dirty, unkempt hair. The men were leering.

"Yes?" Beth asked loftily, repulsed by their appearance. "What can we do for you?"

"You could go on with your story," one of the men drawled. He was the tallest of the three, lanky with angular shoulders. He had a high forehead and a bony, bent nose over a gray-flecked, dark beard. His thumbs were hooked casually in his belt as he grinned at her.

Beth reddened at his words. How long had they been standing there; how much had they heard? Apparently, too much. She had never been so humiliated in her life. "What do you want?" she snapped.

His mouth slipped into a lopsided smile. "Ma'am, we don't wish to bother you, but it's damnably hot. A cool drink of water would be appreciated."

"For heaven's sake—there's a well on the side of the house."

"Yes, ma'am, we saw it as we rode up. But it wouldn't be the same now, would it. I mean there's nothing like a cool glass of water given from a woman's hand."

"Really!" Beth bristled.

One of the other men laughed. "Darn it, Frank! You've upset the lady."

The other men added to Beth's growing unease. The one who had spoken was small and wiry, with restless eyes. The third man, of medium height, did not look particularly bright. He kept glancing back and forth between his companions with an expectant look that suggested a pack dog watching for its leader's first move.

"Just can't help it, Joey." Frank sighed. "Not when I'm faced with such pulchritude."

"Yeah, that's what we got here," the third man said with a happy, leering grin. "Pulchritude."

"Does make a man's blood hot, don't it?" Joey said.

Beth stiffened with outrage as the men took a step toward the stairs. She heard the frightened gasps from the other women, and Teresa had begun to cry softly. Beth rose from her chair to block the men's way. "Ladies," she said with far more calm than she felt. "Go into the house."

"Good idea," Frank agreed, coming to stand on the step below her. "Let's all go into the house."

Beth grew cold, realizing her mistake. The girls must remain exactly where they were. The only chance they had was to remain on the veranda where they might be seen by one of Castro's men. She glanced at the position of the sun. They would return soon for supper; if only she could do something! Without taking her eyes from the man's gaze, she attempted to speak as calmly as she could. "Stay where you are, ladies. Do not move." Francisca had begun to sob. "And be quiet!" she snapped, thinking of the old women in the house. If they awakened now they were likely to try something foolish and get them all killed.

"Come on, don't be afraid of us," Frank said, taking a step closer. "We haven't had the company of women in months. Now why don't we just go into the house for that water? We could talk a little."

Beth swallowed heavily as she fought an overwhelming impulse to scream. She couldn't give in to hysteria. She suspected that if she began to scream, she would never stop. Her alarm grew as the other two men moved past her, and Alicia began to cry. Never in her life had she felt so totally helpless. She understood what it meant to be at the complete mercy of another human being who had total disregard for her as a person—this slimy, filthy representation of humanity. She was suddenly, furiously angry. "You son of a bitch!"

Frank hesitated as his eyes grew wide. "Well, well now. And I thought you were a lady."

"Lay a hand on us and I promise that you will hang," she gritted out.

He seemed to find the statement amusing. "If that happens, and I doubt it, Fremont will level this territory to rubble."

"Fremont?" She felt as if she had been punched in the stomach. "What has he to do with you?"

"We are part of his company—ma'am." He smirked at her stricken expression.

Beth went numb. She heard Teresa cry out, but it did not touch her. Then Frank's arm went about her waist and he yanked her to him, knocking the breath from her.

Suddenly a voice cut through the mixed thoughts of those on the veranda. A threat, vitally real.

"No se mueva! Do not move!"

Beth's abductor tensed. She twisted her head, and her eyes widened with shock. Ariana stood in the doorway, holding a rifle which was leveled at Joey's back. "Let them go. Do it, or I'll blow your damn Yanqui heads off," she said calmly.

Frank glanced at his companions. Ariana smiled at the brief exchange. "Try it. I know how to use this, and you had better believe it."

The three men paled. "You're crazy!" Frank growled.

"Perhaps. It won't take much for me to kill you, gringo. I want to."

Frank began to back off the veranda. His companions followed, their eyes fixed on the rifle. When they reached the foot of the stairs they turned, rounding the corner of the house where they had apparently tied their horses under the grove of trees. It explained why the women had not seen their approach.

"Thank God!" Beth said shakily, leaning against a post for support. "Oh, Ariana, you were magnificent!"

"You were not so bad yourself, Beth." Ariana smiled, lowering the rifle. "I heard you out here—you bought time. The rifle was above Castro's mantle, but I couldn't find the damn shells."

"Really, Ariana!" Beth said, shocked. "Profanity is hardly necessary!"

Ariana laughed. "Beth, you really are too much. I heard everything. You can swear quite adequately when the occasion calls for it."

Beth flushed, remembering what she had said. My word, she wondered silently, where *had* that come from? Then Teresa began to cry. Ariana leaned the rifle against the wall as Beth gathered the sobbing woman into her arms, and went to comfort Francisca and Alicia. Then they heard the sound of approaching hoofbeats. A glance confirmed that Castro's men were returning. In spite of the remnants of her own fear, and the shock of Ariana's cool behavior, Beth gave in to a smile. She had done well, she affirmed, using resources she had not suspected she possessed. In moments, the men would be here, but the truth was that they had simply done quite well without them.

11

"Oh Lord, Beth, when I think of what could have happened—" Jeremy pulled her into his arms.

She let herself be enfolded, preferring that to facing the concern in his eyes. Resting her head on his shoulder, she stared at a vacant point across the room, vaguely aware of his tender words. The moments on Castro's porch had been only the beginning—the realizations that followed were far more important. They burned relentlessly into her thoughts. She was safe with her husband's arms folded about her. Nothing could touch her. Nothing except the disturbing reality that never in her life had she felt more alive than she had in the terrifying moments when she had confronted those men.

She pulled away from him. "It was nothing, Jeremy—"

"Nothing? My God, Beth, you could have been raped or killed!"

"I could have been, but I wasn't," she said tightly. "I would prefer to forget the whole thing."

"Well, one thing is certain, you are not to be in that situation again while Fremont's pack is on the loose. Not that they will be for long," he added grimly.

She turned back on his last words. "What do you mean?"

"Manuel Castro has sent soldiers to Fremont's camp with orders that he leave the area immediately. If he disobeys, he will be subject to arrest."

"He can't do that."

139

He turned to pour her a glass of sherry, missing her sudden look of despair. Handing her the glass, he reached out to touch her face. "Here, drink this. It will help. As for Fremont, it's done. You don't have to worry that such a thing will happen again," he murmured.

"But—surely Captain Fremont cannot be blamed for the actions of a few unruly men," she stammered.

"He can, and should be. An officer is responsible for the actions of his men, Beth. Besides, Fremont was given permission to winter in the San Joaquin Valley, on the condition that he remain there. He accepted the condition, and then he disobeyed the order."

"It seems—rather extreme to exile him."

"Exile?" Jeremy shook his head. "Exile is for someone who is forced to leave his homeland, Beth. Monterey is hardly that to Fremont. Beth—" His eyes softened with understanding. "I am aware that Senator Benton is a friend of your father's. More than that, Fremont is a reminder of home. But this is not New York or Washington. Fremont is not here to grace our parlor. He must abide by the laws of California, which most certainly includes orders given by Commandant Castro."

"Oh, him," she scoffed, sipping from the sherry. "Really, Jeremy, the man is an overstuffed, pompous toad."

"Perhaps," he conceded, his mouth twitching with a grin at the description. "But he is the law, and we all must abide by it."

"Larkin doesn't."

He frowned. "What do you mean?"

"Oh, come now, Jeremy." She lowered herself onto the horsehair sofa as the blue taffeta of her skirt rustled with her movements. "Thomas Larkin does exactly what he pleases, far beyond his capacity as consul, much less as a merchant. The man controls Monterey and beyond. I wouldn't be surprised to learn that he controlled the whole of California."

"I wouldn't go that far."

"I would. After all, the sub-consuls in Yerba Buena and Los Angeles are under his direction. Everyone kowtows to him as if he were some sort of oracle. The man has far more power than appears on the surface. Even the dons—and Castro, for that matter—hang on his every word."

Jeremy stared at her. Though her brief statement was

laden with her usual contemptuous barbs, it had a depth that astounded him. Or was he indulging in wishful thinking? He delayed comment, pausing to pour himself a snifter of brandy as he formed a response. The realization of what had almost happened to her had shaken him deeply. There was so much he wanted to say to her, to share with her, but caution prevailed.

He sat next to her, sipping from his snifter as he studied her. She was lost in thought, he could tell from the wrinkles in her brow and the distant, slightly troubled look in her lovely blue eyes. He could only wonder where her thoughts had led her.

Beth's thoughts had focused on the fact that Fremont had been ordered from the area. She was terribly confused. She knew that Jeremy was right, moreover quite sensitive in his understanding of her feelings about the man. Fremont represented home, with all that it implied. But was that all of it? Why did she feel so devastated by the prospect of his departure?

Lost in thought, she tensed when Jeremy touched her. His brandy had been discarded on a nearby table, and his arm slipped about her, drawing her close to him. She knew that he sought to comfort her, but her first emotion was anger. She didn't want this now; she wanted to sort her thoughts and emotions, all of which had nothing to do with her husband. With her anger came despair. She knew it was his right to have her, whenever he wanted her. Jeremy had never been brutal, or even insistent. She could stop him with a word, as she had so many times before. But this time she couldn't; guilt over her confused feelings for Fremont kept her from doing so. She forced herself to relax as his fingers went under her chin, lifting her mouth to his.

She kept her body still and forced herself to think of something else. Home: the brilliant colors of her mother's garden in the spring. She focused on her father's look of pride and pleasure as he rocked back on his heels, his hands clasped behind his ample back. Dressed for a social occasion, she stood with her two younger sisters in the entry, near the foot of the staircase. They turned before him, waiting for his reaction to their efforts. He frowned, perusing his small bevy clad in rich silk and lace. It was a game they adored, as his declaration would always be the same. A frown, a pursing of lips, a sigh, and at last, "You'll do," as he cast a surprised look at his wife. "Mother, are these beautiful young women your daughters? Whatever happened to those skinny little girls with freckles?" Oh, Papa.

Jeremy leaned against the dry sink in the kitchen and sipped from the steaming mug of coffee. From somewhere outside a rooster crowed, waking late risers from their beds and roosts. The hot coffee was more for warmth than an aid to wakefulness. His mind was alert. He had always had the capacity to awake fully without grogginess, even after a few hours sleep.

"I have eggs for your breakfast, Senor." Selena busied herself about the kitchen, her eyes on Jeremy's cup. It would be refilled before he asked.

"That would be fine, Selena. And some of those biscuits of yours," he added with an appreciative flare of his eyes.

She smiled, pleased. She had learned how to prepare the Yanqui-style biscuits just to please the senor. She had learned many new things for that reason. She did not understand his preference for the doughy, puffed bread in lieu of the tortilla, but if he wanted it, that was enough for her.

Selena had always been terrified of Yanquis. Her parents had warned her that they were evil, corrupting men. If her family had not faced another bleak, hungry winter, they never would have allowed her to work for Senora and Senor Morgan. They had accepted the position for her, agreeing that she would start with only a few hours notice. She had left her family as a dutiful daughter would, while trying her very best not to think of the frightening things that were certain to happen to her.

But senor did not take advantage of her body, nor did he beat her when she displeased him. In fact, to her amazement, he asked her questions about her people, the Costanoan Indians, and listened to her answers. His kindness confused her. She could not explain it to her family or her friends, any more than she could explain the loneliness she sensed in him. If she had tried, they would have scoffed and laughed at her. The Yanqui was important only for the money he offered.

She checked the color of the biscuits in the oven, then cracked the eggs into a pan of frying chorizo sausage as she hummed softly to herself. She liked the life she had found.

She revered Senor Morgan and relished the moments when he sought her opinion. The *nino* had become the light in her life, a babe to care for and love almost as one of her own.

She set the eggs and biscuits before Jeremy and refilled his coffee cup, just as a rapid knock was heard at the front door. She frowned as she left to answer the impatient summons, hoping that the senor would manage to eat before his attention was drawn elsewhere. Her concern was justified as she opened the door to Thomas Larkin.

"Where is he?" the consul asked, stepping into the small entry hall as he handed his cloak and hat to her.

"In the kitchen, Senor Larkin," she answered, allowing an edge to enter her voice. "He is at breakfast." She sighed softly as the consul rushed down the hall.

"Good morning, Morgan." Larkin plopped himself down at the table, ignoring Jeremy's surprised look.

"Good morning, Thomas. Coffee?"

"Yes, yes. Coffee would be good." He nodded at Selena as she entered the kitchen. "Jeremy, we have a problem."

"I rather imagine," Jeremy said dryly as he popped a piece of biscuit into his mouth. He leaned back in his chair and waited while Selena poured coffee into a mug she had set before Larkin. When she had left the kitchen, he turned to the consul. "So what's the problem?"

"Nothing, except that years of work are undone! Everything is lost. The damn fool!"

"Fremont?"

"Who else? Castro delivered his ultimatum, and Fremont seemed to agree."

"What choice did Fremont have? He blundered, badly. He never should have returned to Monterey."

"You would think so—Castro's nieces, of all people! He should have complied without delay."

"He didn't?"

"No, Jeremy, he didn't. That's what I am trying to tell you! Apparently, he was offended by Castro's demands. He considers the order an affront to American liberties! Instead of returning to New Helvetia, he withdrew to Hawk's Peak with his men! What were his words? 'I shall stand here and fight to the finish, trusting to our country to avenge our deaths!' "

Jeremy stared at the consul. "Jesus," he whispered.

Larkin grunted, slurping from his coffee. "Dammit,

Jeremy," he swore suddenly. "He will not take orders from me—the U.S. Consul in California! He presents no written orders, yet his dispatches to me insist that his position is firm! What in the hell is going on in Washington? What *are* his orders? And why haven't I been informed?"

"I've thought about that, Thomas," Jeremy answered grimly, leaning his arms on the table. "Polk has never concealed his desire for expansion. It was part of his platform when he ran for president. Texas and California are vitally important to him. To that end, aside from whatever else he has done, such as sending Slidell to Mexico with an offer to purchase California outright, he engaged the two of us. You, as his consul and confidential agent, myself in the latter post.

"We have been ordered to act cautiously. He and Buchanan prefer a peaceful solution. From our reports he knows that the Californios are leaning toward cession. Therefore, Fremont's appearance at this time offers two possibilities: either the man acts of his own accord, led by his own feelings of ambition, with Senator Benton's patrimony, or he is Polk's ace in the hole."

"That would mean that the president does not trust our reports." Thomas shook his head. "I do not believe that."

"I do not think so. He believes them—that isn't the point." He smiled grimly. "Thomas, you have been in California for many years. You have directed all of your energies to the possibilities for cession that you see here. Perhaps you've forgotten what you left behind. Democratic politics comfort a strange mixture of bedfellows.

"Our orders came from the collective opinions of Polk and Buchanan. But there are others, Thomas, with power of their own. Our secretary of war is not pleased that I am here. Secretary of the Navy Bancroft has long pushed for annexation of California and Oregon. And he is close to Senator Benton, who is an avid expansionist."

"What are you suggesting? That Fremont has secret orders—not necessarily from the president?"

"It's possible. Moreover, the president may not be entirely innocent. If I were in his position I might be inclined to give direct orders based on my strongest position—and others less directly. To cover all bases."

Before Larkin could respond, both men looked up with surprise as Revere burst into the room, waving a paper.

"You were right, Thomas. Castro has committed himself—the rider came in just after you left." He dropped into a chair, somewhat breathlessly. "He is in San Juan Bautista, with a force of over two hundred men. He has issued a proclamation declaring Fremont and his men nothing more than a band of robbers and thieves. He is calling on all Californios to"—he paused, glancing at the paper—"'lance the ulcer that would destroy their liberties.'"

"Oh, my God," Larkin groaned. "What answer did Fremont give to my last message?"

"There was no answer."

"I see. Well, that is an answer in itself, isn't it? The fool won't be stopped, and will be met by one equally as irresponsible. Damn Fremont and Castro! We will probably find ourselves in a war, due to the pompous, self-serving ambitions of two imbeciles."

"It will be the excuse that our hot-headed settlers have been waiting for," Jeremy observed. "Their chance to overthrow the dons."

"And the excuse the *liberalismos* have been waiting for. I imagine that our prefect, Manuel, had something to do with the proclamation."

"Yes," Revere said somberly. "He co-signed it. It will provide a short fuse for this powder keg."

"A powder keg that Fremont wants to go off. I suggest that we take a ride to Hawk's Peak."

The three men rose and left the kitchen. "I'll meet you at your house within a half an hour, Larkin," he said as he walked to the door.

"No—it's best that I remain here, Jeremy. Fremont has chosen to ignore my messages; he will not listen to me in person. However, my presence could complicate matters with Castro. No, you and Revere go and do what you can. I will do what I can from here."

"Jeremy is thought to be a private citizen," Revere said with a frown. "But as a U.S. Naval Officer, I, too, could compromise our position."

"You were to leave soon for New Helvetia," Larkin said. "It would not be suspect if you were to do so now. Return with me, and I will give you a letter for Sutter. I want him to know what is happening. My God, if the Sacramento Valley flares up over this, we are in deep, deep trouble."

As Larkin pulled on his coat, he paused and shook his

head. "Some things continue to come back to haunt us. Of all of the young rebels who fought against the *Rifleros Americanos* back in '40, Manuel was the worst. It is too bad that Vallejo could not have slapped him into a convent as he did Ariana. And thrown away the key."

As he opened the door, Jeremy's head jerked back to the shorter man. "Ariana? What did she have to do with it?"

Larkin chuckled as he buttoned his coat. "Oh, she was in the thick of it, to Mariano's horror. Why do you think she was shipped off to a convent in Mexico? She and her cousin, Rafael, who disappeared soon after, were up to their young, impulsive ears in it."

Jeremy closed the door behind the two men and stood for a long moment staring at it. "Well, well," he murmured. Then a small smile played at the corners of his mouth. Suspicions, words, and facts tumbled into place. "Ariana Saldivar, what *are* you doing? Playing a man's game?"

"Pardon, Senor?"

He turned to find Selena standing in the doorway to the parlor. "Nothing, Selena. Is senora up yet?"

"She is just rising, Senor."

"Good, tell her to come to my room. I wish to speak with her."

"You wished to see me, Jeremy?" Beth paused in the doorway, her eyes widening slightly with mild surprise and distaste. He was wearing buckskin breeches and a wool shirt, an outfit she disliked intensely and one he had begun to wear more and more frequently of late. The surprise, however, was for what he was doing. "Are you going somewhere?"

He was standing by the bed, stuffing his saddlebags with a change of clothes. "Yes, I have business to attend to. I'll be gone for a few days."

"I see. Lumber business, I assume." Her voice was laced with indifferent boredom as she strolled into the room.

He left the statement unanswered, his usual way of handling such situations without actually lying to her. He knew she would not press for more information. In fact, if she had a fear, it would be that he might want to discuss it with her. He finished packing and buckled the straps of the saddlebag. Then he looked up at his wife, who had crossed to the window and was staring out through the sheer curtains to the street below. He studied her for a moment, her tousled hair, and cheeks still flushed with recent dreams. He wondered what Beth dreamed about. His eyes passed over her slim body, outlined through the sheer gown and wrapper.

"You look quite beautiful this morning, Beth."

"Oh really, Jeremy, I haven't even had my toilette. I am perfectly aware of how I look."

"Then may I assume that you are deliberately standing in front of that window for my pleasure?"

It took a moment before she understood his meaning. She quickly moved away from the window, flushing angrily at the sound of his soft laughter. "Really, Jeremy, must you be so coarse."

"Beth, I am your husband, not your beau." With a sigh, he gave it up. "I've arranged for two of Selena's cousins to provide escort for you in my absence. You are not to leave the house without them—even to visit Rachel."

"Jeremy, that is absurd."

"No, it is not. Right now feelings are running high against foreigners. Besides Rachel, you are the only white woman in Monterey." He saw her look of defiance. "I mean it, Beth. While I am gone I want to know that you and Hamilton are safe."

She could barely hide her irritation. She was to be a virtual prisoner in this house! But she did not argue with him; what would have been the point? She had learned that it was best to tell him what he wanted to hear. "Yes, Jeremy. I will not leave this house without your—guards."

He ignored the sarcasm and picked up the saddlebags and a sheepskin jacket. He hesitated a moment, struck with the impulse to kiss her good-bye. But it passed. He was in no mood to give her the opportunity to turn away from his affection. "I will see you in two days—three, at the most." With that, he left the room.

Beth dressed, had breakfast in her room, spent a few requisite minutes with the baby, and settled in the down-stairs parlor with a favorite novel. Then she heard the baby crying. She tried to ignore the sound, but it continued. Irritated, she laid the book in her lap and closed her eyes. Selena! What was the matter with that girl? The crying stopped. Sighing, she picked up the book and scanned the page, but she soon gave up, unable to concentrate.

She dropped the book on the table next to her and glanced about the room. The house was quiet as a tomb, a stillness that was accentuated by the steady rhythm of the pendulum clock in the hallway. She straightened the lace on her sleeve and brushed a wrinkle out of her skirt. She could visit Rachel, she thought, then dismissed the idea. Rachel Larkin had begun to make her uncomfortable. Her visits usually led to lectures from the older woman. Oh, they were not heavy-handed but consisted of stories Rachel thought were subtle. But the messages were clear enough, and Beth had grown to resent them. The message was always the same: if Beth would just try harder, she could be happy in her new life.

Never, Beth thought. Not if she lived to be as old as her wrinkled, aging grandmother. The old crone had lived far beyond the age that any decent person should. Eventually, she could not even walk without assistance, and spittle constantly hung from her puckered, toothless mouth. With it all, she ruled like a dowager duchess, dangling her wealth with the threat of leaving it to a distant cousin in South Carolina if her family were to displease her.

Beth wondered if her mother had ever loved the woman. Perhaps, she mused, when her grandmother had been younger—and a great beauty. It was hard to imagine her as a beauty; she had always seemed old and decrepit. Though the room was warm, Beth shuddered slightly, recalling moments when she had had to kiss that shriveled, spittled face. But perhaps affection had little to do with the way people look, she mused. Her mother was beautiful still, and Beth had never particularly liked her. The feeling was mutual, however. Margaret Hilton had never particularly cared for her daughters. She displayed them, took pride in them, and planned grandly for their futures, but love had never been a part of her character. Only her father had loved her; only Papa had made her feel special.

And her beaus had made her feel special, long before her season, when young men found excuses to visit with her father, and their eyes wandered to the young Misses Hilton. And of the three lovely daughters of Jonathan Hilton, Elizabeth was considered the beauty.

What good were those years now? There were so many things that she had learned to appreciate: the theater, the arts, salons, glorious parties and balls. And for what? To live in this backwater the rest of her life—where people's idea of a social was to eat cow's eyes and snatch the heads off roosters?

There were no women to talk to, except Rachel. The few men who had a sense of society, such as Fremont and Revere, would leave. She wiped away a bead of perspiration from her lip and took a deep breath. Why had the room suddenly grown so warm? Her chest felt tight and it seemed hard to breathe. Needing air, she rose from the chair and crossed to the window overlooking the street. She pulled back the sheer curtain and drew a breath of the cool air.

Two vaqueros on horseback rode by, their strange-sounding words wafting up to her. A shaggy mongrel trotted at their heels, its tail curled in a proud, satisfied arch over its back. As they passed the house, the dog came to an abrupt halt and froze. The hair on its back lifted in a threatening ridge. Across the road, a large pig was rutting at the edge of the dusty street. Growling deeply in its throat, the dog bared its teeth and began to move cautiously toward the pig.

The dog approached the rutting swine and began snapping at its hind legs. The pig swung about, and its small ears began to flap as it lowered its head, swinging it back and forth in a threatening gesture to the dog. Beth stared, transfixed as her hand tightened on the sheer lace of the curtain. The pig grunted, then squealed as the dog leaped up and its teeth made contact. Suddenly, the pig rushed the dog with an agility that seemed impossible for the heavy animal. It began tearing at the dog with its razor-sharp teeth. The dog stumbled, then managed to free itself, yapping in terror. Its shoulder was ripped open, the fleshy muscle torn, trailing blood as it ran.

Stunned, Beth staggered back from the window, her hand still on the curtain. Her heart was pounding, perspiration breaking out on her lip and forehead. She looked vacantly at the torn piece of curtain in her hand. Slowly, she forced her fingers apart and watched as the lace drifted to the parlor floor. Pulling her gaze away from the fabric, she looked vacantly about the room, touching on the pieces Jeremy had purchased with such studied care.

She could still see him standing in this room the first day he had brought her here, his smile full of pleasure and expectation. The steady tick of the clock in the hall began to seep into her brain, each beat growing louder. Suddenly she could not breathe. She gasped for air, drawing it painfully into her lungs. Her hands flew to her face, then to her hair. Pins began to fall to the carpet as she pulled at it. Suddenly she found her breath. She drew it inward in a deep rush. And then she began to scream.

12

Selena rocked in the chair, cooing to the baby. She had been in the kitchen when he had started to cry, and she had hurried to him, knowing that his cries would disturb the senora. She had changed his soiled diaper and fed him from a bottle of goat's milk. It saddened her to know that the senora would never know the joy of feeding her child. Selena did not have children of her own, but she imagined that if one could find such pleasure from holding a babe while it suckled from a nipple on a bottle, how much more pleasurable it must be to hold it to your breast. She had watched her mother nursing her younger brothers and sisters, and it was the only time she had seen her mother content, with a look of true peace on her worn face.

She did not blame the senora for not loving her child; she pitied her. Senora Morgan had come from a world which Selena could not comprehend. She was spoiled and self-centered, and yet Selena knew that she was in terrible pain. Just like the little bobcat she had once found and cherished. To Selena, they were similar as no other two creatures could be. Perhaps that is why she loved the senora.

When Selena was eleven years old, she had been sent by her mother to weed the garden. It was a task that her brothers and sisters hated and avoided at all costs, but Selena enjoyed it. As she was the eldest child, her mother usually had more important duties for her, including the care of the babies, the wash, and helping with the meals. Such responsibility had been part of her life since before she could remember, and she accepted it without complaint. But she did enjoy the garden.

The garden was a vital part of the family's life. A small part of what they grew was for their own use, but, more importantly, it was for the don's familia. Selena's parents were mestizo—Indians. In the California community, only the mestizo could labor. Vaqueros worked the cattle, that was the reason for their existence. The mestizo cooked, cleaned, served, wove, and tended the gardens.

The mestizo was the true Californian. Selena's people had been here long before the first Spaniard or Mexican had set foot upon her soil led by the padre, Junipero Serra. Her parents told her of the missions, the imprisonment of her people, the stern admonishments of the priests, the whippings when they disobeyed or tried to escape, and more punishments—including starvation when they would not forget the teachings of their ancestors and embrace the church.

The missions were gone, but the servitude continued under their new masters. They were no longer whipped for leaving, but there was no place to go. Since before she could remember, the story was the same; there were her father's oft-repeated words: Someday he would be free. He would join with his brothers in the mountains. He would ride a horse and be part of the raids upon the dons and the Yanqui settlers. Once again, California would belong to the tribes, including the Salinans, Costanoans, and Esselens.

Selena loved her father. His father had been a mission Indian, while he had been born on the rancho after the dons had wrestled the land from the church. But her father clung to his dreams, and would do so to his death. And he had taught Selena to believe in her future as well. She remembered the day he had given it to her . . .

She relished the sun; it was part of the privilege of working in the garden. Her fingers moved swiftly through the soft, loose dirt, pulling the weeds in steady rhythm. She had taught herself to work, humming a senseless song under her breath. The soil smelled sweet and rich, and each part of the garden was subtly different. Where the peppers were grown, the soil smelled heavy, contrasting with the sweet aroma where the snap beans were grown. Blindfolded,

Selena would have known which part of the garden she was in, using only her sense of smell.

It was then that she heard it: the soft mewing from the trees just beyond her. The sound had pain in it. She found the creature under a juniper bush where it had been left by a predator. The bobcat kitten hissed at her, lunging, and she barely drew her hand back in time. Then it sunk back into its nest of leaves, whimpering with pain as its yellow-brown eyes fixed on her with fear and anguish. She watched it for a moment, her heart filled with pity and doubt. It might bite her, and probably would, but could she blame it? She wouldn't die from its little teeth, as the creature would if it did not have help.

It did bite her, more than once, but they were superficial wounds, as the kitten was so weak. She bathed the wounds, applying a homemade salve her mother kept on a shelf above the stove, and bound the kitten's wounds with strips torn from her mother's wool scraps.

For two weeks she kept the kitten in a small room behind the chicken coop where old, discarded furniture from the rancho was stored. No one ever came there, except to toss another rejected piece upon the pile. She dared not tell anyone, for fear that her father would kill it.

She checked on the kitten whenever she could, bringing it food and redressing its wounds. To her joy, it no longer tried to bite her, and soon it stopped hissing and spitting when she approached. The day came when it purred as she touched it, and she knew they were friends. She laughed at its antics as it tangled in the blanket or stalked a bug in the dim light from a high window in the small shed. She spent soothing, loving hours with the bobcat in her lap as she stroked it, listening to its answering purr.

She loved the kitten, and her love was bittersweet. A lean-to was no place for a wild thing. It could not live its life there, or it would die. And, she knew that it would tell her when the time had come to let it go.

One morning it accepted her offering of food, and her accompanying strokes of love. It purred, rubbing against her, but as she tried to pick it up it hissed and scratched her. It continued to hiss, arching its back. She stared at it, trying to deal with her sorrow. Fighting back tears, she cracked open the door, peering outside to assure herself that no one was about. Then she stood back and pushed it open, letting the bright sunlight rush into the small shed.

The bobcat moved back into the shadows, as if the sun were a foreign thing. Then it slowly inched forward, sniffing. Suddenly, without looking back, it took off like a shot. She rushed about the door, just in time to see it disappear into the woods edging the shed. Selena slumped down against the door. Sitting in the dirt, she wept.

"Are those tears for the kitten, or for yourself?"

She looked up with a start to find her father gazing down at her. "You knew?" she sniffed, staring at him with wonder through teary eyes.

He hunkered down in front of her, glancing in the direction the bobcat had fled. "There is a saying among our people: to fly with the eagle, one's spirit must be free."

"What does that mean, Papa?"

"It has many meanings, and different ones for different moments in our life."

"If I had not let it go, it would have died," she said sadly.

"Yes, but you already knew that. What does it mean for you?"

She thought about it for a long moment. "That—that if I had not chosen to do what was right, I could not fly with the eagles?"

He smiled, patting her head. As she watched him walk away, his back straight and proud, she began to understand so much more. Her father clung to his dreams because they kept his spirit free. And she learned. Like her father, she would never allow her spirit to be crushed by what others would try to do to her. Only she could deny the eagle's spirit in herself.

Selena looked down at the sleeping baby with a rush of love. His mouth had slipped from the nipple and was covered with milk. She set the bottle on the table next to her, and wiped the milk away with the corner of her apron. Lifting the baby to her shoulder, she patted him until he burped up a bubble. Then she settled him into his cradle. She was covering him when she heard the scream.

She would never forget those screams. They continued incessantly, reverberating through the house. Rushing downstairs to the parlor, she gripped the doorway, staring with horror at the figure who stood in the center of the room. Without hesitation she crossed the room, and with startling calmness, she slapped Beth again and again, until the screaming stopped. Then Selena caught her as she crumbled into her arms.

It took her nearly an hour to soothe the hysterical woman. She managed to lift her off the floor, onto the sofa; when Beth was calm, she fixed some tea, lacing the brew with herbs her mother used for pain. This seemed appropriate. After all, was not the pain of a spirit as acute as that of the body?

Beth seemed to relax with the tea, though her eyes became frighteningly vacant. Even more than when she had been screaming, Selena began to worry about Beth's sanity, never doubting the command she herself took at that moment. After all, she had been responsible for someone's care all of her life, and Beth was a wounded creature, needing her help. "Senora, you must leave here. This is not a place for you." Selena saw a flicker of recognition in the vacant eyes. "You must make Senor understand." She watched the confusion her words caused, and she felt very, very sad.

Monterey was a small community, and she knew that Elizabeth Morgan was disliked. Selena had remained silent as she had listened to what was said about the senora. People did not understand that there were those who simply could not adjust to change. Oh, most could. How else would her people have survived when the missions came, after centuries of freedom? Why else was there a desire among many men to leave their families and all that they had known to find a life in new lands, as the Yanquis had done? And before them, the Spaniards and the Mexicans.

Senor Morgan had left his life behind him, and though he might not know it yet, he had come to embrace his new life. She had watched him; she had sensed his restlessness, seen the distant, regretful looks changing to contentment. But some people did not change, and only the life they knew could be understood, lived, and accepted. They were like wild creatures who could never be domesticated. That was something Selena understood. That was why she had loved the senora in a special way, understanding when others could not.

"Tell him that you must go home," she said softly.

Beth tried to sit up, but she slumped back on the sofa, totally drained. "Selena, I—" she paused, flushing as she turned her face away. She could not look at the other woman.

"I will not tell anyone what happened," Selena said. "If your screams were heard, I shall merely tell them that Senora saw a rat—a large rat."

Beth smiled weakly. "Yes, a rat. Thank you, Selena. Oh, I do so want to go home," she said softly. "I do. But Jeremy will not leave."

"Why can't you go without him, just for a time, perhaps. You cannot stay here, Senora."

Beth turned to look at her. A small glimmer of light came into her eyes. "A visit?"

"Why not? A visit, Senora. Is it not permitted?"

Beth sat up and stared at the other woman. She felt her strength returning. "A visit. Oh, Selena, I could, couldn't I? Why not? But how—Jeremy would never permit it!"

"I think he would, if you explained—"

"No, no." She gazed at Selena with despair. "He wants to keep me here. He'll never let me go." She looked wildly about the room. "There must be a way—yes," she breathed. "There is!" Selena stared uncomfortably at the look that had come into Beth's eyes. "Selena, your cousins—the men Jeremy left as my escort—will they take me anywhere?"

"Anywhere, Senora? Where do you want to go? A ship is not leaving for two weeks. The senor will arrange it. I am certain if you ask him—"

"Forget the senor," Beth snapped, rising from the sofa. She began to pace. "It will work; I know it!" She turned back to the maid, her eyes wide with feverish determination. "Contact your cousins, Selena. I am leaving. When you have returned, you will help me pack!"

Beth rushed from the room and up the stairs, leaving Selena to stare at the empty doorway. *Madre mia,* she thought, swallowing back a feeling of rising panic. What had she done?

"When is something going to happen?" Revere muttered. "This waiting is driving me wild."

Jeremy squinted into the early morning sun. He shared Revere's frustration. It would be at least an hour before the sun would move high enough to afford them a clear view of Fremont's encampment.

"Who knows?" he said at last, shifting his gaze to the

village of San Juan Bautista. "It's the poorest excuse for military readiness I've ever seen."

"I wonder if Fremont shares your opinion," Revere smirked.

"He sees what I see."

They stood in the shadows of the old mission church where they had a clear view of the comings and goings of Castro's forces and, in time, Fremont's encampment in the distance. The topographical engineer had chosen a hill at about two thousand feet, in the shadow of towering Hawk's Peak, for his stronghold.

Across the wide plaza—a makeshift city of tents for Castro's army of about two hundred men—was a hotel and livery stable. The other two sides of the plaza comprised the officers' barracks, with General Castro's headquarters at the far end near the livery, and the church. The fourth side was open countryside.

Jeremy and Revere had been in San Juan Bautista for a long, frustrating week. They had called on General Castro soon after their arrival, prepared to explain their presence. Lieutenant Revere was on his way to the Sacramento, and Jeremy was accompanying him as far as San Jose, whereupon he would double back by way of Santa Cruz to check on his lumber interests. The explanation proved unnecessary. Castro seemed less interested in their reasons for being there than in the fact that he had an audience for his diatribe. He ranted and raved about Fremont's presence, declaring that his army would expel foreign influence once and for all. He seemed oblivious to the fact that he was speaking to a foreign influence.

As the sun rose overhead, they could again see the distant encampment some miles from San Juan, with a flag flying at its peak. Jeremy slipped open Revere's telescope and focused on the encampment. "The man has guts, I'll give him that." He smirked. "He's flying the flag of the Corps of Topographical Engineers."

"At least he didn't fly the Stars and Stripes. Then Castro would have declared war."

"My guess is that he doesn't have one. Otherwise he probably would have."

If this day proved to be like those of the past week, a small contingent of Castro's forces, under the direction of prefect Manuel Castro, would set forth in a great flurry. Approaching the base of the hill where Fremont was positioned, they would spend the remainder of the day shouting threats back and forth, accompanied by a few pot shots. Fortunately, no one had been hit yet.

"Oh, God," Revere said suddenly.

Jeremy followed his fixed stare. Castro had stepped out of his office in his military best. Gold buttons and brushed epaulets glittered in the sun. His hat was plumed, and he was pulling on white gloves. "What is he doing?" Revere blinked. "You would think he was going to a dress review!"

"Perhaps he thinks to overwhelm Fremont with his magnificence."

Revere would have laughed if the picture was not so pathetic. Castro walked among the rows of cook fires scattered over the plaza amid a ragtag mixture of men who leaped to their feet, saluting their commandant, and those who would not stir from the shade of their makeshift shelters.

The steady stream of reports Jeremy had sent to Buchanan ticked off in his mind. He was gratified that his summation of the weak, haphazard preparedness of the Californio military establishment had been on the mark, but his gut tightened as he viewed the prospect of what might come before this conflict was resolved. Unless something was done, it could lead to a bloody end of Larkin's peace efforts, and a beginning of real war.

"When do you think it will start?"

"Not for a while, evidently." Jeremy nodded toward a few soldiers who were stirring up campfires and setting them with pots. "They're going to have breakfast first."

A swift glance confirmed Jeremy's observation. "Jesus," Revere whispered. He glanced back at the crest of the hill. "If Fremont chooses to send men out now, they could pick them off at leisure!"

"He could have done that any time in the past week. No, it's not the type of fight that Fremont wants. He'll wait for Castro to rush him—it'll write better in his next book."

Revere laughed, then fell silent as he watched the slowly waking camp with Jeremy.

As the sun rose it began to spread across Jeremy's shoulders, easing the chill that had set into his muscles through the dark hours before dawn. He rolled his shoulders against the ache and picked up his pack. "Let's collect our horses from the livery."

"Where are we going?" Revere asked as he pushed his shoulder away from the wall and bent to retrieve his things.

"To get a closer look."

Within an hour they were positioned among a cover of manzanita below the ridge of the hill where Fremont was encamped. Below them was a wide gorge leading down through hilly climbs to San Juan Bautista. From their position they had a clear view of the movements of those in the garrison below.

The morning grew warmer, and Jeremy fought a yawn, shaking his head to ward off the temptation to doze. He glanced over at Revere and smiled. Revere's head had slumped back against the rock at his back, and his mouth was open. He was snoring softly. Jeremy checked above and below him; nothing was happening. And nothing probably would, he thought. Apparently Castro was not even going to bother to send Manuel out today. He yawned again, tempted to join Revere in a nap, then suddenly came wide awake. His eyes narrowed as he caught movement across the small canyon. In a position roughly level with his own, two men seemed to be arguing. He reached over to Revere's saddlebags and pulled out the telescope. As he turned back, he saw one of the men lead a horse from the rocks. The man mounted and began to pick his way across the rocky side of the mountain, dropping to a trail leading down the mountain.

Jeremy fixed the telescope on the departing rider. His jaw tensed as he identified the man. Then he swept the glass back to the rocks across the gorge, searching. "Well, I'll be damned," he murmured.

"Joseph," he said, shaking the man's shoulder. Revere came awake with a sputter. "I have something to do. Wait here and keep an eye on our friends." As he settled into the saddle, he glanced back at Revere. "I'll be back shortly. But if something does delay me and anything flares up, get out of here. Don't think twice about it, just get out."

Across the canyon, Jeremy dismounted and tied his horse to a scrub oak. He climbed along the narrow path leading to the rocks above. He knew that he was concealed from anyone above him but that Revere could see him clearly. He could well imagine the naval officer's curiosity—and frustration. At last, he reached a narrow passage where he could drop down behind her.

Ariana heard the falling pieces of crumbling rock and spun about. Jeremy stepped down the last few feet and stared at the gun in her hand. "For God's sake, put that thing away before you kill someone."

"What are *you* doing here?" she demanded. He noted that the gun did not waver.

"I might ask you the same thing."

"You are with them—" she jerked her head toward the mountain.

"No, actually, I'm not. In fact, I'm here with Revere. I imagine he's watching us now."

Her eyes flickered with concern. "Where is he?"

"Across the canyon. Within rifle range," he added with a grin. "If you decide to shoot me, I rather imagine he will not hesitate to return the favor."

The calmly given statement unsettled her. She started to move back into the rocks, then stopped, knowing it would remove Morgan from her line of fire. "What do you want?"

To her surprise, he sat down on a large rock and leaned back against the ridge, crossing his arms and legs in a comfortable position and smiling at her. The insufferable bastard! she thought. "Relax, Ariana. Nothing's going to happen for a while."

She glanced down into the valley, then jerked her head back to him. He was right, of course, and the knowledge irritated her.

"Relax, Ariana," he repeated. "And put that damn gun away. I don't think you want to let anyone know that you are here. A gunshot will accomplish it quite easily. How would you ever explain it?"

She drew a deep breath to calm herself. It was true, she couldn't fire even if she wanted to. She slid the gun into her holster. He studied her, noting the man's cotton shirt she wore and the leather riding skirt that clung to her trim waist and shapely body, which was accentuated by the fit of the holster.

Oddly discomforted by his perusal, she leaned back against the rocky outclimb and crossed her arms over her chest.

"Larkin sent me to observe," he offered with a smile.

"Did Mariano send you for the same reason? You should have let me know—you could have joined us; it is much cooler on the other side of the canyon." He glanced up at the sun. "You should always study the sun when choosing a position, Ariana. Besides the intense heat, you soon won't be able to see a thing from here. The sun will be in your eyes. The position of the mountain—"

"Stop it!"

"I would keep my voice down, if I were you. Sound carries among these rocks." He smiled at her alarm. "Now tell me, who is in charge—that is—who gives the orders, Manuel or you?"

She stared at him, momentarily bereft of speech. "I don't know what you are talking about."

"Of course you do. That was Manuel who just left, wasn't it? You were arguing. Who won out, Ariana?" He paused, noting her reaction. She was good at this, he admitted. "Tell me, Ariana, just what *were* you doing those years when you were thought to be safely cloistered in that convent?"

Her thoughts focused on the gun at her hip. She knew that she could have killed Fremont's men that day at Angel Castro's ranch, without hesitation. But this was different— to kill a man in cold blood, one that she knew. She had never personally killed a man, though in Mexico it had been done, more than once, on her order. Her feelings returned, the guilt she had experienced those nights when she had been forced to face what she had done, for whatever the reason. She felt a shudder of self-loathing. How brave she was, she thought with disgust, when the dirty work was left for others. Her hand dropped to the gun at her side, then she froze, staring at the colt revolver leveled at her. She laughed, a nervous reaction she barely recognized. "You wouldn't."

"Wouldn't what? Kill a woman? I'm not a fool, Ariana. I wouldn't want to, but I have no intention of sitting here and letting you shoot me. I will do it if I have to; you would be wise to believe that."

She did believe it. Her stomach churned, and for a moment she thought she might be sick. *Dios,* she thought, forcing back the bile that pushed into her throat. She couldn't be sick! She would rather die than disgrace herself before this man!

"Why, Ariana?" he said with deceptive softness. "What are you trying to accomplish?"

The question, and the fact that she was struggling not to hiccup, fed her anger. "I do not owe you answers, Yanqui!" she hissed, swallowing. And then she hiccuped.

"Ariana." He smiled. "And I thought you liked me."

The statement left her nonplussed. "Like you?" She fought for control. The anger she felt frightened her. The wrong word, and she could ruin everything. "Of course I like you. Why shouldn't I?"

"Is that why you tried to shoot me?"

"You startled me. It wasn't personal."

"Neither was this," he said, slipping his gun into his holster. "I just don't like guns held on me. Now, I've told you why I am here; let me guess your reasons. It is obvious that Manuel used his position as prefect of Monterey to fuel this confrontation. I can only speculate on your part in it. No matter who wins this conflict, it will fire the Sacramento Valley. The settlers will revolt, and that will force the Californios to take sides. Either way, you win. The dons have been leaning toward cession, and you can't have that. Overpowered by the prospect of war, the dons will be forced to face their heritage, giving their allegiance to Mexico. Your rebels will take control among the confusion. Thus you see yourselves as the commanding force, bringing California to independence, to the republic you see for her."

Ariana stared at him, astounded by his perceptiveness. "You have quite an imagination, Morgan. Yes, I was curious about what was happening here, and came to see it. Manuel and I were arguing because he thinks it is dangerous for me to be here. But I will not deny that I would like to see an independent California. Many Californios wish for it."

He shook his head. "California will belong to the United States, Ariana. There is absolutely nothing you—or anyone can do to stop it. What the *liberalismos* are doing will bring about unnecessary suffering, but the result will be the same. Oh, not from that fool—" he glanced toward the top of Hawk's Peak, "but from what will certainly follow. It could have been brought about peacefully, but it will come, nonetheless." He stood up before she could respond. "Watch, if you must. But what happens here will change nothing. Remember that, Ariana. It could have been done peacefully."

She stared at him, afraid to speak. She had never been more furious in her life. Fortunately, he backed away, disappearing behind the rock outreach. She fumbled for her gun, nearly dropping it as she wrestled it from the holster while she leaped up to follow him. But when she reached the outcrop, he was gone. Frustrated, she clenched the gun, slipping it back into the holster. He was right, she could have shot him, she was certain of it. She stepped back, turning to lean against a rock as she peered down into the valley below. You may be right, Jeremy Morgan, she thought. Perhaps everything will be as you say. But I will fight to my last breath to see that your words do not come to pass.

"Relax, Revere. It's me."

Revere lowered his gun with relief as Jeremy edged his horse into the narrow coppice of rock. "Dammit, Morgan! I almost shot you!"

"Who did you expect?" Jeremy grinned, bringing his horse beside the other man.

Revere grimaced, glancing toward the valley. "I'm more at home on the deck of a ship commanding cannons, than squatting in the bushes with a rifle."

Except for a smile, Jeremy ignored the comment as he glanced down the valley. "Anything interesting happen?"

"No. But our friends above us are awake. I heard them stirring moments ago."

"Then something will begin soon," Jeremy said grimly, glancing above them.

"What were you doing over there? I've probably gone completely crazy, but wasn't that Ariana Saldivar?"

"Yep."

"What is *she* doing here?"

"Watching."

Dumbfounded, Revere stared at Jeremy. Then his breath drew in sharply. "Well, your timing is good. Our other friends are coming."

Jeremy turned to look where Revere gestured. Coming up the gorge was a sizable contingent of Castro's troops, led by the general himself with Manuel at his side. "Well, at least the waiting is over. Let's just hope that it will be another day of bluster and name-calling."

Suddenly a shot rang out. It had come from above and lifted a puff of dust in the gully below, near a soldier who rode at Castro's left. It took an interminable moment for the man to react, as he stared dumbly at the point where the bullet hit. Then he pulled frantically on his mount with a cry that could be heard up the canyon. Another shot followed, then another. None seemed to hit a mark, but the fusillade sent the column scurrying for cover.

"Shit."

Staring hard at what was happening below, it took a moment for the expletive to register with Revere. He turned to find Jeremy untying his horse. "Where are you going?"

"Up there. Get out of here, Revere!"

"Forget it, Morgan. I'm coming with you."

Revere grabbed for his horse, but Jeremy blocked his way. "Revere, you have more important things to do. You have a dispatch that must reach Sutter. He must be warned or the entire Sacramento Valley will rise up, making this skirmish look like a pea-shoot! Now get out of here!"

Jeremy urged his horse into the brush to the narrow trail that led up the west side of the mountain. He glanced back once, gratified that Revere was not following, then concentrated on the steep climb. The horse slipped twice, but he managed to make it to the top of the ridge. He pulled the mount to a halt, murmuring soothingly as he felt the horse quiver beneath him. His eyes swept over the clearing beyond the trees, judging the position of the men who were stationed behind rocks and bushes at the edge of the ridge, their rifles trained on points below. He had no intention of being shot before he could declare himself.

Urging the horse along the edge of the trees, he followed the cover to the back of the encampment, emerging behind Fremont's men. Then he dismounted, leading the horse into the clearing. He was depending on the reason of these men, if they had any. No one in his right mind would react to a dismounted man, leading his horse with his hands in the air. But he couldn't count on it. Fortunately, everyone on the ridge was intent upon what was happening below. He was not noticed until he had walked the entire span of the ridge and had come within a few feet of Fremont himself. The officer was standing behind his forces, his attention fixed on the gorge.

"Captain Fremont?"

Fremont spun about, his hands flying to the pistol at his hip as his face fell with astonishment. He raised his hand quickly against the reaction of the men about him who were reaching for their weapons. "Morgan! Good Lord, what are you doing here?"

"I have a message for you," Jeremy answered.

Fremont shook his head with amazement. "From Larkin, I imagine. Morgan, you are a fool. I almost shot you."

"What in the hell are you doing, Fremont?" The bluntness of the statement froze the captain's face. "Let's discuss this in private," Jeremy suggested. He knew that Fremont would follow him as he walked to the back of the clearing. One thing Jeremy had learned was that an officer of Fremont's ilk preferred awkward conferences to be held in private. Gaining a distance from the others, the two men squared off.

"Say what you have to say quickly, Morgan."

"It will only take a moment." Jeremy smiled grimly. "It is not hard to guess what you are up to. But, you should consider this: you have repeatedly chosen to ignore the explicit orders of the United States Consul. I do not know what your orders are, Captain, or who has given them to you—or even if you have any. However, you would be well advised to think upon the final results of what you are doing here. Without written orders, your decisions are entirely your own, regardless of what you may claim later. Only you will have to live with the results." He saw a slight flicker of doubt in Fremont's eyes, and he smiled. "Larkin's orders from the president are in writing; I have seen them. He acts with full authority. If you ignore his warnings and you make a mistake, what will you do then?"

The momentary doubt disappeared, and Fremont bristled. "Look to the flagpole behind you, Morgan. That is the flag of the United States Army Corps of Topographical Engineers. It is the first flag of the United States to fly over this territory. While it stands I will not surrender! Nor would any officer worth his salt! But then, you could hardly be expected to understand that."

Jeremy glanced at the makeshift pole, a thin, trimmed trunk of birch. He was filled with a mixture of disgust, despair, and anger. He turned back to stare at the pompous officer before him. "Fremont, you are a total ass. You haven't listened to a word I've said. All right, have it your way. First, you should check your history. It is not the first U.S. flag to fly over California. That honor belongs to Commodore Thomas ap Catesby Jones—and look what happened to him. He is up before a board of inquiry. Secondly, it's not Mr. Morgan, Fremont, it's *Major* Morgan. United States Army, on special assignment from the president and Secretary of State Buchanan. And my orders are also in writing." He ignored Fremont's shock. At least he had his attention now. "Thomas Larkin has worked for years to bring California into the Union peacefully. What you are doing here will undo all of those efforts, shedding blood on both sides in the bargain. You are to cease and desist, Captain. That's an order."

Fremont's initial shock passed, and his eyes glittered with anger and resentment. "Of course, Major. We should talk more about this." He smiled slowly. "Perhaps we could discuss this in my cabin. I think you will find it comfortable." He turned and walked away. Jeremy followed him toward a small cabin that had been constructed near a narrow stream. Recalling Fremont's smile, Jeremy felt suddenly uneasy.

Reaching the cabin, Fremont pushed open the door and stepped back so that Jeremy could enter. The calm, cold smile on the captain's face did not add to Jeremy's ease, but he stepped within. Just inside the cabin he stopped short, and his heart sank into his stomach.

"Beth." The name came out of his throat in a strangle.

As he'd entered she had turned with a warm smile that he knew was not for him. Recognition brought shock, and she gasped. The sight of her standing there twisted his gut, and life seemed to leave him. He did not say anything, the words lumped in his throat. He turned and stepped from the cabin, vaguely amazed that he felt so calm.

Fremont was waiting outside. "It seems that she wants me to see her home, Morgan. To New York, that is. Of course, you understand that I cannot possibly accommodate her."

"Of course." Jeremy regarded the other man evenly. "I apologize for any inconvenience my wife may have caused you." Then their attention was drawn to the ridge as another series of shots rang out. Jeremy drew a deep, calming breath. "He won't attack you, you know. You will have to pick his men off, one by one. A rather inglorious campaign. Not to mention the fact that if he doesn't attack, your position with Washington will not be the clearly defined one that you are hoping for." He saw the doubt his observation brought, and he played on it. "You should learn something about your opponents, Fremont. It is the passion for conflict that is important to the Californio. They take up their guns as a last resort. You could well be up here for months. You might think about that."

Suddenly, a strong, irresistible impulse overtook Jeremy. He found himself striding across the compound. Reaching the flagpole, he raised a booted foot, placing it against the birch pole. Then he gave it a shove. The set proved to be shallow, and with a hesitant creak it shimmered, shook, and suddenly toppled. As the pole landed on the ground with a soft thud and a puff of dust, Jeremy reached down and pulled the flag from its tangles. Folding it, he walked back to Fremont who was stunned, as were his men. He handed the folded flag to the officer. "Your flag has fallen," Jeremy said quietly. "There is no reason to remain."

13

Jeremy stared intently into the fire, aware of Beth's proximity, yet there was nothing he could find to say to her. Words lumped somewhere within him. Platitudes came to his mind, but he rejected them with disgust. His father had used those well-formed, useful phrases, and even as a child they had seemed empty and false to him. He was furiously angry, but he could not ignore his own guilt; much of what had happened had been his fault. But he held himself back, unwilling to face the pain that would certainly take him over if he allowed himself to feel. He stared at the snifter of brandy in his hand, suddenly afraid to allow himself the release the liquor would give. It could make him incautious, and at the moment he needed all of his wits about him.

"Why couldn't you come to me, Beth?" he said quietly.

"Oh, Jeremy, you were the last person I could have come to." He was vaguely surprised by the pain in her voice. He heard the rustle of her skirts as she rose from her chair, moving behind him. They were alone, but for the accompanying, steady tick of the clock in the hallway. Selena had greeted them upon their return a half hour past, her warm brown eyes filled with relief. But, as always, she had drawn quick, perceptive conclusions and had withdrawn silently, leaving them to their personal and private war. Jeremy knew that it was a war, one that would be irrevocably decided tonight, but one in which both sides would know defeat. He could only hope that the battle would be conducted with a measure of grace.

"Jeremy, please. Just let me go."

The defeat in her voice tore at him, filling him with inexplicable anger. Suddenly he turned, flinging his snifter at the wall between them. The sound of the breaking glass left them both in momentary shock. "Let you go? Dammit, Beth! When did I ever force you?" The sight of her pale face as she stared at the shattered glass, lifting to him with fear and confusion, only added to his frustration. "I told you to stay in the east! I knew that this was no place for you! But you insisted; you had to come! God—you are so consumed with your fantasy world that you cannot see the real world! Since the day we were married I wanted to show you that reality is better; it feels, Beth! It feels and it is warm and it grows! I cannot be what you need."

She closed her eyes against the pain, and tried to focus her thoughts. "You are—too real for me, Jeremy."

He groaned, leaning against the mantel. "Oh God, what does that mean, Beth?"

"You love me too much," she answered, feeling strangely calm. "I should have married a man more like me. One far more selfish. You give too much. That frightens me."

"I frighten you a lot," he said grimly.

"Yes. You do. I want to go home. Let me go home, Jeremy."

Her words hung heavily in the silence. He stood before the window without seeing. The finality of their life together struck at him, and he couldn't answer her, not yet.

In the impasse, she took a bracing swallow of the brandy he had given her. The last week had been a total nightmare. She had arrived at Fremont's camp with her escort two days after Jeremy had left home. She didn't know what she had expected, but certainly not the reception she got. Within moments she experienced more humiliation than she had ever known in her life. Oh, Fremont was not ungracious; indeed, he was the perfect gentleman. He simply did not want anything to do with her.

Her escort had left her at the edge of the camp, and there was no way to return to Monterey. She became a daily reminder of the awkward position she had placed them in. Then, by the end of their third evening together, Fremont's manner gradually began to change. He began to linger over supper, and found time to spend with her during the day.

She knew that given a little more time, he would accede to her wishes. And, she was fully prepared to do whatever she had to in the bargain. And then Jeremy had appeared.

Beth took another sip of the brandy. Never, she thought, never again would she allow a man to humiliate her. In those last days with Fremont, she had begun to suspect the power a woman could hold over a man. It was a talent she planned to learn.

"I really have little choice, do I, Beth?" Jeremy said suddenly. "I will send you home, but there is one condition. Whether you like it or not, you are the mother of our son." He saw the frown that crossed her expression, and he hardened. "He is a fact, Beth, not a matter of inconvenience. You want to go home, but you will need respectability. What has passed between us doesn't matter anymore—I don't even want to know if you slept with Fremont. But Hamilton does matter. I promise you this: if you fail our son—I will destroy you."

"Destroy me?" She gaped at him. "How?"

His expression was grim, but resolute. "Fail our son and I will divorce you, Beth."

She felt herself grow cold. Divorce? The thought was inconceivable. She would become a social pariah. Even those who would want to remain her friends could not do so. She would never again be allowed to associate with polite company. "You would do that to me?"

She was shocked by the coldness in his eyes. "It is not a threat; it is a promise. You have a lot of growing up to do, and you are going to have to do it quickly. Your behavior must be exemplary, as it will reflect upon our son. Oh, don't look so forlorn, Beth. You really didn't expect that you could return home as the season's virginal debutante, did you? Most of your friends have probably married by now, in any case. As a respectable married woman, you shouldn't have any trouble assuming a suitable social life—within stringent dictates, of course. But I warn you, if one word of scandal reaches me—or touches our son—I will divorce you. You can count on that."

"You could return with me," she countered, controlling her anger. "You are not in the army anymore. You could go into business with your father."

"No, I cannot return with you, Beth," he said coldly. "In fact—I have no desire to."

"How can you be so hateful?" she stammered, anger and frustration filling her eyes with tears. "I am sorry that I went to Fremont. I made a mistake! Why are you punishing me like this?"

"Punishing you? How am I punishing you, Beth? You went to Fremont because you want to go home so badly that you risked your life and made total fools out of both of us. Yet, you've won, Beth. You're going home—"

"Oh yes, with threats!" she cried. "If I do not live my life according to your dictates, you'll ruin me!"

His anger suddenly sloughed away, leaving him feeling drained and terribly sad. He crossed to the sideboard and poured himself another brandy. With his back to her, he stared absently into the amber liquid. It was a long moment before he could collect his thoughts. Finally, taking a sip, he turned back to her. She stood at the center of the room, her face flushed, her eyes bright with frustration and anger.

"Oh, Beth," he said wearily. "We've been poison for each other, haven't we? How did it happen? How could we be so drawn to each other those first months, so certain of our future? This—argument rather sums up what we are to each other, doesn't it?"

"I don't know what you're talking about!" She turned away, plopping down on the sofa. It struck him with a perverted sense of amusement that she had begun to pout. My poor little Beth, he thought. He sat down on the sofa next to her.

"No, I don't imagine that you do. And, I seriously doubt that a few words would explain it to you. I won't even try."

They sat there, a hand's breath apart, without touching. Jeremy sipped from his snifter, staring into the fire, lost in the morose regrets of his own thoughts. Beth was conscious of his closeness, and it made her uncomfortable. Then, as the silence in the room lengthened, her thoughts began to shift, darting back and forth to other considerations. She was going home. Truly, going home! Soon, her life would change again, back to the only reality she knew, understood, or wanted. Her thoughts began to fix on that single thought. Home! After a few moments, nothing else mattered.

Waves crashed against the rocks, leaping over the natural seawall to inch over the edge of the road before they slipped back in wavering fingers to the ocean. Beyond, a spectral shape of a ship could be seen, barely outlined in the morning fog which was gradually pulling back to sea under the warming press of the sun.

Jeremy glanced at the damp feathers on Beth's bonnet. They were hanging in limp defeat, much like his mood, he thought. A little of him would go with her after all.

She turned to him, and he saw the excitement she made no attempt to conceal. Not that it surprised him. He had never seen her so content as she had been in the past two weeks. It was the only time in their marriage that he had seen traces of the woman he had fallen in love with—because she was leaving him.

Rachel and Thomas had arrived moments before to say their farewells and pay their respects. Neither Jeremy nor Beth had told them the seriousness of this parting, but they had sensed it over the past weeks. At the moment, Beth and Rachel were engrossed with a large basket Rachel had brought with her. "Shipboard food leaves much to be desired," Rachel was saying. "This will keep you together in body and spirit. Giving me a similar basket was the kindest thing my mother did for me when I left Boston."

"I remember that basket," Larkin interjected with his natural enthusiasm. "Actually, my dear, it was the reason I spent so much time in your company. That basket brought us together!" He had barely uttered the words when he flushed uncomfortably, fueled by the glare from his wife. "I am certain that you will enjoy it in good health, Elizabeth," he added quickly, with great discomfort.

Jeremy continued to stare out at sea, pretending that he had not heard for the sake of the consul. He was not surprised that the diplomat had made such a thoughtless comment. It was not a comfortable moment for any of them. For any but Beth, he thought. Only she did not sense or care about the gravity of what was happening.

The seamen had finished loading the longboat with the last of the provisions for the ship. Then the senior officer stepped back onto the seawall. He turned to the small party with an expectant look. Jeremy knew it was time. Taking her arm, he drew Beth away from the others. As he faced her, he smiled and reached out to straighten her bonnet in a husbandly gesture that suddenly made him feel uncomfortable. "It will be a long voyage," he said gently, wondering what he could possibly say to her at this moment. He felt that he should say something profound, but he could only fix on the pathetically limp feathers on her bonnet. Then other scattered thoughts occurred. "I want my parents to spend time with Hamilton."

"Of course, Jeremy." She gave him a warm smile. "I promise, as much as they want."

"The transition is bound to be difficult for Selena. I want you to help her, Beth, and make it as easy as possible for her."

He glanced at the young woman who stood to one side, holding the baby. He had been hesitant to ask Selena to accompany his wife and son, and he knew that she was frightened by the prospect. Beth had been appalled by the suggestion, but when it had become one of his "requirements," she had conceded. In fact, once she had thought upon it, she had become quite cheerful about the matter. He suspected that her change of mood had less to do with acceptance of Selena herself than the fact that she would be freer of responsibilities toward their son. Thus, he had made certain that she understood Selena was to remain as the boy's nurse, or he would bring all three of them back to California. He knew that Selena loved Hamilton, and he was comforted that she would be with his son.

"Oh, of course," Beth answered, a shadow of indifference crossing her expression as she looked to the waiting boat. She was almost squirming with impatience. Her reaction confirmed the wisdom of certain steps he had taken. Letters to his father were already aboard ship, including instructions about his son and the nurse. He smiled grimly as he thought of the confrontations between his young, spoiled wife, and his mother. Caroline Morgan would broach any contest between Beth and his son's welfare.

The waiting officer cleared his throat, showing his impatience. Bracing himself, Jeremy faced his wife, turning her to look at him. His large hands gripped her shoulders. His voice was gentle, while he hoped that it did not betray the painful regret he was feeling. "Beth, I want you to be happy." Words of endearment crossed his mind, but he could not bring himself to say them. Under the circumstances, they seemed false. Moreover, he suspected that they would go unheard.

She stared up at him, finally giving him her attention. Her eyes had filled with sudden tears. "Oh, Jeremy," she exclaimed. "My dear, do not look so sad! We shall not be apart for long, I am certain of it! Soon you can have done with all of this and return home where you belong! I have given it a good deal of thought, Jeremy. The very first thing I shall do is to set my efforts to mending your breach with Mr. Marcy. I know that my father can help. Trust me, soon you will be able to return, and it will be as if that terrible time never happened!"

He stared at her. There was nothing more to say. "Goodbye, Beth." He bent down and kissed her gently. Then he turned her toward the waiting sailor and helped her into the longboat.

He found it disturbing that his family disappeared so quickly into the heavy fog. He would have preferred to watch their departure until they were taken aboard the ship, until it became a distant point on the horizon. He flinched as he felt a hand on his arm.

"Come on, Jeremy. They are in good hands. Johansson is an able captain, one of the best. Let's go home."

Larkin had remained beside him on the dock. With a backward glance that was met by thick, gray mist, Jeremy turned and began to walk up the rise to the road with Larkin.

Many thoughts crossed the consul's mind, including that what had just happened was for the best. Women who were suited to contend with the uprooting of their lives did not include Beth Morgan in their company. He commiserated with Jeremy's pain, even as he did not agree with it. In kindness and wisdom, he would never, ever comment with his opinion, but he marveled that a man like Jeremy Morgan had chosen his particular life's mate. He had rarely seen such an unsuitable coupling. It left him in a quandary, as the tenets of his life were firmly grounded in faithfulness. Perhaps, in time, they would find a common ground upon which to base a strong marriage, such as he had with his Rachel. But as much as he wished for it, for Jeremy's sake, he could not bring himself to believe it. For the moment, he could find only one solution: he needed Morgan's full attention on their mutual purpose. And he believed in the solace of work.

"We've had little time to talk these past weeks," he observed, glancing at the other man. "I haven't had the opportunity to express my proper gratitude for your part in bringing the conflict between Fremont and Castro to an end."

"I didn't do that much," Jeremy said, checking his impatient strides to that of the shorter man's. "Nothing I did would have convinced him to leave if he had not been looking for an excuse."

"You are probably right, but then you did provide that excuse. I don't think I would have thought of it. Pushing down that flagpole was a stroke of genius."

Jeremy smirked. "It was an impulse. He had fixed upon the importance of that flag—and I was angry. It wasn't even reasonable. I was humiliated over Beth's presence, and I hated him. In honesty I would have preferred to direct my fist to his self-satisfied face."

Larkin chuckled deeply. "Well, all in all it didn't turn out too badly. Sutter has informed me that Fremont is on his way to Oregon. Meanwhile, Castro has found new meaning in his life. He is heard to recount, at every opportunity, that he was single-handedly responsible for routing the *bandoleros.*"

Jeremy glanced sideways at Larkin and smirked. "If that was all we had to worry about, we'd be in good shape. Unfortunately, it isn't." He noted Larkin's frown at his observation. "Thomas, I may have been somewhat distracted these past few weeks, but I was not incapacitated. I know what's been happening."

"You know about Soberanes and Estrada?" Larkin asked quietly.

"Yes. And more. Fremont is gone and Castro is wallowing in his imagined success, but we are in serious jeopardy of losing the dons' support. They do not trust us anymore."

Larkin sighed heavily. "You're right. Unfortunately. Soberanes and Estrada have been speaking out against us. They are gathering support to oppose any U.S. offer."

"And the rebels are backing them."

"Again, yes. And, of course, there are those who are pressing for association with the English or French."

Jeremy did not answer for a long moment. "Divided, we may yet conquer."

Larkin glanced up. "What are you thinking of?"

"Bring the opposing sides together. Make them face each other openly. This would bring matters to a head, and quickly."

Larkin frowned in thought. "That could work. If we control the situation, at least we would know what they are thinking, instead of all these speculations and rumors."

"There doesn't seem much to lose at this point."

Larkin nodded enthusiastically. "By God, I'll do it. As you said, I don't think there's much to lose."

Jeremy took a long swallow of aguardiente, wincing at the uncomfortable sensation as it burned down his throat. At least it reminded him that he could still feel. He rested the glass on the arm of the chair and stared into the fire. The tick of the clock in the hall accentuated the hollow emptiness of the house. Loneliness wrenched him, though he tried to ignore it. He was unwilling to give in to the feeling of self-pity that it would bring. All of his life he had thought himself committed, working step by step, to achieve worthwhile goals. He had fought injustice whenever he had found it, pledging himself even when he knew it could involve personal loss and pain. He really hadn't asked much for himself; in fact, he had never actually dwelled much upon his needs. Perhaps he had thought that if he did not do so, his needs would be met, without conscious desire on his part. He had lost something invaluable.

He could not make sense of the situation. His wife was gone, his son would probably never know him. Once he had looked upon his life with enthusiasm, promise, and faith. Nothing would ever become too black, certainly never more than he could handle. There were always ways to adjust one's life and control the outcome. Now the world suddenly presented odds that could not be countered, despite all his efforts of reason and will. He had never felt so empty and drained, so totally without hope.

"Senor?"

Jeremy turned at the interruption. Maria, the maid Selena had found to replace her, stood in the doorway to the small study. She was a heavyset, middle-aged woman, timid to a point that left him frustrated and irritable. But he stifled the impulse to snap at her, fearing that he would send her scurrying like a frightened rabbit to some dark corner of the house. He would be left to find her and apologize, and at the moment he simply couldn't handle it. "What is it, Maria?" he asked wearily.

"You have a visitor, Senor. Shall I show her in?"

Her? Jeremy frowned. "Who—"

Before he could finish the question, Ariana came into the room, nodding at Maria as she passed. "I will speak with him privately. Leave us, please."

Jeremy stared at Ariana as the maid swiftly obeyed the curtly given order. He remained in his chair, his rudeness meant as a rebuff for her own. "Well, Senorita Saldivar," he drawled. "To what do I owe the unexpected pleasure of this visit? You will forgive me if I do not stand. Apparently ceremony is not a consideration."

"It hardly matters," she answered, pulling off her coat. She dropped it on a chair and moved toward the fire to warm her hands. "I came to apologize."

"Really." He laughed shortly. His eyes dropped over her, noting the strained look on her face, the tight set to her body, and her brief, constrained words. "For what?"

"I was rude to you when we met at Hawk's Peak. I am sorry for that."

He stared at her. Suddenly the room filled with the deep sound of his laughter. "Rude?" He barely got the word out, he was laughing so hard. "Oh, for God's sake, sit down, Ariana!"

She sat in the chair across from him, her back stiff. This was not the reaction she had expected. "I fail to see what is so amusing!"

"You don't? Good God, woman, you wanted to blow a hole through me! But yes, that would have been incredibly rude, I agree." He continued to grin at her, then it suddenly faded. "Ariana, what devious little plot are you hatching now?"

She stiffened. "I don't know what you mean."

"Give it up, Ariana. I've had a bad day. I am in no mood for your games." He raised a hand as she opened her mouth to protest. "No, I mean it. Oh, lady—I do mean it." He was no longer smiling.

"All right, Senor Morgan, you shall have it. I am very worried about my uncle. I love him very much—I owe him more than I could ever repay. He is deeply involved with what is happening, and that involvement concerns me. I feel that I must do whatever is necessary to help him. He—"

"Bull."

"What?" She blinked.

"You heard me. Oh, I accept that you owe him a great deal. And perhaps you realize that; perhaps you even love him. The rest is bunk, and I have no interest in listening to it. Whatever you are up to it has nothing whatsoever to do with your concern for Mariano Vallejo."

"How dare you—"

"I did not ask you to come here. I don't want you here. However, it seems that you are. If you are going to sit there and lie to me, then leave." He smiled grimly at her flushed cheeks. "You are not here to apologize. You know that I was with Thomas today. You want to know who Archibald Gillespie is, and why he was in Monterey. You won't learn it from me—even if I knew, which I don't."

Archibald Gillespie's sudden appearance in Monterey had answered many questions for Jeremy. Posing as a merchant traveling for business and health, the thirty-eight-year-old Marine lieutenant had arrived aboard the man-of-war, *Cyane*. Apparently, Jeremy was not the only confidential agent working for the president; Gillespie carried dispatches for Larkin. The three men had spent two days discussing his mission, which included delivering letters to Fremont from his wife and Senator Benton. Jeremy and Larkin had exchanged speculative glances on that piece of news. When Larkin informed him that Fremont was on his way to Oregon, Gillespie seemed disturbed. He would have to catch up with him, he said, if it meant going all the way to Oregon.

Gillespie had spent the past four months in Mexico, and his observations began to fit pieces into the puzzle that Jeremy had played with for months. General Mariano Paredes, an avowed monarchist, had led the successful revolt against Santa Anna, and was now the greatest threat against Herrera's government. Gillespie added details of other groups vying for control, including the Federalist party led by Valentin Gomez Farias, Santa Anna's former vice president. But it was the information on Paredes that was of greatest interest to Jeremy. That, and Gillespie's observation of the present Mexican attitude toward California. Herrera's government would not receive Polk's envoy, John Slidell. They were too occupied with their own private interests, including attention toward Texas and the United States, to attend to distant California. Gillespie felt strongly that the revolution in Mexico would assure California's independence. Realizing the seriousness of the situation, President Herrera had provided funds to Paredes with orders to equip a force to subdue California. Paredes used the fund for payment of troops to attack Mexico City. Thus, California remained independent.

In their present mood, the Californios had been quite suspicious of an American civilian arriving aboard a man-of-war. Juan Alvarado threw a ball in Gillespie's honor, and Jose Castro spent the evening trying to ply him with drinks in order to gain information. Even Vallejo expressed an opinion to Jeremy that he was certain the man was a spy. At one o'clock A.M., at the height of the ball, Jeremy and Larkin secreted Gillespie out of Monterey, providing him with supplies and a guide to Yerba Buena.

Jeremy smiled grimly at Ariana's stiff expression. "If you want to tell me the truth, I'll listen." He paused. "No? Fine, then let me try. How's this: you slipped in and out of that convent, however you managed it. It became a convenient cover for more important activities. I don't know the details, of course, but you managed to involve yourself in Mexico's political situation when it would affect California. I wouldn't be surprised if you had been the mistress of some high mucky-muck who was in a position to affect policy. Polk's offers to purchase California failed. And, there was a revolution; in fact, rumors say that there may be another one. You were there at the right time and in the right place, with some influence—my congratulations, Senorita Saldivar.

"You're drunk."

"No, I'm not. Now, what else," he continued. "You returned and rejoined the *liberalismos.* The lovely Senorita Saldivar, niece of Mariano Vallejo. Who would suspect her? She is a woman, after all. A beautiful, sensuous, innocent who wanted nothing more than to learn how to be a true lady from my Yanqui wife."

He raised a dark brow to her cool expression and chuckled. "Well, what shall it be now?" He glanced at the reticule clutched in her hand. "A derringer in there, perhaps? Or is it in your boot? Dare I turn my back? Don't try it, Ariana. I would hate to wring that lovely neck."

She stared at him. As she had listened to his lengthy discourse, her emotions had tossed between anger and shock. Then, suddenly, a small twitch began at the corners of her mouth. Damn the man, she thought. Why did she suddenly find this interesting? "I'd like a drink," she said, relaxing back into her chair.

"Sherry?" he asked, rising.

"Aguardiente."

"Of course."

He returned and handed her the glass. "You are a hard woman, Ariana Saldivar."

She coughed softly, hiding her laughter. Waiting until he sat down, she sipped the brandy, collecting her thoughts. "Even if—your fantastic summations were true, Senor—"

"Jeremy."

"Jeremy. I would hardly admit it."

"Of course."

"However," she continued, "I could only wish to be the woman you've described. I do care about my people, and, in spite of your doubt, I care most deeply about my uncle. You are a merchant and your main consideration is profit. But I do not disrespect that. Larkin is like you, but he has done many things to benefit us. We trust him. Are you to be trusted, Jeremy?"

"I would never lie to anyone about my business dealings," he answered easily. "But then, there is no need. California is an easy country in which to make a profit."

"Si, it is. A land of plenty, which leaves it open to speculators. Men who are not so selective in their motives."

"True. And all the more reason why California must be protected by laws."

"American laws?"

"Why not? They are certainly superior to what you have known."

She let that pass. "I understand that you were in the Aroostook War, with General Scott."

The statement left him nonplussed for more than one reason. How had she learned that he had been in the military? This knowledge had been Beth's entry to an introduction, and he could only imagine what Ariana meant by mentioning it. But then, why should he be surprised, or angry? Women, after all, were the same when it came down to it. "Yes," he drawled. "It was quite a conflict. Brutal. Great losses on both sides."

She frowned with confusion. "Perhaps I am thinking of

the wrong war. It involved a dispute between your country and Great Britain over the boundaries of Canada, and was resolved without armed conflict as I recall."

Her observation surprised him, but not enough to make him into a believer. She knew about one percent more than Beth had. "It was much more involved than that, of course, but basically that was it."

Ariana was used to having men ignore her thoughts and treat her questions as if she were a simpleton or a child. But for that other, secret part of her life, her situation was no different than that of her sisters. But she knew how to use this cover. It was all too easy for an intelligent woman to encourage a man to expound his wisdoms and observations. And, if he talked long enough, she usually heard what she wanted. She had been stunned by his observations. The man was unquestionably dangerous. Yet, he was a mystery, one that intrigued her. She had not told Manuel of the episode at Hawk's Peak. But she often did not tell him everything; he was such a hothead that she controlled him with bits and pieces of carefully imparted information. In the end, Manuel was no more difficult to control than any other man.

But this man disturbed her. Increasingly, it became more and more difficult to believe that he was a typical American merchant. Perhaps she had not told Manuel about him because that would have left only one solution to Morgan's future—a quick and final one. For some inexplicable reason, she had felt it important that he not be harmed. And now, her feelings had suddenly become intensely personal. She stood up and began to pull on her gloves.

"I must leave, but I appreciate the time you have given to me, Sen—Jeremy." She paused as he dropped her cloak over her shoulders. She turned to look up at him, then dropped her eyes suggestively. "I would appreciate the opportunity to speak with you again, Senor. I must hear more of this aura of mystery and intrigue you have woven about me. It is fascinating."

He looked down at her with deep amusement. His hands paused heavily on her shoulders. "Of course, Senorita Saldivar. Anytime."

She stepped away from him and finished pulling on her gloves. "I understand that Senora Morgan left for Boston. Is she returning home to New York for a visit?"

"Yes."

"Muy bien. It is not good to miss one's past as much as she did. I hope that the visit will help her."

He walked her out to the hallway and to the door. "It is late—it will be my honor to see you home, Senorita."

She turned and smiled up at him. He saw the flash of laughter in her large, deep, brown eyes, and he was momentarily transfixed by her loveliness. Careful, Jeremy, he thought. She is a beautiful woman, and you are somewhat vulnerable at the moment.

"You are learning quickly, Jeremy Morgan." She laughed softly, a deep, husky sound. "Soon you will have the gallant manners of a Californio. But it is not necessary that you accompany me. My men are waiting."

"Your men?" he asked as a brow arched in question.

"Three of my uncle's vaqueros." She smiled.

"How disappointing. I hoped they were your fellow rebels. I would like to meet them."

"You do have quite an imagination, Jeremy." She stepped toward the door, then paused as he reached across her to the latch. Seeing her hesitate, he regarded her with question. "Is there something else?" he asked.

"A small thing. Only a thought, but one that has given me some trouble. In regard to our conversation: when the Webster-Ashburton Treaty was signed, ending the conflict over the northern boundary to your country, it seemed that many Americans did not cheer your Daniel Webster's efforts. Some looked upon the matter as a defeat, that too much land had been surrendered to the British. In fact, it was a Senator Benton, I believe, who wrote that the new boundary of Maine should be marked with black stones of mourning. Apparently, the man was quite upset over the prospect of losing any land that might come under the control of the United States. I wonder, was that Senator Benton the same Thomas Hart Benton who is Fremont's father-in-law?" She waited in silence. "Senor Morgan?"

"Yes," he said finally. "One and the same."

"Interesting," she said. "Thank you, Jeremy, for your hospitality. I hope to see you again soon." She opened the door and slipped out, closing it behind her.

Jeremy stood, staring at the door. "Ariana Saldivar," he said out loud, with a touch of wonder. "You amazing little witch."

14

Unfinished letters lay on the desk behind her as Ariana stood at her bedroom window overlooking the street below. Vaguely aware of a draft in the room, she absently pulled the blue silk shawl more closely about her shoulders. The past weeks had been much the same. She attempted to complete necessary tasks but her mind seemed determined to wander.

Ariana had fitted her life into neat little portions, each part to be dealt with in its place and time. Whatever effort was required to deal with each, she would find the inner resources. This method had become vital—the only way she could deal with the shifts in her life. One moment she was the obedient, loving niece, the consummate hostess who managed within stringent dictates to entertain her uncle's political or social friends. These, in contrast with the darker shades of her life: the whore, who gave her body for information. The cold, bloodless woman who controlled men who sometimes respected her, but most times obeyed her out of fear.

She thought of the innocent girl who had once stood at this very window, years before. It was difficult to recognize something of herself in the memory of that young woman. She could not help but wonder what she would be like now, if not for that night when her life had changed so irrevocably. Undoubtedly she would be married with a covey of children about her feet. A dona of a great California rancho whose total purpose in life would be to provide for the comfort of her husband. Perhaps it would not have been such a terrible existence, she thought, if she had found a man to love. But then, the odds against that possibility were too great to contemplate.

She sighed heavily against her morose thoughts. She had never been tolerant of self-pity, in others or in herself. It was a useless, destructive emotion. So why now? Why these lapses into indecision? She knew the answer, though she did not understand it, nor did she want to face it. She could sum up her confusion in three words: Jeremy Randolf Morgan.

He was everything she despised: a Yanqui speculator, part of the comforted American establishment. He had chosen an insipid, bigoted wife. From what Manuel had learned from the Mexican consul in Washington, he had even once been part of their military. She loathed him. So why did she think about him so much? Why would the thought of him enter her thoughts so compellingly and with such irritating regularity? She could accept the fact that she was drawn to him physically. After all, he was an exceptionally handsome man. His self-assurance, even his perceptiveness, though it involved her, made him attractive. Perhaps she should have an affair with him, face her attraction to him and have done with it. But would it end there? She had never had an affair with a man for personal reasons; she didn't know if she could handle it.

She turned away from the window with disgust. Ariana Saldivar, she thought, you're a fool. The last thing you need right now is to involve yourself with someone, for any reason. And a married Yanqui at that. She glanced at the clock on the mantel. Besides, it was time to dress for dinner.

She descended the stairs and crossed the narrow hallway to the study, pausing briefly at the mirror by the front door to consider her reflection. She had deliberately chosen a gown of soft, amber silk, adding a few petticoats to flounce the skirt, and a fichu at the neckline for modesty. She knew that her uncle would be pleased by the suggestion of a more European style, a fact proven as she entered the room. He turned and smiled, regarding her with approval.

"*Tio*, are you certain that you wish for me to accompany you this evening?" she asked, turning her cheek for a kiss. "It does not seem to be a social occasion."

"Nonsense." He smiled. "A beautiful woman's presence can be a great aid in keeping men's emotions in check. Tonight your presence may well prove invaluable."

She returned his smile with sincere warmth. He was a source of pride and admiration. He was educated well beyond men of his time, and he had a true passion for the future. She might not always agree with him, but she loved him, with the deepest, purest part of her heart.

He turned away from her and stepped to a sideboard where he poured two goblets of sherry. As he turned back and handed her one, she saw the concern in his eyes. *"Querida Tio,"* she said softly, "what is troubling you?"

"You always seem to understand, *nina,* when no one else does." He sighed with a mixture of sadness and regret. "This could be a very important evening, for all of us."

"I know," she said gently. "Everything you have worked for, these many years, is in jeopardy of failing. The dons no longer trust the Yanquis or their motives. But do not worry, *Tio.* I have faith in you."

He stared into his glass. "There are many who do not share my visions for California."

"Then you must convince them."

"Does that include you?" Before she could respond, his dark eyes turned to her, and she wondered at the glint of amusement they held. "I wonder, my dear, what you would do at this moment if I left you behind tonight."

She regarded him with some confusion. "Then I would remain, *Tio.* As you wished." His expression made her uneasy, but she tried not to show it.

"But then, how would you learn what you need to know?"

"I don't know what you mean."

"Of course you do, *querida."* He smiled. He sat back on the edge of his desk. "Ariana, I've known about you, Manuel, and Rafael for quite some time."

She could only stare at him. Words of denial rushed to her mind, but she suddenly knew better than to try. *Madre Dios,* she thought, not a little frantically, what was happening? First that damned Yanqui, and now this! "How did you find out?" she asked softly, setting her glass on the table. She was somewhat surprised by the calmness of her voice; her heart was pounding and she felt chilled.

"It doesn't matter how. I've known for years. I knew about General Paredes and the others. I was aware every time you slipped away from the good sisters."

"Why?" she asked breathlessly. "If you knew, why did you allow it?"

He regarded her silently for a long moment, a look at once regretful and resolved. "Allowed it? Ariana, it was I who arranged that first dinner for you with Santa Anna."

She gaped at him. "But how could you know—even I did not know what the outcome of that evening would be."

"Nor did I. But I believed that if you found yourself in a situation to discover things that would be important to us, we would benefit by it."

"That is why you sent me away!" she accused.

"No, *querida*. It was only later when I reflected upon what you had done with the *liberalismos.*" He chuckled. "You were only sixteen, but I saw so much of myself in you. I thought about the woman you would become—"

"The woman I would become!" she flared. "You let me become a whore! You used me. I loved you, and you used me!"

"No, you chose that path; but I never loved you less for it. In fact, I loved you more, understanding the sacrifice you made, the pain you suffered."

Suffered? For years she had held her grief privately within, unexamined, unexposed. Yet he had known and had allowed it. It had not merely been a personal choice, based on conviction. She had been sacrificed by one she loved, revered, and trusted. "You could have stopped me!"

"Yes, I could have. But would you have wanted me to?"

Dios, she thought, turning away. This explained so much! Why he treated her as he did, allowing her freedom that no other woman of her acquaintance could even dream of. Simply, there was nothing more to protect. She turned back, regarding him openly with the hardness that had become so much of her life. "What now? You cannot expect me to surrender my freedom. Nor will I concede what I am fighting for. I fear that we may well find ourselves at odds."

"I am certain that we will," he answered with an easy smile. "But you haven't answered my question. Would you have wanted me to stop you? Should I have brought you home, married you to someone of my choosing?"

It was a moment before she could answer. "No," she whispered. Then she managed to look at him. "No."

"Good." He smiled. "You are very dear to me, more than

you can ever know. And I am proud of you. You contributed greatly to stopping President Polk's effort to purchase California. That could not be allowed."

"But—you want cession!" His words jumbled beyond any measure of reason. "Why would you want to interfere with such an easy solution?"

"Because nothing is that easy. I was aware of what Polk was doing, and if he had been successful the result would have been disastrous. Understand this, Ariana, if nothing else: we have struggled against Mexico's domination and indifference for decades. I have fought, all of my life, to free ourselves from her. There is one thing that can throw us back into the grips of Mexican control, and that is the threat to our liberties by another government. The hardest thing to change, of all of man's emotions, are his loyalties. They are ingrained, and when he is faced with indecision and confusion, he will cling furiously to that which is familiar, even if it is wrong. If we are forced to accept a new master, we will seek the comfort of the old one."

She turned away from him, pacing across the small room. Her skirt brushed the floor, its soft, scraping sound the only disturbance. The thought struck her then, the similarity between her uncle's words and the things Jeremy had said to her at Hawk's Peak. And the similarity was true. It made what she was doing all the more important. "I will not stop fighting for what I believe in."

He surprised her with an easy smile. "I never said that this would be easy. You are the revolutionary that I once was. How can I not feel delight in you, in spite of our differences? Oh, you are wrong, but your motives are good, and I respect that. But understand, my dear, from this point on, I will fight you."

"Really!" She laughed brittlely. "You will have a fight on your hands."

"I suspect so. But for all that you have done, this is what I will give to you: a fair fight. *Nina,* I could crush you in an instant. I could force you into a marriage, or back to that convent, this time to spend the remainder of your life in total seclusion. But I won't do either of those things. I will leave you your freedom, with one word of advice: you would do well to believe that California's destiny is to be part of the United States. We cannot survive under Mexico's dominion, nor as a republic."

"We shall see," she countered.

"Yes," he smiled, "we shall. Now, Thomas is waiting. I understand that Rachel has planned quite a feast for us this evening. I think, my *liberalismo,* she will need your help in the kitchen."

His words gave her pause, and she glanced up at him with a glare, bringing a hearty, sincere chuckle from him that she did not share.

Jeremy stepped to the opened window, hoping for some relief from the stuffy warmth of the room. He breathed deeply of the cool, salty air while listening to the heated conversation behind him. No one had refused their invitation. Hartnell, Spence, Cooper and Garner were present. The Californios were well represented by Estrada, Soberanes Vallejo, Commandant Castro, and former governor Alvarado. Younger men, nephews and sons, had come as well. Jeremy found himself studying them with particular interest, wondering which of them were members of Ariana's *liberalismos.* One thing became quickly apparent: each had come to insure that his point of view would be heard.

Larkin had cleared the large storeroom of its goods, and a trestle table had been set with Rachel's best linens, china, and crystal. Dinner was excellent and the conversation pleasant, though the serious purpose of the evening was never far from anyone's mind. Then the moment came when Rachel rose from her chair, asking the gentlemen's permission for the ladies to withdraw. The tension could be felt in the air. Aguardiente was served, along with finely rolled cigars, but within a quarter of an hour voices were raised, all pretense gone as the men began to argue.

Hartnell stood to give his support to a British protectorate. She was an imperial nation, he argued, and California's people leaned toward a monarchy. David Spence rose to support Hartnell's view. His reputation as a God-fearing man became quickly apparent. He reminded those gathered that Great Britain would not sanction the abomination of slavery. Castro sputtered, rising from his chair as he demanded attention. He claimed that California had only one destiny beneath a ruler, that of Catholic Spain. Only through the bonds of religious belief would California find true peace and prosperity.

From where he stood by the window, Jeremy listened with a mixture of boredom and dismay. He had heard it all before, months before in the report he had shown to Revere. Just "sound and fury, signifying nothing" he thought. But he had learned that his and Larkin's concern had been justified. Fremont's activities had caused a heightening of mistrust and fear. Many of those who once favored the United States now looked for other solutions.

His gaze shifted to Larkin where he sat at the head of the table, listening attentively. Larkin must be as dismayed as he was, but he appeared to be listening with respect for each man's opinion. Perhaps that was the mark of the man, what made him uniquely suited for the difficult role he played. He had patience, a virtue which Jeremy realized he was sorely lacking. Then a cry drew his attention. Young Mariano Soberanes had leaped from his chair, his dark eyes flaring with anger at the older men who had led the conversation. His impassioned voice cried out: *"California libre, soberana, y independiente!"*

Well, Jeremy thought, smiling to himself. At least we have a fresh point of view. It had finally been openly said: California as an independent republic. The room erupted into a mayhem of voices, a medley of protest and support. Jeremy watched with interest, noting those who were likely candidates of Ariana's rebel band.

Voices argued hotly, then slowly, and one by one they drifted off. Vallejo had risen from his chair and waited for silence. Then he began to speak. Jeremy found himself listening with fascination, as if he were hearing the words for the first time. In a way, he was; the man's presentation was spellbinding. Even when his calm declaration for admission to the United States was met by a sudden uproar, he continued, bringing the gathering once again to silence. When he finished, there was a long, palpable silence. And then former governor Alvarado rose, his voice filled with emotion as he began to speak in support of Vallejo's words.

My God, Jeremy thought. Vallejo and Alvarado had been bickering for years, yet they now appeared united. The first *liberalismos,* who had once changed California's history, had joined again in a common cause. At that moment, Jeremy glanced at Larkin, meeting the consul's eyes. An exchange of understanding passed between them, and both men smiled.

As conversation resumed, Jeremy edged toward the door and slipped through it. The kitchen was empty. Apparently the ladies had retired to Rachel's parlor upstairs, a fact which he met with relief. He did not want to meet anyone just now. His thoughts were on the solitude and peace of the Larkins' garden.

The clear, black sky was studded with stars. The night was quiet, but for the faint sounds of men's voices carrying from the house behind him. He stepped into the rose arbor, the sound of his footsteps crunching on the crushed seashells accentuating the stillness. The air was filled with the fragrance of the first roses of spring that grew over the arbor, and he paused, breathing it in.

"You surprise me, Jeremy. Our future is being decided in there. How could you leave?"

She was standing in the shadows of the arbor, a few feet away. Somehow he wasn't surprised to find her there. He closed the remaining steps between them.

"Ironic, isn't it?" he said with a smile.

"Ironic? Why?"

"Because I left, and you would like nothing more than to be in there."

"Me?" She laughed softly. The husky sound of her laughter touched him with an unexpected sensuality. "There is no place in there for me."

"That fact must be very painful."

"Jeremy, you keep insisting that I have some deep, dire purpose for what I do. I can only thank you for bestowing illusion on an otherwise dreary spinster's life."

"Spinster?" He grinned. "I cannot think of a less apt description for you."

"Then you are disillusioned. My well-advanced age and unmarried state reduces me to that sisterhood of aunts, unmarried and widowed, whose purpose in life is dedicated to the protection of our younger women."

"You, a duenna?" He laughed.

"I fail to see what is so amusing," she said.

"It's all right, Ariana. I don't expect you to admit it."

"You are the strangest man I've ever met," she said.

"Strange?"

"Incomprehensible," she amended.

"A challenge, Senorita Saldivar?"

"You overrate yourself."

"Perhaps. But then, it is preferable to underrating oneself —at least on important matters."

She blinked. *Dios,* this man baffled her. He was always saying something unexpected. "What do you mean?" Suddenly she really wanted to know.

He studied her face in the moonlight. Her large, dark eyes were guileless. It was the first time he had seen them so unguarded, almost childlike. She had never looked so exquisitely beautiful, nor so vulnerable, and all temptation to tease her left him. "You really do not know, do you?" he said quietly. "You try to be so hard; you hold to it like a shield. It keeps you from feeling life, Ariana."

"Everyone feels life," she countered, disappointed in his answer. Not feel life? *Madre mia,* she had experienced more than any other woman she knew.

"No, everyone does not. You don't. You are afraid to." His eyes moved slowly over her face to the full, exquisitely formed mouth that was parted in a slight, tempting pout. A deep ache began to stir in him, regret blending with longing for something desperately needed. Without thought, he reached out and drew her to him. Their eyes met briefly, then he bent his head and kissed her. He felt her amazement, yet she made no attempt to draw away as her lips parted under his. He was dazzled by the softness of her body as it pressed against him, her tender mouth as it opened to accept his embrace, the sense of her submission and wonder. "Oh, Ariana," he whispered, kissing her again, drawing from the incredible sweetness of that mouth.

The first touch of his mouth had been met with shock, but her surprise quickly fled as her mind was filled with wonder. His kiss reached inward to consume every inch of her body. Tears gathered, slipping from the corners of her eyes as her mouth trembled at his tenderness, and she moaned softly.

The anguished sound brought him to reason. He raised his head and saw the tears. He touched her cheek. "Tears?" he murmured. "From such a coldhearted rebel?"

"You are making fun of me," she breathed. She tried to pull free of his arms.

"No, I'm not," he answered, holding her tightly. "I did not plan that kiss any more than you did. It was an impulse, for both of us." He released her gently, though he was prepared to stop her if she turned to run from him. The kiss had shaken him as much as it had her. "Come here." He took her arm, leading her to a bench along the path under a large pepper tree.

Oddly, she felt no regret for what had just happened. She didn't know what to expect from him, but certainly not the long silence as they sat, side by side, in the bright moonlight. Any other man she had known would have been pledging his passion and need for her, or begging her forgiveness for what had just occurred. She glanced up at him, wondering why he didn't say something. But his profile seemed to be pensive. There was certainly no hint of embarrassment or regret.

Suddenly, from somewhere among the flowers, a lonely frog complained of his solitude with a deep, rolling croak.

"I know how he feels," Jeremy said.

Ariana blinked at the outrageous comment. Unexpectedly, laughter bubbled up in her. "Are you a frog-prince, Jeremy Morgan?" She laughed.

"Are you looking for one, Ariana Saldivar?"

She drew in her breath sharply.

"No, Ariana," he said softly. "I am not your prince, though you deserve one. I cannot be, we both know that. But I would like to be your friend."

Burning with humiliation, she leaped up. He grabbed for her, catching her arm and spinning her back to him. "What makes you think that I need a friend?" she cried, struggling against his grip on her arm.

"Because you do, and so do I!" he gritted out.

She froze at his words and stared up at him, her eyes wide with wonder. "What—did you say?"

"You heard me," he said. "Oh, I know that it is not a custom among your people—or mine—that a man and a woman could just be friends. But I think we can be. Am I wrong?"

She slumped down on the bench. She couldn't think rationally. It was the most surprising and outrageous offer she had ever had from a man. Friends? With this man? With all that lay between them? She glanced up at him as he stood over her. "Friends do not kiss as we did."

"No, they don't," he answered wearily, sitting beside her. "Ariana, you are a beautiful woman. I'd be lying if I said that I was not physically attracted to you the first time I looked into those exquisite eyes of yours, when you fell into my arms on the Chesapeake. I rather imagine that kiss had to happen, sooner or later. Better now, here—" He glanced at the brightly lit windows overlooking the garden. "I really do not want to hurt you."

She caught her lower lip between her teeth, biting it gently against the confusion of her emotions his words brought. "Is that all of it?" she whispered.

"No. I want to take you to bed. I want to make love to you. But I won't. I think that you have known a lot of pain in your life from men. I don't want to be part of that." Her eyes widened with wonder, and he smiled sadly. "My marriage is over, Ariana, but I am not free, nor will I ever be."

She thought about what he had said for a long moment. "Why—would you offer me friendship?"

"I already told you. Neither of us is prepared for an intimate relationship, yet there is undeniably something very strong that is happening between us. I know you've sensed it, just as I have."

She held her breath for a moment, letting it out slowly. "Friends?"

"Friends."

It was an unusual thought, strange in its concept and somewhat frightening. Friendship meant trust, belief in another. She had never known such faith. She turned and looked at him boldly, studying his face. Perhaps he was right. Friendship was certainly a solution. The idea was tempting. And frightening. "What would you want from me?"

"Nothing that you do not want to give. Take it slowly, Ariana. Friends do not make demands."

No, she thought, friends do not make demands. But false friends did, particularly ones who had deeper motives. But then, there was no reason to worry as long as she was careful. He had discovered her secrets, but he had not told anyone of his suspicions. If he had, she would have known it by now. "Why not?" She shrugged. "Si, perhaps we could be friends. We might learn much from each other."

His easy laughter startled her. "Oh, Ariana, you have much to learn about friendship. I think you are going to be quite surprised."

15

The lumbering creak of the springless carretas contrasted
sharply against the cheerful sounds of meadowlarks and
poorwills. Ariana held firmly on Oro's reins as he shied
away from the oxcarts. Her pleasure in the stallion's eagerness blended with the feeling of immense peace that consumed her. Early rains had carpeted the valley with grasses
of rich, fragrant green. To the west the hills were dense with
oak and pine. To the east the barren, rugged folds of
mountains were fringed by chaparral and chamois bush.
This was the valley of the Napa, and beyond, the Valley of
the Moon and Sonoma.

Throughout her life, each time she came home, the
pleasure was ever the same: deep, fulfilling and rich in its
reward. The party crossed into the valley, through sagebrush dotted with rangy black cattle, past vineyards once
cultivated by the mission fathers. Beyond, the herds
thickened—thousands of animals parted lazily as they
grazed on the thick, nourishing grasses spring had brought.
Her heart filled, and she knew a moment of total contentment. Glancing back at Jeremy as he rode nearby, she
caught his eyes and smiled. Her gaze dropped over him,
proud of the way he looked, the way he moved easily with
his horse. She smiled, wanting him to see what she saw, to
feel the contentment, to know the pride that she felt.

Jeremy answered with a smile. He had joined the party at
Vallejo's request and Larkin's suggestion. He had letters for

Sutter and an intense interest in surveying Sonoma for himself. But Ariana's enthusiasm had been the final, deciding factor. The dons had been soothed for the moment, and Fremont was somewhere up in Oregon. It seemed that they might enjoy a moment of peace.

Suddenly he started, barely controlling his mount as the air was rent by the sound of bloodcurdling cries. A small army of riders swooped down on the party, accompanied by yips and whooping cries. His hand went for the hilt of his rifle. As he spurred his mount to catch up to Ariana, her horse broke into a run, rushing pell-mell toward the approaching riders. In moments, they were surrounded among the riders and a thick, choking cloud of dust. Then Ariana was beside him. Her hand clamped down on his arm as he tried to pull his rifle from the saddle boot. "No!" she cried, laughing. "They are our vaqueros! They have come to greet us!"

Dust swirled about them, cries and laughter rising above the tumult. Vaqueros passed before them in a celebration of dangerous feats of horsemanship, dipping from saddles to touch the ground with feet and hands, swooping back into the saddle just in time to escape flying hooves. Jeremy grinned, feeling somewhat foolish, as well as admiring of the daring feats.

It came as little surprise to Jeremy that Vallejo's return would be celebrated with a fiesta. In fact, he suspected that as often as Mariano was required to be in Monterey on business—and politics—each return offered the excuse for another Californio celebration. The festivities were already well under way. Sighing, Jeremy glanced at Ariana with a comic roll of his eyes. She laughed, edging her horse toward him. "Come on, Yanqui, and brace yourself—it's just begun!"

The morning after their arrival, Jeremy stepped out onto the balcony overlooking the large plaza that was the center point to the burgeoning pueblo of Sonoma. The plaza itself, Vallejo had informed him proudly, was the largest of its kind in California, comprising six hundred and sixty-six square feet. The observation had caused Jeremy to smile. Everything Vallejo did seemed to be accomplished on a grand scale.

In 1835, Mariano Vallejo was twenty-seven years old and the commandant of the San Francisco Presidio. It was then

that Governor Figeuroa ordered him to establish a pueblo
at Sonoma. He did so with a flourish, laying out a gridiron
of streets with 300-foot-square lots about the large plaza. A
110-foot-wide boulevard was built to provide an impressive
approach into the pueblo from the south.

Jeremy's eyes swept over the town from his vantage point.
Bordering the plaza to his right were the two-story homes of
Vallejo's brother, Salvador, and his *cunado,* or brother-in-
law, Jacob Leese. The structures, Jeremy noted wryly, had a
distinctive similarity to Larkin's. It was Leese, another
transplanted Yankee, who had acted as Jeremy's tour guide
since his arrival the day before. Once an Ohio merchant,
Leese had married another of Vallejo's sisters. The Vallejo
women, it seemed, had a penchant for foreigners.

To his left, east of the plaza, were long, low adobe
structures comprising *La Casa Billiar.* The north end of the
long building was a pulperia, or saloon, and a dayroom
where the soldiers from the garrison could play cards and
billiards. Beyond, both east and west, new structures were
under construction, future homes and businesses to meet
the needs of the flourishing town.

But it was the north end of the plaza that dominated the
town. The mission, San Francisco Solano, lay at the most
eastern end, then came the military barracks of El Cuartel.
To the west of where Jeremy stood, Salvador Vallejo had
begun construction on what he called his "post comman-
dandia." In the center of it all was *La Casa Grande,*
Mariano Vallejo's home, an imposing two-story structure
that loomed like the castle of some feudal lord. The main
part of the casa, with its four-foot adobe walls, was over one
hundred feet long. The upper floor was encircled by a wide,
covered balcony, six feet in depth. With a singular, wide
passage—which could be barricaded by heavy eight-foot
plank doors—leading from the front of the lower floor to a
walled courtyard behind, the casa was easily a fortress.

At the west end of *Casa Grande* was a guard house and an
imposing three-story, forty-foot high tower, *El Torreon.*
When asked about its purpose, Vallejo had merely smiled
and shrugged. He had always wanted an observatory, he
said. Observatory? For what, Jeremy quipped, to see ships
docking at Yerba Buena?

The casa's main living quarters were on the upper floor,
dominated by a fifty-foot long parlor which led off to other

chambers. It was furnished in "Down East" tradition: New England pieces of fine mahogany, paintings, and upholstered chairs. Vallejo's pride and joy, however, was his library, which Jeremy completely understood. Considering the disdain Californios traditionally held toward education, the ten-thousand-volume library alone set Mariano apart from his contemporaries.

Behind the casa in the courtyard were the kitchens, well house, orchard and gardens, and a long adobe building to house the considerable number of domestics required to run the Vallejo household. In fact, Jeremy was puzzled as he observed the comings and goings of the extraordinary number of mestizo servants. Mariano Vallejo's wife, Dona Benicia Francisca, saw his puzzlement and explained the familia's need for so many domestics. Each of her eight children required a personal body servant; there were a half a dozen servants each to do the cooking and wash, and a number whose duty was to grind corn for tortillas. Dozens were required for spinning and weaving, and more were needed to clean and tend the gardens.

Below Jeremy, the town was coming awake for the second day of celebration for Don Mariano's return. Smoke trailed from covered pits, evidence that preparations had begun before dawn. Covered tables were set about the treeless plaza, artfully arranged to accommodate the pockmarked landscape. The scattered, deep crevices, Jeremy had been told by Leese, were a result of the ongoing construction in the pueblo. When mud was needed for adobe, it was simply taken from the most convenient source—the plaza itself. Someday, he was assured, the community would fill in the holes. As Jeremy watched the ladies skirt about the crevices in their silks and satins, to the apparent unconcern of their men—and knowing the Californios' disdain for labor—he suspected that the repairs would not be done in the near future.

Facing the prospect of another day of festivities, Jeremy gave in to a yawn. He had played cards with Mariano, Salvador, Leese and Victor Prudon, the don's secretary, until a few hours before dawn. This followed a day of horse races, cockfighting, and even a novillada—an amateur bullfight—in the area behind the barracks. And now, he knew, it would begin all over again. His gaze shifted wearily to the boards that were being set up in the plaza for dancing. Nowhere else on earth, he mused, was there a people so dedicated to the pursuit of doing absolutely nothing, and doing it so well.

"All of this still bothers your Yanqui reasoning, doesn't it?"

He turned to find Ariana in the doorway. As she stepped out onto the balcony, his eyes dropped over the bright yellow gown she had chosen for the festivities. The close fit about her slender, curving body accentuated the lack of petticoats, her bare shoulders, and the deep neckline that outlined the full swell of her breasts.

"The only thing that disturbs me at this moment is the way that you look." He grinned.

"Thank you, Senor." She smiled impishly, swishing her skirts. "I shall take that as a compliment."

"You may."

Her forehead furrowed in thought as she leaned against the balcony railing. "I watched you on the journey here, Jeremy. You cannot reconcile yourself to the thousands of acres used for nothing but cattle—cattle that are allowed to roam free, to forage for themselves. No farms, no orchards —except those left by the missions. No cultivation of any kind. I rather imagine you liken our ways to waiting beneath one of your trees until it fell over and split itself into cut lumber."

He laughed, appreciating her analogy. "You are right— and you are wrong, sweetheart. These things did pass my mind, but I have begun to accept them; moreover, I have learned to respect and admire your people. Tell me, in the vast education Mariano gave you, did you read a book by Richard Henry Dana?"

Her face scrunched with distaste. *"Two Years Before the Mast?* Si, I read it. The man was a bigoted idiot."

"Perhaps," he conceded. "I particularly recall his opinion of a California don—Juan Bandini. He presented him as 'the best representation of a decayed gentleman' he had ever seen. He portrayed him as an accomplished, proud man without any occupation or resources. He even criticized him for giving a ship's steward the last coin in his pocket."

"And how would you portray Don Bandini, Jeremy?" she asked softly.

He shrugged. "Dana was wrong. Bandini was a man of

occupation and resources. He was the don of a rancho; his resources were thousands of acres. He gave his last coin because it had no meaning for him. It was only money."

She walked slowly over to him, with a warm smile. "You are becoming a Californio, my friend." Placing her hands on his chest, she reached up and brushed a gentle kiss on his cheek. Then her hand slid down his arm, brushing the white cambric shirt he wore and taking his hand as she stepped away. Her voice was husky and soft. "Will you dance with me today, Yanqui?" Her eyes sparkled with challenge.

"All right," he conceded with a grin. "Anything but the fandango."

"Oh no," she cried, laughing happily as she led him from the porch. "It must be the fandango! I shall make you into a *true* Californio, Jeremy Morgan, just you wait and see!"

A few hours later, he held her in his arms, gaining life from the steady excitement of the rhythmical music and the bold steps. The brightly costumed gathering stood aside, clapping and laughing, shouting their encouragement. Jeremy had always considered himself an accomplished dancer—of the waltz and other refined steps in polished ballrooms—but he had approached this particular prospect with heavy dread. However, the dance, like the people themselves, was infectious.

He knew, as his heels clicked against the boards and his hands clapped in the rhythm of the steps, that these people would no sooner laugh with cruelty at his efforts than they would refuse him a meal if he was starving and came to their door in the midst of a banquet. As the dance ended, he practically stumbled to the edge of the boards, and was met with slaps of appreciation on his back and laughter from the men. As he joined in the laughter, countering their good-natured barbs with his own remarks, an unexpected feeling settled deep within him. He almost felt like he was home.

Then matters turned serious as an announcement was made that the barbecue was ready. As everyone began to move toward the cooking pits, Jeremy held back. He had been eating for hours and had no appetite left. Suddenly, Vallejo threw an arm about his shoulder. "The first portion shall be for you, my friend! Anyone who dares to make such a spectacle out of himself by dancing the fandango with my niece, she who steps that dance with unsurpassed grace, shall be accorded the piece of honor!"

Oh God, Jeremy thought. It was a bull's head.

The pit was uncovered with great ceremony, and they lifted out the wrapped, steaming head, lowering it onto a plank. Slowly, the coverings were drawn back, to the accompaniment of sighs and "ahhs" of satisfaction. A spoonful of hot, steaming brains was scooped from the cavity and wrapped in a tortilla, which was handed to Vallejo, who passed it on to Jeremy. Fixing on the look of anticipation in Vallejo's expression, Jeremy also noted a gleam of extreme amusement in those dark eyes. With a deep breath, Jeremy tore at the tortilla with his teeth. Juice began to dribble down his chin, which he caught with a quick swipe of his tongue. He chewed, and to his amazement, discovered that it was incredibly tender and delicious.

"Absolutely wonderful," he declared with relief. Vallejo roared with laughter. Wiping his chin with a kerchief Vallejo had extracted from his pocket, Jeremy glanced over the don's shoulder to Ariana. She was smiling as she gave him a slight, approving nod. He answered with a smile and a wink.

Jeremy swirled the fine French cognac in the snifter, fixing on the deep colors reflected in the glass from the candlelight flickering in the iron chandelier above him. He raised the glass to his lips, anticipating the heavy, sweet aroma and the smooth taste as the liquor slipped down his throat. He sighed with contentment, appreciating its rare presence in his life.

He was alone with Vallejo in the library, enjoying a nightcap with the don before they retired. The silence after the past two days of celebration was almost heady.

"I am glad that you accepted my invitation," Vallejo said, rising to refill Jeremy's glass. "While Monterey is the hub, there is more to Alta California. Are you glad that you came?"

Jeremy studied the older man as he resettled in his chair. "Of course. It has helped me to appreciate the vast richness of this country."

"An answer, and no answer at all." Vallejo smiled. "You have seen as much when you've traveled to Santa Cruz for your lumber business. Now tell me what you really think.

You have been in our country for a year; more than enough time to form an opinion. What have you written to your president?"

Jeremy stared at the don, nonplussed. Vallejo's look was steady. Jeremy realized that he wasn't bluffing. "How did you know?" he asked quietly. "Was I so obvious?"

"Quite the contrary; you are very good at what you do."

"What gave me away?"

"My instincts. I knew it the first night we met. Just as I am certain of Lieutenant Gillespie." He smiled at Jeremy's alarm. "Do not concern yourself, Morgan. No one else suspects, of that I am certain. I would know it if they did. Socially, you have managed to balance your political apathy quite well with your consuming interest in profit. Very American."

"I should be insulted."

"Si, you should be. Just as I would be a fool if I supported the American cause believing that such ideals demonstrated the true American spirit. But the ruse works for you, as all too many are ready to believe in what you represent. Just as there are those of your people who consider Californios to be lazy and shiftless."

"Can you deny *poco tiempo?*"

Vallejo sipped from his brandy, considering the question. "The Californio's attitude of 'too little time' comes from the fact that we have too much of it. California is a land of temperate climate; it is difficult to starve here. Not impossible, of course, but difficult if one knows how to live off the land.

"This attitude seeps into all aspects of our life. Conflict takes effort. Oh, our leisure has made us a passionate people—passion for graciousness, honor, beauty—and our politics. But intrigue is met with debate. Compromise is preferable to rebellion."

"I cannot argue with that attitude, Mariano," Jeremy said. "You have created a civil government in California without any experience. And, you have accomplished it with a minimum of bloodshed."

"So far," Vallejo answered somberly. "And now it is your turn, Jeremy. What do you believe in?"

"I support the Larkin Plan."

"As do I. Which may prove that we are both fools.

Though I pray not." He was pensive for a moment, then leaned back in his chair and his expression lightened. "So then, what do you think of my niece?"

The shift in subject surprised Jeremy. "Ariana? She—is a lovely, intelligent woman."

"Si, she is that. And that is also no answer. Are you in love with her?"

"Don Mariano—" The man had left him speechless. "How can I answer that?"

"With the truth." Vallejo smiled easily, sipping from his brandy.

"I am married." Jeremy sputtered.

"I am quite aware of that. I am also aware that your wife has left you, a fact which did not surprise me. In all due respect to your lovely wife, Elizabeth was not suited for the life here. In fact, I do not think she was suited to you at all. Do not look so dismayed, Jeremy. I am a man given to blunt speech. I am a don. In the event that you have not heard—" he added, punctuating his words with a grin, "my word is law. What is the proverb: when at Rome, do as the Romans do."

"What are you suggesting?" Jeremy asked, totally appalled by the turn in the conversation.

The don smiled. "If you were a Californio, the suggestion would be quite clear. My niece is not likely to marry, in spite of the threats I make to her." He laughed softly. "Threats I feel are necessary to keep her in line. But, I am not likely to marry her to anyone. I would never give her to someone beneath her station, such is my love for her. Yet, I have other responsibilities, and they do not allow me to give her to one for whom she would be unworthy. A dilemma, si? Ariana is a favored child, I want her to be happy."

Jeremy rose, staggered by the implications of the don's words. He set his brandy on a table and held himself back as he struggled to remember the reason for his presence in California—his duty. "Don Vallejo—" He swallowed against his surging anger. "Ariana—your niece—is a beautiful, gracious woman. She has become a friend, and I would never dishonor her. Now, if you will excuse me, I am extremely tired." He nodded with respect and left the room, bursting with the things he wished to say in response to the don's outrageous suggestion.

Vallejo watched him go, noting the stiff set of his back.

Any doubt he had held left him. Smiling with satisfaction, he gave his attention to his brandy.

Ariana tossed restlessly and awakened, thoroughly chilled in the cold air of predawn. Shivering, she pulled the scattered covers about her and nestled down into the deep mattress. She tried to force sleep to return, but it relentlessly resisted her. Turning onto her back, she stared at the ceiling above her and the shadows formed by the graying light from the windows on the far side of the room.

Four days had passed since she had returned home. Four days to replenish her soul, which happened each time she returned to Sonoma. Yet, this time peace eluded her. Everything was familiar, cherished, yet it was also different, and all because of him.

Tears of self-pity pooled in her eyes. Angry, she wiped them away. He had offered her friendship and she had accepted it, with more eagerness than she wanted to admit. In the past three weeks he had given her a warmth and affection she had never known from a man. She had spent hours in his company, talking with him of things she had never discussed with another, simple things that she hadn't known were so dear until she uttered them. Memories of her childhood, fears, and dreams. And he had listened, with true interest and understanding.

Friendship? Slowly, over the past three weeks she had begun to realize that, for the first time in her life, she had fallen in love. With a man she could never, ever have. Her body took its own course, and for the first time she felt the deep, aching desire of a woman for a man. She turned in the bed, moaning softly. *Dios,* why now, why him? Men had touched her, taken her body, and not one of them had been felt except in disgust. For the first time she was regretful, wishing that she could offer a man the purity of her body in love. But it was far, far too late. For that—or for regrets.

Even if she could, she would be taking something that belonged to another woman—a woman who did not cherish or want what Ariana so desperately longed for. The fact that Beth had rejected him suddenly made her angry. She rose from the bed, shivering as the chill, night air cut through the thin, white lawn of her gown. She crossed to a bureau and pulled a shawl from a drawer. Dropping it about her shoulders, she sought a chair near the window, realizing that it was useless to try to sleep. As her gaze drifted over the gray predawn landscape, she was struck by the uncomfortable familiarity of the moment. All that time over the past years when she had sat in the early hours of dawn, seeking to calm feelings of repulsion and regret. But there was one distinct difference between those times and now: no man slept in the bed nearby; her body did not recall a recent touch that had left it feeling sullied. Instead, she felt empty and barren, needing a man's touch, aching for it. Wanting him.

Damn Beth Morgan, she thought. She had hurt him, and Ariana hated her for that, hated her for rejecting what she so desperately needed and wanted. Just once, if only . . . Her eyes rose to glance about the room as a small, insistent idea burgeoned. Impossible, she resisted. But yet . . . to know that love, just once.

Her mind raced with doubt, and she couldn't move. She swallowed heavily, unable to leave or to go on. Watching him sleep, she started as he turned suddenly, moaning against his dreams. Indecision paralyzed her. In a few hours it would be light, the household would be awakening. It was now or never again. She almost laughed, she was so incredulous at the position in which she found herself. Ariana Saldivar, with all that she had experienced, and she was terrified by this man. She swallowed heavily and drew a deep breath. She had never known love, and it was for that which she had come, and that which terrified her. What if it proved to be nothing more than she had known before? Somehow the prospect devastated her, more than anything she could contemplate.

Bracing herself, she thought of removing her gown, then decided against it. Leaving it as a small barrier against her pride, she approached the bed. Lifting the covers, she slipped beneath them. She lay still. Her heart pounded so hard that she wondered if it would awaken him. She stared sightlessly into the graying light of the room, listening to the measured sound of his breathing. Then he moaned in his sleep and rolled over, tossing an arm across her stiff body. Startled, she tensed. But when nothing else happened, she became aware of the pleasant sensation of his arm across her body. Perhaps, she thought, to remain like this for a while would be enough. Then she would leave, and he would never know. He moved again, his hand slipping up over her body. As it covered her breast her breath drew in sharply. Stunned by the exquisite sensation of this intimate touch, she closed her eyes.

Then she felt him tense. She turned her head to find his eyes open, staring at her. "Oh, my God," he groaned. He pulled away from her and rose up on an elbow. His voice was raspy, angry. "Ariana, what in the hell are you doing?"

Tears of regret and humiliation filled her eyes. Frantically she rolled away from him. An arm snaked out and grabbed her, yanking her back. "Oh—no you don't!" He was utterly furious. Vallejo's words came rushing back, even through Jeremy's sleepy, half-fogged condition. Astounded and enraged by the don's suggestion, he had found it difficult to fall asleep. And now this. "So, the don has spoken, and I am to take care of you. Very well, then let us be to it."

Unable to understand the way he was treating her, she began to struggle with panic. She managed to roll away from him until her feet hit the cold floor, but his arm dragged her back onto the bed and she fell against him. He rolled over and pinned her down against the mattress. His mind was still fogged with sleep and anger. Why was she fighting him? "Christ, Ariana, hold still!" he growled. She was gasping as she tried to draw a breath under the heavy weight of his body.

Now fully awake, he looked down at the bright, angry eyes that stared up at him in the gray light. The impossibility of the situation struck him, and he laughed abruptly. "It occurs to me that you came into my bed, sweetheart. It would seem rather strange if you were to cry rape just now."

"Damn you, let me up!"

"If you didn't want me to touch you, why are you here? Apparently Mariano did not toss you in here, bound and gagged."

"My uncle? Are you mad?" She began to struggle again, and managed to twist over onto her stomach.

"Are you telling me that he didn't send you?" Jeremy asked, breathing heavily from exertion.

There was a moment of silence. "This is typical of my life," she said, her voice muffled in the bedding. "Of my own free will I have chosen to crawl into the bed of a totally crazy gringo."

He stared down at her, trying to reconcile her words with

his confused emotions. She had done this on her own? The implications focused, and he suddenly became aware of the feel of her body beneath his, her thin bedgown leaving little to his imagination. Feelings he had kept tightly in check fought for release. His body responded, and he closed his eyes, taking a deep breath. Damn. "I think—" he said gently as he shifted, turning her over, "mere friendship is about to be rather short-lived."

Suddenly, hating herself for it, she began to cry. "Let me go, Jeremy, please," she said softly, tears streaming down her face.

"No, Ariana. Not now. Neither of us wants that. I'm sorry, sweetheart, I didn't understand." He kissed the corners of her eyes, tasting the salt of her tears. Then his mouth covered hers, at first gently drawing, then more demanding. She moaned as a deep aching need began to spread through her. Terrified of what she was doing, of wanting him so badly, she trembled.

"It is all right," he murmured. "It's all right." Then he kissed her again, more deeply, until he felt her begin to relax. Her arms slipped around him. He shifted as he reached for the hem of her gown, drawing it up over her head. Dropping it over the side of the bed, he returned to caress her body, gently touching her shoulders and the full, sweet softness of her breasts. He kissed away the tears that began anew, and he murmured gently, caressing her with his voice.

She had never felt such feelings before. Anticipation and need rushed through her body in sharp, bitter contrast to the emptiness she had always known. His arm slipped beneath her as his other hand roamed in butterfly touches that made her skin tingle and sharpen with anticipation. His mouth and tongue played with the corners of her mouth, denying a deeper kiss as she sought fulfillment, then teased lower to her earlobe, her slender neck, finding a tender spot that sent showers of sparks through her body. He traced a path lower, across her shoulder, to a breast as his hand cupped its fullness and his mouth claimed the taut, aching tip.

Her limbs were leaden with desire as her mind spun with the exquisite sensations he was causing in her. Never, never before had lovemaking resembled this. Where before there had been only revulsion, there was now a bright, startling feeling and burning sensations that brought an aching, exquisite ecstasy.

He sensed her need and gave to her all that he knew how to offer. He claimed her body, cherishing it, wanting her to feel. When he covered her, he took her gently. No one, nothing else mattered but the two of them and what he wanted for her. He responded to her soft sounds, her gasps of pleasure, and he built upon them until she cried out, a sound mixed with pleasure, surprise, and anguish. And then he wrapped her tightly in his arms, holding her as she cried.

16

It was midmorning when Jeremy left Casa Grande. He was tired and out of sorts, as much from weariness of the incessant prattle he had been subjected to all morning as from frustration over his delayed start. He had risen late, exhausted from the night spent with Ariana and his own confused emotions. He had no sooner appeared downstairs than he was beset by a bevy of young women: Vallejo's nieces and cousins. There was no polite way he could resist their attentions as they dragged him into the sala, fluttering about him as they vied to see to his breakfast. He had been appalled by the array of food as they set course after course before him. All he had longed for was a cup of strong coffee.

Finally, he impressed upon them that he really did not prefer their thick, sweet chocolate, and from somewhere a cup of coffee was produced. One taste and he wished he hadn't asked. He struggled against a grimace at their efforts to please, while trying to meet their eager, shining faces with a smile of gratitude. The thought occurred to him, at that moment, that there was something to be said for the custom of a young, proper woman rushing out the back door when a man entered the front.

He finally managed to escape and stepped into the warm April sunlight with a heavy sigh of relief. He struggled against a strong impulse to saddle his horse and ride into the countryside where he could be alone with his thoughts. Instead, he turned and began to walk along the rutted, dirt-packed road. Walking east, he reached the barracks, a long two-story adobe built by Vallejo to house the Mexican troops stationed in Sonoma. He wandered about the grounds which had finally returned to normal following the three days of celebration. Affecting indifference, he paused in the shade of a large, spreading oak and lit a cheroot as he noted his surroundings.

Buchanan's report had clearly stated that over a hundred Indian soldiers were stationed at the garrison, along with thirty to forty Mexican cavalrymen from the San Francisco Presidio. From what he could see, he confirmed Larkin's opinion that the pueblo was no longer a threat, as evidenced by the few, ragtag Indians who wandered about. There was a generally circulating fear spread by the settlers in Monterey and the Sacramento Valley, that Vallejo meant to defend Mexican interests from this garrison. The rumor could not be proven by him.

Mentally confirming the report he would send east, he leaned a shoulder against the tree, drawing from the cheroot as he enjoyed the moment of privacy. His thoughts drifted to Ariana, her sweet, passionate body, and the amazing hours of the past night. Once the shock of finding her in his bed had passed, along with the suspicion that Vallejo had been responsible, he had realized, with startling clarity, that he desperately wanted her. The fact that she had come to him of her own will had filled him with an incredible tenderness. He had made love to her, then held her in his arms as she cried with silent tears, declaring a deep, wounded pain that wrenched at him. And then he had kissed her tears away and made love to her again, slowly, wanting nothing more than to heal her memories. The irony of the situation struck him bitterly. When all was said and done, nothing could be changed. For them, there could only be stolen moments. Perhaps they should be enough.

He dropped the cheroot, crushing it beneath his boot, and walked on, crossing the road toward the Mission San Francisco Solano. A glance about the grounds caused him to shake his head. Oddly, he could equate his life with the crumbling mission. Well, as the poet Burns once said, the best-laid schemes of mice and men, go astray.

He would not deny that the hours spent with Ariana had been wonderful. He had needed her as much as she had apparently needed him. She was beautiful, warm, and giving. Her body was as exquisite as it had promised to be, and he had certainly speculated about it. Being with her had been like coming home—holding a willing, passionate woman in his arms. And that was what worried him. He wasn't home with Ariana, and could never be.

He turned, crossing the road. His eyes took in the single-story structure ahead that gave respite to soldiers and travelers. And it was one particular traveler he sought. Earlier, on his way out, Vallejo had passed through the sala. Jeremy had noted that the don neatly circumvented the attentions of his females, pausing just long enough to inform Jeremy that a particular individual had ridden into Sonoma at dawn, having returned from a bear hunt.

He stepped onto the boardwalk and opened one of the double doors, stepping into the large barroom that was the center of the hostel. He paused at the door, allowing his eyes to adjust to the dark room after the bright sunlight, then spotted his prey at a corner table near the back of the room.

Revere was leaning back in his chair, his booted feet propped on the table. Looking up, he broke into a pleased grin. "Morgan, well I'll be damned! Where did you come from?"

"It's rather early to be drinking, isn't it?"

"Not when you've been in the mountains for a week."

Jeremy grunted. "Care to share some of it?" He slipped onto the bench across from the naval officer, who at the moment was clad in grimy, fringed buckskins. Revere's chair legs hit the floor as he picked up the bottle and leaned across the table to pour a glass for Jeremy. "Take it easy—I think they aged this for about two weeks."

Jeremy tossed off a large swallow and shuddered.

"I warned you." Revere chuckled, leaning back in his chair as a boot hit the table.

Jeremy leaned his elbows on the table and studied the other man. "You look well pleased with yourself. Did you bag a bear?"

Revere grinned broadly. "A ten-foot grizzly."

"I presume that since you left me at San Juan Bautista you've had a few more experiences to add to those journals of yours."

"You don't know the half of it." Revere's eyes followed a buxom barmaid who walked by, her dark eyes flaring suggestively at the handsome Yanqui. "You know, Morgan,

I don't know what I really expected to find in California, but I must say that I'm pleasantly surprised. I thought that people here would be more like the Spanish, aloof and condescending toward us Yankees."

"And?"

Revere's eyes flared comically. "Well, put it this way. There's a song that sailors sing when bound for California's golden shores, and apparently it's true:

> Already the senoritas
> Speak English with finesse.
> "Kiss me!" say the Yankees,
> The girls all answer "Yes!"

"Revere, that's disgusting."

Revere's eyes narrowed as Jeremy glanced angrily about the room. "Morgan, you sound like a grumpy old man."

"That's how I feel." Jeremy grunted, taking another drink. The two friends fell silent, Jeremy enclosed in his morose mood and Revere waiting. Jeremy stared into his glass. "Did you ever meet Angustios de la Guerra Ord?"

Revere thought for a moment, then brightened. "Yes, a charming and cultured woman. Another of our Californio donas who settled well upon her Yankee husband. What of her?"

"I dined with them the night before our departure from Monterey. And you are right, she is gracious, and exceedingly intelligent. And very sad. Dinner conversation turned to what is happening in California, eventually leading to Fremont's folly. Comments were offered, opinions on how fortunate it was that 'such a difficult matter' was settled so quickly. They were platitudes, and everyone knew it. Then, in an impasse, she said, very quietly, 'And now it rains on the sheepfold.'" He looked up at his silent friend. "Joseph, what are we doing to these people?"

Revere regarded him somberly. "We haven't done anything to them."

"Oh, but we are going to, aren't we?"

Revere was at a loss for an answer. Jeremy leaned back in his chair, turning his glass in his hand. "On occasion, I used to dine privately with General Scott. Normally he was a reticent man, but when in his cups he would talk of his torments. He recounted, in great detail, the time when it was his responsibility to drive the Cherokee Nation from their lands in Georgia. Listening to him, I swore that I would resign my commission before I was ever party to such an act."

"Jeremy, these people took this land from the Indians."

"But I was not part of that. I am part of this now."

"Well," Revere sighed, leaning forward to refill Jeremy's glass. "Before you send a letter of resignation to Buchanan and Marcy, have another drink."

"I'm serious."

"I know you are." Revere studied Jeremy closely, frowning at the unaccustomed despair in the other man's eyes as he stared at his glass. "What is this all about, Jeremy? What has happened?"

"I told you."

"Shit, Morgan, you haven't told me a thing. This isn't about the Indians, or the Californios. Look, we've known each other less than a year, but I think I've come to know you pretty well. If not, we've wasted a lot of good aguardiente." Jeremy threw a glare at him, but remained silent.

Revere sighed softly, suspecting that he knew what was bothering his friend, but he hadn't the vaguest idea of how to approach the subject. Inside he seethed, furious at what that little chit of a wife was doing to him. He was tempted to tell Morgan what he knew of Beth, of the times she had swayed her luscious hips at him, or brushed her full breasts against his sleeve, batting those faithless, spoiled eyes. But the temptation passed quickly. He knew that Morgan would be stunned, or more likely would not believe him. It would be a swift end to a treasured friendship.

Revere had never been in love, at least not for longer than a week or two. But he knew that he was a romantic, and would someday, in all probability, fall head over heels with some dainty form with flashing eyes. At least he hoped so. The irony was that he could imagine himself in Morgan's dilemma; he had never been wise about the fairer sex. But that Jeremy should be so unwise was astounding. The man was a pragmatist. How Morgan had found himself led on a merry chase, then saddled with a selfish little bitch like Beth Morgan, was a fact Revere could only ponder. But then, he mused, "The race was not to the swift, nor the battle to the strong . . . but time and chance happeneth to them all."

He looked at the man across the table and offered a cockeyed grin. "Jeremy, are you needed anywhere today?"

Jeremy glanced up. "Not particularly."

"Then I'll give you a choice. We can go find a grizzly, or we can get drunk."

Jeremy stood up, grabbing the bottle off the table. "Let's go find that bear."

Fortunately, the bears had headed for the high country. By nightfall a campfire had been carefully laid by their guides. The vaqueros exchanged amused glances, stifling their laughter as they determined that the two Yanquis were not likely to freeze to death, and then retired to their own fire a distance away. They watched their charges carefully across the clearing as they fell into muted conversation, knowing that Vallejo had entrusted the well-being of the crazy Americanos to them. But they kept their distance, totally by choice.

"You're a damn liar, Revere, there are no bears up here!" Jeremy said happily.

Revere reached for another bottle from his pack to refill his cup. "Don't call me a liar, Morgan. Would you," he paused, hiccuping, "doubt the word of a naval officer?"

"As an army officer—in a country minute." Jeremy tried to snap his fingers but gave it up.

"There're grizz up here, Jeremy!" Revere said, sweeping his hand in an expansive gesture.

"Then show me one, Joseph. Right now, I want to see one now."

Revere grinned. "No you don't. We're so goddamned drunk, we can't even stand up. We're bear bait."

The two men stared at each other, then broke into convulsions of laughter, bringing doubtful looks from the other campfire.

They exchanged barbs, which shifted to bawdy stories, answered by bursts of laughter, one upon another until long silences began to stretch, as each turned to his own thoughts. Finally, Jeremy broke the comfortable silence. "You spend much time in Washington, Joseph?" he asked, staring into the leaping flames of the campfire.

"Enough. I live there, remember?"

"Sailors don't live anywhere."

"Yeah, we do. We've got homes. Family."

"You see them much?"

"Not enough."

"Do you ever regret it?"

"Sometimes."

"You ever been in love, Revere?"

"Yeah. About a dozen times."

"That doesn't count. I mean really in love."

"No. Not like you have. But I want to."

"Why?"

Revere turned and looked at him. "It—it's what we all want, isn't it? To love a woman, and be loved. Really loved." Even in his present state, Revere sensed what was behind Jeremy's question, and he tried to clear his mind, wanting to give his friend the answer he needed. "We can only try, Jeremy. If we don't, we'll never find it."

"And if we do, and it's too late? What then, my friend? What if we find someone we can really love, someone who needs us, and wants what we want to give, and it is too late? What then?"

Revere looked at Jeremy with confusion. The words did not fit. Revere stared at him, and slowly they began to assimilate. Comprehension dawned on him suddenly, soberly. "Oh, shit," he said softly. "We're not talking about Beth, are we?"

Jeremy turned to look at him with eyes that were amazingly clear. "No."

Oh, Morgan, he thought, you poor bastard. And then he almost laughed out loud. Why was he feeling sorry for him? He had been worried that Morgan would spend years in useless mourning. "Who is she?" Jeremy only shook his head. "Okay, it doesn't matter—though I have a pretty good idea." He frowned at Jeremy's profile. "You want my advice?"

Jeremy smiled. "From a man who promised me a bear?"

"And I'll give it to you, if you'll stay up here with me for a week, which I know you won't. So I'll give you the advice anyway. Take what you can get, Morgan. And feel sorry for the rest of us poor bastards who may never find love at all."

"Thanks, Joseph. I'll keep that in mind."

* * *

Perspiration threatened to trickle into Ariana's eyes, and she wiped it away with her forearm, pushing back damp tendrils that had escaped from beneath her hat. As she was thus distracted, Oro noticed the steer swinging to her left, and the well-trained horse lurched in the direction of the disappearing longhorn. "Good boy," she whispered, bending over the horse's neck as they raced to cut the steer back toward the herd. The longhorn was running hell-bent for a thick brush of chaparral.

Through the leather of her split riding skirt, she felt the horse's muscles bunch between her legs. She worked with the animal to steady him, using the reins, pressure from her knees, and words.

When she was twelve, Ariana had sneaked away from the casa to join the vaqueros. She had watched them all her life, and she had wanted to be part of their world. It occurred to her that she might not be able to do a man's work, and that she wouldn't be accepted, but those possibilities were not concerns. In one way or another, Ariana had lived her life on the fringe, never quite accepted, except by *Tio Mariano*. And from him she had learned that it was the trying that was important.

At first the vaqueros had been amused, teasing her unmercifully. Then, as she persevered, accepting their barbs and criticism without complaint, working until she could manage the cattle with respectable skill, their attitude began to change. Then loyalty came as they hid the fact of her escapades from Vallejo, and more importantly, the aunts. Over the years, whenever life became unbearable, whenever loneliness struck and self-pity threatened, she had escaped to the vaqueros. Their easy ways, their teasing acceptance bordered with respect and affection, the hours of hard, punishing work, never failed to cure what most ailed her. Thus, she had slipped out of the casa just after dawn, and ridden out to the herd in an attempt to escape from herself and the dark, muddy paths of her thoughts.

For so many years she had not allowed herself to speculate upon what it would be like to be with a man she cared about. She would not allow herself to think of what would never be, knowing that to acknowledge her need would force her to face what little affection she had in her life. The night with Jeremy had brought every hidden desire to the surface of her mind. She had returned to her bed before dawn, awakening a few hours later with a soft, happy smile. She had risen quickly, washed and dressed, eager just to see him again, to let him know how she felt, if not with words, then a touch or a glance.

To her dismay, she had been waylaid at the top of the stairs by *Tia Benicia,* who insisted that she breakfast with her in the aunt's sala. It had been much too long since they had spent time together, her aunt had declared, and Ariana found herself trailing after her while her thoughts pulled her toward the dining room where she could hear her cousins' laughter and Jeremy's deep voice.

An hour later, she managed to escape the elderly bevy to discover that he had just left. She spent the rest of the morning with her younger cousins. She tensed each time the door opened and whenever she heard a man's footsteps. But each time it proved to be one of her uncles or male cousins. Soon the afternoon waned into evening, and still he had not come.

She lay in her bed that night, staring sightlessly at the dark ceiling of the small bedroom, fighting back the tears that threatened to prove what a total fool she had been. It was obvious that he had left without a word to her because he did not want to face her. His departure carried the distinct message that she was not to consider their night together more than it was: a few hours of passion. She had been a fool to expect more.

Memories and recriminations lingered in the back of her mind, though she had struggled relentlessly throughout the day to forget them. She returned the wayward steer to the main herd, then rode across the meadow to the campfire where the second shift of vaqueros had gathered for a midafternoon meal. She slid from Oro, tying him to the cook wagon, then took a plate of frijoles and stewed beef to a shady spot under a scraggly oak.

As much as she wanted to hate Jeremy Morgan, she could not. In fact, for the first time she began to understand the Yanquis a little, though begrudgingly. They married Californio women and took their bride's lands. They sat over gambling tables, winning land, cattle, and homes with a turn of the cards. California was being handed to them, but none of it was taken by force—not yet.

Throughout the past night she had tossed in her bed, wanting to hate him for taking what she had freely given to him. The Californios made it their habit to give away what was dear to them, and she was no different than the rest.

Her chest was tight, and she swallowed against a dull, empty ache. *Madre Dios,* why did it have to be so wonderful? Better that she would have been disappointed. Instead, she had left that room so filled with his touch, his soft words and the pleasure, that she had deluded herself into believing that she had also taken his love with her.

She scooped up the last of the beans on a tortilla. It was then that she noticed a rangy hound who had been lying a respectful distance away. He had risen, with that infallible instinct that dogs seemed to have whenever the last bite was about to be eaten. Sidling up to her, the dog wagged its tail in a nervous whirl of anticipation. She hesitated, looking into the large, brown, hopeful eyes. "Oh, here." She shrugged, tossing her tortilla to the dog. It was caught in midair and gulped down with apparent relish. "If only the answer to my own dreams could be that simple," she murmured, rising to brush grass and dirt off her skirt. But the thought gave her pleasure that at least the poor dog had found a bright spot in its day.

She returned to the camp and joined the men. Their conversation involved matters of cattle, weather, and good-natured ribbing directed toward one of the younger vaqueros who was to be married in a few weeks. Laughter eased the ache inside her, and she regarded the men fondly, glad that she had made the decision to come. At that moment, she spotted the rangy hound as it approached one of the men, wagging its bony tail. Without pausing in his conversation, the vaquero threw it a chunk of beef. Then the dog moved to another man, and the action was repeated.

"Who does that dog belong to?" she asked suddenly.

Antonio Guerra, one of her uncle's best vaqueros, shrugged his big shoulders. "No one—and all of us, Senorita. That old dog has been around for about two or three years now." Then he grinned, scratching the hound behind its ears. "Never could understand this dog. It eats more than two of us put together and still looks like a scrawny old cur. Just like some people, I guess."

For the second time in two days, Ariana felt as though she had been used, and for the second time she knew it had been her own fault. When would she ever learn?

Filled with self-disgust, Ariana was still angry when she rode into Sonoma, sliding from Oro's lathered back at Casa Grande. She tossed the reins to a mestizo, who had appeared at the sound of the approaching horse, and crossed the space between the stable and the house. She felt grimy, covered with sweat and dust, and her thoughts were fixed upon a bath. She would have just enough time before supper, she thought, if she hurried.

She went around to the front of the casa. She was in no mood to face her cousins, not to mention the aunts. The women would be at the back of the casa at this hour, supervising supper as they gathered about in the shade of the courtyard to exchange bits of gossip. It was too early for the men to have returned, so she should be able to slip to her room undetected.

She crept through the passage running through the lower floor and slipped into the shadows of the stairs that faced the back of the casa. She had judged right; the aunts were sitting by the fountain that provided water for the household. She inched toward the foot of the stairs, then rushed up into the hallway above. As she crossed through the long parlor, she suddenly stumbled, wincing with a soft cry as sharp pain shot through her foot. Apparently a pebble had wedged loose from somewhere inside her boot to pierce the tender instep of her right foot. She hopped, wriggling her foot to shift the rock. Then, as she limped past the open doorway to the library, a hand shot out, grabbing her arm. She gasped as she was pulled suddenly into the room.

The door swung shut behind her, and strong arms went about her. Catching her breath, she looked up into deep blue eyes and a wry grin. "Ariana, where have you been all day?" His nose wrinkled. "God, you need a bath—"

"Jeremy—" she stammered with shock. Before she could say more, he kissed her resoundingly, leaving her breathless as her mind tossed with confusion. Then she remembered the disappointment, humiliation, and anger she had carried with her throughout the day, and her temper flared. She pushed her hands up between them and shoved against his chest. Breaking free, she stumbled back and cried out in pain. The stone had become lodged under the ball of her foot and it pierced into the soft flesh. She hobbled backward, favoring the foot, her eyes filling with tears of pain and frustration. "Where have *I* been all day?" she sobbed.

"What do you care? And what do you mean, dragging me in here—"

"Ariana, for heaven's sake, let me help you." He wrapped an arm around her waist and swept her into a chair. Before she could react, he had grabbed her leg and had tugged the boot off. "Your foot is bleeding. You need to soak it—"

She tried to pull her foot away from him. "Only if your head is under it, Jeremy! Let me—" Then she yipped. Through tears, she stared dumbly at his fingers which held up a small, sharp pebble.

"Got it," he said with satisfaction.

"That hurt," she accused.

"I'm sorry for that." He looked up at her, momentarily transfixed, then grinned. She was sitting there with her bare leg propped on his bent knee, smelling like horse and sweat, her hair hanging down from a disordered knot at her neck, utterly filthy, and as prim as a duchess. He felt his heart contract.

At that moment the door opened, and they looked up to find Vallejo standing in the doorway, one hand holding a book, the other on the door latch. His bushy eyebrows arched as his eyes shifted from his niece to Morgan, who was holding her bare leg. They both looked as if they had just been caught with their hands in the cookie jar. His chin quivered as he fought laughter. "Ariana," he said sternly, his eyes sweeping over her. "You've been out with the vaqueros again."

"*Si, Tio,*" she answered, attempting to rise. It did not help matters when Jeremy's arm went about her waist to assist her. She could not protest, as it would only make matters worse, so she leaned stiffly against him while trying to appear indifferent before her uncle. "I had a rock in my boot. Senor Morgan helped me—"

"So I see," the don said, stepping into the room. His eyes dropped to her foot as he crossed to the bookshelf, where he slid the book back into its place. "You are bleeding on my rug, Ariana. Perhaps Senor Morgan will help you to your room, where you may attend to it."

She wanted to murder both of them. Her uncle for his suggestion, and Jeremy for the amusement that flared in his eyes as he swept her into his arms. "I should carry you— after all, one ruined rug is enough."

She wanted to rail at him, and then remembered the

aunts. *Dios,* she couldn't let them see her like this! She nearly strangled on her protest as he carried her through the parlor to her room. Kicking the door shut with his foot, he set her down gently in a chair by the window. Glancing about, he spotted a pitcher and bowl on a table. He filled the bowl with water and placed it at her feet. "Put your foot in there," he ordered.

"I'd like to put my foot in your—"

"Ariana!" he chided, shaking his head. "Don't say anything you'll be sorry for."

"I won't be sorry!"

"Yes, you will. Now soak your foot. While you do, we can talk." To confirm his words, he bent over and stuck her foot in the water, then retired to the wide adobe casement of the window, where he sat down.

"I don't want to talk to you," she said, sulking.

"Yes, you do. You are furious with me for not being here yesterday." The accuracy of his words startled her, but she turned her head away, unwilling to look at him. "Fine. I'll talk, you listen," he said. "Ariana, when I woke up yesterday morning, I did not like myself very much. I've been attracted to you since the first moment I saw you, over a year ago. That attraction steadily grew through a period when I was falling out of love with my wife. When you and I made love, it made me feel things I thought I had lost." Her surprise almost hid a glimmer of fear, but not quite. He saw it and smiled gently. "I don't want to hurt you, but I do not know how to proceed with this. I wish I was free to love you as you deserve, but—"

She pulled her eyes away from his. She was filled with unspeakable hurt. "You—you should go now. I must bathe and dress for supper."

"Ariana," he pressed. "Listen to me. You are very special—"

"You have said more than you need to, Jeremy," she interrupted. "I understand, fully." *Dios,* she didn't want to hear more. She couldn't bear it. "I do not expect anything from you. I am grateful for what we had, but I do not expect anything more. I went to your bed because I wanted a man. That is the end of it."

Staring at her rigid profile, he felt as if he had been punched in the gut. It was a moment before he could speak.

"Then there is nothing more to be said. I shall leave you to your bath." He rose stiffly.

She watched as the door closed behind him, and then she slumped into the chair. Damn him! She swallowed back tears in huge gulps. Damn everything! Then she sniffed as her mouth drew into a pout. Ariana Saldivar, in one day you've been deceived by a dog, you've injured your foot, and you've managed to make a total fool out of yourself with a Yanqui. She drew a deep breath, letting it out raggedly, then sat silently for a long moment. Oh well, she thought, staring at the tepid bowl of water and her swollen foot, some days are just like that.

17

As Californio hospitality was embedded in graciousness,
Ariana knew that her aunts and uncles would be horrified if
she treated Jeremy with anything less than complete courtesy. Thus, under their watchful eyes, there was nothing she
could do throughout dinner but answer as pleasantly as
possible when he addressed her. She could feel his gaze
upon her, even when conversation at the large table was
directed elsewhere. She tried to focus on her dinner, though
she was totally without appetite, and when she ventured a
glance in his direction she found him watching her with an
infuriatingly calm expression. She had to struggle with the
childish impulse to make a face at him.

Jeremy was watching her, waiting. When he had left her
room earlier that day, he had been furious and, admittedly,
somewhat hurt. Later, when he was alone, he realized that
in his attempt to explain his absence and his concern for
their lack of a suitable future, he had been callous. She had
probably thought that he was trying to sever the relationship. Little wonder that her wall of defiance had resurrected
itself. God knew, she had spent enough years dodging
behind it, protecting herself.

It was an impossibly difficult situation. If he ignored her,
it would only confirm her opinion that what had happened
between them had meant little or nothing to him. Then
again, he could not be overly attentive, or else, in her
present mood, she would meet him with sarcasm. He saw

that the only option left was to make her aware of his presence—and of his continuing interest—while leaving her unsettled enough that she would not know quite what to do. He left the dinner table, following her into the parlor where the family gathered for the evening.

Upon leaving the table, Ariana was waylaid by her young, female cousins, who insisted upon a game of monte. They were giggling and chattering, and Ariana fought the impulse to snap at them and flee. But in spite of their silliness, she adored her young cousins, and not even her present mood would cause her to hurt their feelings. Thus, she capitulated and allowed herself to be led to a table in the corner of the room, while the men settled to their cigars and brandy.

The next hour passed pleasantly enough, as she lost herself in the game and the infectious happiness of the young women. Then, suddenly, she was staring at Jeremy across the table. Amid a rush of nervous giggles, he had taken a place at her table.

"Monte is fine, but allow me to teach you a popular Yankee game, ladies," he drawled pleasantly, casting a devastating smile at the breathless young women. "It's called five-card stud."

"Really, Senor Morgan," Ariana protested tightly. "You needn't waste your time in our company."

"Oh, please let him show us, Ariana!" the girls protested, their eyes wide with excitement above dimpled cheeks.

"If you wish it. And if he really wants to. However, I cannot imagine why he would want to participate in a game with women," she said, silently challenging him across the table.

"Perhaps I can teach you something new, Senorita Saldivar. You might even enjoy it," Jeremy responded.

"Play on, Senor Morgan—though I warn you, I play a good game."

"Not the one that I am going to teach you." He smiled as he dropped the deck in front of her.

She cut the cards, pushing them back to him.

"The rules are simple," he said, dealing the cards to the players. "One card facedown, four are played faceup in turn, with an intervening bet on each." He smiled at Ariana. "Of course, you can fold at any time. I advise you to play cautiously, ladies, as I play in earnest, even in this gentle company. And, I shall certainly claim my winnings." He smiled at their giggles, and his eyes locked with Ariana's as she silently met his challenge.

The next hour passed swiftly as a small heap of coins piled up before Jeremy, along with chits of paper. The notes written in feminine handwriting promised food delicacies prepared for his pleasure, and coffee steamed each morning when he arose. His shirts would be mended during the following winter. At last, there were only two players left at the table. The men had gathered about, having long forgotten their conversation as they were drawn to the laughter of their women. For the past quarter of an hour they had been watching, encouraging Jeremy with humor, fascinated by the game and the prospect of the prizes he had won.

Ariana glared at him from across the table. She had managed to lose little, holding back as her cousins had bet wildly. But she now understood the game, and she had begun to play in earnest. On the table next to her, added to the promises lost by her cousins, was his pledge to carry her bath water for the next three days—though she wondered, with some unease, if he had somehow managed to lose that one. But this bet was different. Peering at her concealed card, a king to match the two that were showing with an eight, she wrote her bet on a slip of paper and passed it to him. He picked it up and read it. Glancing up at her, he smiled appreciatively.

"Well, what is it?" Salvador Vallejo asked, leaning over in an attempt to read the note.

Jeremy placed it facedown in front of him.

"Do you accept the bet?" she asked.

"What is it?" Jacob Leese persisted.

Jeremy regarded Ariana calmly. "If I lose, I must leave California."

Gasps were heard about the table. Vallejo's eyes darted to his niece, filling with rage. He reached out to snatch the paper, but Jeremy stopped him, pulling the note toward him. "There was no limit set on the stakes, Mariano. I accept."

"I will not allow such a bet!" Vallejo sputtered, glaring at his niece. His eyes shifted uncomfortably to the pair of fours in Jeremy's exposed hand.

"It is a fair bet." Jeremy shrugged, then he laughed softly. "You might find it a handy way to rid yourselves of foreigners. And now for my bet." He wrote on a slip of paper and passed it to Ariana. She picked it up slowly. Reading it, she looked up at him with confusion.

"What does it say, Ariana?" Vallejo demanded.

"It does not matter, unless I win, Mariano," Jeremy said. He picked up the deck, dealing her a card. It was an eight. Then he dealt one to himself—a four of clubs. The room was deathly silent. Jeremy smiled. "The bet is to you, Ariana."

"No more bets," Vallejo said grimly. "Show your cards, Ariana."

Her eyes fixed on Jeremy as she slowly turned over her hole card. It was a king, bringing a sharp intake of breath from those watching. Her mouth drew into a smile.

"My congratulations, Ariana," Jeremy said pleasantly. "A full house. You do play the game well." Then he turned over his hole card. "However, it seems that I win." Her eyes widened, her gaze dropping to his card. It was a four, giving him four of a kind.

"Yes, Senor Morgan, you do," she answered, staring at him.

Salvador Vallejo reached out and grabbed up her chit. He glanced at Jeremy with amazement. Those clustered about the table waited impatiently, trying to see what was written. Salvador shrugged. "Tomorrow she is to go riding with him."

There were sighs of disappointment, and the group drew apart, suddenly disinterested in the turn of the game. As Mariano Vallejo turned away, retiring to his forgotten brandy, a smile touching the corners of his mouth, he caught Jeremy's eyes, and he nodded slightly. Noting the look of approval, Jeremy glanced away. This is not for you, Don Mariano, he thought, or for your plans. It is for Ariana, and for me.

"Why now—today?" Ariana asked tightly, barely controlling her anger.

Vallejo gave her a quelling glare. "Because I have not been in contact with my majordomo at Rancho Petaluma for weeks. It is important that these dispatches reach him. Besides, it makes no difference where you ride with Morgan; one place is as good as another."

"Of course, it will take a day or two for an answer to your letters. And I am expected to wait for them," she answered sarcastically.

Vallejo dismissed the comment and turned back to the work on his desk. "You made a bargain with Jeremy, and we are people of honor, Ariana. Be satisfied with the fact that I do not address the outrageous bet you offered him. I am still quite angry over it." His final words were said with firm emphasis, and she could only squirm uncomfortably, seeing no way out of the present situation.

"So be it," she said stiffly, taking up the packet on the corner of the desk. Without looking back, she turned and left the room. Changing into her riding clothes, she packed a knapsack for a few days and left the casa. Jeremy was already at the stable, saddling his own mount. As they waited for Oro to be saddled, she stole a glance at him. Then her eyes widened. "That is Taro, my uncle's horse!" she said, staring at the buckskin stallion.

"Yes, he's a beauty, isn't he? Mariano graciously suggested that I borrow him."

So much for leaving Jeremy behind, she thought, frowning blackly. Taro was the only horse that could outrun Oro. Piqued, she began to realize the depth of her uncle's hand in this.

"One would think that you did not want my company," Jeremy said in an infuriatingly indifferent voice.

"I don't."

"You seemed to want it well enough the other night."

Her eyes widened, and she gasped. As the servant approached with Oro, she grasped the reins and swung into the saddle; her only thought was to leave Jeremy as far behind as possible. She pressed Oro, pushing the stallion to a dead run, leaving Jeremy behind in a cloud of dust.

Sonoma had long disappeared from sight when she realized that he was abreast of her, pushing his mount hard. She saw his hand reach down and grab Oro's reins, and she almost tumbled from the saddle as he jerked and brought the stallion's head about.

"What in the hell do you think you are doing!" he roared at her. She looked up into furious blue eyes as he struggled to hold the frantic animal's reins.

"If you cannot keep up with me, then remain behind!" she cried, reaching to take control of her mount.

"Dammit, Ariana! Is it so important to you that you're willing to ruin a good horse?"

It was then that she became aware of Oro's heaving sides, and the foam from the lathered horse that flecked her skirt. She paled, horrified by what he had done.

"Walk him," Jeremy ordered, urging his horse forward as he continued to hold the reins. As they walked the horses, she stroked the animal's neck. The fact that she had almost killed her beloved Oro left her shaken.

"I might have expected this from someone who did not know horses as you do, Ariana. But then, I did not realize that you hated me so much," he said finally, his voice tight with anger. "Even to wasting a good horse."

"I did not think," she said with quiet anguish.

"Obviously. If Mariano had not given me his own mount, I probably couldn't have caught up with you before you killed them both."

She glanced at the buckskin. It did not ease her guilt that Taro was also lathered and spent.

When they had walked the horses for a distance, they stopped beneath an old, spreading oak. Ariana dismounted and went to sit beneath the tree as Jeremy gave the horses water from his canteen. A deep strain had developed between them that was even more difficult than the anger and hurt she had felt for the past week.

They were silent as they rode on to the rancho, the tension remaining under the surface as an awkward, lurking presence. It was broken momentarily as they approached the main buildings and she heard Jeremy swear under his breath. "I had heard that Rancho Petaluma had the largest private adobe in California," he said softly. "Now I believe it."

Following the direction of his intent gaze, she felt a thrill of pride and pleasure. Beyond them, spreading over the crest of a hill, was a massive, two-story adobe fortress.

"He picked a good location," Jeremy observed, noting the strategic placement of the rancho.

"Petaluma means a beautiful view that can be seen well from all points," she answered. "It was originally built to protect the area from Russian fur trappers and hostile Indian tribes. Come, I shall show you." She spurred Oro forward, feeling the exhilaration of a homecoming.

They passed an adobe structure which housed the Indian

laborers of the rancho, another large building which served as a tannery, and then a thick-walled adobe corral for the horses. Approaching the foot of the hill, they rode across a sturdy wooden bridge spanning a deep, running creek. Riding up the hillock, Jeremy took his first good look at the imposing structure, a perfect square. His practiced eye noted the defense of the fortifications, the few heavily shuttered windows set in the outer walls, and, as they rounded the building, the single portal facing a narrow shelf of the hill that dropped off sharply.

The wide doors were open, and as they began to dismount a man came out to greet them, his arms outstretched to Ariana. *"Saludos!"* he cried, enfolding Ariana. She returned the hug then turned to introduce them. "This is the majordomo of the rancho, Jeremy. Miguel Alvarado."

The stocky, muscled man turned to Jeremy and offered his hand. "Welcome to Rancho Petaluma, Senor Morgan!" Servants had already appeared to take their horses and remove their packs. "Some food, heh?" the manager offered affably. "And a siesta, perhaps? It is a long ride from Sonoma."

"No, gracias, Senor Alvarado." Jeremy smiled. "Actually, I would like to see more of the rancho. It is quite impressive."

Miguel beamed. "Si, si, I would be most happy to show you! Come."

Ariana left the two men. She was anxious for a bath and some badly needed moments alone. Perhaps she could face him again at supper, she reasoned, once she had time to herself to collect her wits. But she did not see Jeremy for the rest of the afternoon, nor for supper. Occasionally she caught glimpses of him with Miguel as they crossed the large courtyard, but the rest of her day and evening were spent in solitude.

Jeremy, meanwhile, was thoroughly enjoying himself. He liked Alvarado immediately, and the admiration was mutual, encouraged by the fact that Jeremy was so obviously impressed by the majordomo's domain.

The adobe consisted of four, hundred-foot-long, two-story wings enclosing an immense courtyard. The rooms on the upper floor opened out to a twelve-foot-wide, heavily planked gallery overlooking the compound below. With obvious pride, Miguel painstakingly explained the workings of the rancho. It occurred to Jeremy that if the Californio dons had "a disdain for practical affairs," the feeling was not shared by Don Mariano Guadalupe Vallejo. Set in the two-foot-wide adobe walls were long, wide rooms for every sort of industry: leatherwork—everything from boots to saddles—weaving, and metalwork. There were candlemakers, carpenters, and those who spent their days making soap from the *botas* of tallow. Many rooms were used for storage of the ranch's products: hides, tallow, and produces, such as barley, wheat, corn, peas, lentils, and beans.

As they passed through each room, Miguel proudly recounted the details: "With only two hundred plowmen, we produce barley of over seventy thousand fanegas—or bushels—and over five hundred fanegas of corn . . . our weavers make enough blankets to fill the needs of over two thousand Indians . . . the tannery makes shoes to supply the vaqueros and soldiers with their shoes . . . Indeed, Senor, it would be proper to call this a hacienda as well as a rancho, for we do not just raise cattle on Rancho Petaluma but produce as well."

In the courtyard stood the ever-present, dome-shaped *horno* ovens, and large, copper pots hung over cook fires—which Miguel informed him, with a wry smile, had come from Yankee whaling ships. There was a tahona, or grist-mill, and a blacksmith who worked beneath a thatched roof, manning a large, leather bellows. Another thatched roof located just outside the adobe's kitchen housed a cooking pit, where a full side of beef was sizzling over the fire. There were servants everywhere, scurrying about their duties under the watchful eye of the majordomo.

The upper floors consisted of the sala and the living quarters, Miguel explained. The south end of the square was used to house the more "important" servants, the north wing the rancho's guest room, the Vallejo family's rooms, when they chose to visit, and, of course, his own quarters, he explained proudly. It was there that he and Jeremy retired for some supper and "a bit of aguardiente."

Across the courtyard, in a large, well-appointed sala, Ariana sat alone at the long mahogany table as she picked idly at her supper. Occasionally the sound of men's laughter carried across the courtyard, and she glanced through the doorway which had been left open amid the warm night air. Compulsively, she rose from her chair and went to stand there, leaning against the jamb. Miguel's open windows glowed with the flickering light of a lamp, and again she heard their deep laughter. She tried to be angry that the men had left her to dine by herself, but she could only feel sadness. She had never felt so terribly alone.

Tears filled her eyes and she felt too drained and listless to wipe them away. Nothing made the least bit of sense anymore, not even the cause to which she had once devoted her life. And that was the worst thing of all: the feeling that she had lost her sense of direction. Her memory tripped back and she recalled a night from years ago. She had been alone with *Tio Mariano* in his study, arguing over a passage written by the English poet, Edward Young. Oh, how she had argued, with the fervor of a fifteen-year-old. She recalled the poet's words, and her uncle's patience in the face of the enthusiastic conviction of youth:

> At thirty, man suspects himself a fool;
> Knows it at forty, and reforms his plan:
> At fifty chides his infamous delay,
> Pushes his prudent purpose to resolve;
> In all the magnanimity of thought
> Resolves; and re-resolves; then, dies the same.

She had been horrified. So convinced of the rightness of her dreams, the certainty of accomplishment, she had been repelled by what she concluded were mere ramblings of one who had not been strong enough to accomplish his own purpose. She wiped away a stray tear and smiled sadly. She had been so filled with pride. She was not yet twenty-six, but she now suspected the truth of the poet's words.

She stepped out onto the gallery and sat on the long, wide bench outside the room. Turning her face to the slight breeze that lifted over the peaked roof, she closed her eyes and allowed the tears on her cheeks to dry. *To die the same* . . . words once rejected now tentatively accepted, with all of their sad implication.

She was so deeply weary. She had sacrificed so much, fought so hard, turning her back on a safe, secure life because she thought she could make a difference. Yet it all seemed to move forward on some unseen, uncontrollable mechanism, the dream crushed beneath ponderous, rotating life-wheels. If the dream could not be realized, was the life then worthless?

Had she suspected the truth, somewhere inside of herself? Is that why she had gone to him? A last chance to feel—to discover something wanted, yet so long rejected as part of the sacrifice? But direction escaped her, lost in the futility of wasted years, mistakes, and lost dreams.

She tensed at the sound of a closing door. Lifting her gaze she saw him across the courtyard as he stepped into the moonlight on the opposite gallery. Knowing that she was concealed in the shadows, she watched as he lit a cheroot, the flare of the match illuminating his face for a brief moment. He leaned against a roof support, casually smoking as he stared at some distant, unseen point, lost in his own thoughts. She watched him, wondering what he was thinking. What secret dreams do you have, Jeremy Morgan?

He threw down the cheroot and crushed it with his foot, then began to walk down the length of the gallery. She felt a surging rise of panic. He would round the far corner, then walk along the adjoining side to his quarters, which were less than twenty feet from where she sat. She could not move or he would see her. If she were to dart back into the sala, he would think she was fleeing from him. And she would be, she thought, with an unhappy smile. She realized, not without irony, that for the first time in her life she knew how her nieces and cousins felt when an attractive man entered their presence. She, a twenty-five-year-old woman who was no innocent.

As he approached his door, he paused and looked directly at her. She would have given a good deal to see his expression, but it was hidden in the shadows. She offered what she hoped was a pleasant, noncommittal smile. As he paused she glanced away, holding her breath as his footsteps approached. Her heart began to pound in anticipation; her neck and cheeks grew warm. Then she heard his door close. Her head jerked about and she stared, not believing. *Dios!* He hadn't even said goodnight! She leaped from the bench and fled into the sala. Slamming the door behind her, she winced at the reverberating sound. *Dios,* he probably heard that. *Madre,* what was happening to her?

18

Ariana kept to her room throughout the next day. It began with a simple need for solitude, a time to sort her feelings. She was determined to rid herself of the complications that had changed her life, to regain the single-minded direction that had filled her life since her second year in Mexico. By midmorning she found herself wallowing in self-pity.

Self-pity was an underrated emotion, she reasoned. There were moments when it could be quite satisfying. She deserved it; who was to say that she didn't? Certainly not that pig-licking, reprobate Yanqui! Just once in her life she had wanted something for herself; but nothing had changed. Apparently it wasn't allowed; not without humiliation and disappointment.

She soaked in a bath, crying. She ate the meals brought to her, alternately devouring them with relish and picking at them through a blur of tears. She rummaged through her wardrobe, rejecting most of the garments left at the rancho for her use, tossing them about the room in a disarray that matched her mood. By early evening, the room was in shambles. She glanced about at the scattered clothes and abandoned meals and felt a contrary pleasure. Flinging herself back on the bed, she cursed everyone who ever had claimed control over her life.

At dusk, the door swung open, and she turned her head at the sound. Jeremy was shadowed in the dim light from the lamp that one of the servants had lit when she had brought dinner.

He glanced about the room with disgust. "This room is a pigsty." His gaze shifted back to where she remained sprawled on the bed. "I assume that you feel better?" Then, before she could respond, he continued, "You have had enough time to wallow, Ariana. A supper will be served in fifteen minutes. I expect you to dress and present yourself appropriately. If you are not at the table by then, I shall return and dress you myself." The door closed behind him.

Sitting up, she glared at the closed door. Who did he think he was! Misbegotten foreigner, seducer, pillager—goddamn Yanqui! Supper? With him? Let him come back, she'd show him what. Then it struck her that he could do exactly what he promised. She couldn't resist him physically, but she wouldn't submit to his insufferable male dominance! Slowly, a smile crept over her mouth. On the other hand, she had learned other devices—oh, how she had learned them! And what better time than this to apply her skills.

Jeremy poured two glasses, one of sherry, the other of brandy for the bracer he suddenly needed. The closed door to Ariana's bedroom became a challenge, and he steadied himself against what would soon emerge. His thoughts turned back to the moment he had ridden in pursuit, hell-bent to catch up with her, when they had left Sonoma. He had been furious with her abuse of the horses and fed up with her petulant attitude.

Thus, he had become determined to ignore her for a while; it seemed a safe, noncombative alternative to throttling her. It wasn't hard to guess what her problem was, but he needed time to decide what to do about it. Vallejo's suggestion had become less and less outrageous upon reflection. The night in the mountains with Revere on their ridiculous bear hunt, and mostly Ariana herself, had made the decision for him. But he knew that before Ariana could begin to accept what he could offer her, she had to begin to accept herself. He had not expected to start quite the way that he had, but now he fully intended to carry his plan through.

He heard the door open, and he braced himself. Turning, he caught his breath, then expelled it slowly. What in the hell did the little chit think she was doing? She had dressed, all right, in a provocative gown of red satin, trimmed in jet black lace. The bodice was skintight and cut so low that her slightest breath would threaten what little was left of her modesty. As she stepped closer, his eyes widened slightly. Damn if he couldn't see the top of her nipples. Her tactics were blatantly clear, and the battle lines were drawn. However, while it was a war he fully intended to win, he was quite interested in observing her maneuvers.

"Is that sherry for me?" she asked in a husky voice.

"Yes." His gaze slipped over her gown. "Or would you prefer something stronger?"

"No, the sherry is fine."

She sipped the wine as she looked up at him through thick, lowered lashes and noted the glazed indifference of his expression. So, he was not going to be an easy mark. Actually she was not surprised. But she promised herself that by the end of the evening he would either be wrapped around her little finger, or he would be willing to remove himself from her life, once and for all. Either way, she would win. She would finally be able to put her life back together and concentrate on truly important matters!

The outside door to the sala opened, and two servants came in with their supper. One of the women happened to glance in their direction, and her eyes widened with shock at Ariana's gown. She stumbled, nearly dropping her tray. Her fellow kitchen maid had set her own tray on the table and turned to help, when she, too, spied her mistress's décolletage. She gaped, her young face flushing to a deep, rosy red.

"That will be all. I will serve Senor Morgan myself!" Ariana said sharply. She heaved a sigh, realizing that gossip would soon sweep through the kitchen and throughout the rancho.

"Careful."

She looked up, perplexed, and found Jeremy observing her neckline.

"I wouldn't take any more deep breaths, if I were you."

She flared at the deep amusement in his eyes and turned away, crossing to the table where she began to set out their supper of roasted beef, enchiladas, and fried oysters.

"Do you play?"

She blinked. Straightening, she turned back to him. "What?"

He repeated the question, while his mouth worked with laughter. Then he nodded to the large piano in the corner.

"Oh," she said, and laughed softly. "Yes. That is one of only three pianos in California; my uncle is very proud of it. When he learned that no one in Sonoma knew how to play, he hired a music teacher from Fort Ross. For giving us four years of lessons, Professor Hoeppener was paid with a three-thousand-acre rancho."

"Not a bad bargain." Jeremy smiled. "Perhaps, after supper, you could entertain me."

She answered with a slight lift of a well-arched brow. Her mouth turned up into a slow, seductive smile. "Perhaps, if you wish it. I am quite accomplished."

He placed his brandy on a table and walked slowly toward her. "I know," he said. His eyes touched on her full breasts before sweeping over her body. As he came closer, his eyes grew warm with promise, locking with her own steady gaze. She felt her heart pound, and her lips parted, anticipating his kiss. As ever, she thought, it was all too easy.

"Let's eat." He reached behind her and pulled back her chair.

"Si, of course," she stammered, momentarily flustered.

He took the chair next to her and poured the wine. Then, without hesitation, he began to devour his meal with considerable gusto. After a moment he glanced up at her stiff expression. "Not hungry?" he asked, chewing.

"Not particularly."

"Too bad. It's delicious." He grunted, taking another bite. "Quite good. Although—" he glanced at her gown. "I can understand why your appetite would be stunted. I'm surprised that you can breathe in that thing. In the east, Ariana, such gowns are worn only at balls when ladies expect to nibble from buffet tables—standing up. Although, in any case, that one is a mite low for good taste."

"I do not need a lecture on fashion from you!" she said, bristling.

He glanced at her and shrugged. "Have it your way. Since it's just the two of us, it really doesn't matter. But I caution you, Ariana," he said, taking a sip of wine. "Do not wear that gown, or any other like it, except when we are alone."

She gasped with outrage at the calmly given order. The reaction was a mistake. Calmly, he reached over and yanked the bodice back up to cover an exposed breast. "Modesty, sweetness." Then he returned his attention to the meal.

It took her a moment to regain her ability to speak. "Who do you think you are? Are you telling me how to dress, and whom I may or may not dress for? How dare you assume this proprietary attitude!"

"Those are four questions; which would you like for me to answer first?" he said, taking a large bite of enchilada.

"The questions were rhetorical! The point is obvious!"

"The questions were not rhetorical. I am the man whose bed you crawled into. You cannot ignore what happened between us that night, no matter how hard you may try. It won't go away, and we're going to face it." He pushed his plate away, pulling his wineglass toward him as he leaned back in his chair and regarded her with a steady gaze. "When you walked through that door just now, I was tempted to let you play your game. In honesty, I was intrigued to see how you would do it. But let's get one thing clear, once and for all. I did not ask you to come through my bedroom door, but you did. And now, without question I feel a certain—proprietary interest, like it or not."

"And if I choose not to like it?"

"Why would you?"

The question left her breathless. "You mean, why would a whore be averse to the attentions of a man—any man?" she suggested tightly.

"No, that's not what I meant," he answered calmly, swirling his glass. "Ariana, what is this fixation you have on your past?"

She frowned, confused by the question. "It is not a fixation, it is merely a fact. Can you deny your past, Jeremy?" she added defensively. "Can you forget your wife so easily?"

"No, I have not forgotten her."

"Nor the fact that you are married?"

"Nor the fact that I am married. The society I come from is not so different from the one you know, Ariana. Divorce is totally unacceptable. Not for the religious reasons of your people, but for social ones. If I were to divorce Beth, she would become an outcast. It would destroy her. However, among our social milieu, separation is a civilized and totally accepted option."

"If Beth came back to you tomorrow, would you resume your life together?"

"She won't."

"But if she did?" she pressed.

"My opinion that she won't is not merely wishful thinking. Our marriage was a disaster from the beginning. In this, perhaps, Beth was much wiser than I. She made the decision to leave, and I accepted it. We both knew that if we remained together, we would destroy each other."

"What will you do now?" she asked softly. Suddenly she really wanted to know.

"The same as you, sweetheart." He smiled. "Get on with it. That is the only choice we have, isn't it? Put on a brave face and discover what is ahead."

"Bits and pieces," she murmured.

"Yes, that, and perhaps much more." She looked up to find him watching her. "I would like to think that there will be much more for both of us. I think we deserve it."

Her eyes widened, and she could only stare at him. It was a thought that had never occurred to her before. So simple, yet beyond her—that she deserved to be happy, to be loved.

He watched her stricken expression and smiled gently. "Ariana, first you have to give yourself permission."

"Permission?"

"Yes. Permission to believe that you deserve this. You allowed yourself to believe in causes; you gave up everything for them. Why can't you believe in yourself, in your right to find some happiness?"

"To believe that I deserve it," she said absently, lost in thought. His words were frightening.

"Well? Are you going to play that thing for me? You did promise, as I recall."

She glanced up, her eyes fixing on his smile. This evening was certainly not turning out as she had planned it. But then, nothing had been since the moment she had met him. She realized that he was waiting. Yes, she would play for him; at least that would give her time to compose herself.

She smiled and rose from her chair, crossing the long room to the piano. As she stared at the keys, wondering what she might play for him, she heard him settling in a chair near her. Avoiding his gaze, she began to play the first thing that came to mind, a Mozart concerto that she particularly loved. As she played, she began to deal with the things he had said during dinner.

How could she be so angry with the man, then love him so

much the next moment? The night before, when he had shut the door to his room, she had felt that he had closed it against her, against her love, and all that she had needed, wanted, and hoped for from him. Yet tonight, that was what he was offering her, plainly and without pretense or apology. Give herself permission to be happy, he had said. But his love frightened her. It made her vulnerable.

Lost in her thoughts, she was unaware of the moment when he came to stand behind her. "You play beautifully," he said quietly as she played the final notes. "But there is a terrible sadness in it."

He laid his hands on her shoulders, and she trembled. He felt her response and let his hands slip to her bare arms above the gown, drawing her up from the piano stool. "I never meant to hurt you, Ariana, never," he said softly. "On my life, I only want to love you. You have to trust someone, and I want that person to be me." Gently caressing her shoulders, he dipped his mouth to the tender spot at the base of her neck. Her breath drew in sharply and she closed her eyes, leaning back against him as doubt gave way to her deep, growing need of him.

"This gown does have definite advantages," he murmured. His hands slipped around her, covering the full swells of her breasts above the lace. Then they moved downward, effortlessly pushing the fabric before them. His hands slid beneath her breasts as his thumbs began to tease her nipples, which tightened swiftly in response. She moaned softly, leaning her head back against his shoulder.

He watched her, his own pulse quickening at her soft moan, at the sight and feel of her satiny flesh beneath his hands, the taut peaks of her breasts arching to his attentions. "No darkened room tonight, Ariana," he said softly. "No fear of discovery. Just our own, long, leisurely time."

She sighed softly, and he smiled at her apparent acceptance. He was determined that, by morning, Ariana Saldivar would no longer think of herself as anything but a beautiful, desirable woman. He lifted her into his arms over the stool and set her down before him. "Do you want me to make love to you, Ariana?"

She opened her eyes with confusion. He was watching her steadily. He was asking, not demanding? "Si—yes," she said, her voice catching.

"Are you sure?"

And then she realized that she had a right to decide. "Oh, yes. I am sure," she said softly, unaware that her heart was in her eyes.

He drew her to him, folding her into his arms with a kiss. At first gentle and encouraging, it deepened, drawing from her a response that left her heart pounding. He drew away slightly, his mouth leaving hers to travel to the corners of her mouth and eyes in light, butterfly kisses.

"Dios," she whispered. "Love me, Jeremy—"

"I plan to, sweetheart." He kissed her again, gently. "We have all night." One, he hoped, that would be healing as well as satisfying.

He was enough of an expert on woman's garments, at least in regard to their removal, to know that his plunder would now prove more difficult. He had never been a particular fan of whalebone stays, and knew that the gown had been pushed as far as it could go. Viewing the prospect of an endless row of tiny buttons at her back, he reached behind her and grasped the fastenings in his hands. With a quick jerk he ripped the dress open. The rending sound caused her eyes to flare open with shock. "I don't much care for this gown anyway." He grinned. "It isn't nearly good enough for you."

The comic gleam in his eyes caught her humor and, in spite of her initial shock, she laughed. The throaty, deep sound reverberated through his senses, reacting with intense pleasure in his groin. "I trust that you can breathe now," he said. But he did not give her a chance to respond, having no intention of relinquishing control of the situation. His fingers caught under the sleeves about her shoulders, and he drew them down, slowly and deliberately, as he watched the progressive departure of the remaining fabric. He knew that she was watching his reaction as her body was revealed, and he made no attempt to hide his pleasure. He pushed the gown over her hips, where it descended to a silken pile on the floor about their feet. Then he swept her into his arms and carried her into the bedroom, closing the door behind him with his foot.

A gentle breeze from the open window played across their bodies, adding to the exquisite sensations of their lovemaking. Ariana had never felt such total and consuming emotion. That first night with him had been one of discovery, but a mere promise of what she was feeling now. She was stunned by the feelings his hands and mouth evoked as they played over her body. Memories of men in her past faded against the pure, sensual pleasure she was feeling, and her mind spun with wonder at the difference between this man and the others.

He rose up above her on his elbows, kissing her tenderly in light touches around her full, swollen mouth. "Your body is delicious, love, just like the rest of you," he murmured, burying his face in the nape of her neck.

She squirmed against the tickling sensation. "The rest of me?" She laughed huskily. "What is left?"

He answered between light, tender kisses. "Your humor, your conviction, your passion for the things you care about."

"Is that all?"

"For starters. And, I plan to learn every part of you. Like this . . ."

He had pinned her down against the soft mattress with a splay of arms and legs, and he deepened his intense pursuit, leaving her gasping. She arched her hips, filled with a need that began to flame and then burn steadily through her until she cried out softly, begging him for release.

When he parted her soft flesh, she arched her hips to meet him. She drove against him wildly, claiming what he was offering, her moans mixed with gasping sobs of exquisite pleasure and wonder. Then she burst apart in a shattering release that wracked her body.

The silence in the room was gentle, claiming them in a deep, sated feeling of peace. He had drawn her into his arms, holding her close as he kissed her slender neck and stroked her soft hip.

"So," she said dreamily, her voice soft with sleepy humor. "You like me for my mind."

"That—and other things," he murmured lazily against her ear. "If breasts controlled thought, you would be a genius. As for your—" he whispered in her ear.

She gasped, then giggled, turning in his arms to look up at him. "Your Spanish has improved, Senor Morgan. Wherever did you learn such a word?"

She felt him shrug. "It comes to one, when needed."

She snuggled into his arms, sighing peacefully. "Jeremy?" she said softly.

"Humm."

"Did you cheat in that card game?"

There was silence. "That, my love, you will never know."

A longer silence followed. "Jeremy?"

"What?"

"There is one thing I know now—" She hesitated, grateful that the room was dark and he could not see her clearly. "I—I never knew what it meant—to be satisfied. Until you." When he didn't answer, she took a deep breath. "I always faked it."

His arms tightened about her, and he kissed her temple gently. "Sweet dreams, *querida.*"

Light played against her closed eyes and, gradually, she opened them. She stirred, awakening with a contentment she did not fully understand until she remembered the past night. Sighing softly, she turned with a smile. He was sitting up against the head of the bed, awake.

He looked down at her and smiled as he reached out to pull her up against him. "Good morning."

"Good morning," she returned warmly, flushing contentedly with the remembrance of the past night. "Jeremy, I'm famished." Her eyes glittered with pleasure and expectation.

"For food?"

"For the moment," she answered happily, flinging herself from the bed.

They made their way downstairs to the kitchen, where Ariana tossed orders to one of the three cooks. "We'll eat outside, Maria, and quickly! We're utterly famished!" She grabbed his hand, pulling him from the overheated room into the courtyard.

"I believe that we are the subject of some gossip, my dear," he murmured as they crossed the busy compound.

"I know," she answered. "We'll eat over there," she added, indicating a small, rough, wooden table set beneath a thatched lean-to in the far corner.

"In view of everyone?" he observed, peering at her.

"Everyone!" she whispered fiercely.

He sat with her at the small table, and glanced about at the industry that had begun hours before they had risen. The forge was shooting red-hot sparks as the smithy pumped the bellows with one foot. His muscular arms moved in counterpoint as he struck the iron rod he was

shaping with his hammer, sparks flying against the anvil
with each sure, ringing stroke. A carcass of a sheep turned
over the pit near the kitchens; laundresses tended fires
under large, steaming, copper pots. Others scrubbed over
soapy buckets or carried newly washed garments through a
narrow corridor to the lines outside the adobe. Open doors
along the walls of the lower story revealed weavers at their
looms, leatherworkers shaping new saddles. A cluster of
women sat near a far wall, in a congenial circle as they
carded wool. Smells assailed him in a heavy mixture of
roasting meat, lye, leather, and boiling tallow.

He leaned back on the bench, against a support pole of
the thatched canopy, and regarded Ariana through narrowed eyes. As her gaze passed over the activity, it was filled
with contentment—and determination. "Ariana," he said
quietly, "why do you want to deliberately subject yourself
to criticism?"

She turned her head and looked at him steadily. "Jeremy
there is nothing that goes on in this place that doesn't
become common knowledge within hours. Even if I hadn't
worn that gown last night. Even if you had crept to my room
after everyone was sleeping. I can't stop them from disapproving." She glanced about, her voice becoming firm. "But
I can remind them that I am a Vallejo; I do not subject my
decisions to their opinions."

"Does that include me?" He grinned.

"Absolutely, Senor Morgan." Laughter danced in her
eyes.

"That, Senorita Saldivar," he said, his eyes filling with his
own amused determination, "remains to be seen. But we
shall discuss it at another time—in private."

Their breakfast approached in the arms of a sturdy
large-bosomed kitchen servant who laboriously bore the
tray across the courtyard. Her expression clearly showed her
disgust at having to cater to two late risers who had nothing
better to do than loll about over a breakfast picnic. But her
attitude changed considerably after a moment, and the
round-faced woman returned to the kitchens beaming with
pleasure, a two-dollar coin tucked safely between her ample
breasts.

"You should not have done that," Ariana observed as she
attacked the food spread on the table before her. "It was
unnecessary and far too generous. Now they'll all be

expecting you to tip them, for each little thing they do for you, not to mention the arguments you will cause over who will serve the generous *bostonio*."

"Well, you know how it is," he drawled, wrapping a large chunk of shredded beef into a tortilla. "We filthy-rich Yankees corrupt wherever we go." Her mouth was full of empanada, and she grunted. "I particularly anticipate the opportunity to corrupt a certain lovely Californio of my acquaintance. And quite thoroughly, just as soon as I get some strength back."

As sauce dripped from her chin, she darted a glance at him, but he was attacking a large burrito. "I thought you wanted to ride this morning."

Swallowing, he leered at her. "Oh, querida, I plan to."

19

There are moments in one's life that seem suspended. The mind draws them out, holding them, releasing them reluctantly. Such moments replayed in Ariana's thoughts as she soaked in a tub and reflected upon the past, glorious week she had spent with Jeremy. Suddenly she shivered, not from a chill, but from the prospect of loss. Could she ever bear to live without him in her life? Why couldn't she just accept these moments of happiness without worrying about the future?

Determined not to become morose, she quickly finished her bath and dressed. She left the bedroom, eager to find him. She knew that he would allay her fears as no one else could, as no one ever had. An expectant smile on her lips, she paused at the doorway of the sala and frowned. The upper gallery of the casa was filled with people, lined along the railing as they stared down into the courtyard expectantly. Moving to the railing she glanced down and blinked.

A large crowd had gathered, apparently from every recess of the casa. Onlookers ringed the large courtyard, and at the center of the open space was Jeremy with an equally intent majordomo. The two men were squared off in a puzzling stance as they stared at what appeared to be an inflated goat's bladder lying on the ground between them. Behind them, two lines of vaqueros and the sturdier of the male servants were poised. Thirty-four grown men, staring intently at a goat's bladder. Suddenly, to the uproar of the watchers, Miguel kicked it. It twisted wildly to Jeremy, who managed to send it back with a swift kick past Miguel's shoulder. The field broke into bedlam, men bunting and pushing, battering opponents, inflicting bloody noses and bruises, issuing yelps, profanity and laughter as they bore down on the bouncing, crazily veering bladder.

A half-hour later, Ariana had managed to make her way down onto the playing field where she offered Jeremy a ladle of water. "We're winning!" he said happily, his clothes torn, one eye blackened.

"How can you tell?" she asked with a smirk.

"We made four goals!" he said, gesturing to the stakes that had been pounded into the ground across the court-yard, opposite a matched pair at the other end.

"This was your idea, wasn't it?" she asked, glancing doubtfully at the other battered men who were standing about, eager to be back into the thick of it.

"They're loving it." He grinned. "It's called football, Ariana—a good old Yankee game."

"You are a totally deranged gringo."

"Yep," he said happily. "We've been playing this at Harvard since '26. It began as a game between the freshmen and sophomores, each year on the first day of the new term. Used to call it 'Bloody Monday.'"

"I can see why," she said, dabbing with a kerchief at the trickle of blood from the split above his eye.

"Of course, Yale plays it against us now," he added as an imperative observation, ignoring her comment. "They call it the Annual Rush—"

"Hey, Boston!" Miguel called, holding up a bladder. "We got a new ball!" The game had been called because the ball had suddenly disappeared, deflating as it flew through the air to slap down in a rubberized wrap on a squawking, terrified chicken, almost smothering the bird before some-one could extract it.

The game resumed, concluding seven to three, with only one seriously fractured arm.

It was the first afternoon in memory, beyond holidays and fiestas, when there was no sound of industry at Rancho Petaluma. In fact, strenuous work was curtailed for the next few days, due to the bruised condition of the rancho's most experienced vaqueros, not to mention a slow-moving, but totally happy majordomo.

Jeremy eased himself through the following afternoon, moving as little as possible. In the face of his stiffness, accentuated by occasional pauses and winces, it was difficult for Ariana to understand the self-satisfied look he wore. But she was most forbearing. She had never known a sane man in her life. More importantly, she learned not to question him about the game. It led to conversations that left her dazzled with boredom—and little chance of escape. After listening to a detailed accounting of one Joseph Settermore, class of '31, and how the sophomore phenomenon had carried the ball past battering obstacles, pounding the ball through a seventy-four-yard streak to the goal, she silently promised herself that she would never, ever approach the subject again. Besides, if left alone, the brutal, stupid game was bound to follow the way of man's other follies, never to be heard of again.

However, she did discover that there were some advantages left from the game. As Jeremy healed slowly, but apparently not too slowly, a strange bloodlust was caught and suspended at a peak, not unlike what a soldier experiences after a battle. She found that while he might begin with a tedious recounting of the objectionable game, his enthusiasm built until it led to his making wildly passionate love to her. Thus Ariana found herself lolling through lazy afternoons with a building contentment she had never known before. Occasionally, she wondered if Joseph Settermore had had a sweetheart. Never in her life had she felt so cherished.

The morning of the end of their third week at Rancho Petaluma, Ariana awoke slowly. She had become accustomed to the delicious pleasure of rising late, with Jeremy's arms wrapped about her, his hard, warm body against her back. She nestled against him, wallowing in a sleepy contentment as she waited for his response. His arms tightened gently, and his legs drew up under hers with an unmistakable stirring against the soft flesh of her hips. Sighing, she turned, slipping her arms up to wrap about his neck. "Good morning, my love," she whispered softly, taking joy in the total lack of restraint she felt as she silently requested his attentions.

He grunted sleepily as his arm tightened about her and a hand slipped up to claim a warm, full breast. His head dipped to the nape of her neck, his mouth giving light, teasing kisses about the sensitive nerve endings. "You're so warm," he murmured, cuddling closer.

She laughed softly, feeling the sound in a deep, contented part of her, and she shifted slightly to allow his hand free play.

They both were startled at the sudden, insistent pounding on the door of the sala. "Damn," Jeremy uttered the single, controlled expletive and rolled from the bed, grabbing his robe as he stumbled sleepily into the other room. Ariana nestled back under the covers, trying to hold the warmth of his body until he returned. She sighed happily, thinking of how her people had accepted their relationship. The early looks of disapproval had changed to amusement, then acceptance. How could they not understand, she mused sleepily, when they saw how much she and Jeremy were in love? She smiled to herself, realizing how much that silly football game had done to endear Jeremy to her people.

She heard the door reopen, and she turned in the bedding with a dreamy smile. Her smile faded slowly at the expression Jeremy wore. He paused in the doorway, then crossed to the bed, reading the letter he carried. "What is it?" she asked with rising dread as she sat up. She gathered the covers about her in an instinctive attempt to hold off what she saw in his face.

"It is from Larkin," he answered, coming to stand by her. Very slowly he looked up, fixing her with a steady, unwavering gaze. "Ariana—the United States has declared war upon Mexico."

She moved through the next hour with steady deliberation. She dressed quickly and made certain that Jeremy had a substantial breakfast, knowing that it would be the last full meal he would have for days. She checked his supplies as they were fixed upon her uncle's buckskin—she would allow no other mount for him—and then faced him with composure as he made ready to depart. He gripped Taro's reins, holding the horse firmly as it skittered nervously after the weeks of confinement to a corral. Only she among all of those who had gathered fully understood the importance of what had happened. Miguel stood nearby, his weathered face heavy with deep, constrained grief.

"Take the road to the Embarcadaro," she said firmly. "Leave Taro with Mario Gonzales. He is a tanner, and works for my uncle. Please, Jeremy, you promised. Do not attempt to ride all the way to Monterey; find an American ship at the Embarcadaro—it is only four miles. I cannot say how the Californios will react to this news, and many of the Indian tribes will be even more unpredictable." She forced a smile. "They'll be looking for you Yanquis."

"Don't worry, *querida.*" He smiled, reaching up to touch her cheek. "I'll get back—that's not what's worrying me . . ."

"I know," she said softly, turning to kiss the palm of his hand. Looking up at him, her eyes filled with the words they had not been able to say to each other. "I know. Jeremy—" Her breath caught, and she forced a smile. "I love you, Yanqui. I—"

"I love you, too." He smiled, bending to kiss her, his arm wrapping around her waist as he drew her to him with a sudden fierceness. Reluctantly, he drew away, his eyes feasting on every contour of her face. "No matter what happens, do not forget how beautiful you are, or how much I love you," he murmured.

"Senor—" Miguel approached and he took the buckskin's reins, his eyes pleading.

Ariana stood with Miguel at the crest of the hill, watching until Jeremy disappeared. The majordomo left her silently, feeling her grief, sensing her need to be alone. She was unaware of the tears that streaked in a steady course down her cheeks. Fear and desperation fed a deepening sense of loss within her—she was terrified that she would never recapture the closeness she had known with him in the past weeks.

She was a Californio, and Jeremy's country was at war with Mexico. Oh, the war had been declared over Texas, but Ariana knew that California would be the prize. And, unlike most of her countrymen, she knew what that could mean. This would not be a war of bluster and diatribe as her compatriots were accustomed to, but real war, by a nation who knew how to wage it. The Californios would panic. Even those who had claimed preference for union with the States would react. They would return to their Mexican loyalties embedded within their souls, which they had not had time to extricate. Confusion and fear would turn them back to an instinct they had spent twenty years struggling against: a need for the familiar, the understood.

And Jeremy knew it, too.

That day she returned to Sonoma. She avoided everyone, rudely when necessary, particularly her inquisitive cousins and disapproving aunts who attempted to inquire about the absent Senor Morgan. She found her uncle in the library, bent over his desk as he penned a letter—one of many, judging by the stack.

"Welcome back, Ariana," he said gently, leaning back in his chair. "I presume that Jeremy is on his way to Monterey?"

"Si." She sighed, taking a chair across from him. She told him of the advice she had given to Jeremy, adding: "I hope that he—arrives safely."

His eyes narrowed at the simple understatement, and he studied her face. "Do you want to talk about it?"

"The conflict?" she asked.

"Si, Nina, the one between you and Morgan."

"Oh," she whispered. "Well—" she flushed, drawing a speculative look from her uncle. "There is no conflict there, *Tio."*

His eyes warmed with pleasure. *"Bueno, me querida.* I am pleased for you. He is a good man."

Her eyes rose to meet his. "I love him, *Tio."*

He grinned. "I assumed that when you did not return for almost weeks."

"Dios," she murmured. "The aunts must be scandalized."

"Si," he said, his eyes twinkling. "But they now keep their comments well out of my hearing. It was a matter I settled with Benicia; she will handle the others."

She smiled at him, and they exchanged a glance of understanding. Then she sobered, glancing at the letters on his desk. "And now—what is going to happen, to all of us?"

"Time will tell us," he answered wearily. "But I fear that we do not have long to wait."

The quiet atmosphere in Sonoma that greeted Ariana upon her return soon proved to be a thin, nervous shield that swiftly disintegrated. Tensions increased, neighbors drawing into polarized groups to discuss rumors, their eyes fixed nervously upon those who had once been trusted friends and now were looked upon with suspicion. Yanquis became Americanos in the eyes of the Californios, and the settlers began to draw into clusters of their own kind. Word began to infiltrate the community every day, bringing rumors of skirmishes in Yerba Buena, Santa Rosa, Monterey, and throughout the Sacramento Valley: Indian attacks upon settlers; ships that sailed up the coast with fresh troops from Mexico; the American government sending companies of men on ships and overland. Rising panic boiled just beneath the surface of daily life.

Vallejo worked daily to soothe fears and counter the rumors on both sides. Dispatches came and went to Sutter, Larkin, and Castro with regularity, and he knew that there had been no open conflict. Moreover, neither Mexico nor the United States had yet to make any overt action toward California. Along with his American allies, he still nurtured hope that the situation could be resolved peacefully.

Ariana received dispatches as well, from Rachel, and more importantly, from Jeremy. They both confirmed what her uncle's correspondents had reported, but it was other news in their letters that interested her. Rachel's tone, beyond mention of the war, was light; her firm humor subtly pressed between the lines. One American lumber merchant of their mutual acquaintance, she wrote, appeared to be in rather high spirits of late, in spite of the ominous threat of war. He tended to smile, and there was a peculiar look of satisfaction in his handsome blue eyes that she had never noticed before. "I cannot imagine . . ." Rachel wrote, bringing a soft smile from Ariana as she read. ". . . what has happened to place him in such a strange mood. However, it appears to agree with him, and I can only hope that it continues."

Jeremy's letters sustained her. They were cautious, as he sought to protect her should they fall into the wrong hands, but they were filled with subtle references to their closest moments, and hinted of his need to be with her again. She was somewhat surprised when he wrote that he had closed down his lumber business. His reasons were understandable —difficulties with travel and shipping—but she could not but wonder what effect it would have upon them. She did not want to consider the possibilities, but she fell into a morose mood that took her days to overcome. It was only when her uncle noticed her despondency that she finally discussed the situation with him.

"With his business gone, and the possibility of war here, what is to keep him?" she observed.

"You fear that he will return to the east?"

"Yes, it seems a possibility, *Tio*. After all, his wife and son are there."

Vallejo wanted nothing more than to allay her fears, but he would not lie to her. "Yes, it is a possibility. And, if he does, it is something you will have to live with. At least you will have had your time together; it is more than most have, *querida*."

It had certainly been more than she had ever dreamed of. As she moved through the next few days, she realized that she had never expected to have him forever. She knew that the day would come, in spite of his assurances, when he would return to his wife and son. And she began to accept the idea, gradually placing her memories away in a deep, inner part of her. Slowly, she began to rejoin life.

Transition did not come easily, but she accepted that fact and was patient with herself. Manuel's response to her first letter was angry. He had been trying to communicate with her for over a month, but his couriers had returned each time with the same message; that she was "away" and no one knew when she would return. Did she not realize the importance of what was happening? Her answer was terse, but she modified her outrage at being questioned. She still believed in their cause as strongly as ever, while accepting that love had tempered her emotions. She no longer saw life in the stark colors she had before, but had begun to understand the misty edges of doubt—and compromise.

The situation in the Napa and Sacramento valleys steadily worsened. The previous March, as Fremont and his men had passed through the area on their way to Oregon, they had suggested to the settlers that his expulsion was only the beginning. Eventually, Fremont had assured them, Castro's demand would include the removal of all foreigners from California. At the time, the suggestion was met with little credibility, but with the rumors of war, talk sprang anew. Settlers armed themselves, and grogshops were filled with hostile speculation. Lines were drawn as fractions continued to polarize. Then, in late June, a letter from Sutter warned that John Charles Fremont had returned to the Sacramento Valley. He had been there since May.

The letter had remained unopened on Vallejo's desk for a

full day. When he finally managed to read it, he could barely focus upon it. Listlessly, he handed it to Ariana and asked her to forward it on to Larkin. She took the letter from him, her heart squeezing painfully as she shared his grief. That morning, a week after the onset of a sudden, terrible fever, her little cousin, a cherubic, bright-eyed four-year-old, the joy of the Vallejo household and the brightest spot in his father's eye, had died.

The house had descended into deep mourning; soft sounds of grief could be heard from the dining room where a vigil had begun beside the tiny casket. Ariana's eyes were blurred with tears as she set to the task of penning a letter to Larkin, enclosing the note from Sutter before sealing the correspondence. She bypassed the mourners who had come to pay their respects, a line which moved through the house throughout the day and into the night, and made her way to the stables. There she roused one of the vaqueros, his own, dark eyes wet with tears. Instructing the man, she saw him off to Monterey, then entered the house to take her place by the impossibly still form of the little boy.

The mass and funeral were the following day; the rest of the afternoon and evening were spent grieving with family and friends. Finally, in the small hours of the morning, the last family members managed to find their beds, falling into exhausted sleep.

It was not yet dawn when something awakened her. Ariana rose up on an elbow and listened intently in the graying light, wondering if someone in the household was unable to sleep. And then she heard it again; the distinct sound of horses—and men's voices. They were right under her window, which faced out to the street. Slipping from her bed, she pulled on a robe and went to the double doors which opened to the wide gallery. She stepped into the shadows of the overhanging roof and her breath drew in sharply. Backing into her room, she shut the doors quietly and dressed as quickly as she could.

As she reached the top of the stairs, there was a pounding at the door. "Raul!" she hissed halfway down the stairs. The servant had come into the hall below and was crossing to the door. He stopped at the sound of her urgent whisper and looked up at Ariana with wide, frightened eyes. "Wake the don. I will see to the door. Now!" she added, pushing the man on his way. Bracing herself, Ariana stepped to the door, pausing for a moment to draw an even breath, then opening it.

In the shadows stood three grim-looking Yanquis. Behind them, still on horseback, was a large group of men. She only recognized one of the men, his red hair familiar in the half-light of early morning. It was Kit Carson, Fremont's scout.

"May I help you?" she asked, regarding the men with composure.

"We're here to see General Vallejo," one of the men said gruffly.

Inwardly, she stiffened with alarm at the use of the title. "The family is in bed, including the don. Besides the unsuitability of the hour, this is a house in mourning. I suggest that you come back at a later hour—"

"We will see him now." A tall, angular man dressed in buckskins interrupted, stepping forward.

"That is quite impossible," she answered. Her hand slipped into the deep pocket of her gown to the gun she had dropped into it before she left her room. Her fingers closed about the handle, and she bent the barrel upward. She was fully prepared to shoot at the first one who tried to step into the house. Her fingers closed about the trigger . . .

"What can I do for you, gentlemen?"

She tensed at the sound of the voice behind her. Then she felt his hand on her arm, gently drawing her hand from the pocket. Glancing up, she saw the flicker of warning in her uncle's eyes before he stepped by her. "There is no need for trouble. You are welcome to my home." To Ariana's horror, he stepped back and gestured for them to enter.

Vallejo led the three spokesmen into his office downstairs, pausing to instruct Ariana to bring a few bottles of cognac. She brought them quickly, along with extra glasses, setting them on a table by the window where she could see what was happening on the street beyond.

"Brandy, gentlemen?" Vallejo asked affably.

"We are not here to socialize, General." The taller of the men scowled. "In fact—"

The door opened and Vallejo smiled at the group of men who entered. "Ah, yes, thank you for answering my summons so quickly. Gentlemen, I would like to introduce Jacob Leese, Victor Prudon, and Salvador Vallejo. I took the liberty of sending for them because I suspect that our conversation will interest them, as well. Ariana, my dear, would you pour us some refreshment?"

Reluctantly she obeyed, as she marveled at her uncle's capacity for managing a situation—even one as strained as this. There was no doubt in anyone's mind as to why these men were here. The fact that they had addressed him as general was enough to give alarm.

The tall, rawboned man frowned uncomfortably. "It is just as well that they are here, we would have looked for them anyway. General, I am Ezekiel Merritt. This—" he said, indicating the largest of the trio, "is Robert Semple. And he is William Knight. We have ridden from the Sacramento Valley to inform you that we mean to establish California as a republic. Furthermore, we are prepared to fight to support that position. I regret to inform you, General, that you are under arrest—as is your brother here, along with Leese and Prudon."

"I see," Vallejo answered, returning the other man's intense stare without flinching. "Well then, if it must be, I assure you that there is no need for violence. We will accompany you, if that is your wish. However, after your long journey you must be exhausted. Please, share my hospitality and rest yourselves. It is an equally long journey back."

The three men exchanged doubtful looks while each of their thoughts were the same. It had been a long, exhausting ride, one of considerable strain, as they had anticipated a reception far different than the one they were experiencing. They were standing in the parlor of the richest man in California. And, the general was famous for the quality of his wine and liquor cellar. They eyed the cognac with interest.

Ariana was already pouring the glasses. She carried a tray across the room, offering each man a glass which he took with only a moment's hesitation. As she passed her Uncle Salvador, she noted the fury in his dark eyes and the dangerous clenching of his hands. Her glance caught his, and she stared at him for a moment as she laid a hand on his arm. To her relief, he seemed to relax a little, and she passed on, offering cognac to the others. However, for the first time in her life, she thought that perhaps Salvador was right. She had absolutely no idea of what the don hoped to accomplish by being gracious to these intruders. Her own thoughts were focused on the gun in her pocket.

A full hour passed, sixty long minutes that had left her emotions ragged. She had refilled glass after glass and was half-crazed by the don's small talk as he entertained the men with amusing stories. She had moved to the window overlooking the street, drawn by the sound of raised voices. Understandably, the men outside were growing restless, and she became truly frightened, wondering where this was all going to lead.

Then they heard more pounding on the front door. A few moments later, two other men entered the room. John Grigsby and William Ide were introduced by their fellows, who, to the outrage of the newcomers, were decidedly drunk. Ide ordered coffee to be brought, barely containing his fury over the idiocy of their elected spokesmen. "General Vallejo!" he said with tight control. "As the military governor of this area, you are under arrest. We demand that you turn all armaments in this garrison over to us and proceed with us to Sutter's Fort, where you shall be incarcerated."

"So I have been informed," Vallejo responded calmly. "As for the armaments, there is little here. As you must know, this has not been a formal military garrison for many years. You are certainly welcome to whatever we have. As I have assured the others, there is no need for violence. Ariana," he added, "I believe that we are in need of coffee."

She hesitated, unwilling to leave him. "Go on," he said firmly. "Do what I say."

She left the room with a thick lump in her throat. It couldn't be happening! That thought ran through her, over and over, mixing with a chilling fear for what they might do to him. She crossed the courtyard to the kitchen, where she found Raul standing in the shadows, staring at the casa.

"Quickly, Raul, the don has ordered coffee for the Yanquis," she said, pulling him by the arm toward the kitchen. The Indian stared at her for a moment, then turned and disappeared into the small adobe, emerging with a pot which he set into the *horno*.

They both stood, watching the pot as they waited for the water to boil. Then, as it began to bubble, Raul returned to the kitchen for the ground coffee. As he crossed the short space back to the outdoor oven, he paused suddenly, staring at something on the ground. Bending, he picked up the object of his interest, and joined her by the fire. His dark face broke into a grin as he wordlessly held up a filthy sock someone had dropped in the courtyard. Without a word, he proceeded to stretch the grimy object over a kettle, and he dumped the grounds into it. Ariana gasped, then began to laugh, quickly stifling the sound with her hand as she glanced toward the casa. She grinned as she watched the servant pour the hot water through it.

Ariana carried the kettle back into the casa, bearing it like a standard. In spite of the night's events, and the tenuous, sorrowful days that preceded it, she felt renewed. Because of one spiteful act by a beloved family servant. She would serve the coffee, along with some plans of her own.

She entered the room, sensing the tension that had built in her absence. She poured the steaming coffee, shaking her head slightly at her own men when she passed by them. Mariano frowned, but Salvador's eyes widened in expectation. She watched with stifled amusement as the Yanquis gulped it down and asked for another cup—a request she unhesitatingly filled. And she bided her time, waiting for the right time to proceed with her own plan. In the moments that had passed, she had formed it carefully. Her hand slipped into her pocket. If she could hold them off, it would give her men enough time to escape out the back and over the walls. If they made it as far as El Cuartel, they could hold off the Yanquis indefinitely.

"Gentlemen," Vallejo addressed them, rising from his chair. "We will be ready to go with you whenever you wish. I would make only one request: to have a moment alone to speak with my niece. I promise you, upon my honor, that I have no plans to resist you. I only wish to instruct her on personal matters in my absence. Upon your arrival, my wife and children were ordered to remain upstairs. They are certain to be concerned for my welfare and I wish to leave words of support."

Ide regarded Vallejo silently for a long moment, then shrugged. "It is a reasonable request, General. We shall wait for you in the hall. But I advise you not to attempt to escape," he added, glancing at the window. "The rest of our men are just outside, and they are in a rather nasty mood."

"I have no intention of escaping, Mr. Ide."

When they were alone, Ariana spun on her uncle with frustration. Before she could speak, Vallejo stopped her with a quick gesture of silence, glancing at the door. He stepped to her, taking her shoulders in his hands. "It would have been very foolish for you to do what you planned." He smiled, with a sadness that struck at her heart.

"It would have worked!" she said, fuming, glancing at the door. "You could have made it to the barracks—"

"And then what?" he interrupted. "How long would we have withstood them when they held our families?"

"They would not have harmed us," she insisted.

"Could we have taken that chance? Besides, *querida,* there is another matter, as dear to me as those I love. And this is why I wanted to speak with you alone. Our visitors cannot know, but they have done me a great favor, solving a problem which has been plaguing me these past many weeks."

"Favor?" She frowned. "By arresting you?"

"Exactly so. Now be silent and let me speak; we have only a few moments. This rebellion is not unexpected; matters are far worse than you know. You, perhaps above all others, know how I feel about California's destiny. I have shared my dreams with you since you were a child. I know that you have taken your own path, and I will not debate that with you now—there is no time. But if you love me, you will help me now."

"How, *Tio?*" she asked. "Anything."

"I am an officer in the Mexican Army. True, for the past many years it has been a title of honor. But I have no doubt that the next dispatch from Pio Pico will be one reestablishing my military command, with orders to strike against the Americans. This matter, as distasteful as it may be, alleviates that conflict. Thus, I go and gladly. Do you understand?"

She hesitated, not wanting to accept what he was saying. Then she sighed heavily. *"Si, Tio,"* she answered raggedly. "I understand. I will try to make Tia Benicia understand. And I will care for the others—"

"No, that is not what I am asking of you. Benicia understands already. You have another duty to perform, something much harder." He smiled at her confusion. "Benito is waiting for you—I sent word to him by Raul before I joined you to greet our guests. Once we have departed, you are to leave. I want word to reach Larkin as swiftly as possible, along with the letters that are in my desk. Tell him what has happened here, and what I have said. Will you do this for me?"

She drew a steadying breath. "Of course," she answered, though her eyes were filled with concern for him.

"Good," he grunted, drawing her into a swift embrace. Just then the door opened.

"You have had enough time, General," Ide said, stepping into the room. "We must go."

"I am ready." Vallejo bent forward and kissed her forehead. *"Vaya con Dios, mia querida,"* he murmured. He drew back and smiled at her. His request had been truthful, if not complete. She was the only one who could carry his message to Larkin, particularly because she had heard the details of his arrest firsthand. But there was another reason he had chosen to send her away. Left to her own devices, Ariana was certain to get into trouble, particularly now that hostilities were certain. Only in Monterey, under Larkin's care—and Jeremy Morgan's—was there a chance that she could survive the inevitable storm of future events—and her own volatile nature.

20

"What in blazes is going on up there!" Larkin roared, throwing the letter on his desk.

"If Revere knew more, he would have told us," Jeremy said reasonably. "As he said, he's been unable to leave Yerba Buena. It's unsafe to travel; moreover, Sonoma is virtually sealed off. Unless he was to take a large contingent of marines off the *Portsmouth*—"

"Oh God! Don't even suggest such a thing!" Larkin groaned as he resumed pacing.

"It's that, or wait." Jeremy shrugged, while keeping his own emotions in check.

Larkin paused, glancing again at the letter as his forehead wrinkled into a deep frown. "Could it be true that they actually took Vallejo prisoner?"

"And raised their own flag," Jeremy muttered, leaning over to grab the letter. He scanned Revere's astounding words. ". . . sewn from a piece of muslin, with a red strip at the bottom. They put a star on it, like the star of Texas, and a grizzly for strength and courage." Jeremy paused, remembering the drunken night he spent with Revere when they were hunting grizzly bears. He wondered how much liquor had fueled this particular venture. "From what he has heard, the bear looks more like a pig. Bear Flaggers, they're calling themselves."

"Yes, and that William Ide and Ezekiel Merritt were behind it!"

"Perhaps—" Jeremy said slowly. "But I think we both know that there was someone else who, at the very least, encouraged it."

Larkin turned and looked at him. "Fremont?"

"Who else? Vallejo's last letter said that our esteemed engineer had returned to New Helvetia. Ide and Merritt are from the Sacramento Valley."

"Yes." Larkin sighed wearily. "And we have good reason to suspect that Fremont was involved in the raid of Castro's horses."

Weeks before, Jose Castro had sent men north to buy horses. They had gathered a large herd and were returning south, when they were attacked by the very group of settlers from whom they had purchased them. Manuel Castro was one of the survivors of the mission, and he had reported that their attackers had mentioned Fremont's name.

"I had preferred to believe that Manuel's prejudices had influenced his opinion," Larkin said reluctantly.

"But Fremont was in the area at the time. And now this."

"There is no proof, Jeremy. I prefer not to jump to conclusions."

You might not, Jeremy thought, but I can. He did not believe in coincidences. He rose restlessly from his chair and walked to the window while trying not to pace. He had been half-frantic with worry about Ariana since Revere's letter had arrived that morning. If Vallejo had been taken, God only knew what she was doing. He fervently prayed that she had remained at Rancho Petaluma.

"Rachel said that you received a letter from Beth," Larkin commented, pouring them each a measure of brandy.

It took a moment for Jeremy to swing with the shift in conversation. "Yes. She and Hamilton are fine. Both sets of grandparents are doting on the boy, and he promises to become thoroughly spoiled."

"Splendid!" Larkin grinned. "That is the responsibility of grandparents." When Jeremy did not smile, the consul became solemn. "I know it is difficult to be parted from your son, Jeremy. The saddest days of my life were those when I sent the boys away to school. Rachel and I miss them terribly. I'll never forget when Thomas Junior was six, he wrote to us saying that a little boy should not be so far from home." Larkin's eyes took on a faraway look of regret, then he sighed. "But there was nothing to be done for it. I tried to establish a school here, as did Vallejo and Hartnell. It soon became apparent that the only way the boys would be able to prepare for their futures was by going away."

"Well, at least I can try to console myself with that," Jeremy said, placing his glass down. He picked up his sheepskin jacket, slipping it on.

"It's been a long day, Morgan," Larkin said, walking him down the stairs and to the front door. "I'll send another rider out in the morning to see if we can find out what is happening up there."

Jeremy paused at the door. "I swear, Larkin, if this one does not get through, I'm going up there myself."

Larkin's eyes darkened with amusement at the determination in Jeremy's voice. "Not in uniform, I trust."

"No," Jeremy answered, then he glanced back at the consul. "Not yet."

He walked the few blocks to his house. The air was cool and the night dark from a quarter moon. A dog barked, and a ship's bell could be heard from a merchantman in the harbor—lonely sounds that added to Jeremy's restlessness. He missed Ariana; he missed her laughter, her teasing, her temperament. He had thought about her almost continuously since he had left her, and with those thoughts had come deep regret. He was not morose, he was too much of a pragmatist to waste time on destructive emotion, but a large part of him still regretted that he had been unable to make a successful marriage with Beth. And he regretted that he could not give more to Ariana. He was married to a woman who did not love him, and he loved a woman he could never marry. The only thing he did not regret was his son. For Hamilton, if not for Beth, he would be compelled to continue his farce of a marriage.

Beth's letter had been revealing. She was happy. A contentment shone through her letter, a mood that he had not seen since their courtship. The once-successful deb had become the toast of New York society, a fact that he had learned in a letter from his mother, laced with edges of disapproval. Caroline Morgan had suggested, quite strongly, that Jeremy come home immediately and take his wife in hand.

A separate letter from his father had assured him that Beth was behaving herself. He had added that she was stretching her activities to the limits of propriety, but thus far had not crossed the line. Frankly, Jeremy was inclined to believe his father's opinion. If anyone knew who was dallying with whom, it would be his father and the cronies in his club. As for his mother, he rather imagined that she would disapprove of anything his wife did. Thus, the situation was difficult to judge and would likely remain so. In any case, he knew that Beth was quite content to do without sex; in fact, she preferred abstinence. She was not likely to risk her social position on a messy affair.

Then there was Ariana. The thought of her brought him an involuntary smile. It would seem that, in spite of his resolve, he had assumed the role of his father. Had Hamilton Morgan loved another woman as he loved Ariana? God, were they condemned to love only women they could never have, could never openly cherish? He made a silent promise that he would make her life as full and content as possible. And—it was a moment before he could complete the thought—if another man came along who could make her happy, he would gladly step aside. Well, not gladly, but he would do it. In fact, he would encourage it. He thought of her as he had left her: her lovely slender hands clasped tightly in front of her, her back stiff with natural pride, the breeze lifting her dark, silky hair, her large, dark eyes filled with unshed tears. Tears that would fall for him. Never in his life had he felt this way about a woman, and his feelings were returned. Silently, he reaffirmed the promise he made to Larkin. If word did not come soon, he would go to Sonoma himself, whatever the consequences.

Ariana gathered her skirts about her, trying to keep them from brushing across the filth of the floor as she followed the guard down the dimly lit hallway. He stopped before a thick, banded door, and fit his key into the lock, clicking it open. It swung back, and he gestured for her to enter. "Fifteen minutes, that's all," he said briskly.

She brushed past him and hesitated, swallowing back the gorge that rose in her throat from the overpowering smell of the filthy cell. The room was completely bare but for a sagging rope cot, a small table with a single stool, and a revolting bucket in the corner. *"Tio,"* she whispered.

Vallejo stood facing the small window that looked out to

the compound beyond. He had ignored the opening of the cell door, thinking it to be the guard with his supper. He turned at the sound of her voice, his face falling into unmasked surprise. "Ariana! What are you doing here?"

She waited until the door was closed and locked behind her, then she set the package she carried onto the table. "I have brought some things for you." She kept her face from showing her dismay at his surroundings, knowing that the last thing he would want was pity. Instead, she smiled with a rueful smirk. "It looks as if you could use just about anything."

"Why are you here?" he repeated, though he could not help but grasp her to him in a fierce hug. "Have you returned from Monterey already? What news is there?"

"I only left Sonoma yesterday," she answered grimly, pulling away from him. "For the past fifteen days I have been held a virtual prisoner in La Casa Grande."

"What did you do to warrant that?" he asked, frowning.

"Absolutely nothing. None of us was allowed to leave after your arrest. The men—including Benito—were gathered up and locked into the barracks."

"Benicia and the children?"

"They are well, and send you their love. No one was harmed, just restrained."

He expelled a relieved breath. He backed up and sat on the edge of the table, gesturing for her to take the stool. "Tell me what has been happening."

"For us, not much more than that. I think the worst thing, besides not being able to carry your message to Larkin, was viewing that damnable flag from my window each morning. They stuck the thing in the plaza right across from the casa." Seeing his puzzlement, she smirked. "They have their own flag now—a ridiculous rag with a star and a pig on it. Oh, before I forget . . ." She nodded to the box she had brought and her voice lowered. "*Tia* sent you a cake. I suggest you eat it gingerly. There's money in it for you to purchase—" she hesitated, glancing about, "some luxuries." Her eyes grew hot with sparks of anger. "How can they do this to you?"

He shrugged. "It does not matter. It is Captain Fremont's little joke."

"Fremont?" she asked. "Then it was he."

"Ide protested my conditions, but our esteemed captain

insisted that I be given no comforts—in retribution for the insults I caused him."

"You caused him? What did you ever do to him?"

"I believe that he has me somewhat confused with Jose. But then, I am rather certain that he sees us as one and the same."

"What of the others?"

"They are in cells nearby. Leese and Prudon are doing well, but I worry about Salvador. His temper has already caused him more than one beating, and I fear more will come. Moreover, I suspect that he will never forgive the Americans for this insult."

"Well, I wouldn't."

"None of them? Not even a certain lumber baron we both know?" he asked, a twinkle in his eye.

"He has nothing to do with any of this," she said stiffly. "Nor would he. He is as innocent of the actions of his government as we are. But I don't want to talk about that now; I came to tell you what is happening. Your precious Mr. Ide has declared himself president of California. In his official proclamation, he stated that while his 'companions' were led into this country with the promise of land, they were oppressed by military despotism. He even went so far as to suggest that he was throwing off the yoke of oppression that had robbed the 'good people' of California of their missions and its land."

"Is he giving California back to the Indians?" Vallejo grinned.

"Not quite." She smirked. "He promises liberty to all; however, I doubt very much that it will trickle down to the Indians. A main theme of his proclamation was to encourage 'virtue and literature.' Perhaps he's going to give them books."

"Enough sarcasm, Ariana. Now, dare I ask what Castro is doing?" This was his major worry, one that had begun long before his arrest. The dispatches he had left in his desk included suggestions to Larkin of how he might control the uncertain commandant. Ariana's hesitation deepened his feeling of dread.

"He . . . Two days ago he sent a force of fifty men under the command of Joaquin de la Torre to recapture Sonoma. They were met near Santa Rosa. A few Americans and five or six Californios were killed. At last word, de la Torre and his men were retreating toward Yerba Buena. Fremont, however, is declaring it a great victory."

"Fremont?"

"Kit Carson led the attack. Also, it was Fremont's arrival in Sonoma two days ago, following the battle, that allowed for my release. He has declared himself military governor and has joined his men with the 'Bear Flaggers.' He calls it the 'California Battalion.' Lieutenant Gillespie is his adjutant."

Vallejo was silent. He closed his eyes for a moment then opened them to regard Ariana calmly. "You are free now?"

"Yes. Fremont acted like our great benefactor. He even had the audacity to imply that if he had known we were so cruelly restricted, he would have acted sooner. Obviously, we mere women are of no concern to him."

It occurred to Vallejo that this was one woman he probably should have kept locked up. "How will we get word to Larkin?" he said absently.

She regarded him with surprise. "I know that I let you down, *Tio*. I did try to find a way to escape, but the casa was heavily guarded. But I am no longer restricted. I promise you that I will get word to Thomas as quickly as possible."

He looked puzzled. "Is Benito with you, or some other?"

"No. I was escorted here by Fremont's men. But do not worry. Once they delivered me they headed for Sutter's grogshop. It will be easy for me to slip away."

"By yourself? You cannot!"

"Of course I can." Then she saw his doubt. *"Tio,* there is no vaquero on Rancho Petaluma who can ride better than I can. As for that—" She laughed softly. "One of the Yanquis tried to take Oro for himself. They finally decided to leave the stupid, crazy beast for me. Moreover, I can live off the land as well as any good Californio. With a canteen of water—"

"Ariana, there are other dangers," he interrupted. "Especially now. Besides the Yanquis, there are bandits—"

"You mean Juan Padillo, or Three-fingered Jack? Yes, they are in the area, using the confusion to cause their usual mayhem."

"Then there is all the more reason—"

"Tio." This time it was her turn to stop him, and she sighed. There were things she never wanted to tell him, but she would not have him worry about her, especially now

that he had so much time to worry. "I will not be in any danger. Upon occasion both Padillo and Garcia have worked for me."

He looked stunned. It was one of the few times in her life when she saw her uncle lose his composure. "Someday, Ariana, when all this is over," he said, clearing his throat, "I want you to tell me all about it."

No, *Tio,* she thought, you don't. I will never tell you everything. "Of course," she said. "Someday. But for now, just trust me. And do not worry about me."

"I have no choice." He sighed, standing up. "Fremont is likely to make slow progress to Monterey; he has too much to prove here first. You still have time. Word of this must reach Larkin. But I still worry, Ariana," he added, pulling her into a hug. "There are those you may come upon who are not simpatico. I fear what they could do to you."

She pulled back. *"Tio,"* she said with emphasis. "Do not worry about me. The sooner I go—" she glanced about with distaste, "the sooner we get you out of here."

The morning of July 2, 1846, began like any other day. In the early morning hours, Jeremy walked with Larkin along the road edging the bay, having left the Custom House moments before. Dispatches for Polk and Buchanan had been sent aboard a merchantman due to leave that morning, and there was little more that they could do. They had both spent the past few days closeted with Castro, trying to persuade him to act reasonably, to little avail. The commandant continued to make furious threats.

Understanding that Castro's patience had reached its limits and also feeling fearful and frustrated, Jeremy had made his identity known to Castro and assured him that the United States Government was supporting Jeremy's opinion and actions. Jeremy and Larkin declared that this was a time for cool heads, that a peaceful solution could still be found. Both men remained certain that Polk did not want to take California and cause bloodshed, and nothing had happened to change that view. They assured the commandant that the actions up north were the results of frightened and disgruntled settlers, led by a United States military officer who was acting without official orders.

Castro listened, his beefy face clearly displaying the distrust he felt. But he listened. Larkin reminded him that he was speaking as the official representative of his government. Moreover, he declared, Jeremy had been sent by Washington to aid Larkin in finding a peaceful solution to the problems in California. Would they have not been told of orders sent to John Fremont?

"I don't really think Castro cares whether we are right or not," Jeremy observed, watching an otter play in the swelling waters near shore. "This time he is determined to provoke conflict. He's already proven that, by sending de la Torre to retake Sonoma."

Larkin shook his head. "Castro values his own neck. He will not wage a major offensive without adequate support. He will only have that if he joins with Pio Pico in the south. Until then, he will continue to bluster and threaten, as he has always done."

"Good point." Jeremy paused, smiling at the furry animal as it rolled over on its back and floated on the surface of the water, leisurely scratching its stomach. "If I had had Fremont within my grasp in San Juan Bautista, I would have humiliated him and run him out of California once and for all."

"Yes, you would have mounted a proper military attack and had done with it," Larkin observed. "But then, you are not Castro."

An agreeable silence fell between them, both men watching the antics of the otter, which had been joined by another. The two animals began to play, wrestling in the water. "That reminds me," Jeremy said suddenly. "Thomas, I am leaving for Sonoma tomorrow."

"*What* reminds you?" Larkin asked, arching a brow as he watched the animals. He laughed. "Never mind, I don't want to know. As for your departure—I don't see why not. You probably should have done it sooner—"

"Sooner?" Jeremy turned and glared at him. "I would have left ten days ago except that you constantly insisted that you needed me here!"

"Calm down, Morgan. I did, and I do. Point in fact, it was the revelation of your position that mollified Castro. Not that he was too pleased to discover that you have been working for the U.S. Government all of this time. But he has learned to trust you—unlike someone else we know. Yes, you should go. I have begun to suspect that it is the only way we will learn what is really happening up there. Besides, it is not likely that anything will happen here." He paused, frowning at Jeremy, who had suddenly grown pale. He turned, following Jeremy's horrified gaze to a point beyond the bay. "Oh, my God," he breathed.

Coming out of the fog, rounding Point Pinos with shortened sail, was an American man-of-war. It cut through the water, sailing into the deep water harbor with four sister ships, all flying the Stars and Stripes from their masts. The men stood watching, aware that an audience had begun to gather.

"As an army officer, I only had a brief course in flags of the navy," Jeremy murmured. "However, if I am not mistaken, that is the flag of the Commander of the Pacific Fleet."

"I am not in the military," Larkin said quietly, "but I am certain of it."

"Well," Jeremy said, turning to look at the consul. "In that event, I suggest that you get that damned consular uniform of yours out of mothballs, Thomas. It would seem that you have finally found a use for it."

Ariana rode into Monterey with mixed emotions. She knew she should go directly to Larkin, but there were more personal matters pressing on her mind. She had kept thoughts of Jeremy at the back of her mind the past five days, as she had concentrated on survival. Her senses had been alert to everything about her, in an effort to avoid danger. Garcia had suddenly appeared the second day and rode with her for a time, then left her just as suddenly in the late afternoon. She didn't want to know where he was going and didn't ask.

She was hungry for something besides wild beans and mustard leaves. And she dreamed of a soft bed; a dreamless sleep to make up for the brief, guarded naps that had made up the last week. Most of all, she wanted Jeremy's arms about her. As she had passed through Salinas, she had finally allowed herself to think of him, that she would actually be seeing him before the end of the day.

Since those moments when she had allowed herself to dwell on the subject of Jeremy Morgan, his image had consumed her. She smiled, slowing Oro to a steady gate, remembering how blue Jeremy's eyes were, the tiny laugh lines that radiated from their corners. And so much more.

His house came into view, and her heart began to beat in a heavy, steady rhythm. The sorrel that her uncle had given him was tied up in front at a standing post. The realization that he was there, that she would be in his arms in a matter of moments, left her pleasantly light-headed. She slipped from Oro's back, and tied him next to the other horse. Then she rushed to the door, pounding on it impatiently. At last it opened.

"Maria—where is he?" she said, stepping past the startled maid. She tore off her gloves, throwing them on a hall table, and glanced back at the maid impatiently.

"He is in his room, Senorita Saldivar. Shall I—"

Ariana gave her no time to finish as she began to run up the stairs, ignoring the maid's scandalized protest. She wanted to laugh out loud as she envisioned Jeremy's expression when he saw her. She opened one door, only to find it empty, and moved on to the next, throwing it open, and then the next. And then he was there, standing before a pier mirror.

"Jeremy!" she cried, her eyes feasting on him. Then they began to widen with shock. The next moments seemed to pass in slow motion. Her senses were bombarded with thoughts, feelings, and impulses that tossed confusingly. She realized that he was smiling, as his first, stunned surprise turned to pleasure. Part of her thrilled at the sight of him, and she had to repress her joy as a feeling of horror consumed her, destroying the happiness that had sustained her throughout the day as each mile had brought her closer to him. She could only stare.

Across the room, illuminated by the sun from the window, his hands lingered on the top button of his tunic. His face finally registered the horror in her own expression. Jeremy, her beloved Jeremy, stood there in the blue, brass-buttoned, epauleted uniform of a major in the United States Army.

"Ariana!"

She heard his voice calling to her, but she was already stumbling down the steps, running toward the door. Lies followed her, raced ahead of her, filling her with a pain she would have thought impossible for a human being to bear.

21

Jeremy and Larkin were led to the commodore's cabin immediately upon coming aboard his flagship, the sixty-four-gun Savannah. As the two men entered the spacious cabin, a slender, silver-haired man in his mid-sixties, dressed in a trim, bedecked naval uniform, rose from his chair behind a massive desk.

"Consul, I am honored to meet you at last." John Drake Sloat, Commander of the United States Pacific Fleet, held out his hand.

Larkin grasped it firmly. "As I am to meet you, Commodore. May I present Major Jeremy Morgan—"

"Ah yes, Major Morgan. I have had good reports on you from Washington, Major."

"Thank you, sir," Jeremy responded, shaking the Commodore's hand.

Sloat gestured for the two men to sit. "May I offer you some refreshments, gentlemen? Coffee—or something stronger, perhaps?"

"Coffee would be pleasant," Larkin answered. "Thank you."

Sloat nodded to his adjutant, who left the cabin. Then the commodore turned back to Larkin. "As you may know, Mr. Larkin, I sent word ashore offering to fire a salute to the Mexican authorities, but we have been waiting, and there is no flag visible."

"It was a gesture that was met with a great deal of relief,

Commodore." Larkin smiled. "It will help me to assure the locals that your presence is no threat."

"I have no intention of repeating the mistake of another member of my naval fraternity." Sloat smiled grimly.

"Ah, yes." Larkin nodded. "Coincidentally, I recently received a letter from Commodore Jones. A much delayed verdict was issued from his Board of Inquiry, exonerating him of all responsibility in that unfortunate event. He hopes to return to California as early as next year."

"I am glad to hear it." Sloan paused as the door opened and his aid reentered the room carrying a tray of coffee, which he set down on the desk between them. "Gentlemen, I would like to introduce you to my adjutant, William Tecumsa Sherman. Lieutenant, please remain. Now," he added, "as for the other matter. Does General Castro wish for me to salute his flag, or not?"

"I am certain that he would," Jeremy answered. "If he had one."

Sloat frowned, regarding the two men with puzzlement. Larkin shrugged. "The Presidio's flag disappeared some time ago, and there are no funds to replace it."

"Are you serious?" The commodore stared.

"Totally," Jeremy answered. "Nor is there powder to answer your salute."

"Are there cannon?"

"Three. But only one works. My reports to Washington have detailed the conditions of the military establishment here, as well as in the north. The guns at Presidio San Francisco have not been fired for almost forty years and are totally inoperative."

"Now sir," Larkin interjected. "May I presume to ask what your orders are? I am certain you understand, considering the situation between our country and Mexico, that the presence of your squadron is causing considerable alarm."

"Of course. I wish to assure you, Mr. Larkin, that I do not wish to cause concern among the inhabitants." He looked uncertainly at the other men. "Frankly, I am not sure what I am doing here. My orders were that, in the event of war, I was to capture the ports without alarming the inhabitants."

Jeremy exchanged a look of incredulity with Larkin. Take the ports without alarming the inhabitants? "Then we are at war," he said.

Sloat's expression deepened into a frown. "Major, I rather imagine that my information is the same as yours: that we are at war. However, that information has come from Mexico. I have not received official word from Washington. And that, gentlemen, is our dilemma. There is a British squadron somewhere between here and the Sandwich Islands, under the command of Admiral Seymour. If I take official possession of California and we are not actually at war, I will find myself in the same situation as my predecessor, Commodore Jones. If, on the other hand, we are at war and I do nothing, the British may take possession before I can act."

"I believe, Commodore, there is something that you should see." Jeremy reached into the dispatch case he brought with him and extracted Revere's letter, handing it across the desk to the naval officer. "It is from Lieutenant Joseph Revere, of the U.S.S. *Portsmouth*. He has been working with us for the past few months."

The commodore opened the letter, glancing at Larkin and Jeremy with a frown, then began to read. After a moment he sat up straight in his chair, his expression one of disbelief. "John Charles Fremont? He is behind this?"

"We are not certain of that, Commodore," Larkin said quickly. "At this point it is merely rumor."

"There is a way—" Jeremy began, glancing at Larkin. "Ariana is in Monterey."

"Ariana?" Larkin's eyes grew wide. "Here? Where is she?"

"She—came to my house this morning. I was unable to talk with her. I tried to find her, that is why I was late. She's disappeared."

Sloat cleared his throat, gaining their attention. "This woman is of importance to this matter?"

"She is Mariano Guadalupe Vallejo's niece," Larkin explained. "She was in Sonoma when the event occurred. Good Lord, Jeremy, why did she disappear? We've got to find her!"

"We will," Jeremy assured him.

"I don't understand," Sloat said. "What has Captain Fremont to do with any of this? I had understood that he was on a mapping expedition in the Oregon territory!"

"So did we," Jeremy said grimly. He proceeded to explain the episode at Hawk's Peak that led to Fremont's expulsion from California. "Apparently, he has returned and is somehow mixed up in all of this."

"Damnation," Sloat swore. "This is terrible. It's worse than I thought." He seemed to visibly age. "Well, there is nothing to do for now but wait."

"Sir—" Jeremy interjected. "The Californios and the settlers are primed for each other's throats." He paused, glancing at Larkin. "Thomas, in this instance I must disagree with you. Commodore, I believe that your presence here is timely. If you act swiftly, you can diffuse this situation. What has happened cannot be undone, but your authority can undermine Fremont's actions."

"Jeremy, what are you suggesting?" Larkin said with alarm. "The commodore is correct in using caution."

"No, not now. If he had arrived a few weeks ago, before that damnable Bear Flag incident, yes. Commodore, even if we are not at war, we might as well be. But Fremont will have to back down if you take command. Then you could appease—"

"We shall see, Major," Sloat said abruptly. "However, I have already stated my position on this matter. I will not—I *must not* act until I have official orders from Washington! Now then, there are other matters which must be seen to at the present time. My men have been at sea for many months. I am anxious to give them liberty. Lieutenant?"

Jeremy was stunned. Sloat had totally ignored him.

Sherman stepped forward. "Yes sir," the officer said officiously. "With your permission, Mr. Larkin, we plan to send the men ashore in small groups of about one hundred. They have been given strict orders not to molest the inhabitants, or cause undo mayhem. However, in order to avoid any possible problems, my men will be given stipends in the area of $1,000 to $1,500 each. We would like to send the first party ashore in the morning—if that is agreeable with you, of course."

In spite of his mood, Jeremy noted that Larkin stiffened at the enormous amount of money that had been allotted for shore leave. "Of course," the consul agreed.

"Well then, gentlemen," Sloat said affably, rising from his chair. "I feel that this meeting went surprisingly well, don't you agree?" He stepped around the desk to shake their hands. "Major, you will find out about the situation up north, I trust?" he asked as he took Jeremy's hand.

"Without question, sir," Jeremy responded, unsettled by the abrupt end to the meeting. He glanced at Larkin who seemed unruffled by the fact that they were being summarily dismissed.

They did not speak as they were rowed to shore. Stepping from the longboat, Jeremy swore. "Smile, Morgan," Larkin said in a low voice. "People are watching."

A large crowd had gathered about the Custom House, their voices lowered in an expectant, nervous hush. Larkin strode down the dock, turned up the street, and, with a pleasant grin, headed directly toward the crowd. Jeremy followed, his face stiff with a smile he did not feel. Sloat's uncertainty, his obvious indecision, and his reluctance to listen had not impressed him. It was true that the commodore was aging, and that could account for his mood; he had to be close to exhaustion from the long voyage. However, he was Commander of the Pacific Fleet. Age notwithstanding, for good or ill, should the matter come to a head, he was the man who would take possession of California.

Jeremy joined Larkin, who was assuring the clustered citizens that there was no need for concern. Some moments were spent explaining Jeremy's uniform, to people who had known him for the past year as a businessman. Larkin fended most of the questions, explaining that Major Morgan had worked for him as an assistant consul, whereupon there was no need to exercise his military position. His choice of wearing a uniform today was purely a matter of courtesy for the visiting commodore. In fact, he added with a grin, Jeremy's choice had allowed him to wear his own uniform, something he had been wanting to do for over a year. Laughter met the comment, along with a few blatant looks cast in Jeremy's direction from the younger women as they appraised the handsome American officer. One young woman of Jeremy's brief acquaintance leaned forward, smiling up through her lashes as she commented on how wonderful he looked and expressed her disappointment that he had never chosen to wear the uniform before. Jeremy smiled, but inwardly he was seething with anger.

He had been playing cat and mouse for over a year. That morning he had made the decision finally to declare his position for two reasons: one, that he was sick to death of acting as a spy. And two, that by doing so he would now be in a better position to have some control over Fremont. In spite of Sloat's indecisive reasoning, Jeremy had no doubt that they were at war. Like it or not, the Larkin Plan had failed. Oh, not completely; Larkin's work might help keep bloodshed to a minimum. But vacillation at this point could ruin even the chance for that. He saw fear in the eyes of the people above their hopeful smiles, fear that could turn to panic without assurances from a strong presence.

It was then, as his eyes passed over the heads of the crowd, that he saw her. She was dressed in a long serape and a wide-brimmed, flat-crowned hat. Larkin paused mid-sentence, turning with surprise as Jeremy suddenly pushed by him, disappearing into the crowd. He pushed and shoved, murmuring apologies as his eyes were fixed on her just beyond him. He knew that if she saw him she would bolt, so he did not move toward her directly, but by a slower, roundabout path. He came up behind her and reached out.

As he grasped her arm, she spun about, pulling away instinctively. Her surprised expression turned to anger when she realized who he was, her large, dark eyes filling with rage. "Let me go," she exclaimed.

"Not on your life," he said grimly. "We are going to talk."

He pulled her to his side, wrapping an arm around her waist. He pushed her ahead of him through the crowd to the Custom House, ignoring the curious glances of people they passed. They stepped into the dark, cool interior, and he smiled pleasantly at the customs agent who looked up with interest. "Good morning, Mario. I would appreciate it if I could use your office for a moment."

The man's eyes widened, both at the grip Jeremy had on a furious Ariana, and at Jeremy's uniform. "Si, Morgan—ah, Major Morgan. Of course, if you wish."

Jeremy closed the door behind them and released her. She stepped away, glaring at him as she rubbed her arm.

He saw the gesture and frowned. "I'm sorry, Ariana, I did not mean to hurt you."

"Cabron!"

A smile twitched. "I know what that means, sweetheart."

"Bueno. And you can forget the endearments. I suppose that you have brought me here to explain the fact that you are an American army officer. A small matter you have chosen to overlook all of these months. You needn't bother, Major Morgan; I am not interested."

"Yes you are. And I will give you reasons for my omission if you want them. But nothing suggesting an apology."

She turned quickly, walking to the window on the far side of the room. "I would not expect one. Why did you bring me here?"

"Why did you return to Monterey?"

She closed her eyes against the pain that rushed through her. To see you, damn you, Jeremy Morgan, she thought. "To bring Larkin word of what has happened in Sonoma."

"And that is why I brought you here." She spun back on him, unable to hide the effect of his cold words. Her eyes filled with tears, adding to her anger. "Ariana, we do need to talk about us."

"There is no *us*, Major!"

"Yes, there is. Ariana, as much as I wanted to, I could not tell you about me until this morning."

"Why now? Because I know—after seeing you in that!" she said vehemently, gesturing at his uniform.

"No. Because of that squadron of ships in the harbor."

"Oh! And how have they changed the fact that you lied to me!"

"I have never lied to you. Their presence changes my position here."

"Not lied to me? You've lied every day I've known you!"

"Not directly. Only in the same way that you did to me, until I discovered what you were doing." He smiled suddenly, shrugging. "Admit it, Ariana. I'm just better at this than you are."

"Oh! *Cabron!*"

"You're repeating yourself." He grinned.

She glared at him. "How about a loathsome, miscreant whore-hound?"

"It's more inventive." He smiled. "Ariana, you're just upset because you didn't figure me out for yourself. We both were doing our jobs. But they have nothing to do with how we feel about each other."

Suddenly, her anger faded. "No, Jeremy," she said quietly, sorrow filling her eyes. "It is much deeper than that. That uniform—" she swallowed, her eyes passing over him, "is the uniform of your country." She held up her hand to silence him as he began to speak. "No, it is not because the United States is at war with Mexico. I knew that when you left Petaluma, yet I came to you. I thought—that no matter what happened there would be a chance for us. That you had embraced my people, our way of life . . ." She paused, laughing sadly. "I even fantasized that you might join with me . . ." Then she looked at him with clear, cold eyes. "Major Morgan, there is no us. Your orders will be clear: California is to become part of the United States. That fleet of ships out there, in spite of what Thomas assured the people outside, is here to achieve that end, and you will be part of it. And I will fight you, Jeremy. I may not win, but I will fight you."

He stared at her. "You still envision California as an independent republic? Ariana—"

"Ariana! Good Lord, child, where have you been?"

They both turned at Larkin's entrance. "Are you all right?" Larkin said, coming into the room. "Why didn't you come to me immediately?"

"I am fine, Thomas." She smiled, accepting his embrace. "I was—delayed this morning. Besides, it would seem that you had other obligations." Her eyes lightened with humor as she glanced at his uniform. "It looks splendid on you."

Jeremy watched with amazement at the swift change in her. Larkin visibly puffed. For the first time, Jeremy began to truly appreciate her talents—and her commitment. The thought struck him uncomfortably.

"So then, tell me!" Larkin pressed. "Oh, do sit down, we have a lot to discuss." He looked miserable as he forced himself to ask the next question. "Where is Mariano?"

"At Sutter's Fort—in prison," she answered grimly.

He shut his eyes for a moment, shaking his head. "I was afraid that was true. Is he all right?"

"Yes, he is well enough, if you discount the fact that he is being held in a cell without any comforts. He is given enough to eat, and he has a blanket to warm him."

Larkin's expression turned hard, barely concealing the outrage he felt. "Tell me everything."

Jeremy stood aside, leaning his shoulder against a wall near the door as he listened. He watched Larkin's reaction to her story, gratified to see the powerful anger in the consul that Larkin was usually so adept at hiding. And he listened to Ariana, watching for some indication of her own plans.

"Kit Carson was part of the group that arrested him; you are certain?"

"There were at least thirty of them, but there was no

mistake. He was one of them. He also led the force against de la Torre."

"Then Fremont is involved," Larkin said unhappily.

"Involved?" Jeremy laughed with disbelief. "Thomas, the man has declared himself military governor! May I point out that he cannot even be certain that we are at war? You only received word of that possibility two weeks ago. Fremont returned to New Helvetia in May. He was brewing his plans long before I left Petaluma."

"He might have his own sources."

"Oh, God, Larkin. He was in Oregon. The only person he saw was Gillespie!" Jeremy pushed away from the wall and came to stand in front of him. "Look at the facts. We both know that Gillespie was convinced war was imminent. Those were his own conclusions drawn from his time in Mexico, beliefs he carried to Fremont."

"He had dispatches for Fremont," Larkin argued.

"Thomas, why are you defending him? Either of them, for that matter. Gillespie clearly said that he had letters from Fremont's wife and Senator Benton, nothing more. Would you prefer to believe that Washington is dealing a double message? That the president is sending one set of orders to us, and another to Fremont? Polk's orders, as well as Buchanan's, have always been the same: find a peaceful solution! Why would they pit Fremont against you, under-mining your authority and everything you've done here?"

"Jeremy, I understand your feelings about Fremont—"

"My personal feelings have nothing to do with this! I do not blame Fremont for Beth's mistake, if that is what you are thinking."

"I believe that, Thomas," Ariana said.

"Thank you, Senorita Saldivar." Jeremy smirked. "The point is, Thomas, I believe that Gillespie carried only two letters to Fremont. One was from his father-in-law. If there was any suggestion of how Fremont should proceed, it could have come from Benton."

Larkin stared at Jeremy for a moment, his face working with his thoughts. Then he turned back to Ariana. "Where was Fremont when you left?"

"In Sonoma, declaring himself the victor of a great battle, in defeating Castro's forces."

Larkin suddenly took on a strange look. He leaned back in his chair, sighing with deep weariness. "Oh, yes. Castro. I should explain why I was delayed. Castro is gone."

"What?"

"He is gone. Vanished. I was going to arrange a meeting with the commodore, but he has left with his men. There is no one in the Presidio."

"Damn," Jeremy swore. "He is on his way to Pio Pico; I'd bet my life on it."

"Without doubt," Larkin agreed, rising from the chair. "And if that is true, may God help us."

For the next five days, Monterey was kept on tenterhooks. The American sailors came ashore, and there were few altercations, all minor, while the money they spent gained the favor of the merchants and ladies it was lavished upon. There were daily conferences between Larkin and Sloat, though there was little disagreement between the two men that caution was the byword. Left to itself, the tenuous peace might have lasted indefinitely, but word began to drift down from the north. There were reports of Indian raids and of settlers who were burned out, along with stories of atrocities committed by the newly formed California Battalion, under the command of John Charles Fremont.

Ariana, at Rachel's insistence, was staying with the Larkins. She resumed her contacts, joining secretly with the radical faction that met daily to discuss California's future. The young dissidents were joined by many of Larkin's former allies as their concerns were fed daily by the actions of Fremont's brigade.

Jeremy resumed his visits to the local grogshops and was not disappointed. If he had entertained any thought that his new position would curtail a flow of information, it became quickly apparent that, if anything, he encouraged the opposite reaction. The settlers who gathered in the grogshops gravitated to him. Each had his opinion of what the military should do, ranging from proclamations to armed hostilities. More than one suggested that all Californios should be summarily sent back to Mexico, leaving the territory to those who knew what to do with it.

Often, in such moments, Jeremy had to remind himself of his duty and that he was seeking information. He often struggled against a strong impulse to hit someone. Instead, he usually ordered another rum. But the entire situation sat like bitter bile in the pit of his stomach. He began to visualize Winfield Scott's tormented eyes as he talked about the Cherokees.

Jeremy also visited the Californio haunts, where he was accepted with reserve. At first he was met by silence and distrust from those who had once been accepting, but gradually he noticed a change. Conversations became more open as anger fed courage. It did not surprise him when they began to talk freely in front of him; he knew he was being used. And he remembered what Vallejo had told him about the Californios' passion for debate—until it failed and they reached for their guns.

He had entered the small establishment with few expectations. In fact, he was totally exhausted and planned to have one short measure of rum then go home to bed. Choosing a table in the shadows, he ordered his drink and leaned his chair back against a wall as he waited. And then he saw her.

She was sitting with a group of young men at a large table at the other side of the room. She was wearing a serape and a flat-crowned hat. Jeremy smiled as he picked up the rum that was set down in front of him. Apparently, it was her *liberalismo* outfit.

Suddenly his attention was caught by raised voices at the table. One of the men stood up, gesturing with anger. It was Mariano Soberanes. "The Yanquis in the north say they are liberating California from uncivilized men!" he exclaimed. Then he turned and stared directly at Jeremy. "Morgan, you have known us, how can these *leperos* call us uncivilized?"

Jeremy was aware that everyone in the room had turned toward him. Well, well, he thought. So I am to be the main attraction in this drama. He smiled easily, keeping his voice even. "Simply, Mariano, because they must justify their actions. Either they are liberators, or they are thieves."

Jeremy's words were met with silence. Soberanes looked confused by the blunt honesty of the statement, but Jose Estrada leaped up. "They lie to cover their own acts! They know that the Indians act of their own accord, as they have always done! And Castro did not steal horses to be used by his troops to force the settlers out of California, as the Yanquis have claimed, but to wage war against Pio Pico in his dispute with the governor over the treasury!"

"It is apparent that you have come among us to gain information, Major," Soberanes said. "You wear your uniform; is it meant to threaten us?"

Jeremy smiled. "Threaten you, Mariano? Hardly. I am wearing my uniform because I happen to be an officer in the United States Army—"

"But you did not choose to wear it until now," Ariana interrupted, staring at him evenly.

"No, not until now," he agreed. "I was sent here by President Polk to determine the situation and report to him. He wanted to know what the attitudes of the Californios were in fact, not just speculation or rumor. He wanted to know how you felt about cession, and most of all, how cession could be accomplished peacefully. These were matters I could answer only as a civilian. I wear my uniform among you now to give you a message. Beyond what is happening up north, there are those who have the authority to offer that peaceful solution. There is no need for bloodshed."

"No need—if we accept the rule of the United States!" Ariana said sharply.

"Yes," Jeremy answered, regarding her steadily. "In spite of the fact that the rebellion in Sonoma was led, or at the very least influenced, by an officer in the United States Army, I am here to assure you that my government has no plans to take California by force. The settlers are acting on their own accord and have caused considerable grief. Moreover, I have no doubt—nor do you—that the so-called California Battalion will continue to cause grief unless they are stopped. You cannot do it; you have not the resources nor the experience."

"But you can?" Manuel Castro was sitting next to Ariana. The prefect stood to face Jeremy, his face grim.

"Yes," Jeremy countered calmly. "My government can."

"And if we reject your offer?"

"Manuel, it is not an offer. It simply will be done."

"That is a threat!" Ariana exclaimed.

"No, it is not. The settlers were not sent here by my government. They came on their own, or by Mexico's invitation. Now it is time that you looked at the facts. The United States has long looked upon California and Oregon as part of its Manifest Destiny. We have tried to negotiate for California, and we have offered to purchase it. We are now at war with Mexico over Texas, and California and Oregon are certain to become part of the final prize. Mexico cannot defend even a part of California. Your concern should be with those settlers within your borders who truly threaten your liberties. Thus we are back to the issue of the California Battalion."

"Well said," Soberanes answered grimly. "Your fine words would have us overlook how we have been betrayed! For years we have listened to your consul and believed in his words. We believed that we would be aided to overthrow the tyranny of the Mexican Government. Yet now, what has been the result? Do we find ourselves pitted against men of honor, men worthy to fight against us in this struggle? No! We are to fight men who are exiles, yet we are not even considered by them to be civilized!"

Jeremy understood the depth of Soberanes's words. If he had learned nothing else in the past year, he had come to understand the Californio sense of honor. Mexico had always treated California as *la otra banda,* the other shore. And now, their opponents considered them mere barbarians.

"Mariano, they will be dealt with, I promise you. Your honor will be met, not with arms, but with diplomacy. There will be much to do to build this country into what it can be, and we can best effect it together."

"Lies!" Manuel turned to the group, his eyes flaring with rage. "In spite of the Yanqui's false promises, it is the present we must deal with! The Yanquis have chosen a flag with a bear on it, an animal who represents to us a thief that steals our cattle, our very lifeblood! It was not innocently chosen, but with insulting deliberation! They placed a star on it to represent their belief that California would become another Texas! Have we forgotten Isaac Graham, when he and his *Rifleros Americanos* declared 'California next'? It is obvious that this has been a well-developed plot! They have taken Vallejo, imprisoning him!" He placed a hand on Ariana's shoulder, looking down at her with sympathy. Jeremy had to give him the moment, it was an effective gesture.

"They are expecting us to attack in an attempt to release him!" Manuel continued. "It will give them the excuse to retaliate! And meanwhile, they commit every atrocity, no matter how grievous!" He paused, as if he was reluctant to go on. "Three days ago, the despot Fremont and his men murdered Jose de los Ryes Berreyesa and his nephews, Francisco and Ramon de Haro."

Cries of shock and outrage went up, and the room erupted into bedlam. Manuel waved his hands for silence, shouting above the din. "Listen to me! Hear me! Fremont was patrolling with his men near Suisum Bay. They came across the three unarmed innocents and, without warning, they shot them. Ramon was killed instantly. When his brother fell across him to protect the body, he was shot as one of his attackers cried, 'Shoot the other bastard!' When Jose cried out against the outrage, he said, 'Why do you kill them for no reason? I am an old man, you should have killed me instead!' They obliged him. And Morgan asks that we deal peacefully with these people? We are asked to deal with savages!"

Jeremy struggled to remain calm in the ensuing uproar, forcing his expression to remain placid as he privately dealt with his own rage. He had no doubt that the story was true. Manuel would not have chosen to use an incident that could be easily discounted. At that moment he wanted to murder Fremont. His gaze shifted, traveling over the anger and despair he saw in the eyes of those gathered, and finally settling on Ariana. She nodded imperceptibly, a calm smile on her face. Glancing at Manuel, then back at her, Jeremy wondered who had planned the young rebel's effective speech. It was brilliant, and beautifully timed. Then, as his eyes locked with Ariana's, he no longer had any doubt.

22

Jeremy entered the Larkins' dining room, pausing by Rachel's chair to bend and brush her cheek with a kiss. "You look particularly beautiful this morning, Rachel," he murmured. "When are you going to leave that good-for-nothing and run away with me?"

"Don't tempt me, Jeremy Morgan." She flushed with a pleased smile. "Sit down and have your breakfast."

"Keep your hands off my wife, Morgan," Larkin said with a mouthful of biscuit. "If she runs away with you, I shall be left with that unruly pack in her nursery."

"*My* nursery?" she asked, a brow arching. "It seems to me that you had something to do with it."

"When were they relegated back to a nursery?" Jeremy asked as he slipped into a chair.

"After the food fight at dinner last night," Thomas said, passing Jeremy a bowl of fruit.

"A food fight?"

"Now, Thomas," Rachel countered. "They were just feeling their spirits."

"Explain that to my good coat. It now has permanent gravy stains." He looked up suddenly. "Come to think of it, it was your fault, Morgan."

"My fault?"

"Yes, our eldest resident son chose our dinner hour to demonstrate how you taught him to throw a football." Larkin picked up a biscuit and tossed it to Jeremy.

"The boy has a good arm on him," Jeremy observed, dropping the roll onto his plate. "Definite Harvard material."

"After last night, I'm sending him to Yale."

"Eggs, Jeremy?"

Jeremy took the hint and accepted the plate from Rachel. "Yes, ma'am," he said somberly, winking at Larkin.

"Morgan," Larkin asked suddenly, leaning back in his chair. "What would you think of a ball?"

"I thought that subject was changed."

"Not that kind, a full-dress ball. A dance, you fool."

Jeremy spooned eggs and chorizo sausage onto his plate and reached for the butter. Lathering a generous amount on his biscuit, he glanced at the consul. "What do I think of it? That depends upon why you want to do it."

"A celebration."

"What are we celebrating?"

"The entrance of California to the United States."

Jeremy's biscuit paused halfway to his mouth. "What?"

Larkin removed his pocket watch, flipping back the cover to note the time. "In approximately forty-five minutes, a contingent of marines will depart the *Savannah* to raise the Stars and Strips over the Custom House. Eat up, Morgan, we don't have much time."

Jeremy stared at Larkin. "What happened?"

"Sloat called me on board last night to discuss the matter. Oh, your name was not mentioned but his words were—ah, rather familiar. He has finally come to the decision that Fremont's activities have lit a slow fuse on a powder keg. Moreover, he is growing more troubled, thinking that the British may arrive any day. Frankly, I think that he wants to see an end to the affair. He is not a well man. The past five days have convinced him that the people have accepted the presence of his men, and he hopes to conclude the matter peacefully . . ."

"If he acts quickly."

"So he has finally concluded."

Peacefully, Jeremy repeated to himself. "Where is Ariana?"

"She is not up yet," Rachel answered. "Why do you ask?"

"Are you certain that she is here?"

"Yes." Rachel frowned at him. "Is there some problem?"

I hope not, he thought. "Does she know of this?"

"No," Larkin answered. "At this moment the only people ashore who know are in this room."

"Good," Jeremy grunted. As he turned his attention to his breakfast, the Larkins exchanged a puzzled glance. Just then a loud crash was heard from the direction of the kitchen, followed by youthful shrieks of rage. Larkin sighed, rising from his chair.

"Jeremy, I will say this for children: they keep a man humble." The consul of California squared his shoulders and strode away, readying for battle.

When the door closed behind him, Rachel turned back to Jeremy. "Why are you concerned about Ariana, Jeremy? Is she in some sort of trouble?"

"Why would you ask that?" He shrugged, taking another bite of egg. In the silence that followed, he glanced up at her. She was watching him with a steady regard. "Is there anything that escapes you, Rachel?"

"Not much."

"Don't worry about it; I'll handle it."

"Will you?"

"I'll try, Rachel."

"See that you do. That girl needs you. We all do," she added.

They exchanged a glance that left Jeremy genuinely touched. Coming from this woman, it was a deeply felt compliment. He sighed softly. Laying down his fork, he leaned back in his chair. "I don't deserve your faith, Rachel. I don't feel very good about myself these days."

"Because of Beth?"

He smiled at her bluntness. "Partly. I'm a man who has allowed his wife to leave him, taking his son. I am trying to live with the fact that I don't want her back. I'm an adulterer. I am in love with a woman I have no right to love. I thought, for a while, that I could be good for Ariana, but I know now that was merely wishful, selfish thinking. I hurt her deeply, and I know now that it could have been the only outcome." He glanced at her, expecting disapproval.

"Jeremy Morgan, you listen to me. You are a fine man who has made some mistakes in his life. That only makes you human. Would it shock you to learn that I fell in love with Thomas the moment I met him? I did not know then that my first husband had died. Yes, I know what you are going to say: that I did not pursue the relationship until I was free. That is true, but know this as well: I had deep affection for my first husband, but following that voyage, I knew that I would spend the rest of my life thinking of Thomas. And I spent a good deal of time thinking about that over the years, with a good deal of guilt. Gradually, I came to realize those feelings were wrong. I had not wished my husband dead; you did not wish for Beth to leave you. Deal with what *is,* Jeremy, not how you would wish it to be."

After a long moment, he gave into a reluctant smile. "Thank you, Rachel. I promise to think about what you have said."

"That is all that I ask," she said briskly. "It would be nice to think that at least one man listens to me."

He laughed. "With that, Rachel, I shall direct myself to my next objective." He rose from the chair, dropping his napkin on the table. "As for you—I would recommend that you rescue your husband. Time is growing short and I am certain that he would rather deal with Sloat and a group of angry citizens than the bloody war in the kitchen."

As he left the dining room, he did consider her words. He knew she meant well, but the differences in their pasts could not be overlooked. There was no doubt in his mind that Rachel Larkin would have stayed with her first husband, no matter how much she had loved Thomas. His thoughts of Beth had increased over the past month, and guilt had grown steadily. Perhaps the Scottish poet, Campbell, had been right when he wrote: "Tis distance lends enchantment to the view."

He waited for her in the hallway near the foot of the stairs. Within moments she came down, and his brow rose speculatively. She was in her *liberalismo* outfit. As she reached the last few steps she saw him. "What do you want?" she said peevishly.

"Good morning, sweetheart." He smiled. "I missed you at breakfast."

"Oh? Were you here? I am glad I missed it."

"Are you? Well, it doesn't matter. We're going to spend the day together."

"What makes you think so?"

"Come on." He took her arm firmly and escorted her

through the store to the front door.

"Jeremy, if you do not let me go this instant, I shall scream!"

"Feel free." He grunted. "I'll simply tell anyone who cares that you are under arrest."

"For what?"

"Insurrection. No one will question this uniform, *querida,* not anymore."

"Where are you taking me?" she gasped, trying to keep up with his long strides.

"To the Custom House, so you can have a firsthand view."

"Of what?"

"Of history, my love. And I have no intention of allowing you to make a disastrous mistake at such a portentous moment."

They arrived at the Custom House, where he plopped her down onto a bench and dared her with a warning look not to move. She glanced about at the crowd which had gathered, wondering what it meant. Then, as they were joined by the Larkins, she noticed that everyone's eyes were focused on the harbor. No! she cried silently. *Madre, no!*

A large party of uniformed marines had come ashore, falling into a neat unit at the harbor landing. Before them they carried the American flag. The crowd fell silent as the contingent began to move, their steady cadence pounding in Ariana's brain. The marine officer shouted curt orders, and the formation moved in military unison, quickstep and double time, up through the streets.

Ariana was aware that Jeremy was watching her. Stiffly, she stood up and stared rigidly at the approaching formation and the standard they held before them. Just then Jeremy stepped forward, taking her arm. He led her to the small group of naval officers that stood by the Custom House door.

"Commodore Sloat, may I present Senorita Ariana Saldivar, niece of Don Mariano Guadalupe Vallejo."

Lieutenant Sherman, who was standing at the commodore's side, frowned. "General Vallejo, Major?"

"If he were here to greet you himself, I believe he would prefer the title of don, Lieutenant. Unfortunately, as you know, he has been detained. Under the circumstances, and as General Castro has decided to absent himself, may I suggest that Senorita Saldivar might represent her uncle in his place of honor?"

Stunned, Ariana's eyes flew up to Jeremy's profile. But before she could respond, the aging commodore stepped to her side. "Your suggestion is an excellent one, Major." With that, he took Ariana's arm and led her to an elevated reviewing stand that had been hastily erected at the corner of the building next to the flag pole. Jeremy followed behind with the Larkins.

"I hope you know what you are doing, Jeremy," Larkin said quietly.

"So do I, Thomas."

As they took their chairs in the reviewing stand, Sloat regarded Ariana with interest. "Senorita Saldivar, I understand that it was you who brought word of what was happening in Sonoma."

"Si, it was my uncle's wish," she responded coolly.

"It must have been a difficult journey; you have our deepest gratitude."

"In all due respect, Commodore, it was not done for you." Her gaze went past his shoulder to the ships in the harbor. "I had no idea that you would be here."

"Point taken." The Commander of the Pacific Fleet smiled. "Would you have come, if you had known?"

"Probably not," she answered without hesitation.

The officers about them stiffened with indignation. Larkin's gaze became fixed, and Jeremy rolled his eyes. The commodore, to everyone's surprise, merely laughed. "I cannot say that I blame you, Miss Saldivar. But let me assure you that everything possible will be done to expedite the prompt release of Gener—Don Vallejo. Moreover, the information you brought will aid me in settling the unfortunate matter up north." He paused as the marines arrived at the foot of the platform. He nodded to his adjutant.

Sherman stepped to the edge of the platform, where he stood above the apprehensive crowd. They watched with a mixture of anger and defiance as he unrolled the parchment and began to read, first in English, then in Spanish. "From John Drake Sloat, Commander of the Pacific Fleet, Governor General of California, to the People of California: Greetings. Although I come in arms with a powerful force, I do not come among you as an enemy. I come as your best friend. Henceforth, California will be a portion of the

United States, and its peaceful inhabitants will enjoy the same rights and privileges they now enjoy . . ."

Ariana watched and listened, her thoughts echoing those of the citizens of Monterey. Was this to be it, so simply done? How quickly were a people subjugated, from one tyrant to another. But as Sherman continued to read, their expressions softened, first with wonder, then with guarded hope. It was announced that all imports from the United States would henceforth be duty free and the imports of other nations would be taxed at a fraction of what was demanded under Mexican customs regulations. Thus new trade would bring an era of unprecedented prosperity to the new territory. Further, persons in rightful possession of land would have their titles guaranteed, and no supplies, or other private property, would be taken without fair compensation.

As he concluded, Sherman nodded to Captain Mervine of the marines. With military precision, the marines stepped forward, attached the flag of the United States, and raised it over the Custom House. The crowd watched silently, then murmurs began, floating as the Stars and Stripes rose, catching the wind until it began to furl and snap. As it reached the top of the flag pole, the cannons on the flagship answered, sixty-four guns firing in succession. As the last of the cannons fired its powder, the troops gave out three boisterous cheers, and the marine band struck with drums and brass.

A quarter of an hour later, Ariana stood by herself in the shadows of the Custom House, watching the goings on with shock and anger. Within moments after the band had begun playing, the citizens had joined the Americans in their celebration. The situation shouldn't have surprised her, but it struck hard. It had become a fiesta.

"They are fools," she murmured under her breath.

"Are they?"

She started and turned to find Jeremy at her side. *"Si!"* she snapped. "They think that a few words will change everything. They have not yet learned how worthless the words of Americans are!"

"Brava, *querida."* He smiled grimly, lowering his voice. "Such a brave statement by one who is afraid to face her own truth." With that, he turned and left her. She watched him disappear into the crowd, clenching her hands tightly as she tried to control the rage she felt.

"Ariana, there you are!" Rachel appeared at her side, her handsome face beaming. "My dear, we have been invited to a dinner aboard the commodore's flagship this evening."

"What? Oh, no Rachel, I couldn't." She sighed, collecting herself.

"Of course you can! You must. Remember that you are representing Mariano." Rachel's shrewd eyes noted the look of frustrated anger as Ariana stared at Jeremy's departing back. Her voice became lower. "Ariana, whatever problems you are having with Jeremy, you must put them aside. Commodore Sloat is concerned about Mariano; your presence could go a long way toward helping your uncle."

Rachel's words gained her attention. "Of course, you are right," she answered as her gaze shifted to the large group that had gathered about the commodore. Her mind began to churn with possibilities. "Of course," she repeated softly, "that is exactly where I should be."

"My love, since that first dinner with Sloat five days ago, you have enraptured the poor old commodore, as well as his entire contingent of officers." Rachel chuckled, sipping from her sherry. The two women were enjoying a quiet moment before the beginning of a night which would undoubtedly reach into the early hours of morning. They were in Ariana's bedroom, comfortably settled in their wrappers until it was time to put on their ball gowns. Ariana's maid, who had been brought from the Vallejo home, had just finished dressing her hair. It had taken over an hour to complete the coiffure as Ariana insisted that it be done and re-done until it was perfect.

"You never cease to surprise me, Ariana," Rachel commented, studying the results of the past hour. "You have always resisted foreign fashion. Why this sudden desire to look so—American?"

Ariana looked into the mirror on her dressing table, critically appraising the results. "You don't like it?"

"It is beautiful. It is just very different for you."

Ariana's shining black hair was parted in the middle and pulled to the sides over her ears, where cascades of long curls fell to her shoulders. Garlands of tiny white silk roses held the curls back. The effect was striking against the golden hue of her skin and accentuated her large, dark eyes.

"Ariana," Rachel observed, shaking her head, "you'll have the officers falling all over each other."

Ariana smiled at Rachel's reflection in the mirror as she applied a light touch of blush to her cheeks and lips. She rose from the stool and joined the other woman, curling up in a chair near her. "We are part of the United States now," she said, picking up her glass from the table between them. "I merely want to remind the men of what they left at home."

"I hardly think that will be the result." Rachel smirked. Lost in thought, she idly ran her finger around the rim of her glass. "I do believe that half the officers in Sloat's command would rush to Sonoma to rescue Mariano, if you but gave the word."

"That would be foolish."

"Indeed, it would. Many men, including Mariano, could be hurt. But Sloat has kept his word. He has begun negotiations for the release of those captured during the rebellion. And, as for that distasteful matter, Lieutenant Revere marched into Sonoma three days ago and took control, replacing the 'bear flag' with the Stars and Stripes. He is now acting governor for the area."

Ariana thought of the infectious, likable lieutenant. He was one of the few Yanquis she had any use for. But she wondered how effective he would be with Fremont, who must be bristling under Revere's command. She didn't believe for a moment that they had heard the last of the California Battalion.

Rachel sipped from her sherry as she studied Ariana's pensive expression. "Your suggestion to Thomas was brilliant," she said. "However did you think of having a cascaron ball?"

"Because I think that our visitors will enjoy it." Then Ariana laughed. "I know that our people will. No one will be safe tonight."

Rachel smiled. "Not even Jeremy?"

Ariana's smile faded. "What do you mean?"

"Nothing." Rachel shrugged innocently. "Only that there are quite a few young ladies who have been looking for just such an occasion where he is concerned."

"That has nothing to do with me," Ariana answered stiffly, draining her glass.

Rachel let it pass. Setting her glass on the table, she rose from her chair. "It's getting late, and I must dress. However, I am not leaving this room until I see that gown you have had two of my maids working on for the past four days." She went to the door and opened it, calling for Ariana's maid.

Clad only in a demi-corset, camisole, and linen drawers, Ariana was helped into layers of petticoats: one of flannel, one of heavily padded horsehair, and two of starched muslin. Then the gown was carefully dropped over her head, adjusted, and the last tiny button was hooked.

As with the coiffure, the gown had been painstakingly planned. It was of heavy ivory velvet with short, puffed sleeves worn off the shoulder, tight at the waist and cut low at the bodice. The back of the skirt cascaded in garlands of roses to match those in her hair. It was utterly feminine, innocence blending subtly with sensuality.

Rachel regarded her for a moment, then her eyes rose to meet with Ariana's deep brown gaze. "Ariana, you are a dangerous woman."

Ariana laughed softly. "And you, Rachel, will be late unless you dress."

When Rachel left the room, Ariana dismissed the maid. She grimaced at the thought of the sweet sherry and sighed, wishing she had a brandy to brace herself for the evening ahead. Turning, she kicked the heavy skirt around, and crossed back to the sherry decanter. Carrying the glass to the window, she parted the lace curtains and looked down on the street below. Cloaked couples were already making their way to the Custom House for the ball.

Fools, on a fool's errand, she thought. It would be a night of gaiety, one remembered in celebration of California's position as a new territory of the United States. During the past week there had been talk of statehood. Ariana's expression grew grim. There was only one suitable outcome, California as a free republic. During the past week of festivities, strides had been made in that direction, although the celebrating citizens had been too occupied to notice. But tomorrow—she smiled, hearing laughter from the street below—tomorrow they would awaken to discover what had been done, and it would be too late to stop it. A new beginning.

Leaning against the window frame, she sipped the sherry and thought over what had been accomplished, and what would happen tonight as the Yanquis and their allies were distracted by the cascaron ball. Indeed, she had promised Sloat and his men a night they would remember, and it would be that.

She laughed softly, recalling Rachel's comments on her choice of hairstyle and gown. Poor Rachel. In spite of her warm, giving nature, she was terribly, honestly simple. Tonight Ariana would remind the Yanquis of home, not to draw their attention but to gain their trust. It was a lesson learned early, one that had ultimately led her to success. A man could be so easily led to see what she wanted him to see. Thus they would be comforted, and she could extract information like child's play; there was always more to be learned, to use.

A knock at the door broke through her thoughts. "Enter," she said, setting her glass on a table. Rachel reentered, with a maid carrying two baskets. "You look lovely," Ariana said sincerely, noting how the soft, blue satin of Rachel's gown complemented her fair complexion.

"Thank you, my dear. And here are our cascarones," she added, handing a basket to Ariana.

Ariana accepted it, taking one from the basket. She tossed the hollowed-out eggshell in her hand, and smiled mischievously. "Let's go down the backstairs."

Rachel grinned. "Attack from the rear?"

"And split our forces. We'll come in from both sides. Thomas won't have a chance."

Ariana pressed herself against the wall in the darkened storeroom, edging toward the door with an egg clasped in her hand. Estimating the time since she had left Rachel by the back door, she crept closer to the light that streamed from the open doorway. She forced herself to wait another moment to give Rachel time to secrete herself under the stairwell, then she turned, springing through the door. Her hand crashed down on an unsuspecting dark head, accompanied by Rachel's laughter and the deep sounds of male protest. Bright pieces of colored paper exploded from the eggshell, floating about them as heavy perfume infiltrated the room. Suddenly, strong arms clamped about her and her feet were whisked from the floor, thrashing in midair as she fought to escape.

"No, you don't," Jeremy laughed, "I've caught you."

"Let me go!" she squealed. From the corner of her eye she saw Thomas's form pursuing Rachel down the hall.

"Oh no, the prize is mine." He grinned down at her. His hair was sprinkled with bits of colored paper.

"I thought you were Thomas!" she protested.

"Your mistake."

"Let me go!"

He set her down abruptly. "For the moment, sweet. But beware, I'll get even in my own time."

She was breathing heavily and sought to calm herself as she brushed out her gown. "What are you doing here?"

"I am your escort for the ball—or had you thought of going without one?"

"I am going with Thomas and Rachel," she said bristling.

"And with me," he finished for her.

"You seem terribly certain of yourself."

"I am. Besides, Sloat expects it."

"Oh, I see. Then this was an order, Major Morgan."

"No. My orders do not come from the navy. You may consider it a presidential order, if you like."

"I prefer not to consider it—or you—at all."

His eyes passed over her appreciatively. "In any case, you look absolutely beautiful."

"You needn't sound so surprised."

"I thought you might wear that red number. Now that wouldn't have surprised me."

"You ruined it, remember?"

"So I did." She was suddenly aware that his eyes were passing over her slowly. They rose to meet hers with unconcealed curiosity. *"Querida,* what are you up to?"

"I am going to a ball," she said stiffly.

"And what else?"

"Do I look like I am dressed for anything else?"

"You are primed for something."

She opened her mouth for a retort, but just then the Larkins reentered the hall. "My word." Rachel laughed, her face flushed. "The evening has taken a rather fine start. Wouldn't you agree?"

Ariana and Jeremy laughed at the happy leer Thomas gave them. "Morgan, you've got confetti in your hair. Here is your basket, Ariana; I almost tripped over it by the back door. By God, I haven't slowed down; I caught her before she made it to the garden!"

The sound of music floated over the harbor and through the streets, accompanying them as they walked down toward the Custom House. Children had gathered at the windows of the building to peer into the brightly lit room. They gawked at the colorfully gowned senoritas and senoras, accompanied by their handsome escorts in the heavily embroidered costumes of the Californios and the crisp military dress uniforms of the Americans. As the Larkins entered the building they paused, turning puzzled glances to Ariana and Jeremy who had stepped into the room behind them. The marine band was playing to a crowded room, but no one was dancing. The people stood about in clustered groups. The atmosphere was hushed and decidedly uncomfortable. The commodore was there, standing aside with his officers as they talked among themselves.

"What in the world is the matter with everyone?" Larkin murmured.

"This hardly looks like the culmination of five days of celebrating," Jeremy observed with a frown.

Studying the scene before her, Ariana noted the baskets hanging from the arms of the ladies as they stood apart from the Americans. She glanced down at her own basket. Her brow furrowed with thought as Rachel touched her husband's arm and whispered, "Thomas, what is wrong? Do you think that there was an argument?"

"Creo que no," Ariana said softly, then she smiled. "I think I know what the problem is." Her mouth turned up impishly and her eyes glittered with sudden mischief. "Thomas, shouldn't you be forming a receiving line with the commodore?"

"Yes." He hesitated, glancing about. "Although I don't think it will serve to thaw this crowd."

"Go ahead, Consul." She smiled. "You might be surprised."

When the Larkins had left them, Jeremy drew Ariana into the shadows of the doorway. "All right, Ariana, what's in that devious little mind of yours?"

"Nothing you would disapprove of, Jeremy. And since we seem to be stuck with each other for the moment, you might

as well help. As they say, nothing ventured, nothing won."
She grasped the sleeve of his coat and began to edge through
the crowd toward the receiving line.

A dark brow arched as he looked down at her warily.
"Another saying comes to mind."

"What is that, Jeremy?" she asked distractedly.

"Beware the hind-part of a mule and the mind of a
woman," he murmured.

According to Ariana's master plan, Jeremy adroitly cut
into the line, to the disgruntlement of those behind, particularly a full-bodied senora who glared up at him—a matter
he soothed with a devastating smile and a wink. Shaking
hands with the commodore, he ignored Larkin and Rachel's
look of surprise as he proceeded to launch into a conversation with the startled man. He also ignored the glares from
those who were waiting, including the large-bosomed dona
who was no longer amused by the tall, handsome, and
particularly rude army officer as he doggedly persisted in
engaging Sloat's attention.

Sloat tried twice to dismiss Jeremy politely, to no avail.
When Jeremy continued to stand his ground, Lieutenant
Sherman finally stepped forward from his place behind the
commodore. "Major, perhaps these are matters you could
discuss with me. The commodore has many people to
greet—"

"No thanks, Sherman," Jeremy said happily. As the
lieutenant moved from behind the commodore's guarded
back, Jeremy saw a flash of ivory velvet, and his smile
broadened. "Commodore, have you ever been to a cascaron
ball?"

"No, I cannot say that I have," Sloat answered, somewhat
irritably as he glanced with a sincere look of apology down
the receiving line.

"Do you know what a cascaron is?" Jeremy grinned.

"No, as a matter of fact—"

The commodore's eyes widened as suddenly two eggshells were broken over his cranium, showering him with
confetti and cologne. Sharp gasps and soft cries were heard,
and Sloat and his officers were momentarily frozen with
shock. Sherman began to protest as the commodore, obviously shaken, began to brush off his dress tunic. He picked

some bits of the colored paper off his shoulder and stared at them for a moment, then looked up at Jeremy. "Would you care to explain this, Major?"

"That, sir, is a cascaron. To have a lady strike you with one is a great honor."

"Indeed."

"Yes, sir."

"And what do I do about it?"

"You retaliate, sir."

"Retaliate? With what?"

Jeremy pulled two eggshells from his pocket, handing them to the commodore. "With these."

Sloat examined them as Sherman began to protest. "Really, Major Morgan—"

"It's a matter of self-defense, sir," Jeremy interrupted, still smiling at the commodore.

Sloat looked up, his mouth twitching. "Well then, Major, I have been attacked, I certainly have no intention of retreating."

"No sir." Jeremy's eyes shifted slightly over Sloat's shoulder. The commodore smiled, nodding. He turned quickly, his hand shaking out with an agility that amazed Jeremy. Thinking herself to be well concealed with Sloat's officers about her, Ariana squealed as the new Governor General grasped her arm and in a single motion, broke the eggshells over her head, spraying colored paper over Ariana and the people nearby. "I believe, Senorita Saldivar, that the final assault is mine!" he quipped. The crowd broke into laughter.

"Oh, no, Commodore." She laughed, her eyes bright. "It has only begun."

Sloat looked down at the basket on her arm, and then glanced about, noting that all of the women carried their own arsenals. "And where are we to gain our own powder and ball?" he asked good-naturedly.

"Why, Commodore," she said sweetly, smiling up at him. "You steal them—if you can."

Sloat glanced about at his men, whose eyes were bright with speculation as they looked about at the senoritas' most promising smiles. "Well, gentlemen, the battle lines are drawn. I expect you to show your colors and give no quarter."

"Yes sir!" Sherman grinned, nodding at his fellows. The cascaron ball had begun.

By midnight, the floor of the room was covered with colored paper and cologne. The Americans had learned the game rules quickly, becoming swiftly adroit at stealing the eggs and applying them, though no frontal attacks were allowed, and the dance floor was off limits for theft. The marine band soon gave way to the Californios, who struck up with guitar, horn and violin, and waltzes were replaced by fandangos and contredanses.

Jeremy avoided Ariana throughout the evening, contenting himself with a string of lovely senoritas who were enthusiastically eager to dance with the handsome officer. Ariana spent the majority of her time with Sloat's staff officers, in particular Lieutenant Sherman, who appeared totally susceptible to her considerable charms.

As the marine band took their place once again and struck up a waltz, Jeremy made his way across the room, smiling congenially at Sherman who was approaching Ariana for yet another dance. "I believe that this one is mine, Lieutenant." Before she could react, Ariana was encircled by Jeremy's arms and swept out onto the dance floor.

"I don't want to dance with you," she hissed.

"You did not seem to mind my company when you needed my assistance," he answered calmly.

"That was different!"

"You needn't concern yourself, Ariana. This is business."

"Business?" She glanced up at him as he turned her smoothly through the waltz. Seeing the amused look he wore, she bristled. "You and I have no business together!"

"Oh, but we do. You needn't have wasted your time tonight. I probably would have told you anything you wanted to know. Sloat's plans are not secret."

"I don't know what you are talking about," she said stiffly. But she betrayed her true reaction with a misstep.

"I just polished these boots, sugarplum. I would appreciate it if you didn't dance on them."

"Marano!" she hissed, calling him a pig.

"Sugar-cured, sweetheart." He chuckled, swinging her in the wide circles of the waltz. As the last strains of the dance were played, he pulled her tightly to him and looked down at her, all his attempts at humor gone. "Ariana, about whatever you are planning. It won't do any good and will only cause grief to those involved."

Her mouth slackened as she stared at him, a flush creeping up her cheeks. Over her shoulder Jeremy saw Sherman approaching, and he reached up, placing a finger under her chin to close her mouth. His eyes lingered on her lips and, for a moment, she thought he was going to kiss her. She swallowed heavily. Her eyes fixed on his mouth, and her lips parted involuntarily. Reading the gesture, Jeremy fought a smile. He stepped back. "Lieutenant." He nodded, to her horror and humiliation. "She's all yours."

23

Commodore John D. Sloat's normally indecisive face was flushed with anger. "Major Morgan, did you know about this?"

"Yes, sir. I suspected it."

"And you chose not to warn me? May I presume to ask why?"

"Sir, the Californios do not look upon these matters in the same way that we do. Principles of honor decide most issues; confrontation is deplored. There was no reason to believe that the matter would go beyond a debate. They wouldn't have actually signed and distributed the document unless they had felt desperate. If it hadn't been for the arrival of our visitors this morning . . ."

"You are blaming this on Fremont?" Sloat raged, waving the proclamation at Jeremy.

"Yes. It is a direct result of his actions in the north, as well as his untimely arrival."

"I sent for him!"

"For him, not the ragtag group of over two-hundred men he led through the streets of Monterey this morning. They looked like buffalo skinners, and just as threatening to the citizens. Not to mention the fact that he paraded those men through the streets like an invading conqueror—"

"Morgan, must I remind you that thus far your information has been totally unsupported. Until I receive Captain

Fremont's report, I can consider it only a rumor."

"Ariana Saldivar was there, Commodore."

"She is a civilian, Major. Moreover, she is General Vallejo's niece. Her testimony is not without prejudice."

"Commodore—"

"That is all, Major. I have requested that Captain Fremont report to me in the morning, along with Mr. Larkin. I wish for you to be here as well. You may make these accusations at that time, in the proper manner. That is all."

Jeremy left the ship, barely able to control his anger. He reached shore, leaping onto the dock, and strode down its length to where his horse was tied. He rode past the Custom House, which had been cleared after the ball and was now used to quarter over one hundred of Sloat's men. Sherman had taken residence in the small house behind the Larkins, which had been Jeremy and Beth's home those first few months in Monterey. It was evident that Sloat was establishing his command, but this fact gave Jeremy little comfort. The uncertain commodore seemed to retreat one step for every two he advanced.

He arrived at the Larkin house, tying his mount to a porch support, and went inside. He found Larkin in the storeroom wearing a leather apron, his hands full of invoices. Larkin opened his mouth to give a greeting, but the words never came out.

"Dammit!" Jeremy exploded. He began to pace as he fought for control. "The fool is about to pardon Fremont, I know it!"

"Bad morning, heh?"

"He claimed that Ariana's testimony was prejudiced! Oh, I know what he's thinking! We still haven't heard from Washington. I'd bet a month's wages the fool is hoping that Fremont has official orders that will absolve him of a possible blunder in taking possession of California! Dammit, Thomas, will you stop playing merchant for a moment and listen?"

"Playing?" Larkin asked, peering at Jeremy over the tops of his eyeglasses.

The comment went unheard as Jeremy continued to pace. "That resolution of loyalty to Mexico totally threw him."

"What resolution of loyalty?" Now he had Larkin's attention.

"The one that Manuel Castro, de la Guerra, Estrada, and

the rest of their group wrote while we were breaking eggs over our heads. You know—" He suddenly paused, regarding Larkin strangely. "You didn't know?"

"No, I didn't."

Jeremy looked confused. "But I thought—when you were not on the ship when I arrived, I assumed that you had already seen Sloat."

"I haven't seen him since yesterday. But I did hear from him. I am no longer consul, Jeremy."

Jeremy gaped at him. "What?"

"It comes as no surprise." Larkin shrugged, putting the invoices down on a packing crate. "Would you like some coffee?"

Jeremy sat down heavily on a barrel. "Yes, I think I could use a cup."

The two men sat silently, drinking from steaming mugs. Finally, Larkin broke the silence. "California is no longer a foreign country, Jeremy. There is no longer need for a consul. Keep in mind that this is what I've worked for."

"Not like this," Jeremy grumbled. "Has he assigned you a new position?"

"No. He has appointed his chaplain, Walter Colton, as alcalde. Colton will administer civil government in Monterey."

"He has no experience!"

"Neither did I, once." Larkin shrugged. "He's a good man. He'll do well. Besides, he has help."

Jeremy glanced up, waiting. He wondered at the strange look in Larkin's eyes. The man seemed as if he were going to pop.

"Will Garner is to be his secretary."

Jeremy looked away quickly, his mouth twitching. "Well," he said, after a moment. "Will can teach him a lot."

"Yes."

The two men stared at the floor, afraid to look at each other. "Who—" Jeremy asked, clearing his throat, "recommended him?"

"I did."

The two men broke out in laughter.

"Well, Thomas—" Jeremy said when he could finally compose himself. "What are you going to do now?"

"Do? What I've done for the past ten years since coming to California. I'm going to 'play' merchant." He chuckled at

Jeremy's chagrin. "I plan to write to my agent in Boston, order a new vessel, and stock it with every manner of merchandise it can carry. Jeremy, people are going to flood into this territory. The possibility of profit fairly boggles the mind. We are watching the birth of a new state, my boy, I'd swear to it." He let Jeremy digest that for a moment. "Now then, tell me what those young radicals have done."

"It's not just them, but many of the dons who once supported Vallejo. They've been talking about it for weeks, and until today, it was the same old rhetoric. Some pressed to join Castro in the south where he is forming a resistance. Others were crying for British support, while others wanted to approach the French."

"I dined with Admiral Seymour aboard his ship the other night," Larkin said. "We have no need to worry about the British."

"I know, I spoke with him the day he arrived. The British are definitely hands-off on this. He said that he is here only to observe, and I believe him. No, it was Fremont that caused this!" His face flushed with renewed anger. "They're camped in the pine forest just outside the city. God, one look at that troop riding through the streets in bloodstained buckskins, and the Californios beat a hasty retreat to El Cuartel where they signed a resolution declaring their loyalty to Mexico!"

"My God," Larkin said quietly. "I was afraid that was what you meant. But I'm not surprised. The way things have been going, this was bound to happen, sooner or later."

Jeremy snorted. Then a new thought dawned on him. Turning to Larkin, he smirked. "Come to think of it, you aren't out of this yet. Sloat wants you on board the *Savannah* in the morning when he confronts Fremont."

A heavy eyebrow rose slightly at the news. "That ought to be interesting." He sipped his coffee. "Particularly in that I am no longer a diplomat."

The next morning found Jeremy and Larkin in the commodore's cabin, a full fifteen minutes before Fremont was expected. Larkin had plotted their arrival with his usual finesse. He had no intention of allowing Jeremy and Fremont to meet on the dock or share a boat out to the ship. He was afraid that Morgan would drown the engineer before Sloat could confront him.

Sloat had ordered coffee, which Jeremy declined as he stood staring out of a porthole. Sloat made small talk until the door to the cabin opened and Fremont stepped in. Larkin glanced at Jeremy, who continued to stare out to sea. For a moment Larkin was afraid that Jeremy was not even going to acknowledge Sloat's introduction, but he did so at the proper moment, nodding briefly at the other man. Sloat, fortunately, did not appear to notice Jeremy's rudeness. He began to chat affably with the "Pathfinder of the West," as Fremont was reverently called in the east.

The friendly conversation continued for another quarter of an hour, until Sloat apparently decided it was time to confront matters. He sat at his desk, riffling through his papers, bringing one from the pile. He spread it out with his hands, then leaned back in his chair. "Your report, Captain," he said expectantly.

"Yes, sir," Fremont replied, glancing briefly at Jeremy with a look of satisfaction. "I am pleased to report that the northern portion of Alta California has been secured. The unrest between the Mexicans and the settlers placed me— and my men," he seemed to add as an afterthought, "in a position to come to the defense of the American settlers. Following the Battle of Olompali—"

"Battle of Olompali?" Sloat frowned. "I am unfamiliar with any such conflict."

"I believe that he is referring to the skirmish with Castro's men near Sonoma," Larkin observed, regarding the officer steadily. "Castro's men were under the command of Joaquin de la Torre—"

"Yes, now I recall." Sloat nodded.

"It was more than a mere skirmish, Mr. Larkin," Fremont countered. "They were attempting to retake Sonoma. However, we routed them handily—"

"Along with unarmed civilians, whom you handily murdered," Jeremy interjected.

"Major, your interest in these people mystifies me," Fremont said, bristling.

"Gentlemen, please!" Sloat interrupted. "Continue, Captain."

"Yes, sir. Following the battle we proceeded to the Presidio of San Francisco at Yerba Buena, reaching it on July 1. There we immediately took possession of the garrison and spiked its guns—"

"You spiked the cannons?" Jeremy blurted out incredulously.

"Yes, of course," Fremont answered imperiously. "I can assure you that they will never be used against our forces."

Jeremy burst out laughing. The fool had spiked inoperative cannons that had not been fired in forty years! Larkin struggled for a second to control himself—then remembered that he was no longer a diplomat. Sloat looked stunned, then his mouth began to work in laughter. Fremont glared uncertainly at the three men, totally puzzled by their reactions. Once Jeremy and Larkin had themselves under control, Sloat thought it best to change the subject. He picked up the paper before him.

"I have a report before me compiled from a number of sources, Captain Fremont," he said grimly. "It tells of your activities, beginning with the first visit you made to Consul Larkin. It concludes with your recent activities in Sonoma. Along with what you have just told me, I must ask you one question. Your answer, of course, will settle any question about the validity of your actions. Under whose orders did you act?"

Jeremy watched the officer with interest, waiting for the answer. Fremont did not flinch at the question. In fact, he answered it clearly, without hesitation. "Solely on my own responsibility, sir."

Sloat visibly froze with shock. Jeremy sighed softly, and then glanced at Larkin. Their thoughts were the same, a mixture of anger at the ambitious officer's audacity, and relief that they had not, after all, been dealing with double messages from Washington.

"Do you realize what you have done?" Sloat gasped. Then anger overcame his initial shock. He stared at the officer, his face working with rage, when suddenly he grew pale. Jeremy quickly stepped forward, thinking that Sloat was going to be ill.

"Commodore, are you all right?"

"Yes, yes," Sloat said, waving him away. But he seemed to have aged in the past few moments. "Captain Fremont, return to shore. I will deal with you later." The three men fixed their eyes on the door that closed behind Fremont, then Sloat slumped back in his chair. "My God," he said distantly. "I had hoped that his orders would justify my actions here. Instead, they have compounded the problem!"

Jeremy barely heard him. He was stunned. Fremont's easy dismissal was tantamount to approval! "Commodore, by Fremont's own admission he did not act under official orders. What he has done here has undermined everything that has been accomplished in the past two years . . ."

"It is not too late," Larkin added. "If you discipline Fremont, the Californios will take it as a mark of good faith. The need—"

"It is too late, gentlemen," Sloat answered wearily, waving off the protests. "The damage is done."

Jeremy stared at him, aghast. "Too late? He is here with his confounded California Battalion! If he is allowed to continue—"

"Major, I said enough! One more word and you will be facing censure!" He sat up in his chair, clenching the desk as he glared blackly at Jeremy.

Larkin quickly stepped forward, drawing the angry commodore's attention from Jeremy. "There is one other matter of grave importance, Commodore." He was relieved as Sloat seemed distracted by the interruption. "Mariano Vallejo. It is imperative that he be released as soon as possible. He has long been our staunchest ally for cession. His incarceration is being used by his supporters and his enemies. His supporters use it as proof of our duplicity, evidence that we are not to be trusted. His enemies claim that it is his just desert, proof of his misjudgment, that he was wrong to support us. In any event, we need him now more than ever."

Sloat listened, but he looked openly annoyed. "I have pledged to do what I can on that distasteful matter, Mr. Larkin. As for Fremont, I have already instructed Captain Mervine and his marines that they are not to acknowledge the presence of Fremont or his men. For the time being they shall be treated as civilians, without any official authority. More than that, I shall advise you in my own good time of my decisions on this entire situation. That will be all, gentlemen. Good day."

Commodore Sloat made his decision when Commodore Robert F. Stockton sailed into port two days later. He turned over his command and retired from the navy.

Nodding at a servant to refill their glasses, Ariana smiled at the three men who graced her parlor. As many times as she had dealt with it, she never ceased to be amazed by the self-centered pomposity of a truly ambitious man. Fremont did not remember her. Of course, she had only met him once, briefly, that night when Beth had introduced them. And apparently he did not recognize her name from the letter she had sent to him in Sonoma, requesting permission to visit her uncle in prison.

Her gaze shifted to the other two men: Commodore Robert Stockton, the new commander of the Pacific Fleet and new governor general of California, and Archibald Gillespie, Fremont's adjutant.

It had not been difficult to make Stockton's acquaintance, and for that she could be grateful to the departing Commodore Sloat. Sloat's last official duty was to give a dinner aboard his flagship for the new governor general, and Ariana had been one of the guests. It made little difference to her which Yanqui was governor general of California, as long as she had his confidence. In that regard, the swaggering, pedantic Stockton had, by far, proved easier prey. By the end of that first evening, she had totally charmed him. By the third day she had deftly convinced him that her parlor could offer him the comfort—and privacy—needed and deserved by someone of his station. Mexican or Yanqui, it made no difference. History would repeat itself, and she would learn what she needed to know. The *liberalismos,* and thus California, would benefit.

The first evening they spent alone over a quiet dinner. She soothed the commander with succulent foods and fine wines, learning a great deal about his plans, information which she passed quickly to Manuel. Then, the second evening, he stunned her by arriving with Fremont and Gillespie in tow. Alarmed, she was extremely uncomfortable for a few moments, until she realized, impossible as it seemed, that Fremont simply did not remember her.

Over the past four evenings, it had become quickly apparent that none of the three men was a womanizer. At least not for the moment. For once her presence was required only to set a fine table and assure them a relaxing atmosphere for their conferences.

She sipped her cordial, listening to the conversation without apparent interest. Over the course of the past four evenings, she had learned a great deal. Immediately after assuming his command, Stockton had dealt severely with those who had resisted American authority. He began by arresting those who had signed the proclamation of loyalty to Mexico. Fortunately, Stockton had spoken of his new plan in front of Ariana. Her quick warning had enabled Manuel and Rafael to escape. Information continued to travel through Ariana to the *liberalismos,* including the detailed plans Stockton made with Fremont and Gillespie for their "southern campaign," causing many of her *liberalismos* to go into hiding, a cause she had aided by the information she had gained. Stockton then began to plan a "southern campaign" with Fremont and Gillespie.

The three men had met well. Unlike Sloat, Stockton had been in total agreement with what Fremont had done. He approved of an aggressive policy for the conquest of California, and quickly incorporated Fremont's California Battalion into the plan. The new policies formed by the three men had made her job that much easier. Larkin, and those who supported him, were simply dismissed. Including Jeremy.

She glanced at the clock on the mantel. Upon arriving, Stockton had informed her that there would be another person for dinner—if it was convenient, of course. She had assured him that it was, and had instructed the servants to set another place at the table. But it was growing late, and she was concerned that the meal would soon be ruined. Tapping her foot impatiently, she was just about to suggest that they dine when she heard a knock at the front door. She smiled at the three men who glanced toward the hallway, and then turned to greet the additional guest.

"Good evening, gentlemen." Jeremy entered the parlor. "I apologize for being late."

"Morgan, I'm glad that you could come!" Stockton stepped forward, extending his hand. "You've met the others I know; may I present Senorita Saldivar, our hostess."

Somehow, Ariana managed to find her voice. "Major Morgan," she said, holding out her hand.

"Senorita Saldivar." He smiled, brushing her hand with a light kiss. She trembled, and he squeezed her hand lightly. "How good to see you again."

Stockton looked surprised. "Do you know each other?"

"We've met," Jeremy said. "Good evening, Fremont. Gillespie."

"Morgan," Fremont acknowledged. Gillespie nodded.

"Well, now that you are here, we can dine," Stockton said with enthusiasm. He turned and took Ariana's arm in his, leading her toward the dining room. "I must say, my dear, that it has been rather torturous waiting for the major. The aroma coming from your kitchen is tantalizing. I trust that you have prepared another excellent meal."

As Ariana took her place at the end of the table, Stockton settled into Vallejo's chair without preamble. Jeremy took the single chair across from Fremont and Gillespie. Fremont barely sat down before saying what was on his mind.

"Well, Morgan, since you have accepted this invitation, can we assume that you have decided to join us?"

"Charley, let us not spoil Miss Saldivar's efforts with dreary table talk," Stockton said. "We are here to enjoy ourselves. Business can wait until later."

Jeremy enjoyed himself thoroughly. Though he couldn't say the same for Fremont, Gillespie, or Ariana. In fact, the prospect of witnessing their discomfort was the reason he had finally accepted Stockton's open invitation to dine with him. He seriously doubted that Stockton would continue to wear that self-satisfied, smug expression if he knew why he had come. Unlike Larkin, he had not been released from his duties to Washington. In fact, that morning a dispatch had arrived from Buchanan with rather terse inquiries. In response to Jeremy's information about what had been happening, including Fremont's and Gillespie's actions, Buchanan wanted a full accounting. Furthermore, he stated that General Stephen Kearny was on his way overland to take command. Across the bottom of the dispatch, in his broad, scrawled hand, was an added note from Polk: "What in the hell is going on out there?"

He knew that Ariana was nervous. He hadn't expected her to be pleased to see him, but neither had he expected the shock he read in her expression when he walked into the room. It was obvious that his presence had caused her more than discomfort. She was panicking.

He had been surprised and angry when he had learned that she was entertaining the American officers. There was only one reason why she would do so, and it left him astounded. What could Mariano Vallejo's niece possibly think she could learn from John Charles Fremont? The only reason that Fremont would tolerate her would be to humiliate her. It had also left Jeremy somewhat alarmed. Stockton had severely clamped down on the rebels—particularly those who had signed the proclamation. While her name might not be on it, it wouldn't take much investigation to discover that Ariana had been involved.

The situation made even less sense now that he was here. Dinner progressed smoothly, except that Ariana steadfastly refused to look at him. Fremont, on the other hand, like Gillespie and Stockton, were perfect gentlemen, treating her as they would the finest hostess in the east. As the hour went by, Jeremy's confusion deepened.

He studied Stockton, recalling the only thing he really knew about the man. The scandal had become public knowledge. In 1844, Stockton had worked with John Erickson, a naval designer, developing plans for the "*Princeton*," the first warship to be driven by a screw propeller. Stockton had personally designed its guns, which were to be the largest in the naval fleet. Upon completion, the guns were demonstrated for the government, whereupon one of them exploded, killing two visiting cabinet members. Eventually, following an inquiry, Stockton was exonerated and promoted.

Fremont—well, Fremont was Fremont. Gillespie—Jeremy's gaze shifted back to Ariana. He wondered what she would say if she knew that Gillespie had been the biggest stumbling block—more so than either Sloat or Stockton—to Mariano's release. And the three of them were as thick as thieves. It had only taken Jeremy a few hours in Stockton's company to know the man's mind. Following that first visit, he had given up any lingering hope for peace. Stockton wanted a campaign, and he was fully supported by the other two across the table. Jeremy was here to find out the extent of their plans and report them to Washington.

"Miss Saldivar, I haven't eaten food as fine as this since I left the east." Stockton smiled contentedly, nodding to a servant to refill his wineglass. "Wherever did you learn to cook Yankee food so expertly?"

Jeremy's gaze shifted to her with interest.

"From Rachel Larkin. We have been friends for many years."

"Ah, yes. Mrs. Larkin. A refreshing breath of home in this wilderness. But what of you; have you lived in Monterey all of your life?"

"Most of it," Ariana answered, giving attention to her own wine.

"And the rest?" Jeremy asked.

Shimmering with anger, her eyes darted up to him. Then she looked at the others and smiled. "On a rancho further north. Captain Fremont, your glass is empty. Anita, bring another bottle."

"Well, I for one am gratified that the commodore found you." Fremont smiled as his glass was refilled. "As he said, your table is a refreshing breath of home. Not to mention what I must say are, ah, eastern manners. You would grace the finest salon in the States, Miss Saldivar."

Jeremy, dumbfounded, suddenly understood. It couldn't be. Incredulous, he stared at Ariana; then his gaze shifted to the others. I'll be damned, he thought. Suddenly, he struggled against the impulse to break into laughter. Fremont had spiked another cannon. However, he mused, this one could still fire. The last thought sobered him. The little fool. He turned and looked at Ariana who was watching his reaction.

"Tu pequeno la bruja," he murmured.

She forced a smile.

"Heh? What did you say, Morgan?" Stockton asked.

"I was merely complimenting her," Jeremy drawled, turning his attention to his caramel custard.

As dessert was cleared away and brandy and cigars were produced, Jeremy noted that Ariana was giving no evidence that she intended to withdraw. Well, he thought, tonight, sugarplum, you will. "Miss Saldivar, the dinner was excellent. My congratulations. I hope to see you again in the near future."

"Are you leaving, Major?" she asked. Her voice was hopeful.

"No. Not yet. But I must soon, and I doubt that I will still be here when the gentlemen join you later."

Her eyes widened, a reaction she struggled to suppress. She rose from her chair stiffly, forcing a smile. Jeremy knew that she was trapped. Regardless of the fact that the others had apparently accepted her presence on previous evenings, she could not remain after such a blatant hint. She turned to leave the room. Their eyes locked, and hers were burning with anger. He rose from his chair, taking her hand, brushing it with a kiss. "Miss Saldivar," he murmured. She pulled it away as quickly as she could and swept from the room.

"A beautiful young woman," he said as he resettled in his chair.

"Indeed," Stockton agreed, clipping off the end of a cigar.

"I am surprised, however," Jeremy added, clipping and lighting one of his own.

"About what, Major?" Stockton asked, puffing on his cigar as he lighted it.

"Nothing really. After all, if you find her presence acceptable, why should I question it?"

"What are you trying to tell us, Morgan?" Gillespie asked. "And why did you call her a little witch a few moments ago?" He smiled at Jeremy's surprise. "I speak Spanish fluently."

"You knew her before, didn't you, Morgan?" Fremont accused.

"I told you that I did, when I arrived." Jeremy shrugged, pouring himself a brandy. "I assumed that you knew who she was. I certainly thought that you would, Fremont."

"Me? Why should I know her?"

"Because you met her once before at the Larkins'. Moreover, later you gave her written permission to visit her uncle where you incarcerated him." He smiled at their puzzled frowns. "Ariana Saldivar is Mariano Vallejo's niece."

Stunned, Stockton turned to glare at Fremont. "Is this true?" Fremont looked confused, then slowly, he remembered and blanched. The look was enough. "My God!" Stockton stormed. "How could you forget such a thing? We've—" he sputtered. "We've spent the past four nights discussing our campaign in this house—at her table!"

"Commodore, I would not worry about it," Jeremy said easily. His manner mollified Stockton, whose look of outrage relaxed to a glower.

"And why is that?"

"I know the lady quite well. She is beautiful and gracious but—well, she is rather politically inept. She is completely a social creature. I seriously doubt that anything you have said here would have much meaning for her." He smiled at the others with a look of shared male superiority. "It seems that women everywhere are the same. I know that our own lovely ladies are disinclined to understand the more serious aspects of their men's lives. Isn't that so, gentlemen?"

The three men seemed to relax as they nodded in agreement and understanding. "You are right, Morgan. Except for my Jessie," Fremont said. "She is the most political creature I know."

"Yes, but she has Hart Benton for a father." Jeremy smiled. "Your wife is quite the exception." Then he added, somberly, "In truth, Fremont, I have never known another woman like her."

"Yes, just so. I am a lucky man," Fremont agreed.

"I still do not feel easy about this." Stockton frowned. "Why would Vallejo's niece wish to entertain us, except to spy?"

"I think you answered it, Commodore," Jeremy said breezily. "Vallejo is her uncle. I rather imagine that she hoped to find a way to plead for his release. What better way than by wining and dining you?"

Stockton thought about that for a moment. "That must be it," he said with relief. "Of course. Naturally, however, we cannot continue enjoying her company—under the circumstances."

"I should think not," Jeremy agreed.

"Well, I must thank you for this information, Morgan," Stockton said, reaching for the brandy. "This is an excellent example of why I asked you here." He poured himself a glass and leaned back in his chair. "You know these people. You know who they are, their customs, and how they might react in a given situation. I realize that you have been working with Thomas Larkin for the past year and you have developed a close relationship." There was no doubt from what source he had received that information, as he glanced meaningfully at Fremont. "However," he continued, "the Larkin Plan, as it has been called, is now a moot issue. There is only one way that we can bring peace to California, and that is by force.

"General Castro has gathered his troops in Southern California, near Los Angeles. He means to join with Pio Pico. It is there that we must strike to put a final end to the rebellion." He proceeded to launch into a detailed plan of his campaign, pausing only when Fremont or Gillespie interjected their thoughts, or when Jeremy asked a question.

Finally, he concluded the discussion with the suggestion that they refill their glasses for a toast. The men raised their drinks. "To our campaign, gentlemen. And Major, I must say that I am gratified that you will be joining us."

In the silence that followed Jeremy set his brandy on the table and put out his cigar. He had come for two reasons: to gain information for Washington of their plans, and to do what he could to extract Ariana from certain disaster. Both had been accomplished. Now he would have the satisfaction of a third. "Commodore, since the day I left West Point—" He glanced pleasantly at Fremont who, not unexpectedly, frowned. Jeremy knew perfectly well that the engineer had twice been refused admission to the academy, and it was a sore point. "It was my intention to make a career of the service. I have spent the past year serving as an agent for Washington, in the hopes of finding a peaceful solution for California's cession to the Union. A hope which the president shares. I still believe in Larkin's plan, unfortunately an effort of many years that is now—as you put it, Commodore, quite moot."

"Major—" Stockton frowned.

"You were correct, Commodore—" Jeremy continued easily, "when you said that I know these people. I will not aid you in suppressing them. I do not agree with your plans."

"Major, as your superior officer—" Stockton bristled.

"I am not under orders to the navy, but only to Washington," Jeremy countered calmly. "Moreover, my term of enlistment was up before I left the east. I am free to resign my commission at leisure." He stood up. "My resignation, along with my final report, will be on its way to Washington in the morning. Good evening, gentlemen."

He turned and left the room, shutting the front door quietly behind him.

Larkin sighed softly, placing his pen down and removing his glasses. Obviously his accounts were going to have to wait. He smiled indulgently at Rachel, who had entered his study a few moments before with her needlework. She sat quietly in the chair on the other side of his desk, as she often did to keep him company as he worked. But he knew the signs. The petit point lay idle in her lap, and she was staring out the window—sure signs that she wanted to talk.

"What is it, Rachel?" he asked.

She turned with surprise. "Why nothing, Thomas. Please, do not let me disturb you."

"You are not disturbing me, my love."

"Well . . ." she hesitated. "If you are certain."

"I am certain."

"In that case . . . Thomas, I had a letter from Dona Benicia this morning. Ariana is not in Sonoma."

Larkin frowned. "Has she had word from her?"

"No. It was bad enough when she was spending her time entertaining Stockton and Fremont—alone, in her own home! I knew we never should have allowed her to move back into Mariano's house!"

"There was little that we could do to stop her."

"Well, we should have thought of something! Now she's gone!"

"She is not a child, Rachel."

"But we have a responsibility to Mariano. Until he's released from that dreadful prison, he would expect us to watch out for her."

"Rachel—" He paused, choosing his words carefully. "My dear, remember that Mariano allowed her to travel all the way from Sonoma without an escort. He must have confidence that she can take care of herself."

His voice was heavy with implication. She stared at him. "Oh my," she said at last, her eyes widening. "Well, it doesn't matter. I care about her."

"Of course you do, as do I." He thought for a moment. "Perhaps Jeremy knows where she is."

"Jeremy? Do you think so?"

"I don't know." He shrugged. "Those two may have declared that they don't care a twit about each other, but I, for one, do not believe it for a moment. The fact that Jeremy did not return east when he resigned his commission two months ago has more to do with her than he would admit. I understand that he is developing quite a rancho in the Salinas Valley—" He paused as there was a knock at the door.

"I'll see to it," Rachel said, rising from her chair as she laid her forgotten needlework on the corner of his desk. "Don't go away; I want to talk more about this."

"I'll be here." He smiled, hoping to use the impasse to complete another page in his accounts. The moment proved brief, however, as Rachel returned minutes later. "It was one of Jeremy's men," she said, closing the door behind her. "He brought you a letter."

"It's about time." Larkin smiled, taking it from her. "Now perhaps we can find out what's going on. He might even have news of our errant Ariana." He ripped it open, settling back into his chair. She watched as he began to read, growing impatient as he glanced back at the date, then began to read again. "Well I'll be damned," he said softly.

"What is it?" She gaped, alarmed by her husband's uncharacteristic profanity.

He looked up, amazed. "Rachel, apparently Beth has divorced him." He glanced back at the letter, swearing again for the second time in Rachel's recent memory. "Well, I'll be damned."

24

The wind swept through the valley, raising topsoil, lifting tumbleweeds to roll and careen wildly until they caught among brushes of scrub oak and chamois brush. Cattle huddled, turning their backs to its persistent punishment. Fine, powdery dust lifted, covering fence posts and wire in a thin, brown blanket, seeping through walls and sifting into corners. A candle on the table flickered from a sudden gust, but Jeremy didn't notice. He was more than slightly drunk.

He rose from the table and walked unsteadily to the door, stepping out onto the porch and drawing heavily of the cold night air. It was November, he thought, yet no matter how cold the days were, that damned wind came up. He had been told that the wind stopped from November to March, but with his luck it would probably blow all winter. At the moment, however, it helped to sober him, and he leaned back against a porch rail and took a cheroot from his pocket. It took three attempts to light as the wind blew out his match.

He drew from the cheroot, then watched as the smoke dissipated into the wind. A movement caught his eye, and he turned his head to find a small patch of ground stirring near him, not a foot from the porch. After a moment a hole emerged and a pocket gopher popped his head out. It looked about with its poor eyesight, unaware of the enemy standing a few feet away. Jeremy stared at it. He probably should go back into the house and get a gun and shoot it, he thought. Then he laughed softly. He'd probably miss.

Maybe he should walk over to the bunkhouse and get one of his men to shoot it. No, he'd have to face the whole bunch of them in the morning knowing that they would be thinking that he had to get help to shoot a gopher. Besides, he didn't feel like walking that far.

He watched the rodent creep from the hole. Then he flicked the cheroot at it with his thumb and middle finger. It made a direct hit, causing the gopher to scurry back into the ground. He grinned happily, feeling better than he had in weeks. Couldn't have done better with a cannon.

His brief euphoria faded, and he stared at the empty hole. Then he went back into the house. He noticed that the candle had gone out. He had been out of kerosene for a week; he really should send someone to Salinas tomorrow for supplies, he thought. He stumbled to the foot of the stairs, tripping over a chair in the dark, and made his way up to the bedroom where he fell onto the bed.

He lay there, staring at the shadows wavering across the ceiling from the sycamore outside the window. Its branches bent in the wind, illuminated by the full moon and cloudless sky. Suddenly he was wide awake, left to face the long hours ahead, until dawn would allow him the release of another day's work.

Everything seemed clearer during the day, when he entertained no doubts about why he had made certain decisions. During the day, he was able to push disturbing memories from his mind and fix his thoughts upon what needed to be done. But the night was different; his mind echoed with memories he had once thought of as dreams.

His marriage seemed to symbolize his life, beginning so well, though he often wondered how much of his own fantasy his marriage had been. From the first moment he had seen Beth, he had not doubted his love for her. The doubts had come much later. She was a woman of her time, and he was irrevocably drawn to her beauty and her insecurities. God, he thought with the clarity of reflection, he had actually seen himself as some sort of medieval knight, rescuing her from her self-doubts and the limitations of her moral dilemmas. What he had not counted on was that she hadn't realized she needed any help.

He had plotted, plodded, and worked—all for nothing. He had played the game alone. Those letters locked away in his desk downstairs had finally caused him to doubt his own vision of reality.

The first letter had come from his father, informing him that Beth had applied for a divorce. He had read it three times before he could assimilate the words, thinking them to be a mistake. More the fool. One last time he had tried to protect her. God, he had given his protection as a sacred offering! Beth, he thought, my congratulations. You had the last word.

She had divorced him to run off with a lover to Europe. A lover! His frigid, unaffectionate Beth. He became curious, wondering what her lover had offered her that he had not. What part of her succulent body he had touched, how he had touched it, to make the difference . . .

He threw himself off the bed and poured himself a brandy from the decanter on the table by the window. He took a deep swallow, shuddered, and stared from the window at the moonlit landscape beyond. He knew that there was no use castigating himself; he would only become a self-inflicted eunuch. He had had enough women in his life to know that he was a good lover. Just as he knew that lovemaking was not just a physical experience. He had never been able to arouse Beth's emotions. As, apparently, her lover had.

His thoughts shifted to the one woman with whom he had felt fulfilled. And had lost. Perhaps he should have told her about himself before she found out the way that she did. But when? By the time he had become involved with her, it was already too late. Besides, she was so intent upon her own commitments that there was never a time when the information would have made a difference. The results would have been the same. Well, he had done what he could for her—the little fool—and now she was safe. At least for the moment.

He stared moodily out of the window, seeing only the shadowy outlines of endless grasses and scattered trees. Why in hell did he stay here? Life had its own rules and it laughed at any attempt to change them. Men are like that pitiful gopher, he thought, they emerge into a broad world filled with endless promise, only to get hit by a cigar butt.

Beth, wherever you are, he thought, find all the happiness you can. Ariana, take on the world; fight it and learn to bear what you cannot change. As for me—he drained the glass—I am going to bed.

25

Lieutenant Joseph Revere, United States Navy, looked about the silent streets, feeling the emptiness that accompanied a leave-taking. He had written letters, said his farewells, and there was nothing more to be done. Nothing but to take his memories with him—those thoughts that would be added to his journals. There was one parting left undone, and he deeply regretted it. However, the *Portsmouth* would sail by noon, and he was expected on board within an hour.

He crossed the wide, dusty street, pausing to greet acquaintances. He knew that he would carry the memory of these people with him, moments of remembered warmth and comfort. He had been a sailor long enough to know that such experiences were all too rare. He would never forget California or its people. Or its women.

Grinning at that last thought, he passed an open-air grogshop. It was little more than a lean-to with a thatched roof and crudely built tables that served as a meeting place for less than selective residents. He was drawn, one last time, but struggled against it. His captain was not "simpatico" to last-minute celebrations. He would hardly look with favor upon his first officer reporting four sheets to the wind. Fortifying himself, he bravely strode past, taking only one last brief glance of longing. Then he stopped dead in his tracks.

"Is this party private, or can anyone join it?"

Jeremy looked up into a broadly grinning face. His

stomach tightened in intense, surprised pleasure. "I'm not selective, Revere."

Revere gestured to the bartender and sat down across the table. "What is it?" he asked doubtfully, glancing at the cloudy liquid in Jeremy's glass.

"Rum," Jeremy answered, taking a drink. "It is the only thing they serve now, in honor of the American sailors. Drink up, Revere, you qualify."

When his glass was brought, Revere tasted it gingerly. He shuddered. If it was rum, it was only a distant relative. He glanced up at Jeremy, noting his forbidding expression, and he suddenly wondered what to say. But then, subtlety had never been part of his makeup. "I heard you got your divorce."

Jeremy glared at him. Then he shook his head and laughed. "Revere, if you had to depend upon your diplomacy, you'd starve to death."

Revere grinned. "I'm glad to see you, Morgan. We sail this morning. I wrote you a letter, but I didn't think I'd get to see you before I left."

"This morning?" Jeremy stared at him for a long moment. "My best, Revere. I'll miss you."

Revere returned the steady gaze. "Me, too. I thought you kept yourself to that ranch. Why are you here?"

Jeremy shrugged. "There is a ship due in this morning— my son is on it."

"Hamilton?" Revere stared. "She sent him back to you?"

Jeremy glanced at him briefly as he turned his glass in his hand. "She didn't want him."

Christ, Revere thought. That goddamn bitch. He glanced down at the table, having seen the brief anguish in Jeremy's eyes. The pain he saw shook him, and he glanced toward the harbor, knowing that in a few moments he would have to leave. There was little of the world he hadn't seen, and change always suited him. Shifts allowed him new experiences, in spite of the few lasting friendships they made. But, unexpectedly, there had come one. Somehow he sensed that he would never see Jeremy again, and he wanted to leave the friendship intact. He could leave and walk away and it would be done. But suddenly it became imperative not to deny the truth, even if what he was about to say caused him to lose Jeremy's friendship.

"Don't grieve for her, Jeremy. She wasn't worth it."

Jeremy looked up at him slowly. His eyes grew hard.

Revere ignored the warning. "You want to remember her as some delicate creature that you failed. It wasn't your fault, Jeremy. She was rotten. Go ahead, glare at me, but it's true. She didn't just find love when she left you, she was on the hunt long before she left you. I know, she tried with me. Each time she was with me. Each time you left the room—and sometimes even when you didn't. If I hadn't cared about our friendship I could have buggered her in a minute. So, go ahead and punch me out if it makes you feel better, but it won't change the facts. You're well out of that marriage."

Jeremy glared at him for a long moment. Then he sighed raggedly. "No. I don't want to hit you, Revere."

"Good. I value this extraordinary face." He grinned. Then it faded. "On the other hand, maybe it would be better if you did. At least it might help you to get rid of it."

Jeremy looked up at him. "Get rid of what?"

"That cross you're carrying. Why can you accept the fact that she could be unfaithful, but not the fact that it wasn't your fault? Jeremy, you are not responsible for the happiness of everyone you care about."

"Revere, go to hell."

"Not yet. Morgan, you are the best friend I've had in a long, long time. I may never see you again, and so I'll give you this as a farewell: there's a woman out there that you deserve, and she's about to destroy herself. I'd like to sail off from here thinking of you two together. But it's unlikely. You are both too bullheaded, stubborn, and just plain stupid to know what's good for you."

"Ariana?" Jeremy asked.

"Who else?"

"How did you know?"

"Jeremy, I've known for a long time. Probably before you did. And she's in danger."

"How?" Jeremy frowned.

"Don't you know what's going on? What do you do on that ranch—stick your head in a hole? Fremont's returned. He's here gathering forces and mounts for his glorious southern campaign. It's said that he has a large herd and is returning through San Juan Bautista. Ariana is there with Manuel and the *liberalismos*. They are planning to take him on." Revere watched, waiting for a response.

"I heard you," Jeremy said finally, taking another drink.

Glancing at the harbor, Revere heaved a heavy sigh. He stood up, throwing a few coins on the table. "I have to go."

Jeremy stood and faced the other man, reaching out his hand. "Take care, you old bear hunter. I say that generously; you never did find me one."

Revere grinned. "No, I didn't. But they're still out there, Jeremy. You just have to be patient and find one."

They exchanged a long look, then suddenly Jeremy grasped him in a hug. "Take care of yourself," he said, stepping back.

"I will. You can write to me in care of my family. Let me know what happens."

Jeremy watched as Revere walked away. He would miss him; but he knew that Joseph wasn't meant to stay in Monterey. Jeremy pictured him with sea-foam and waves, a plunging ship cutting through the water, docking in distant, exotic lands. The image seemed appropriate. And he preferred it to his memory.

Six hours later, Jeremy was on his way back to the Salinas Valley, having watched one ship sail and another arrive, each tormenting him with different emotions. He held the reins firmly as they rode along the hard-packed road, guiding the carriage around the deepest ruts and bumps so as not to wake his son. He afforded himself a brief glance at the sleeping child and the woman who held him. Selena looked drawn and weary, but her happiness at being home kept her awake. She wore a half-smile on her face, and her eyes were bright as she visually devoured the passing landscape, as if to confirm that it was all really happening.

The boy's small face was peaceful in sleep, but Jeremy had been shocked by the fear he had seen in his son's eyes earlier. As Selena had stepped from the longboat, he had reached for the child. Hamilton's face had scrunched up with tears, and he had buried it in his nurse's shoulder, his small hands clutching at her cloak as he whimpered in pathetic, soft little mews. Jeremy had expected that the boy would be frightened of him at first; after all, he was a stranger to his son. But there was something in that terrified reaction, and in the two hours that followed as they visited with the Larkins—Rachel had insisted upon seeing the baby—that made him uneasy. The child would not allow

Selena out of his sight, his large blue eyes following her everywhere. If she left the room, Hamilton's eyes would become glazed with fear. Perhaps the child was just shy, Jeremy thought. After all, he assumed that Beth had spent little time with him. Except for the time with his grandparents, his entire world would have revolved around Selena.

It was that world that interested Jeremy now. "How was the journey home, Selena?" he asked gently.

She turned to him and smiled. "As I told Senor Larkin, his supercargo was very good to me. He made sure that Hamilton and I had everything we need."

"And how about the time you spent in New York? Were you treated well?" She looked away, but not before he saw the uncertainty. "Selena?" She did not answer. "Selena, you must tell me."

"What do you want to know, Senor?" she asked quietly, staring down at the sleeping child in her arms.

"Was anyone unkind to you?"

She hesitated. "Most people were very kind to me."

"Who was not?"

"Senora Morgan's friends did not like me much." She shrugged. "But it did not matter. I rarely saw them. When they came I stayed in the nursery with the *nino*."

"Then what were you afraid of?"

Her eyes widened at the question, and she looked away. "I—I was not frightened."

"Then what was my son afraid of?"

She looked back at him with surprise, then her plain face grew hard. "He is a good boy, Senor."

The statement, the emphasis of her voice, took him off guard. "Of course he is. Answer my question, Selena. I must know." To his shock, her large brown eyes filled with tears. He took the reins in one hand and reached over to touch her arm. "You are home now," he said gently. "No one is going to harm you or my son. You must tell me everything."

She swallowed heavily and adjusted the blanket about the child protectively. Her voice was barely a whisper. "You are right; you must know. Forgive me. I was wrong. She is a bad woman, the senora."

Jeremy felt his gut tighten. "What did she do to you?"

"She—she did not do anything to me. She slapped me sometimes, when she thought I was slow or disrespectful."

He was stunned. "She hit you?"

"Si, Senor. But—I did not mind, until—she hit the *nino*."

Jeremy jerked hard on the reins, and the buggy lurched backward as the horses protested, then stopped. "She hit the baby?" he asked hoarsely.

"She would slap him when he cried. He was not supposed to cry when she had company."

"But, if you were in the nursery, why should her company have been disturbed?" It didn't make sense. He thought of his house in New York; it was much too large for the sound of a crying baby to have disturbed her guests.

"She—the senora would—" She hesitated, flushing deeply. "Her bedroom was next to the nursery," she said softly. "Until she moved us upstairs."

Upstairs? From the nursery? "To the attic!" Jeremy blurted. His hands tightened on the reins, wishing they were about his ex-wife's white neck. The exhausted baby stirred restlessly, whimpering in his sleep. He forced himself to be calm. "Do not worry, Selena. Whatever you and my son have been forced to suffer, it is over. You are home now."

She returned his smile timidly, but her eyes were bright with gratitude. "I know, Senor. Everything will be all right now, as you say."

The remainder of the trip was silent as Selena managed to sleep, leaving Jeremy alone with thoughts he would sooner have not faced. He knew that there was so much she was not telling him, perhaps endless days of neglect and abuse. No wonder his father had not known of Beth's affairs. She must have threatened Selena, then conducted them in her own home when the other servants were given the evening off. With no witness who would tell.

They spent the night in Salinas, and arrived home the following day. It was an overcast day, with the threat of a storm. When he had first received word that Selena and his son were coming home, he had brought Maria from the house in Monterey. Jeremy was pleased with the decision, and the house was well lit and warm.

As he showed Selena to her room on the second floor where she would stay with the baby, Selena gasped, turning back to him with a face filled with pleasure.

"Oh, Senor, it is so *bonito*!"

He smiled, happy that she was pleased. "Senora Larkin helped me when we knew that you were coming home."

"Ham will love it!" She smiled, glancing down at the sleeping baby.

"Ham?"

She smiled at him shyly. "Forgive me, Senor, but Hamilton seems such a big name for one so little. I call him Ham—when senora was not about."

He smiled warmly, glad that his son had had Selena with him these past months. "I will send Maria up to help you unpack."

Jeremy spent hours each day with his son. It was three days before the boy would allow his father to hold him without crying, and another two before he was able to coax a smile from the small face. It came in a moment when Jeremy was holding him on his lap after a bath. Selena had gone to fix the baby's supper, and Jeremy had been struggling to put on Ham's nightgown. Each time he tried to pull the narrow sleeve over Ham's arm, the baby watched him with an innocent expression and then, just prior to success, he opened his hand, flaring his tiny fingers to catch them in the folds. After the third attempt, Jeremy swore softly, feeling totally out of his depth. Obviously, the child was smarter than he was.

"Ham, you're doing that on purpose. Why do you want to make a fool out of your father?" Jeremy leaned back in the chair, staring at the ceiling with frustration. The baby turned in his arms, grasping his father's shirt, and gurgled. The sound drew his attention and Jeremy glanced down, instantly fascinated with the bubbles his son was making. Impulsively, he made a face at the child. Ham studied the odd expression for a moment, then broke into a smile. And laughed.

Jeremy stared. The vice that had gripped his heart suddenly released. That smile was stunning in its power.

Later that night, careful not to disturb Selena who slept in the room next to the nursery, he slipped in to watch Ham sleep. "Someday," he whispered, his heart full, "your dreams will be rid of those memories, as you have rid them of mine. I swear it."

In the following days, Jeremy's life became richer than ever before. He moved through each day with new purpose, a commitment to his future and that of his son. Even the land, which he had purchased as an investment, took on new meaning. It was no longer merely a western addition to the Morgan Investment Company. It had become, in Jeremy's mind, the Morgan Land and Investment Company. And the land became the pivotal part. He began to see what he had glimpsed when he first came to California, sensing the richness of the future and its promise. Within the past year, the frustrations and disappointments had receded, leaving Jeremy a renewed determination to succeed. All because of one small boy and his smile, gifting his father with a paternal feeling of immortality.

With some reluctance, Jeremy conceded to the request of the tall, rangy cowhand standing on his porch, acknowledging that in the past week he had been somewhat remiss. Before the change in his life brought by the small child asleep in the room above, he had spent the majority of his nights with his men across the yard in the bunkhouse, or in Salinas, lifting a glass. Thus, he walked with his foreman, Dirk Lucas, across the dark compound to the bunkhouse. Why not? he thought. Just because he had become a full-fledged and willing father didn't mean he had to become a monk as well. He found himself looking forward to a few hands of poker and an evening in the company of his men.

"You owe me two bucks, Jake." The foreman grinned as they entered the bunkhouse. "He's going to sit in."

A broad-shouldered, ruddy-complexioned cowhand swore good-naturedly, to the laughter of the other men in the room. Jake sat with two other men at the round table centered in the room, while others lolled about, some trying to sleep in their bunks. The foreman grinned in response to Jeremy's puzzlement at the laughter. "I bet Jake two bucks that you wouldn't come."

The statement unsettled Jeremy; he hadn't realized that the change in his life had made him so unapproachable to his men. But, he realized, he had hardly spoken to them in a week, except to give them orders. "Well, Jake—" He smiled, taking the vacant chair next to him. "Would I miss the opportunity to win back your wages?"

"You can try, boss." The large man chuckled. "You can try." He pushed an empty glass over and filled it with whiskey.

The first hand was dealt and taken by Jake, who chortled

gleefully as he scooped the chips toward him. The ensuing hands broke evenly, drawing the game into the night. By eleven o'clock, they were drunker than they were rich. Jeremy had paced himself, no longer needing the release that liquor would bring, preferring to enjoy the men's company. He recalled another game, many months before in Vallejo's parlor, accompanied by the soft laughter of women, a sharp contrast to the present deep laughter and profanity. It had been a similar game with far different stakes. But when he wanted to become maudlin, the temptation was swiftly curbed.

"I hear that bastard Fremont is back," Dirk drawled in his thick Texas accent as he dealt the cards around the table. Jeremy glanced up at him in surprise.

"With luck, he'll cross Morgan land," a lanky cowboy added from his bunk.

"We could use more horses." Another laughed.

He shouldn't be surprised, Jeremy thought as he spread his cards. The men were firmly settled here, adjusting much more easily than he had when he first came to California. It wasn't surprising that they knew more than he did about what was going on. "Fremont is nothing to us," he said. "Don't go looking for trouble." But inwardly he was pleased and satisfied with his decision to hire these men.

When he had first considered buying this land from William Richardson, it had been a major decision. The land was south of Richardson's Los Coches rancho, the nine-thousand-acre rancho Maria Josepha, the eldest daughter of Feliciano Soberanes, had brought to her husband when she married him. Normally the purchase would have been impossible by Alta California law. Jeremy was not a Californio, he was not Catholic, and he was not married to a Californio woman. The fact that the purchase was not questioned was an indication in itself that times were changing, to the detriment of the Californio landholders. Over the past two years, the tallow and hide business had begun to fail. William Richardson, unlike his Californio father-in-law, knew that the Soberanes land he held in trust for his wife was in jeopardy of being lost to the inevitable changes that would come with United States possession. In the past few months, new settlers had already begun arriving in alarming numbers. Richardson knew that only the

strongest would survive, and that meant money to ride out
the hard times.

Jeremy truly liked Richardson and his gentle Californio
wife. He was glad his purchase would help them. However,
it was not enough. As Jeremy observed the operations of the
Soberanes' land, he grew concerned. Jeremy knew that as
much as he revered the Californio vaqueros, and as impressed as he was by their extraordinary abilities with cattle
and unsurpassed horsemanship, more than their talents
would be needed for survival. The Californios were not
prepared for what was coming, what was already here.
Larkin's words passed through his brain, as they often had
in the past months: "These are the halcyon days, Jeremy.
We shall not see their likes again."

A solution came when he recalled that a brother officer
from the Point was stationed at a garrison in Texas. He had
written to him immediately, and the letter resulted in the
men in his employ: Texas cowboys left unemployed by the
war. His brother officer had chosen well. These cowhands
were rough, crude, and expert in their jobs, with talents that
surpassed their horsemanship.

"It's to you, boss."

"I'll take two," Jeremy said.

"I'll stand with these." Four heads turned to the speaker,
a slow-talking, potbellied cowboy with gray hair by the
name of Jasper, whom the entire outfit held in quiet respect.
Jasper's face was bland as he quietly offered his wisdom.
"It's no good to go lookin' for trouble, but we'll be here if it
comes."

"Amen, Jasper," Jake said. "Gimme one."

Jeremy re-spread his cards, his own face placid as he
noted a full house. He glanced at Jasper. When the bet came
back, he raised the pot two dollars. "Fremont is north of
here. We're not likely to see him."

Dirk studied his cards, then met the bet, raising it one.
"Nope," he agreed. "We're not likely to. That outfit in San
Juan will probably see to the matter."

"What outfit?" Jeremy asked casually, tossing down a
whiskey. He missed the exchange of glances at the table.

Jake met the raise and upped it two. "That greas—" He
paused, glancing at Jeremy, knowing how Jeremy felt about
the term, and he quickly amended it. "That Californio,

Manuel Castro. He's got a band of his compadres at San Juan Bautista. They say in Salinas that he's fixing to take the Yankee horses."

Jeremy kept his eyes leveled on the cards. Revere's warning came back, words he had forgotten in the past week, and his stomach churned. Forcing down the warning that pressed on him, he called. In a quick turn his full house was lost beneath Jake's straight, then Jasper's royal flush. Jasper smiled slightly as he swept the chips to the pile in front of him.

Jeremy drew from a cheroot and stared into the dark, quarter-moon night. He had crossed halfway back to the house only to pause beneath the large sycamore that stood centered in the large compound. A few days before he had decided that he would hang a swing from this tree for his son. Now he contemplated the tree in a moment of privacy.

"They're likely to get themselves killed, you know."

Jeremy's head turned to find Dirk standing near, as the foreman lit his own smoke. "Who?" Jeremy asked, knowing the answer, but asking anyway.

"Manuel Castro, and everyone with him."

"How much do your men know?" Jeremy asked. He had heard that cowboys were incurable gossips, and now he knew it.

"We've heard some." Dirk shrugged.

"Go on."

"You know, boss, I've only been in this country for about three months, but I've gotten to know the Californios pretty well." He laughed softly. "We've certainly spent enough time drinking with them in Salinas. You get to know a man pretty well that way." He fell silent for a long moment, drawing from his cheroot.

"I remember a time in Texas, during the early days, after the Alamo," he said. "An entire village I knew was wiped out fighting Santa Anna. Men, women and children. It hit me hard; I knew a lot of those people and I liked them. They were warned, but they went ahead anyway and fought. I know that Fremont's ours, but he kinda reminds me of Santa Anna."

He dropped the cheroot on the ground and crushed it with his foot. "Just wanted to let you know. The boys and I are ready to do whatever you want us to."

Jeremy watched Dirk stroll back to the bunkhouse. He swore softly, tossing his own cheroot away. Manuel Castro could go to the devil for all that he cared. And, dammit, Ariana didn't want him. And he had no interest in a woman who was determined to reject him. She had her own dreams, as she had been so fond of reminding him, and they were diametrically opposed to his own. Besides, she would reject any attempt to save her, if he were fool enough to offer help.

As those thoughts crossed his mind, he glanced at the main house and thought of what it held. He had been given another chance. And then Revere's words came back to him. Suddenly he swore again, violently. Damn her, it was none of his business! But as he held onto that thought, reaffirming it, he was already crossing to the stables. There was no way that his men would be involved with this, not yet. And he meant it; Manuel could go to the devil. But despite his denials, his mind was forming a plan that would, in all probability, backfire right in his face.

26

Candles flickered in the small, iron chandelier overhead, casting irregular, moving shadows over what had once been Jose Castro's office in the military garrison of San Juan Bautista. A map was spread on the desk. What remained of Castro's wine cellar was being passed among the four men who sat around the desk as they studied the sketched terrain before them.

"Here—" Manuel Castro tapped his finger on a point marked Natividad, a position southwest of where they sat. "The hills will provide cover. At the pace he is moving, he should arrive by the day after tomorrow."

"How can you be certain that he will pass through there?" Rafael asked.

"It is the only pass that will accommodate the three-hundred horses that he has collected for us."

The others laughed at Manuel's observation. The usually reticent Rafael grinned, encouraged by the mood of the others. "Ariana chose well." He smiled. "Her plans usually work."

Staring at the map, he missed the jerking muscle in Manuel's jaw, but his next words were clear enough. "This was my plan, not hers." Rafael blanched at the controlled fury he saw in Manuel's face. He doubted the truth of what Manuel said, but there was no way he would contradict him. Instead, he merely nodded.

Manuel glanced about at the others, his eyes hard and angry. "Understand me, for many years Ariana has served our cause. I am grateful to her, as we all are. But it is no longer a time for spies but for action. War. A time for men." Then he paused, as if regretting his next words. "And there is another matter. It grieves me to say this but—I fear that she no longer can be trusted."

Rafael's shock and outrage were emphasized by one of the others, a thickset Californio who did not know her well, but revered her reputation among those who for so long had struggled for their cause. "What are you saying? She has risked her life for us, many times!"

Manuel sighed with heavy regret. "Si, it is so. It makes it all the more difficult. I was present when she visited Vallejo upon his release from the Yanqui prison." He recalled the conversation, choosing to overlook the fact that the conversation in question was from a bitter Salvador Vallejo. But the words were true and suited the moment. "Vallejo was angry, demanding that reprisals be taken against the Yanquis for his imprisonment. Ariana protested, declaring that he must find a way to deal with what he had suffered. That some common ground must be found to deal with the Yanquis." He omitted her additional words, to which Mariano had agreed, that to act rashly while unprepared would lead to certain disaster. All could be lost because of the indignities suffered by one man.

With horror and outrage, the men stared at the regretful look on Manuel's face. Rafael felt ill. But his love for his cousin made him bold. "You must have misunderstood her," he stammered. "She has not changed. She spent that time with the Yanqui commodore and even Fremont himself, bringing us information. We were able to escape because of it—she would not make peace with them!"

Manuel stifled his anger and glanced at the other man unhappily. "Rafael, if I had not heard it myself I would not have believed it. I do not want to accept it even now, but I must. I cannot allow my regard for Ariana to weaken our cause—thus I must to tell you what else I know. You know that she returned with Vallejo to Sonoma before the so-called bear flag revolt. It seems that during that time she was not in Sonoma with the don, but at Rancho Petaluma—with the Yanqui, Jeremy Morgan." He allowed the impact of his words to settle in. "He is her lover. He who, upon his return to Monterey, revealed himself as a major in the Yanqui army."

"Perhaps . . ." Rafael glanced at the others, still not wanting to believe the implications of what Manuel was saying. "Perhaps she was with him to learn information."

"When I first learned of her affair, that is what I had hoped," Manuel said, shaking his head. He did not add that he had learned of it from spies he had paid to watch her, hoping that she would make such a mistake. "But I gave her every opportunity to report what she had learned from the Yanqui. She told me nothing. In fact, she did not even offer the information that she had been with him. She was angry that I questioned her about her whereabouts when I could not contact her."

A heavy silence followed as the men dealt with the possibility that one they had followed, revered, and trusted had turned traitor to their cause. For the love of an enemy. Manuel watched them, smiling inwardly as he observed the turn in their emotions. "That is why she is not here for this briefing. She does not know that we are meeting to finalize our plans."

He looked at the map, controlling the anger he felt that she had, indeed, formulated the plan he had presented as his own for the capture of Fremont's horses. But, if his own plans worked, and they seemed to have just taken a large step forward, nothing else would matter.

He glanced at the others, judging that the moment was at hand. "There is another matter, one that could not be presented if she was here—considering the unfortunate circumstances. There are two, not one, objectives that are about to be accomplished. The first, you are aware of: the capture of the arrogant Yanqui's horses, which will cause him great humiliation and lead to his downfall. But it is not enough. The Yanquis must be shown the depths to which we reject their government. They must know, once and for all, that California is meant to be a republic under the rule of the Californios. To capture a herd meant for the United States military is one thing; the capture of their foremost official is another." He smiled at the astonished looks that met his statement. "Their former consul, he who has lived among us for many years, plying us with his lies and promises, is within our reach. Thomas Larkin is at Rancho Los Vergeles, just southwest of here. He is on his way to join his family at Yerba Buena. It is up to us to see that he does not reach it."

Ariana slipped beneath the warm water, sighing from the deep comfort it brought. She had spent most of the afternoon arguing with Manuel, until he finally accepted the wisdom of her plan to attack Fremont's forces at Natividad. The fool had argued to attack in the open plains below San Jose, assuring certain defeat. She knew that Manuel's reluctance to consider her plans stemmed from his abhorrence to suggestions from a woman; she had certainly dealt with the problem for enough years to expect it. Manuel had always been difficult, but it was a fact she had long accepted. With the exception of Rafael, the machismo of her men put up constant resistance to the opinions and wisdom of a woman.

The warm weather offered her soothing comfort, easing the aching problems of the day. She laid her head back on the edge of the tub, determined to enjoy the respite until the water grew uncomfortably cold. Her eyes closed and she shifted in the water, vaguely aware that a chill had descended on the room. She pouted, dipping deeper into the water. Then, suddenly a large hand clamped over her mouth. Instinctively she began to fight, sloshing water over the sides of the tub.

"Quiet!" a deep male voice hissed. Arms dragged her out of the water. She struggled frantically as they wrapped about her, drawing her dripping from the tub. Forcing her head back, she stared into the deep blue of Jeremy's eyes.

She squealed against the grip of his hand over her mouth as he dragged her across the floor. The arm about her waist released her for a moment and she fought, swinging her bare legs as he pulled a cover from the bed and tossed it over her. "You are not going to be part of this insanity; you'll only get yourself killed. You are coming with me, sweetheart." He grunted, pulling the cover about her. "Dammit, Ariana, stop struggling! It's cold out there; you want to go bare-ass naked?"

As he pulled her through the open window, she realized the source of the chill she had felt in the tub. He managed to extract her from the window and she felt his hand replaced by a kerchief, effectively gagging her. Then she was hefted, coverlet trailing, onto a horse. He swung up behind her, then tucked the cover about her legs. His arms went about her tightly, holding her as she jerked with the sudden movement of the bolting horse.

It was all too simple, she thought dismally, realizing that more guards should have been posted to counter such an event. It did not help to realize how much this man knew. In the months she had spent with him, she could have learned from him, knowledge that would have been useful to her. Hot tears bit at her eyes as she realized how innocent the *liberalismos* must appear, how desperate their situation.

They rode for what seemed like hours, though it was impossible for Ariana to judge the time; she was cold and miserable. In spite of her determination not to do so, she dozed, awakening with a start as he stopped in the foothills north of Salinas.

He lifted her from the saddle in a small clearing of scrub oak and chamois brush. Suddenly, he yanked the cover from her. *"Dios!* What are you doing!" she cried. She tried to cover herself with her hands and immediately she began to shiver.

"You're not likely to run away like that," he said. Then he proceeded to gather wood for a fire.

"You can't leave me like this!"

Kneeling to start the fire, he threw down the kindling and glanced up. His eyes swept over her. "I don't plan to. You'll be warm in a few minutes."

When she was settled by the fire, wrapped again in the blanket, he saw to the horse. When he finished feeding and watering the animal, he pulled some extra garments from his saddlebag and returned to the fire. She was curled up under the coverlet, sulking as she stared into the fire.

"Here," he said, dropping the clothes into her lap. "Put these on."

She stared at them for a moment. She clenched her teeth in rage, then stood up, glaring at him. He just stood there, one thumb tucked into his belt, waiting. "You could at least turn around!" she flared.

"Not likely, sugar. Don't worry, I've seen you before, in fact, just a few moments ago."

Somehow she managed to struggle into the oversized shirt and pants, while revealing as little to him as she could. Then she stood there, clutching the pants in her hands to keep them from falling.

"You need a belt," he said.

"I need a gun."

"Would you prefer the blanket?"

"I would have preferred it if you had minded your own business!"

"I am certain that before this is over I will agree with you."

"Then why did you bother?" she spit out.

He stared at her over the campfire. "Do you really think you would have accomplished anything by taking Fremont's horses? You would probably have gotten yourself killed."

"What does it matter to you?" she cried.

"God knows. But you are going to stay with me until it is over."

"It won't ever be over!"

"Ariana, it is already."

"No it isn't! We will fight to the death—"

The sharp sound of his laughter stopped her. "Dammit, Ariana, stop the dramatics. This is one battle you are not going to be part of. It is destined for disaster."

"Jeremy Morgan, the seer?" she said sarcastically.

"Hardly. I did a little investigation of my own on my way to San Juan Bautista. And once I arrived there, it took all of fifteen minutes to discover your plans. Your men talk too much," he said grimly. "Christ, Ariana, *I* discovered what was going on. If Fremont doesn't know, then he is a total fool. And in the slim likelihood that Fremont hasn't heard, your plan is bound to fail. There is an echo in the pass you've chosen. If one of your men so much as coughs, it will be heard for a quarter of a mile."

"How do you know that?" she asked, stiffening with alarm.

"Because I passed through it on my way to you. A good officer—" he added with a smirk, "notices such things."

She was horrified. "Would—" She swallowed, forcing herself to ask the question. "Would the plains below San Jose be a better place to attack?"

"In the open? No."

"Then where—"

"Ariana, do you honestly expect me to answer that? Forget it. What in the hell made you think that you could plan a military campaign against experienced forces? You have about a hundred men—"

"How did you know that?"

"I saw them," he answered grimly. "It's easy to calculate —as a spy for Fremont would do." He hesitated as she groaned, turning her face away. "Ariana, can't you see? You are pitting men who are ill-prepared against men who are hardened and experienced soldiers. From what I could find out, Fremont has about fifty men with him—"

"Two to one?" she gasped, turning back to him. "Those are good odds!"

"In this case they are no odds at all," he said roughly. "Fremont's men will slaughter Manuel's."

"You just want to believe that!"

"Why would I?" he countered, his voice rising. "Fremont's shit! So is Manuel! I hope that neither of them comes out of this! Perhaps then we can find a solution to this mess! And, by God, you are not going to be part of it!"

"You're yelling at me!"

"Goddamn right I am!"

His last words echoed, finally leaving them in a heavy silence.

"Jeremy Morgan, you are a bully," she said.

"Only toward people I care about."

"Then why did you betray me to Stockton?" she asked tightly.

"Betray you? Ariana, how long do you think it would have been before they found out who you were? What do you think would have happened to you when they did? Do you know what they do with spies in war?"

The question struck her uncomfortably. She had never really thought about it. She couldn't think about it. "Why did you leave the army?"

"Stockton wanted me to join them for his southern campaign." He shrugged. "I was fed up with it. And those are enough questions for tonight. I am tired, and we still have a long ride ahead of us."

He dropped a blanket next to her and lay down on one of his own. Pulling it over him, he wrapped an arm about her. "If you recall, I am a light sleeper, Ariana."

It was his final word. She stared into the dark, moonless night, and her thoughts kept her awake for a long, long time.

She groaned as a hand shook her awake.

"It's almost dawn. Wake up."

Her nose twitched at the smell of coffee. As she sat up, he pressed a cup into her hands. "Drink this. We leave in five minutes." She frowned at the hot beverage. "Sorry that we don't have chocolate, princess. That will have to do."

She looked up at him. She hadn't realized that he could still hurt her. "I am not spoiled, Jeremy."

The defeat in her voice caught in him. "No, Ariana, you're not. I'm sorry. You didn't deserve that." He hunkered down next to her, handing her some jerky. "Breakfast."

She took the dried beef and began chewing on an end of the hard strip. He stared at the ground between them, regretting what he had said to her. He hadn't meant to hurt her, but then he had never meant to hurt her. And he knew that there would be much more pain ahead before this was over.

"Ariana," he said hesitantly, wondering why he was attempting this. "I won't humor you. Everything is going to change, and there is nothing that you or I can do to stop it. If you fight a lost cause, you are certain to lose."

She turned and looked at him. Her eyes were flinty. "Could you give up everything you believed in, Jeremy?"

"I already have."

Oh, Dios. She swallowed, hard. "And then what?"

"Take a chance, begin again. But you can't if you're looking back."

He straightened and turned to saddle the horse. At least she hadn't thrown his words back in his face. He wasn't sure if he could have blamed her if she had. Jeremy realized that everything was falling apart around her. He glanced at her over the back of the horse. She was staring into the fire, her forehead wrinkled in thought. She should have stayed in Sonoma when Mariano was released, he thought. Stayed away from this whole damn mess. But he would have been surprised if she had.

"Ready?" he asked a few moments later.

"Do I have a choice?"

"No, *querida.* You don't. Neither of us do."

27

Ariana stood at the bedroom window, watching the dust lift from the compound and swirl about the trees that were permanently bent before its force. The wind had blown throughout the night. The aching moan crept through the rafters of the house, accompanied by protesting creaks and shifts of the wooden frame, adding to the lonely depth of her mood.

She tried to remain composed in the face of all that had happened. Any other emotion would be destructive, she reminded herself. Time, she needed time to sort it all out. He had done so much, she thought, gazing from the window. Barns, corrals, a bunkhouse and stable. And this house. Built not of adobe, but of redwood lumber he had brought from his mill in Santa Cruz before he sold it. That much he had told her upon their arrival last night.

It would not stand against the wind with the rigidity of adobe, she thought, but it would move with it. It would bend instead of crumble.

She had wakened late in the morning to find a dress and a chemise on the chair beside her bed. She recognized the clean but faded dress as one she had once seen Selena wear. Fortunately the woman was full-busted, but the waist was too big and the skirt barely reached to her ankles. Once dressed, she braced herself and left the room, going downstairs as she wondered what this day would hold for her. If it went as the past months had, anything could happen.

She entered the kitchen to find Maria stirring a large pot of what smelled like stew and Selena sitting at the end of a long table near the warm stove with a plump, rosy-cheeked baby in her arms. The child turned at the sound of her footsteps. It studied her intensely for a moment and then suddenly broke into a totally disarming grin. Surprised, Ariana laughed.

"What a beautiful baby, Selena," she said, sitting down next to them. Impulsively she held out her hand and the baby grasped her finger. Then the smile faded and her eyes grew wide with surprise. "Selena! You are here!" Her eyes darted back to the baby. "Hamilton?" she whispered.

"Si, Senorita." Selena exchanged a puzzled look with Maria. Why had the senorita grown so pale?

Ariana felt a tightening in her chest. What did it matter? It meant nothing to her if . . . She forced a smile. "Senora Morgan is here?"

Selena frowned as she struggled with the baby who was trying to stand in her lap. "The *nino* came home with me, Senorita. The senora did not come." Then slowly, Selena realized why Ariana was so pale. She did not know! She smiled. "Senora Morgan left the senor," she said with satisfaction. "She divorced him."

Ariana gaped at her. "Divorced?"

"Si."

Ariana felt her heart turn over. It didn't matter, she told herself, except that she was glad Beth was out of his life. She looked back at the baby. "He has grown so much," she said softly. "May I hold him?"

Selena hesitated for a moment, unsure of how the baby would react to a stranger. To her surprise, as Ariana reached for him, he held out his arms to her. Well, perhaps she shouldn't be surprised, she thought. Ariana was a Californio woman; babies had always been part of her life—accepted and cherished.

Ariana took him into her arms, folding them about his soft body. He was so warm, she thought, and smelled slightly like spit-up. He reached out a small finger and touched a faded flower on her dress. Then he glanced up, studying her face with serious blue eyes that looked startlingly like Jeremy's. Her heart caught in her throat.

Selena watched them for a moment. Then she smiled, satisfied. "Would you like some chocolate, Senorita?" she asked, standing up.

"That would be nice," Ariana said vaguely without looking up. She was totally occupied with the baby, who was playing with the heavy braid on her shoulder. As she cooed to the child in her lap, Ariana was struck by a strange, distant longing. Had her mother ever held her like this, feeling such a sudden rush of love? And with all the babies she had held, why did the thought strike her now? She bent and kissed the soft cheek. "Is Senor Morgan somewhere about?" she asked as she bounced the child on her knee.

"He is out with the cattle, Senorita," Selena answered, setting the hot beverage on the table out of the baby's reach. "He left over two hours ago."

Ariana stiffened imperceptibly, and her heart skipped a beat. He was gone? She handed the baby back to Selena and turned in the chair. Picking up the steaming chocolate, she sipped it slowly, blowing gently between tastes to cool it. The man confounded her, she thought. He kidnapped her, brought her here, and then left her with two women servants while he left to see to his cattle! In spite of the sentimental feelings she had just experienced, his confidence was galling. Didn't he think she'd worry about those she had left in San Juan Bautista? He had quite successfully impressed upon her the danger they were in. And it was her fault, as much as Manuel's. Did he think she would simply stay here because he had ordered her to?

She finished the chocolate and rose to place the cup in the dry sink under the window. She couldn't see anyone from where she stood, but she dared not ask the women if there was anyone else around. If someone had been left to watch her, she had no intention of making her plans obvious.

She moved casually toward the door, placed her hand on the knob, and opened it. To her surprise, neither of the women even seemed to notice, much less care, as they went about their duties. Encouraged, she stepped out onto the porch. The wind had died down, though a soft breeze lifted her skirt and wrapped it about her legs. Her gaze swept over the ranch buildings, and still there was no sign of anyone. She fixed her sights on the stable and stepped down off the porch. She did not even want to consider the probability that the stalls would be empty—though it was a distinct possibility, she realized as she glanced with dismay at the empty corral.

She moved quickly amid the shadows of the roof over-hang, opening each stall door, only to find them as empty as she had feared. Then her heart quickened. As she approached the end of the long building, a large chestnut gelding stuck his head out over the half door. She quickly found a length of rope and fashioned a hackamore for the horse, then led it from the stall. With luck, in a few hours she would know what had happened . . .

"Pardon me, ma'am. Can I help you?" said a deep voice behind her. She spun about to find herself staring into friendly blue eyes in the weathered face of a lean, rangy Yanqui. "You must be Senorita Saldivar." He smiled, touching the corner of his hat. "I'm Dirk, Jeremy's fore-man. He told me to look out for you until he got back."

Disappointment melded with anger. "Guard me, don't you mean?"

"Ma'am?"

"Make certain that I don't escape!"

The man took off his hat and ran his fingers through his damp, auburn hair. "Well, it wouldn't be a very good idea if you left just now, would it? Considering how unsettled things are." He reached over and took the horse's reins. "Let me put 'im away for you. The boss'll be back shortly, and you can discuss the matter with him."

He took the horse and led it back to its stall. Her cheeks burned with fury. The boss? Furious, she headed for the large sycamore centered in the compound, plopping herself down in the shade of the spreading branches to await Jeremy's return. Damn him! she thought. No wonder he had felt secure leaving her to see to his cattle; he had left her with a watchdog!

Unaware that she had been dozing, she was suddenly awakened by the steady beat of hooves. Jumping to her feet, she shielded her eyes against the sun as she tried to make out the riders that were approaching. They disappeared from sight for a moment, then came into view once again as they galloped up the rise leading to the ranch. There were three riders, one whom she did not recognize, but the other two were Jeremy and—Rafael!

She watched them approach, filled with both joy and dread. She was almost weak with relief that Rafael was still alive, but feared the reason that could have brought him here. How had he found her? They pulled up and dismounted. Rafael and Jeremy approached as the other man took the horses, leading them toward the corral. Her eyes searched Rafael's face as she tried to predict what he was going to say to her.

"*Rafael! Que pasa?*" she asked.

Jeremy took her arm, turning her about. "Let's talk in the house," he said grimly.

As anxious as she was, she had difficulty keeping up with his long strides. But when they entered the kitchen, she pulled herself from Jeremy's grasp and spun impatiently back on Rafael. "Tell me! What happened?"

"Selena, take Hamilton upstairs. Maria, find something else to do for a while," Jeremy said calmly. "Ariana, give the man a chance, he's exhausted." He poured Rafael a glass of water, setting it on the table as he gestured for them both to sit.

"How did you find him?" she asked, glaring at Jeremy as Rafael emptied the glass.

"Early this morning I sent one of the hands out to discover what he could about the skirmish at Natividad. He found Rafael."

Both of them turned to Rafael. The slender, young Californio looked terrible: unshaven, exhausted, and desolate. Ariana watched him expectantly.

"Just tell us," Jeremy said quietly.

"It was not what Manuel said it would be," he said, his voice betraying the wonder he felt. "He said that it would be a great victory. We killed maybe two or three of the Americanos. We lost many of ours—maybe a third."

Ariana's eyes filled with horror, then closed for a moment as she tried to steady herself. "So many?" she whispered.

"I think so—there was so much confusion. Maybe some ran away. We did not even get the horses," he added miserably. "We fled. Some were going to Mission Soledad—"

"Where is Manuel?" she pressed, leaning forward.

"To Los Angeles, with some of the men, to join with Pio Pico and General Castro."

"You are certain?"

"Si. That was the plan—although they thought they would have the horses, too. But now they will negotiate.

This time, Yanqui will have to listen," he added, his face breaking hopefully.

Jeremy frowned. "Negotiate? Why will they have to negotiate now, Rafael?"

"Because they have Senor Larkin."

They both stared at the Californio. "What are you saying?" Ariana demanded.

"Senor Larkin. Manuel discovered that he was on his way to Yerba Buena, and had stopped for the night at Rancho Los Vergeles. We took him prisoner."

Jeremy's eyes hardened. Ariana grew pale as she stared at Rafael's self-satisfied expression. "Whose idea was it to take Larkin?" she asked coldly, though she already knew the answer.

"Manuel's—" Then he hesitated, remembering what Manuel had said about Ariana. He had spent so many years following her, trusting her, that throughout the horror of the past day he had simply forgotten. In fact, after he had become separated from the others and Jake had found him, his only thought was that he was being taken to her. He knew that she would know what to do.

"There's a mistake. It can't be Thomas," she whispered. "He knew it was dangerous to travel. Why was he going to Yerba Buena?"

"Because Rachel is there with the children," Jeremy said, barely able to control his anger. "A month ago he sent them north for safety. The baby, Adeline, is very sick, and Rachel sent for him."

She closed her eyes. *"Dios,"* she whispered. Then her eyes opened and she turned on Rafael. "You took him last night?"

"No," he answered, with less confidence than a moment before. His eyes shifted nervously between them. "The night before. Around midnight."

"Then you planned this before I left."

"Si," he said, looking more uncomfortable. "Manuel convinced the others that you were not to be trusted—" He swallowed. "Because of your involvement with Major Morgan."

She stared at him for a long moment. Then, slowly, her eyes darkened to flint. "Rafael, you will rest yourself for a few hours, then you are going to Los Angeles." Rafael visibly squirmed, recognizing that voice. Jeremy watched her face harden, as she transformed into someone he barely knew. "You will take a message to Manuel for me. Tell him that he is to release Thomas, unharmed. Remind him of the old friends I have there, and in Mexico. Remind him of Garcia and Padillo. Give him this promise: if Thomas is harmed, there is no place that Manuel will be safe."

A few moments later, with Jeremy's urging, a shaken Rafael left for a few hours of sleep in the bunkhouse. They were alone in the silent kitchen. "I don't suppose that you would mind if I did a few things on my own, such as sending word to Stockton?" he asked grimly.

"No, do what you must," she answered. The expression she turned on him was resolved. "But none of it will matter, Jeremy. Your people will never find Manuel, unless he wants to be found. There are always those who will hide him. More than that, if a Californio has a horse, a lasso, and a knife, he will never go hungry. They know every pass, canyon, and valley. They can move about, shifting from one place to another and never be seen.

"You write your letters," she continued wearily. "And I will write to *Tio Mariano* as well. He still has influence with Pio Pico." She stared off into space, her eyes focusing blackly on some unseen point. "This is my fault. I knew Manuel better than anyone. I knew he was capable of something like this, but I didn't watch for it. Just as I know that the only thing that will make him see reason is fear."

He stared at her. "Garcia and Padillo?" He shook his head, not wanting to believe what he was thinking. "I don't doubt your influence, Ariana. But would you really do what you threatened?"

She returned the look evenly. "To save Thomas? To use one of your Yanqui expressions, Jeremy, in a country minute."

Jeremy stepped out of the stuffy warmth of the house into the cool evening. It had rained buckets for two days, and the steady downpour had eased only in the past few hours. He paused on the porch to have his evening cheroot, then saw her standing in the shadows of the sycamore. He watched her for a moment, wondering what she was thinking, how she was feeling after all that had happened the past three days.

He had given her time to come to grips with her feelings and emotions. She had even been somewhat amiable last night when he had tempted her with the prospect of a game of poker with the men. There was little else for the men to do during such weather. But for the few who took shifts to check on the herd, they remained in the bunkhouse with their cards.

Jeremy had assured her that the men would welcome such an easy mark—a statement that enlisted an indignant glower—and she had agreed. Then, as they had stepped into the bunkhouse, she had stopped inside the door and stared. Her eyes passed over the men, who began to grow uncomfortable under the intensity of her silent regard. Suddenly, she spun about and went back into the downpour to the house. She had not spoken to him since.

He watched her now, as she leaned against the broad trunk of the tree, staring out over the valley. It was the way she looked, so alone, that drew him off the porch. He knew she was tormented by Thomas's capture, worried for his well-being, and troubled by the knowledge that her own men had excluded her. He didn't know if he could possibly help, but he was determined to try.

She was filled with self-recrimination and doubt. How could everything turn out so badly? she wondered. She had been so certain . . . The flare of his match drew her attention, and she realized that he was there. But there was nothing to say. She continued to stare into the dark, cloud-covered landscape.

"He is much too important and has far too many friends for them to harm him," he said quietly.

"Neither Pio Pico nor Castro would harm him. But I'm not so certain about Manuel," she said.

"I think I've learned a little about him myself, Ariana. He blusters, as he did when he delivered the commandant's ultimatum to Fremont to leave the area. Fremont faced him down. Kidnapping Larkin is his style, but Manuel knows that he is important only as long as he has Larkin. If he harms Thomas, he would not dare face Pio Pico or Castro. The last thing they want right now is a martyr."

"You may be right, but I can't take that chance, not with Thomas," she said tightly.

Just then a mockingbird protested above them, mimicking a crow-owl. The sound came out as a garbled screech-who, and they laughed in spite of themselves. "Is that agreement or disapproval?" Ariana asked, glancing upward.

"Who knows? But then, who needs an opinion from a birdbrain?"

"I've certainly had to deal with enough of those," she said with a smirk.

"I trust that I am not included in that company," he said wryly.

"Would I be foolish enough to say so if it were true? Particularly when I am your prisoner—which reminds me. When are you going to let me go?"

"When I am certain that you are not going to do something stupid."

"Nice. But it doesn't matter now, does it? The battle at Natividad is over."

"Ah, if that were all," he said.

"I don't know what you mean."

"Give it up, Ariana."

They exchanged a long look. "I could do it, you know."

"Probably. But you could also put Thomas in more danger."

"How?" She glared at him.

"Think, Ariana. It is one thing for you to put pressure on Manuel—yes, I know you sent messages with Rafael to others besides Manuel. But it is another thing for you to suddenly confront him. This is his moment of glory. Bullies are only dangerous when they panic. That's why I want to keep you out of there."

"Meaning?"

"Meaning," he said impatiently, "that you are the only one who can cause him to act impulsively. You are the threat, don't you know that?"

She did know it. She didn't want to, but she did. "You really think I'm depraved, don't you?" she asked, glancing at his profile.

"No," he said, drawing from his cheroot. "I've never thought that. I think that you are carrying the weight of some pretty heavy responsibilities. But you would do it all over again, given the same circumstances and choices."

"And what does that make me? A murderess? A whore?"

"You already know how I feel about that," he said. "I'm

tired of belaboring it. But don't overlook the fact that you've been fighting a war, Ariana, for a long time. Only you can judge yourself and what you've done. No one else counts." He turned and looked at her. "Tell me, what have you been fighting for all this time?"

"You know the answer to that. For the rights of my people to govern themselves."

"They can have that now."

"Oh yes, as part of your union," she said bitterly. "And to your country we will become another *la otra banda*. They want what we have, not what we are."

"I wonder how the Salinan and Costanoan Indians feel about that—if anyone thought to ask them. Shall we ask Selena?"

"I accept your point," she said irritably. "So now we are to stand aside. Our time is done."

"The time has changed. It could be for the better."

"Ah, yes, changes. Is that why you've hired Yanquis to work for you?" she said angrily.

"So that's why you left so abruptly last night," he said. "Because of the men."

"You are a hypocrite, Jeremy Morgan. You claim to care for the Californios, but they are not good enough to work for you!"

"Ariana, listen to me." Careful, Jeremy, he warned himself, trying to deal with his own anger. This entire conversation was exhausting. He could understand her anger, but could she understand his reasons? "No man is more skilled on horseback, or with cattle, than a vaquero. No one. That is not why I brought these men here. Before this is over—"

"Don't bother, Jeremy," she flared. "Your actions speak for what you truly feel. I have no doubt that when your barn starts to stink, you will hire one of my people to clean it!"

He drew a calming breath, reminding himself that she was hurting. "I will let that comment pass for now, Ariana. We'll talk about this again when you're ready to listen."

She watched him walk back toward the house. How could he leave her like that?

Ariana went to bed that night wishing it had all been just a bad dream—a nightmare sent to cause her to wonder about the deeper currents of her life. She would awaken to find that the past years had never happened. She would be a child again: when life was endless years of discovery, when every dream could be realized. No doubts, no guilts, no regrets. But now they persisted.

Ariana stood at the cast-iron stove, stirring the pot of beans that Maria had begun just after dawn. Looking for something to do, she had offered to help in the kitchen. For the past three days she had felt totally useless. She stirred the pot of the tasteless, bland beans that Jeremy preferred. She was bored, and her eyes wandered about the silent, warm kitchen. There were curtains on the windows and flowers in a small, earthen pot on the large table centered in the room. A woman's touch, thanks to Maria and Selena. It had begun to look like a home.

Beth was gone . . . forever gone. What that would have meant to her months ago! She might have even dared to wish for impossible things . . .

Dios! She hated this feeling of uselessness! All her life she had met her problems head-on and dealt with them, wrong or right. She was worried about Thomas. She was furious with Manuel, concerned about what was going to happen to her people. She didn't even know what was happening in the south. Perhaps she had made a mistake by rejecting Jeremy's men so quickly. If they were typical vaqueros, they would know the local gossip. *Madre mia,* she thought, except for Selena and Maria, she was surrounded by Yanquis!

She glanced at the shelf near her left shoulder and then stared biting her lower lip. Her conscience struggled against her desire for amusement and lost with little effort. She reached up for the glass bottle and its distinctive red powder. Yanking off the stopper, she smelled the contents gingerly and grinned. With a flourish, she liberally spiced the beans, adding just enough of the cayenne powder to whet the appetite of the hardiest vaquero.

The rains had moved to the south, leaving the morning fresh, the air cleansed and sweet. High, wispy clouds moved above as a gentle wind brushed over the landscape in a cooling breeze. Ariana paused, turning her face to the air, breathing deeply as she crossed the compound. She had offered to feed the chickens, something she had not done since she was a child. The prospect filled her with an odd, simple sort of happiness. She paused at the gate of the coop.

Watching the chickens as they moved about the small yard, scratching, strutting in their jerky rhythm, she recalled a distant, forgotten memory of a more innocent time. Once, when she was seven, there had been a special chicken; she had named her Pilar. A red hen, with bright orange wing feathers.

Remembering, she felt deeply sad. She had loved that chicken. She opened the gate, moving into the coop, and began to broadcast corn from her apron to the gathering, clucking brood. Damn chickens, she thought. She had loved that hen. She had carried it about like a baby. Then, one day, she had entered the chicken coop to collect eggs for a cascaron celebration. She had repressed the horror of that moment until now.

Moving a nest to find an elusive egg—hens liked to hide their brood from their collectors—she inadvertently exposed a nest of baby mice. The coop suddenly became bedlam as roosters and hens clucked and squawked, flying about as they fought for the bounty, carrying tiny, hairless, pink, squiggling mice away in their beaks. Ariana had merely stood there, screaming. She screamed and screamed until Raul suddenly appeared to pick her up, carrying her away as she sobbed into his shoulder. The vivid memory of Pilar fighting with the rest for the plumpest mouse-treasure stayed with her for a long, long time.

Damn chickens. It had been a full month before she could eat eggs again. It was Dona Benicia who first noticed that she grew pale when eggs were set on the table. Finally the dona found a moment alone with her. With little prodding, the story came out. It was met with a gentle smile of understanding. "To each creature in life there is given a purpose, little one," she had said, holding the child in her lap. "Chickens, like every creature, must follow their instinct, what is best for them."

"To eat mice?" Ariana asked, blanching with the memory.

"Even to eat mice. For them it is not wrong. Pilar did not mean to offend you, she was just doing what she was meant to do. She would be very sad if you did not understand."

Ariana had tried very hard to understand the dona's meaning, but she never felt the same way about Pilar again. She cared about her, and she was grateful that the hen was allowed to live a full life. She knew that Raul saw to it that

Pilar was overlooked for the pot, and she eventually died of old age. But from that day, Ariana's affection was given from a distance.

Poor Pilar, she thought, favoring a red chicken as she threw the corn. She had been so rigid that she had never forgiven her, even later, when she came to understand what Dona Benicia had told her. Then, slowly, Ariana's eyes shifted to the house and she frowned.

28

Ariana was sitting in the kitchen, feeding the baby, when Jeremy came in the back door. They both looked up as he stepped into the room; there was a warm, happy smile on Ariana's face and Ham's eyes were full of mischief, his face covered with food. For a moment Jeremy was transfixed. The scene slipped somewhere inside of him, touching a place he didn't want to think about.

"I'm afraid that your son is smarter than I am." Ariana laughed.

"That makes two of us," he said, crossing to the sink. He pumped water into the bowl in the sink and bent to splash his face. As he dried his hands and face on a towel, he watched Ariana trying to coax Ham to take another bite. "You don't have to do that, you know," he said quietly. "Where is Selena?"

"Washing his clothes. And yes, I know. I wanted to." She paused, glancing up at him. "Do you mind?"

"Of course not. I just don't want you to be—bothered with it."

"I'm not bothered, Jeremy. He's a beautiful baby. But he doesn't seem to want his dinner."

Jeremy glowered at his son with a warning frown. Ham regarded his father with serious eyes over a face smeared with yellow goop. Then his large, blue eyes seemed to laugh, and he busied himself with rubbing food into the table in front of him.

"What is it?" Jeremy asked suspiciously, looking into the bowl as he sat down beside them.

"Mashed apples and corn mush."

He grimaced. "I don't blame him."

Ariana frowned, then took a taste. "It isn't bad."

Ham slapped his hand into the bowl, spattering mush on Ariana and Jeremy.

"That does it." Jeremy got up and grabbed his son from Ariana's lap. He crossed to the back door and bellowed for Selena. A few moments later she appeared in the doorway, and Ham was thrust into her arms. "Here. His nibs needs a bath."

Ariana was standing at the sink, wiping off her shirt. As Jeremy took another towel to tend to his own splattered clothes, his eyes moved over her. She had given up wearing Selena's ill-fitting dress for trousers and shirts he had borrowed from one of the hands, a young cowboy not much larger than Ariana. The pants were loose, but this particular shirt was snug about her breasts. As she wiped off the cornmeal the rubbing caused a reaction that made Jeremy swallow. He watched a nipple harden under the thin fabric. Fascinated, he couldn't pull his eyes away. He didn't even try.

She looked up, her lingering smile fading at his expression. She glanced down and flushed. As she looked up again, their eyes met. Neither could look away. Memories came rushing back—thoughts both had struggled to forget. Slowly, his hand reached out, resting on her hip. Then it slid about her, gently pulling her to him. She made no effort to resist, and his eyes questioned her, watching for a response that would tell him to stop. It did not come.

He kissed her as her soft body folded against him, and the kiss deepened. She opened her mouth and moaned as his hand slipped down her hip, pressing her against him as his other hand moved up to a breast, stroking its full softness under the thin fabric. Then they both heard footsteps on the back porch.

Reluctantly, they pulled apart as the back door flew open and Jake burst into the kitchen. With one look at the man's face, the passions of the past few moments receded. "What's happened?" Jeremy demanded.

"They took everything, boss!"

"Who?"

"The Soberanes' rancho . . . Fremont came."

"Fremont?" Jeremy started, fixing on the name as he heard Ariana gasp. "What are you talking about?"

"They took everything," Jake repeated. "We were working the north boundary and one of Richardson's men came riding hell-bent for help. We rode back with him to Rancho Los Coches, and it was just like he said. Fremont and his men had ridden in at dusk last night and—boss, when they left this morning they took everything; mules, food, money. They even searched the house—"

"What about Richardson's family?"

"They're all right. But Richardson wants to take after them—he's sent out for his vaqueros."

"No! He mustn't do that!"

"What?" Ariana exclaimed. "Are you suggesting that Fremont get away with this? Just let him do anything he wants, even to—"

"Quiet, Ariana! Jake, get a couple of the men and go to the storehouse. Take what the Richardsons will need to get by. And for God's sake, don't let them go after Fremont!"

Jake nodded and left. He was barely out the door when Ariana spun on Jeremy. *"Cabron!* You don't care about them—or any of us! You just want to hide here and . . . Where are you going?"

"I have things to do. And so do you. Tell Maria that the men will need something to eat. Now!"

She stared at the door that closed behind him. *"Pinchi! Cabron!"* she swore. Something to eat? *Dios!* Her eyes flew with impotent rage about the room. Suddenly her head jerked to the stove. Her expression changed to grim pleasure. Si, she'd give them food.

Calling for Maria, she informed her that the men were going to eat. Then she hefted the large pot of beans off the back of the stove as Maria rushed to gather the rest of the meal into a basket. Carrying the pot to the bunkhouse, Ariana clunked it down on the table, then stood back as Maria set out tortillas filled with shredded beef. She watched as the hungry men filled up their plates, then began to devour the meal. On first bite, one of the hands looked up, his eyes growing wide. Ariana held her breath. Gasps were heard about the room. Jeremy stepped into the building at that moment.

"Kee-rist!" a cowboy gasped, glancing with watery eyes at the others.

"Hot damn!" another wheezed. "Now these are beans!"

Puzzled, Jeremy frowned as the men dove into the beans, sucking in their breaths between spoonfuls as they grinned at each other. Stepping forward, he took a spoonful from the pot. He chewed a moment, then his eyes grew wide. "God!" he swore, as he grabbed up the water pitcher, bringing the room to an uproar of laughter.

"Them are good Texas beans, boss!" one of the men shouted.

"Too bad you're such a wimpy northerner!"

Jeremy tried to smile, but he couldn't manage it. He saw Ariana's satisfied grin and caught her arm, pushing her from the bunkhouse out onto the porch, slamming the door behind them.

"Dammit, you did that?" he accused, still trying to draw breath.

"Yep," she said, in a slow Texas drawl.

"Why?" he wheezed.

"I only know how to fix food for vaqueros," she answered primly.

"Really," he countered, beginning to feel his tongue again. "I've eaten at your table, Ariana. Remember?"

"I recall," she said, trying not to smile. But his eyes were still watering.

"You put *serano* chilies in that pot," he accused.

"Cayenne pepper," she countered.

"Brujita." He grimaced, calling her a witch.

She smiled.

"You must be disappointed that they liked it."

"I didn't count on that," she acknowledged.

"That's apparent." With that, he stepped back through the door and snapped orders. Soon the men appeared, passing by her as they crossed the compound to their horses.

"Where are they going?" she asked, puzzled.

"The same place we are," he answered grimly, taking her by the arm. "I think that it is time that you took a ride."

They rode out over the rise beyond the ranch yard and into the valley along the Salinas River. The ground was still muddy from the recent rains, and Ariana had to concentrate to keep her mount on solid ground. She was dumbfounded by Jeremy's actions and kept glancing at him as they rode. His expression was resolute while the men seemed easy, resigned. Apparently, he was not going to offer any answers, she realized. Soon she was only aware of how good it felt to ride, and of the measure of freedom it offered. But just as she was beginning to enjoy herself, Jeremy called them to a halt. She glanced about, wondering why he had chosen to stop. There was nothing to her right or left but mud, sagging, wet grass and tumbleweed. Beyond was a narrow ridge angling off to the Salinas River.

"This is the border to Morgan land," he said simply.

Without another word said, the men began to spread out, spacing themselves to a quarter of a mile. She was bursting with questions, but when she noticed the nearby men checking their pistols and rifles, she could only stare. Many vaqueros wore guns, for rattlesnakes and bears. And there were Indian raids and bandits. But watching these men, she suddenly realized what was so different about them, aside from their language and manners. It was the way that they wore their guns, with the same familiarity her men had for their lassos. She had noticed this quality, but had not understood—not until this moment. They were preparing, waiting for an enemy.

There was no dust to announce their arrival from beyond the ridge. But she could hear the steady pounding of hooves moments before she saw the pack of moving horses and men. She glanced at Jeremy, but his eyes were fixed on the approaching party, his expression surprisingly calm.

"Come on," he said suddenly, spurring his horse forward. It only took her a moment to respond. She was aware that Dirk was on his right, moving toward the approaching herd.

They met them a quarter mile ahead. For some reason she couldn't have explained, at the last moment Ariana held back. Jeremy rode ahead of her with Dirk, and they met the small group that broke off and rode out to meet them. Fremont was in the approaching party. Waiting to see what would happen, she pulled her hat down to shade her face while fixing on the proud bearing of the American officer.

"Morgan," Fremont said with a smile. Apparently this was meant as an affable greeting.

"Fremont," Jeremy answered grimly.

"Yes, well . . ." the officer said, clearing his throat. He

glanced down the line of men who were spaced along the boundary line. "I presume that you have found this life preferable to that of serving your country?"

"I am serving my country," Jeremy answered with an easy smile.

"You may have a point. I have my eye on some land of my own. I've written to Larkin requesting him to purchase it for me when all this is over."

"Larkin is in Los Angeles. You might see him there. Manuel Castro has taken him prisoner."

"What?" Fremont exclaimed.

"You heard me. You should keep yourself better informed, Captain. But that is another matter. The issue at hand is the fact that you are on my land."

Fremont looked momentarily confused. "I don't understand."

"It seems simple enough. You are on my land. I want you off it."

Fremont stared at him as his face worked with confusion. "I must have misunderstood you. I have over three-hundred horses here, Morgan. They are needed for the southern campaign against Pio Pico and Castro."

"You didn't misunderstand me," Jeremy said easily. "If you attempt to cross Morgan land, I will take those horses from you."

Ariana was stunned. Without being aware of it, she moved her horse closer to better hear what was being said.

Fremont coughed and then laughed, incredulous. "You are insane, Morgan. God, man, you are an officer in the United States Army!"

"No. I resigned, remember?"

"I see," Fremont said, his eyes growing dark. "I swear, Morgan, I shall report you for this!"

"As you wish. Though I do wonder who you will report it to. Washington? Feel free. Stockton? Fine. Or better yet, how about General Kearny?"

"Who?"

"General Stephen W. Kearny. He should be arriving any day now."

"Kearny?" Fremont stiffened. He had confronted General Kearny in the past, with unfortunate results. Kearny despised him.

"That's right. My last dispatch from Washington said that

he would soon arrive with his troops to take control of the situation here."

"You're lying!"

"Now, Charles. Why would I lie about that?" He smiled at the discomfited officer. "Now then, turn your herd and go around my land."

"Backtrack around the Salinas River? That will take another two or three days!" Fremont protested.

"Yes, it probably will."

Fremont's gaze shifted to Ariana, who had brought her horse abreast of Jeremy's. "Now I understand," he said grimly. "You have taken that spy to your bed! You've become a damn Mexican, Morgan. Comforting that woman proves that you are a traitor!"

"How typical of you, Charley," Jeremy drawled, smiling. "All this time in California, and you still don't know the difference between a Mexican and a Californio. Perhaps if you had bothered to learn, we wouldn't be having this discussion. In any case, yes, I consider myself a Californio. You, on the other hand, are not. Get off my land."

"I warn you, Morgan, I am going to cross."

"Have it your own way." Jeremy sighed. Then he turned and nodded to Dirk. The foreman grinned, then gave a sudden bloodcurdling whoop. The horses shied and shots reverberated down the line on either side of them. Unaware that the herd had begun to turn and move behind him, Fremont brought his horse under control as he glared furiously at Jeremy. "What are you doing!"

"Can't say until I check it out." Jeremy shrugged. "But you should understand something. I've got thirty-four Texas cowboys along this line, and you can be certain that they've found a handy spot to stand you off. You're not going to cross my land, now or ever."

"Sir," Fremont's lieutenant protested, pulling his mount to the officer's side. "The horses are stampeding."

Fremont hesitated for a moment, glaring at Jeremy. His face was contorted with rage and, to the astonishment of his lieutenant, he ordered the herd to be turned. As he jerked his mount's reins about, he glared blackly at Jeremy. "You have not heard the last of this, Morgan."

"Anytime, Captain. But there is one more thing—" He paused until he had Fremont's attention. "I heard what you did to the Soberanes. I'll make you a promise, Fremont, and you can take this to heart: as long as you remain in California, you should look over your shoulder—because I'll be there."

Ariana rode back to the ranch house alone. Half the men were sent to their normal duties with the cattle, and Jeremy remained with the rest to make certain that Fremont did not double back. She was mystified by what she had heard and seen. She simply couldn't absorb it all at once. Instead, she focused on the simple pleasure she felt at seeing Fremont lose face before his men. It did not make up for all that he had done, including what had happened to the Soberanes, but it helped.

She found herself riding back across the ranch, feeling strangely free for the first time in a long while. To the west a herd of black, rangy cattle grazed on new, tender blades of grass nurtured by the recent rains. She pulled her horse to a stop and watched as the cowboys moved among the herd. They worked with their cow ponies, cutting the steers and cows into small groups to judge those who would stand a winter, and those who could not. She had watched such work all her life. It was as much a part of her as the land itself. Yet, she was filled with the strange feeling that she was seeing it from a totally new point of view.

Her gaze rose, moving over the valley to the mountains. They were covered in green velvet, like a deer's spring antlers, beguiling the spirit with their deceptive softness. Those mountains, the Santa Lucia, were home for bear, hawks, mountain lions, eagles, and boar. The mountains themselves tested a man's will, and more than one Californio had disappeared into them, never to be seen again. And yet they were life-giving, gathering the rains to be brought down through their gullies and canyons to the valley below. Majestic blue-green mountains, graceful in their rolling climbs, forested pockets, and breathtakingly beautiful passes that seemed to catch the sun, illuminating their twists and angles, drawing man into their reaches.

So many had come, glimpsing this valley and its protective mountain ranges for the first time. The Indians, centuries before; the mission fathers and their Spanish escorts, who had settled and become the Californios. And now the Americans would come, and once again the valley would change under their hand. As the Indian tribes had given their lands to the cattle, so, she suspected, the great ranchos would give way to Yanqui enterprise. The halcyon days would be no more.

She watched Jeremy's men working in the shadows of the mountains with an ease she had always seen in her own men. Finally, she allowed herself to think of what had just happened. Jeremy had stood up to Fremont in a way that her people had not—perhaps could not. That is what Jeremy had tried to tell her, why he had hired these men.

More men like Fremont would come—and those like Manuel would continue to fight them in the old ways. And they would lose. The Indians had lost everything to the missions because they could not fight back. Just as her people would lose unless they could change.

Tio Mariano had been right all along. Had he seen this? She had never believed in his dream, but she believed in him. Could the answer be just that simple? Trust—to believe in those we love, to have the courage to change with them, to share their vision? While all else in life changed, the land remained. Each man was given his time upon it, but only those with the courage to change could embrace the land and leave it better than before. With Ariana's thoughts came words she had not thought of in many years, words she had once believed in: "There were new worlds to conquer, life was challenging, expanding. Each tomorrow was a beginning."

A slow smile spread over her face as a glimmer of that forgotten dream began to glow in her eyes. Suddenly, she laughed, spurring the horse forward. She rode toward the herd, bringing the nearest cowboys to a halt as she gave out a cry that had been used by vaqueros further back than her memory, than her grandfather, or his before him.

It was dusk when Jeremy rode in. Over the mountains behind him, the sunset glowed red with jutting streaks of pink and orange. He rode up to the corral, where his men were unsaddling and wiping down their horses. Slipping from the saddle, he led the sorrel to the fence. "Dirk, be sure there are plenty of men left with the herd tonight. All hell may still break loose."

"Already took care of it, boss," the foreman answered as he continued to rub down his horse.

Jeremy pushed aside the rump of a horse with his

shoulder, making a path to the watering troth. A feminine oath came from the other side of the roan. The oath was in Spanish. As his horse stepped forward to dip his muzzle into the water, Jeremy let the reins drop and bent under the roan's neck. He straightened and stared.

Ariana was sitting on the edge of the troth, rubbing her foot where the horse had stepped on it. "There *is* another watering troth, you know." She glared.

He gave a short laugh of disbelief. "What have you been doing? You're filthy!"

"What does it look like I've been doing?" she snorted, bending to pick up the brush she had dropped.

"I know what it smells like," Jeremy observed.

"She can work cattle with the best of 'em," Dirk drawled, constraining a grin as he led his horse away.

"You've been working with the men?" Jeremy's eyes grew wide.

"Yep," she said, working the brush over the roan's haunches, its skin rippling in pleasure at her touch. "Sure have, boss," she added in a good imitation of Dirk's drawl.

His eyes narrowed with suspicion as he looked down at her slender form, clad in the oversized pants and the form-fitting shirt. The thought crossed his mind that she had been out with his men dressed like that, bouncing around on a horse. Tomorrow, they would go to Salinas to do some shopping. "Looks like you spent more time in the mud than on horseback," he growled.

She threw him a grimace as she continued to groom the horse. "There's one thing your cowboys have in common with vaqueros—they consider anything they cannot do from the back of a horse beneath their notice."

"Seems to me you've always shared that notion."

She hesitated, then continued stroking the horse. "There were two late calves caught in a mudhole under a bunch of sagebrush. We couldn't get a rope around them and . . . well, I couldn't just leave them there."

"Dirk wouldn't have left them."

"No, but your men just sat around discussing the merits of the problem until I thought I'd scream."

"I see." He broke into a broad grin. "Bothered you, did it? What happened to *poco tiempo?*"

Her hand paused on the horse's back, and she turned her head slowly to look at him. Before she could respond, he walked by her, jerking his thumb behind him. "Since you're a cowboy now, you can take care of my horse."

She spun around and watched him walk away with an easy stride back to the house. *"Coche!"* she hissed. Then she glanced at the sorrel, who had turned its head to regard her with large, brown, inquisitive eyes. "It's all right, boy," she said softly. "I'll take care of you. That man was an officer for too long. The first thing he has to learn about being a vaquero is that a man always takes care of his horse—" Then she smiled. "But we'll teach him." She stepped to the horse and threw up a stirrup to release the cinch. "Besides," she said, laughing softly, "it's better than having to cook another pot of beans."

She entered through the kitchen, not wanting to walk on the rugs in the parlor hall, and went up to her bedroom by the backstairs, ignoring the astonished looks from Selena and Maria as she passed through their domain. All she wanted to do was to take a hot bath and tumble into bed. She couldn't remember the last time she had felt so physically exhausted—it felt absolutely wonderful.

As she approached the door to her room, she realized, with a sinking feeling, that she was going to have to carry buckets of water up those backstairs for her bath. Suddenly she no longer felt wonderful but totally defeated. Opening the door with a sigh, she came to an abrupt stop. Still clutching the doorknob, she stared. There, in the middle of the room, was a tub filled with water. Hot water. Her eyes fixed eagerly on the steaming trails lifting from the surface. On a chair next to the tub lay a nightgown, soap, and a towel.

She closed the door behind her, her eyes filling with exhausted tears of gratitude. No one had to tell her who had done this for her. That's why he had left her to finish with the horses, so he could prepare her bath. No other man she knew would have done this. Not for her.

She stripped off the offending garments, dropping them on the floor at the edge of the rug so they wouldn't soil the heavy wool. She felt the water, then stepped into the tub and sat down gingerly. Sighing with pleasure, she sunk down until the water covered her shoulders. Then she eagerly scrubbed her body and hair, laid her head back against the edge of the smooth wooden tub, and closed her eyes.

She heard the door open, but she kept her eyes closed as

she tried to restrain a smile. She heard it close and then his footsteps crossing the room. The chair next to her creaked. "Feel better?" he asked.

"Much better," she answered, her eyes still closed. "Though now I understand the reason for your thoughtfulness."

"And what's that?"

"You wanted to catch me disarmed."

"There is that," he agreed in a serious voice. "And then there is the fact that I knew I couldn't be in the same room with you until you had a bath. You smelled like a cow-pie."

"That which we call a rose, by any other name would smell as sweet," she said, quoting Shakespeare.

She heard him snort. "The rankest compound of villainous smell that ever offended the nostril."

She laughed. "I give. You win."

"Do I?"

His voice had softened. She opened her eyes to find him watching her intently.

She returned the look evenly, her voice barely a whisper. "Must one of us win, Jeremy? It would suggest that one must lose."

He stared at her for a moment, then rose from the chair to cross to the window. It was a long time before he spoke again. His eyes fixed on the landscape and the last glimmer of light that had turned the world to gray. "Ariana, I've never stopped loving you. But it's not enough. Our relationship has been a continual contest, exhausting and draining for both of us. I know what that can do to two people. Yes, one of us has to win, or there's nothing for us, not together. I can't make you happy, not as long as there is such a difference in our goals. I can't go through that again."

"You are not responsible for my happiness, Jeremy. Not before, not now, not ever." He turned and looked at her, his brows gathering into a frown. She was standing by the tub in the bedgown, and she had wrapped the damp towel around her wet hair. Crossing to the bed, she sat on a corner and began to dry her hair. "Jeremy," she said, patting the other side of the bed. "I think it is time to talk."

He picked up a hairbrush from the bureau and tossed it on the bed as he sat on the other corner, pulling one long leg up under him, thinking that, frankly, their proximity was too close for comfort. Ariana's thin gown hid little from his imagination. "What did you mean just now—that I'm not responsible for your happiness?" he asked, clearing his throat as he tried not to look at her. He had to force himself to ask this question; it seemed, after all, clear enough. She didn't need him now any more than she ever had.

"Jeremy, no one can make another person happy. That has to come from inside ourselves. We can only offer someone else our own happiness—and our love."

He turned to look at her. He was startled by the soft pleasure that shone from her eyes. "Do you love me, Ariana Saldivar?" he asked quietly.

"With all of my heart and soul, Jeremy Morgan. I have never stopped."

"Well." He sighed deeply. "There we are, we love each other . . . but it's never been enough for either of us, has it?"

"No, it never has. And you are right—for love to last there has to be more: a common sharing of goals, belief in the future, in dreams. Even sharing the same view of reality."

He smiled sadly. "So now we both know it."

"Jeremy, I hated you when I saw you that day in your uniform. I thought you had betrayed me because your beliefs were different from mine. I thought that you had used me."

"And now?"

She picked up the brush and began to pull it absently through her hair as she thought of how to answer him. "Now . . . now I believe we both have the same goals, the same dreams, the same vision of reality. We always did, I just didn't know it."

He looked puzzled. "You had better explain this."

"You already know the answer. Tell me about your dreams, Jeremy Morgan."

"They haven't changed." He shrugged, not knowing what else to say. Then, slowly, he looked up at her with amazement. "But they have, haven't they?" he said, his voice touched with wonder. "I said it to Fremont—I've become a Californio."

"What does that mean?" she prompted.

He stared at her for a moment. "It's become home," he said quietly. "I feel roots going deep. My life—my old life—seems so distant. When I think of my future, I think of myself here." His mouth worked, hinting of a smile. "Thomas was right; California will become a state, I'm certain of it. I want to be part of that."

Her smile became warm. "I realized today that you love the land as much as I do. After I left you, I watched your men work the herd and thought upon the moment when you confronted Fremont. I knew then that the old ways were gone; there is a different kind of struggle ahead.

"Your people will come, with their Yanqui ambitions—" she sighed sadly, "something my people will never understand. I care about my people, Jeremy; I will never stop fighting for them."

"Still the *liberalismo?*" He smiled.

"Yes, but in a different fight: to bring my people into this new world, this new way of life. Will you help me?"

"Yes, *querida,*" he said softly, with feeling. "I swear it."

Her eyes grew warm and sparkled with sudden mischief. "Then it would seem, Jeremy Morgan, that we have, at long, long last, found something to agree upon."

"I thought that there were a few things that we agreed on—at least shared agreeably," he said with feigned hurt.

"You fool." She laughed. "I mean something besides that."

"Ariana." He sighed heavily, shaking his head in dismay. "Ever the political animal."

"Ah!" she blurted. "And you are not? My love, it is almost the most satisfying thing we share!"

"Including the arguments?"

"The fights," she responded, her eyes flaring with pleasure.

He peered at her through narrowed eyes. "Does this mean that I must continue to allow you a difference of opinion?"

"Allow me?" she parroted, her eyes flaring.

"Ariana, I expect it," he laughed. "And I welcome it. I must admit, that upon occasion you do present a different, and sometimes interesting point of view."

"Marano!" she muttered.

"As I once said, sugar-cured, sweetheart." He chuckled. Then he sighed again with a roll of his shoulders. "Well, all of this would suggest that you plan to stick around."

As she struggled to maintain her annoyance, her mouth twitched with a smile. "Yep, apparently so."

"Well then." He sighed heavily. "I guess that's the way it

is. I suppose I could find something for you to do. You seem to be pretty good with cows."

She laughed softly. "You're right about that. I'm very good. I'm pretty good at a few other things, too."

"No," he countered somberly. "There you are wrong. You're fantastic at other things." He moved suddenly. The brush went flying, followed by the towel. She found herself pinned under him. His gaze moved over her face with blatant hunger and complete happiness.

She laughed softly, squirming under him as she shifted her body to fit to his. Her face became radiant with the prospect of the coming hours. His mouth dipped to take hers, possessing it in an eagerness that she met in full measure. At this moment, they communicated to each other a sense of utter joy, and they laughed together with the knowledge of their shared delight. Their laughter filled the room; and then Jeremy rolled over, collapsing next to her.

"Oh, God," he gasped. "My love, we are either damn lucky, totally crazy, or both."

"I know." She sighed heavily, trying to catch her breath. She turned to look at him, feasting on his adored profile. Her voice was soft but touched with determination. "We're going to be unbeatable, aren't we, Jeremy?"

He turned his head. Smiling, he rolled over and pulled her into his arms. "That, *querida*," he murmured, "is the one thing that is certain in this life."

AUTHOR'S NOTE

Thomas Larkin was held captive in Los Angeles until the California forces surrendered at the Battle of Cahuenga, in January, 1847. It was not until then that he learned that his little daughter, Adeline, had died.

Upon Larkin's return to Monterey, he once again became active in California's affairs. He was appointed Navy Agent for the Territory of California, profitably supplying the Quartermasters Department. During the Gold Rush, which began the following year, he kept Washington apprised of the rapid changes occurring in the territory. In 1849, he was a delegate to the Constitutional Convention, held in Monterey, which led to statehood.

Ever sensitive to the winds of change, Larkin sold his business interests in Monterey, and moved his family to the burgeoning city of Yerba Buena, now San Francisco, where he quite profitably capitalized on the changes brought by the gold rush.

The surrender of the Californios at Cahuenga began another conflict, a bitter dispute between Commodore Robert Stockton and General Stephen W. Kearney, over who should control the territory—the Army or the Navy. Washington gave the decision to the Army. Stockton, relieved of his command, resigned from the service.

John Charles Fremont, who had achieved the rank of colonel, then Military Governor under Stockton, was relieved of his authority by General Kearney. Fremont returned to the east to face Court Martial in June, 1847. He was found guilty of the charges involving his conduct, but was later pardoned by President Polk. His part in the California conflict, his motives, and the confusion regarding his orders remain questions that are still hotly debated by historians.

"FAST-MOVING EXCITING PLOT
AND FINE, TRULY LIVING
CHARACTERS. A PAGE TURNER!"
—Roberta Gellis, author of *Fires of Winter*

"A PLEASURE TO READ!"
—Laurie McBain,
author of *When the Splendor Fails*

A DIFFERENT EDEN

KATHERINE SINCLAIR

*For Eleanor Hathaway, destiny and desire
are inextricably bound. From turn-of-the-century
Boston, where an aristocrat's twisted needs
force her to flee with her devoted governess…to the
treacherous shadows of a rambling Welsh estate,
where jealousy and madness nearly defeat her search
for one true love…Eleanor vows to never
surrender her dreams…*

___ A DIFFERENT EDEN   0-515-09699-7/$4.50
     Katherine Sinclair

Please send the titles I've checked above. Mail orders to:

BERKLEY PUBLISHING GROUP
390 Murray Hill Pkwy., Dept. B
East Rutherford, NJ 07073

NAME_____

ADDRESS_____

CITY_____

STATE_____ ZIP_____

Please allow 6 weeks for delivery.
Prices are subject to change without notice.

POSTAGE & HANDLING:
$1.00 for one book, $.25 for each
additional. Do not exceed $3.50.

BOOK TOTAL $_____

SHIPPING & HANDLING $_____

APPLICABLE SALES TAX $_____
(CA, NJ, NY, PA)

TOTAL AMOUNT DUE $_____
PAYABLE IN US FUNDS.
(No cash orders accepted.)